The Bargain

Irene Bennett Brown

WOLFPACK
PUBLISHING
— EST 2013 —

The Bargain
Paperback Edition
Copyright © 2023 (As Revised) Irene Bennett Brown

Wolfpack Publishing
9850 S. Maryland Parkway, Suite A-5 #323
Las Vegas, Nevada 89183

wolfpackpublishing.com

Paperback ISBN 978-1-63977-755-6
eBook ISBN 978-1-63977-756-3

For my maternal great-grandparents Frank and Mary (Weed)
Pickering of New Hampshire and Kansas
All I know of you is deep in this story

"The past is never dead. It's not even past."

— William Faulkner

Acknowledgments

In the making of this book I owe a debt of gratitude to several people. My husband Bob was with me every step of tine way, from research in New Hampshire and Kansas—to finished book in hand. You are a blessing of a mate! Alec McDonald, formerly editorial assistant at Browne and Miller Literary Agency, made a suggestion for revision that resulted in my favorite scene in the book. Judy Lilly, Kansas librarian at the Salina Public Library read the manuscript for accuracy of details concerning Kansas. Any errors that may have slipped through are purely mine. I must thank my daughter, Shana Chandler for the beautiful window painting on the cover, and cover design. Your artistic expertise comes through for me, every time. I'm indebted to my cousin Deb Ellis, who provided the lovely photo of a field of Kansas flowers that is the backdrop on the cover. A salute as well to my cousin Bob Keller, who has read all of my books and is man enough to admit he tears up at the touching scenes. You make my day, cousin! Thanks, always, to my family for their love and support, and to my faithful readers who continue to ask for my books.

The Bargain

Chapter One

May 1885—Sandwich, New Hampshire

IT WAS HARD COUNTRY AND NOWHERE NEAR WHAT HE WANTED to offer the woman he loved. Sweat dripped from under Larkin Wade's hat band and blurred his vision as he guided his oxen-driven cultivator between the rows of young corn struggling to survive his rocky hillside field.

He muttered under his breath as the cultivator bucked against a rock that had worked up through the thin soil he'd earlier cleared of stone. He tightened his calloused grip on the wooden handles and his slate gray eyes glared with angry fire. As suddenly, his expression softened to reverence. He shook his head.

Lord, but it was beautiful country, too. He'd never seen prettier in his twenty-three years. He stopped a moment and pushed his hat back, breathed deep of springtime air sweet as berry wine.

In the circling distance heavily forested mountains heaved massive shoulders into a crystal blue. Far behind them snow-cap peaks gleamed. Wrens and a wood-thrush sang and built nests in the brush alongside his field. He returned to his toils. Glory to the senses didn't put food on the table!

Most of his farmland was deep granite below a skiff of soil. A man laboring to make it pay could turn hard as that granite in time. He didn't want that. With a weary "whoa there, Gov'nor, whoa Big

Red," Larkin halted the beasts at the end of the row and wiped his sleeve across his eyes, wondering what he was going to do.

They got the farm free and clear through Ma's inheritance, but maybe coming there was a mistake even so.

He'd allowed to Ma just a few days ago that he'd gladly stay in Sandwich township til the day he died if he could lay hands on a better farm, sell or trade this one for interval and rare good loam. Might be he could take Ma, the boy, and Clare out west. Paradise For Sale, advertisements said. Miles and miles of rich, flat, tillable land could be had for next to nothing. For all his work this morning ridding the upper field of pesky weeds that sapped what nourishment the rocky soil held, there would be blessed few ears of corn come summer harvest.

Would Clare go with him? Would her family grant him the right to make her his wife? Likely not, unless he could somehow prove himself, change their minds about him. His handsome face glowered as he rotated his aching shoulders and then unhooked the cultivator to leave it. Goading the lumbering oxen ahead of him, he strode downhill toward the stone-fenced pasturage behind the barn. He freed the beasts from their yoke and watched them move heavy-footed toward the stone trough to drink.

His glance then roved the handful of miles southeast toward the mills, fields, and homes that made up the family settlement called Hobb's Mills. His heart became a pile-driver in his chest. His gaze locked on the largest house at Hobb's Mills where his beloved Clare lived.

Clare Hobb. Funny day-dreaming Clare was as beautiful and sweet a woman as a man could wish for. The best thing ever to come into his life and a gift he thanked God for every day. In an hour or so they'd be meeting at their secret place. His blood tingled in anticipation.

One minute of Clare's presence, a sweet kiss or two, could cure days of worry. He smiled to himself, and with long strides and breaking into a cheery whistle, he headed toward the small log house built many years ago by Ma's people. He stopped at the well to wash up, and took a long cool drink from a gourd hung there for that purpose. Licking his lips, he hummed the final bars of the song he thought was called Kitty O'Neil.

The tune was being fiddled at a community picnic held on the grounds at Hobb's Mills last summer. He'd seen Clare around the village a few times before, but that day they'd spent hours together, happily getting acquainted and each liking very much what they learned about the other. From that day on, it had been impossible to get the tune, and Clare, from his mind. He'd never be content in life without Clare at his side.

At the table eating the noon meal with Ma and young Nick a short time later, Larkin was dressed in a clean shirt, his thick dark hair in wet waves. He was all too aware of Ma's eyes on him in suspicion and sympathy. He grinned at her, and winked.

She had loved him like he was her own from the market day in Portsmouth when a guilt-faced young girl burst from an alley and pushed into Ma's hands a wicker basket containing his infant self. The girl ran away like fire was at her heels. Ma trundled after as fast as she could with the basket full of babe, but never again saw the young woman who'd borne him. Over the years, Ma's family became his family. Although all that were left of them now was Ma and her grandson, Nick, nine years Larkin's junior.

"Nick," he said, "would you be a good man and take the sharpening stone to the cultivator blades for me this afternoon? The confounded rock in the upper field has nicked and dulled them."

"What you doin' then?" Nick's youthful voice cracked, his adam's apple bounced in his tan throat. He had missed a smudge of dirt at his hairline when washing up. His brown eyes flashed with eagerness. "You plannin' to go fishin' this afternoon?"

Larkin, thinking of meeting Clare, hid a smile. "Not fishin'. But you and I will go catch some of those trout in Little Pond soon. Please pass the bread."

"We could go fishin' in Swift River above Hobb's Mills. Got some big ones in there." Nick passed the bread. Ma set the butter in front of Larkin.

"Ayuh, we could, but not today."

"You know it ain't right," Ma scolded Larkin later, as he prepared to leave the house. "Nick told me what's going on. He's seen you."

"What's not right, Ma? What does the boy think he's seen?" He grabbed at Nick as the boy darted guiltily past him and outside. Larkin kissed Ma's cheek.

"Meetin' that girl, that's what." She slapped at his hand that caressed her shoulder.

"You don't think she's pretty enough for me?" he faked amazement behind his wide smile. Truth was, Clare's lovely face seemed stamped back of his eyes for all time.

Ma scowled, but her warm hazel eyes held love for him, too. "We both know Clare Hobb is the most beautiful girl in Carroll county. And the most high-born, too. I worry for you, son. You're headed straight for heartache and disappointment if you think for one minute those uppity Hobbs will consent to her becomin' your wife. I know what I know! If they find out you two have been slippin' off to meet, sparkin' secret from their knowin', there will be big trouble, I vow!"

"Ah, Ma," he said huskily, turning serious, "there's no call for you to worry that I'm going to get my heart broke. That there will be trouble." He grasped her shoulders fondly. "You'll see, the day will come when Clare Hobb will become my bride. She's going to be Mrs. Larkin Wade, I'm certain-sure. She loves me, Ma!"

"Her bein' in love with you ain't the same as her family sayin' yes to her marryin' you, an' you know it. You're a hardscrabble farmer, not born to a silver spoon in your mouth like them, an' they won't see past that to how good a man you are, inside and out. How good a husband you would make for their young miss, an' pappy to their grand-young'uns. I'm sorry, Larkin, but that's how 'tis."

"I can make myself worthy of her, even in their eyes."

"How, son? How you goin' to do that?"

"First off, if you're agreeable, I'm going to sell this farm and buy a better one, a more farmable place that'd bring profit. More money than you could dream of. Ma."

She wouldn't crush his dreams in spite of doubts. She asked on a sigh, "You did it then? You put up a notice down in the village that this farm is for sale or trade? Like you said you was goin' to do?"

"Ayuh, I did. You've always believed in me, Ma. Can't you now?"

———

STATELY AND SERENE, the white, three-storied mansion known as Homestead House sat on a knoll surrounded by rich green fields and backed by a small grove of white pine and alder trees. A few yards out front of the verandah stood a grand old maple tree under which the first Hobb couple to that country camped while choosing their land.

Down the stone fenced lane from the main house and across the road, on the banks of Swift River, large wood-framed mills turned out flour, lumber, and cloth. Three other cottages dotted the property to the north, east, and south. Square white houses with picket fences and yards overflowing with honeysuckle, larkspur, asters and petunias.

Inside the main house, the huge, steamy kitchen was fragrant with the noon meal of roast beef and vegetables being prepared by a covey of Hobb women.

Clare, her mother, grandmother, aunts, girl cousins, and her two sisters bustled about getting in one another's way in the rush to get the food on the table for male members of the family.

Clare's lovely face flushed in confusion as she turned in a circle and tried to remember what it was she'd been about to do.

I must get Larkin off my mind for the short time now until I can be with him at our private place. Breathing was difficult, thinking of him. She chewed her lip, her flurried gaze going to the other women and girls busily scooping potatoes, vegetables, and sauces into serving dishes from huge pots on the stove.

Her mother, Eugenie, a small woman of fading beauty and nervous disposition, nudged Clare's slender back and whispered in her ear, "Enough wool-gathering Clare! Mind what you're doing. Take the tureen of gravy into the dining room."

"Of course. Momma. Sorry." She took the hot, dish towel-wrapped bowl from her mother.

Uncle Samuel's wife, Polly, eldest of the Aunts, a woman devoted obsessively to church and her husband, reminded Clare with a scolding glance, "The menfolk are waiting to eat!" Dessert dishes clattered as she stacked them next to the enormous cherry cobblers on the work table. "Afternoon work is piled up for all of 'em." She muttered under her breath, her eyes dismissing Clare as near useless, "Flibbertigibbet!"

Clare stiffened, ready to protest the unflattering description she personally held untrue. The fact that most of her extended family had as much imagination as a patch of parsnips was no call to defame her for enjoying a few innocent pleasures.

Aunt Juliette, Edward's meek, thin-faced wife, spoke up quietly, "Clare is just...different. A...romantic. A bonny girl with her head sometimes in the clouds, but that's not so terrible is it? She's a practical girl, too, when need be. Works as hard as any of us."

Clare thanked her with a brief smile for understanding. The tureen of gravy was growing heavy and hot.

"She needs to be check-reined, is what I'm thinking," Aunt Polly's comment was flung at Clare's back as she turned to leave the kitchen. "Wandering over the hills, climbing a tree to read a book, picking flowers like some feather-brain with nothing better to do. What kind of wife, and first lady of our state, will she make with those habits, and day-dreamer that she is?"

It was more than Clare could take. She turned back, picturing with distaste the man she was expected to marry. Elderly, bearded Dr. Plummer with his Prince Albert coat straining at the buttons on his stout form, strands of gray hair on his balding head flying away when he lifted his stovepipe hat to her on the street. Physician to their family, he was a deacon of their church and was also deeply involved in local business and politics. To her dismay, and the surprise and satisfaction of her extended family, he had recently expressed matrimonial interest in Clare.

Her glance now circled the room of females. "I grant you that Dr. Plummer is a wonderful doctor, a good man, and highly respected in our community. I know how you all feel about him." She took a deep breath and gathered her courage. "But I would never marry him and you can get that right out of your minds. He is too old—three times my age. He's worn out enough wives already and I don't want to be the next. Not to mention that when he talks his false teeth clatter and rattle like a mouth full of squirrels!" *Regardless, I love another.*

Aunt Polly's round face was rigid in shock. "You would speak of a fine man like that! You have no idea how fortunate you are that he mentioned his fondness toward to you, to your Uncle Samuel. You've no notion of what you could be throwing away by rejecting Dr. Plummer."

Livia, Uncle Simon's aristocratic much younger wife deplored, "Don't be a silly goose, Clare. Don't you see that Dr. Plummer is the catch of a lifetime? It's possible that you could eventually be first lady of New Hampshire."

I could be throwing myself away for someone I don't love.

"Clare is young, not ready—" Momma murmured with a wave of her hand in an attempt to smooth the situation. "Although no one denies that Dr. Plummer is a fine man."

"And rich!" Livia said. "You could have servants." Livia didn't hold with the Hobb family moral code that healthy women should do their own work when they could easily pay others to wait on them.

"Enough chatter!" Grandmother Hobb said sternly from where she piled sliced bread on a plate. Tall and angular, gray hair in a loose bun, she waved a bony hand for the women to tend to their tasks. "The men and boys are hungry."

Clare fled the room, carefully balancing the bowl of gravy in her hands. She admired Dr. Plummer as a physician and leader in the community but it made her ill to imagine herself wife to him. If she was too "feather-brained" for him, thank the heavens for it! Anyhow, she decided stubbornly, an occasional escape into one's imagination was wonderful respite from the boredom of repeating the same dull chores day after day, and from being held down under the constant rule of family men-folk.

Of course none of them. Momma included, would approve of her dallying with handsome Larkin Wade. Personally, she hoped their romance lasted forever and she intended not to miss a single moment she might possess. It was unfortunate that her iron-minded uncles, in ruling the roost, disapproved of Larkin. He should be allowed to come calling on her properly.

Neither she nor Larkin liked having to sneak about to be together. Unfortunately, the men in the Hobb family, excluding her poor father of course, ruled, and the women obeyed. Well, that was not for her. She simply couldn't live every day of her life that way, and she would run away from all of them before she'd marry Dr. Plummer.

In the dining room, with a gentle, violet-eyed smile at her father, Clare placed the tureen of gravy on the lengthy table where assorted Hobb males sat talking to one another in short, clipped sentences concerning work to be done that afternoon in the mills and on the farm. Spring sunshine through the lace curtains lit the room.

Her father, Frank, youngest of the four Hobb brothers but more faded-out looking than the rest since his head injury two years before, returned her smile and reached to touch her hand as she passed his chair. "The flowers are pretty, girl," he whispered, nodding at the porcelain bowl of wild bluebells and apple blossoms that she'd placed on the sideboard earlier that morning.

She nodded and affectionately touched his shoulder. She moved out of the way as her quiet, dark-haired older sister, Alice, came with a huge platter of steaming roast beef to place on the table. Only Poppa, and possibly Alice who'd had her own tragic affair of the heart, would understand about Larkin, Clare was thinking when Alice gave her a nod and mouthed, "water."

Clare smiled a brief thank you and swept to the sideboard to take up a heavy cut glass crystal water pitcher. She should have thought of this herself. She proceeded to industriously fill each tumbler around the table, the glittering water she poured reminding her of Larkin's shining eyes when he looked down at her.

She smiled privately to herself, couldn't help it. She loved Larkin's eyes. She adored his strong calloused hands, his wide shoulders that looked as if they could hold up the world. Their world, at any rate.

A splash of water on her hand as she poured brought her mind back to the present. Rosy-faced, she looked to see if anyone noticed her lack of attention to her task. Thankfully, the attention was on her eldest uncle.

Uncle Samuel, his weathered face grim above his short wispy beard, was biting off words, "Henry Brewer wants a load of lumber. To his place in Center Sandwich. This afternoon. Wants to finish that addition to his house."

"Thought he got lumber for that addition," Uncle Edward stated. Next oldest to Samuel, a slight frown marred his square handsome face. He cut his beef, ate a large bite, wiped his chin with his linen napkin.

Uncle Simon, the dandy of the brothers, answered him, punctuating delicately with his fork, "That skinflint Brewer should have ordered enough of those two-by-fours in the first place. Always worries he's spending a penny too much. Man should do a better job calculating his needs." Although nine months older than Poppa, Simon looked much younger. A dapper fellow who didn't care for physical work, he kept Hobb's Mills financial affairs in order.

"Ought to charge him double, teach him a thing or two," Samuel agreed dourly. He shoveled in several bites of meat and potatoes and then he turned on Clare's father, who'd been sitting silently, "You listenin', Frank? I want you to hitch up and deliver ten of those new-sawn two-by fours down to Brewer in Center Sandwich." His dark eyes glinted. "You understand?"

"Think I do." Poppa's expression was earnest, desperate to understand and please his older brother. He licked his lips and struggled for further words that would satisfy Samuel, but came up blank. His eyes darted worriedly in his face, his fork nervously tapped the edge of his plate.

Clare hesitated, empty water pitcher in her hand, her heart going out to her father. Poppa didn't deserve to be treated like an imbecile! He wasn't stupid, he was just slow-thinking and sometimes got confused.

At one time, he'd been a strong, sharp-witted man, hard-working and fun-loving. A talented harness-maker, blacksmith and machinist, his duty was to keep all such in meticulous order and condition on the prosperous Hobb farms and in the mills. Then, two years ago, while shoeing a horse of volcanic nature, he'd been kicked in the head. He lay injured and alone for more than an hour before Samuel and Edward found him.

There was little Dr. Plummer could do for him and Poppa lay in a coma for days. A coffin was built and prepared for his passing. To everyone's surprise, and due no little to his wife and children's loving care and fervent prayers, Poppa slowly recovered. He would never be the same, however. He was left with a scaly purplish dent in his head at the temple and forehead where the horse's hoof had struck. His hair, beard and moustache turned silver. Although not an old man at age forty-five, he walked slightly stooped. Mentally and emotionally, he was very different from the man he'd been before the accident. But he was alive!

Samuel turned on Poppa, shaking his head in disgust. "Ya

mink! Now listen, I'm not tellin' ya again. You're to load up that lumber and take it down to Brewer and I don't want no mistakes. Do you understand?"

"Think I d-do," Poppa quavered again. He began to twist his right ear between thumb and forefinger as he often did when unsure of himself.

Clare's young male cousins at the table snickered and she gave them a stony look. "I—I—I can do it, S-Sam," Poppa said. "Lumber. Down to Brewer. Center Sandwich."

"Ya better!" Sam snorted. "An' do it right."

Clare wanted to order Samuel to leave her father be, to not be so hard on him. It wasn't that Poppa couldn't handle the simple-enough task, of course he could. She wanted to tell Uncle Samuel that if he and her other uncles weren't so mean to Poppa, he'd make lots fewer errors.

It was wrong to mistreat him for his mental weakness that was not his fault. They only made it worse. With Eugenie and his children he was calmer, more content and capable. They loved him for the man he used to be and the man he was now and they made allowances for his shortcomings.

Sometimes it was as though the others didn't want Poppa around at all, if he couldn't handle a full share of work at Hobb's Mills. His deficiency was an embarrassment and an irritant to them, and it was so wrong for them to feel that way. Poppa was still a Hobb and a good man to his core. He was her beloved father.

There was so much she could say, but Uncle Samuel's word was law in the family and he'd abide no back talk or contrariness especially from a Hobb female. And that's how he'd see her defense of Poppa: as needless, silly argument from a young woman who ought to know to keep her mouth closed and to behave properly.

While she seethed inside, and later helped to serve dishes of cherry cobbler with thick pouring cream, Clare considered that she could miss meeting Larkin. She could go with Poppa and help him with delivery of the lumber. But it really wasn't necessary. Poppa could do the job, and the accomplishment on his own would make him feel better.

When the men and boys had left the house to go back to their work, the women and girls ate at the second table. Afterward, busy hands made short work of clearing the table, washing dishes and tidying the kitchen. Then Clare's aunts departed to their own homes to tend afternoon tasks there. Grandmother retired upstairs. Alice and Hallie got out their samplers they were embroidering and sat stitching in the light from the dining room window. Momma remained in the kitchen to start a cake for the evening meal. Clare, disliking that she had to fib, but wanting to see Larkin so much her head spun, told Momma that she really should see to the newest calves in the barn, and after that she wanted to search and make sure there were no late motherless lambs in the far pastures.

"Don't be long. We have several baskets of mending to do this afternoon."

She gave a guilty, noncommittal nod. Before going to the barn she stopped in the wash room off the kitchen to wash her face and tidy her dark hair. The looking glass reflected the telltale flush in her cheeks, echo of her feelings. Larkin. He had no doubt finished his own noon meal long since. She'd better hurry or she would miss him and who knew when they'd have another chance to meet?

Chapter Two

CLARE MADE HER WAY FROM THE MAIN HOUSE THROUGH THE
attached chain of outbuildings—summer kitchen, woodshed, milk
house—and into the barn.

The calves were sleeping clean and sweet in fresh straw in
their pen. She hurried from the bam through a side door north.
Holding her skirts, she flew through a pasture of buttercups,
catching her breath when she reached the apple orchard just
coining into bloom. She ducked from tree to tree, keeping her eyes
on Simon and Livia's tidy cottage at the edge of the orchard and
whispering a prayer that Aunt Livia wouldn't look from her
window and see her.

It was hard to feel kindly toward Aunt Livia, who constantly
lorded it over the other women, considering herself superior due to
her city upbringing. Uncle Simon, who had lost his first wife to
childbirth, the infant dying, too, spoiled Livia terribly. Clare had to
admit that Livia was pretty, spirited, and had a certain charm and
grace. At the same time, Livia didn't hesitate to be cruel if it served
her means or fed her ego. Unfortunately, Clare's younger sister,
Hallie, admired Aunt Livia and wanted to be just like her.

Despite the warm sunshine, Clare shivered as she considered
the trouble know-it-all Aunt Livia could cause if she knew of
Clare's trysts with Larkin, a young man the family deemed totally
unsuitable. Clare could be forced to marry Dr. Plummer, or she

would be banished to elderly Aunt Zilpha in Manchester for as long as it took to rid Larkin from her life.

The latter had happened to Clare's older sister, Alice. When she was seventeen, Alice had made the unforgivable mistake of failing m love with their cousin Everett Uncle Samuel's oldest son.

Although Everett cried himself to sleep for a week over his loss of romance with Alice, within a month or two he was well over it and a year and a half after Alice's banishment, Everett married "sensibly" and moved to Gilford.

Alice, once a pretty, light-hearted girl, was eventually allowed to return home to Hobb's Mills, a drab, withdrawn young woman, seemingly destined to become an old maid and not minding if she did.

dare took a deep breath, ran the last mile up Young Mountain road to the meeting place, a huge boulder just off the side of the road and halfway between Hobb's Mills and Larkin's farm. She had so frightened herself with thoughts of what would happen if she were caught, if she was never to see Larkin again, she went faint with relief when she spotted his tall, broad-shouldered figure waiting for her in the shadow of the rock.

Happy tears stung her eyes, and she gave a small cry as she ran into his arms.

"I thought you weren't coming," he said huskily against her temple, his arms tight about her.

"Of course I came," she said, snuggling close.

He murmured her name softly, tipped her chin and kissed her. She felt weak as his lips made trails from her brow to her cheeks and back to her mouth. She returned his kiss, both of them making up for those terrible moments when they were apart.

Staying away from Larkin is no more possible than denying my next breath. She drew back to look at him and told him breathlessly, "I'm sorry I'm late. Today's noon meal took longer than usual. Uncle Samuel was fussing at Poppa—but let's don't talk about that."

For the next several minutes they held one another. She stood on tiptoe and caressed the strong planes of his face, while his hands caught in her hair and he murmured soft words of love.

Realizing the import of her racing heart, and strange deeper feelings, she knew they must stop, now. "Larkin," she murmured, "we—must stop."

He groaned in disappointment but agreed with her. "We better."

Breathing deep, smiling blissfully, they moved apart.

He took her hand, kissed her fingers, and told her, "I have a plan that I need to talk about with you."

"What is it?" Leaving her hand in his, she moved to lean back against the boulder, her eyes closed and the bright sun washing her face. He leaned back beside her.

"I intend to sell the farm. It's never going to pay a decent living, no matter how hard I work it—"

She whirled on him, her eyes wide. "You're not leaving?" Her hands gripped his. "If you ever went away from Sandwich, Larkin, I would die, I truly would." Each time they were together only cemented further the feeling that she couldn't survive without him. That he was her destiny. Worry coiled inside her.

He chuckled happily. "You'd suffer my absence that much? Can't say that doesn't please me, my darling!" He pulled her to him and kissed her again, soft, feathery kisses. Her senses swam and with difficulty she managed an inch or two between their bodies.

His voice was husky, "Leave? Leave you, Clare? Never! No, I only want to sell the farm or trade it for a better one. Somewhere here in Sandwich if I can find a place with good loam. I'm tired of fighting rock and boulders big as chicken coops to try and raise a crop!"

"It's not fair that you have to work so hard, but please don't ever leave this place, Larkin." With a sigh of contentment at his closeness, she laid her cheek against his chest, felt the rhythm of his heartbeat like music under her cheek.

His arms pulled her tighter and his lips brushed her hair. "I wish I could court you properly, Clare. Hiding, meeting this way in secret is shoddy, not right for my girl."

"It's the only way for now," she said, lifting her eyes to meet his worried gaze, "and I don't mind. Although finding an excuse to leave the house alone is getting to be more and more difficult. Each time, I'm afraid someone will suspect."

"Ma knows we're seeing each other."

Clare jerked back. "She won't tell, will she?"

Ma Wade, a truly wonderful, kindly soul, sometimes helped out at Homestead House when someone was sick, or when extra help was needed at harvest and preserving time. "She won't give us away, will she?"

Clare's own mother would be disappointed if she knew what Clare was doing. But her response would be insignificant compared to how Clare's uncles' and their wives' would react!

To consort secretly with someone below the Hobb family social standing would be shocking in the extreme. She'd be pegged an immoral outcast, bring shame on Momma and Poppa. She didn't want that, but neither could she give up Larkin. What they were doing was not wrong, she loved him and he loved her. It was the others who forced this unnatural situation.

Now she ducked her hot face and pressed it against his shirt-front. "Oh, Larkin, what are we going to do?"

He caressed her gently. "Ma won't tell. She'd never do anything to hurt me. Or you. But that doesn't mean she doesn't worry." He chuckled, a catch in his throat. "She fears I'm in for a broken heart."

Clare grew very still. "I'd never want to hurt you, Larkin. And I wish, too that we didn't have to meet this way." Reluctantly she told him, "I can't stay but a few more minutes. If I'm missed, someone might come looking for me."

"It's never long enough," he growled, leaning toward her before suddenly jerking back. "What's that?"

She listened to the muted sound that was like distant thunder. As it grew in volume there was something else, a screeching sound. "Dear God!" They moved away from each other. Clare whirled past Larkin, hurrying toward the road.

He reached for her too late. "Go back to our rock and wait!"

She ignored him and with her skirts gripped in her trembling fists she ran alongside him in the direction of the noise. Like a horrible phantom, a white horse pounded up the rise in the road iii a cloud of dust. The empty wagon the animal pulled ricocheted back and forth nearly turning over. The screeching, which she recognized now as a human being screaming in pain, suddenly stopped.

"Larkin, be careful!"

"Stay there!" he said hoarsely. He ran into the road in an

attempt to catch the frightened horse. Eyes rolling, the horse reared, hooves pawing the sky, then swerved off the road toward a copse of trees to avoid Larkin. The wagon, with a wrenching yawl of wood and metal thudded against a tree. The lathered horse, lunging but anchored by the weight of the half overturned wagon slowly surrendered and stood with front legs apart and sides heaving.

"Nabby!" Clare cried with sickening horror. The runaway mare was the one Poppa would use to make the delivery to Center Sandwich in the opposite direction. Where was Poppa? Dread formed a fist in Clare's mid-section. What had happened? At first her feet wouldn't move and then she stumbled to join Larkin who cautiously caught the animal's cheek strap.

"There now," he crooned, reaching carefully to stroke the nervous animal. "There now. Nothing to be afraid of, be calm, be calm." Nabby rolled her eyes in fright and cocked an ear toward Larkin.

"Where is Poppa?"

In cold fear, she started back toward the wagon but Larkin grabbed her arm, and rasped, "Clare—don't look, stay here."

Despair trembled in her voice, "I have to know—! I have to help —!" She jerked away and rushed to the wagon caught against the tree. Dust still filtered the air and it took a moment to recognize the bloodied bundle of rags to be a human form caught by the legs in the whiffletree, the pivoting crossbar at the front of the wagon to which the traces were attached. A stricken whisper tore from her throat, "Poppa!" The world spun dizzily. She took several deep breaths and fought to stay on her feet and not faint.

Larkin's voice broke through, "I need your help, Clare. Come hold the mare and keep her calmed while I untangle the pour soul. His boot must have caught, somehow, or his pants leg on the hooks for the tugs— Hurry now, girl. There's no time—"

Fighting to hang onto her senses, she hurried to Larkin's place at the animal's head and stroked Nabby's long nose with trembling fingers. "Is Poppa alive?" she begged, as Larkin worked gently to free him. Dear God, let Poppa live, please don't let him die. She buried her face in the crook of her arm to still her swimming mind, waited on rubbery legs for Larkin to tell her Poppa was not dead. She wanted desperately to be the one seeing to her father, caring for him, begging his forgiveness that she hadn't gone with him. "Larkin, will he be all right?"

"Clarie!" She heard her name, Poppa's voice. Startled, she whirled to look Limping, coming abreast of the overturned wagon where Larkin was freeing the crumpled victim, was her father. Poppa, unhurt except for a limp and a look of terrible distress and confusion. His hat was off and his eyes were wild in his pale face as he mumbled and sobbed words she couldn't understand.

And then, "I've killed him, Clarie, I killed my brother Samuel."

"He's still breathing," Larkin called as he lifted the bloodied figure and carried him to a soft grassy patch at the side of the road. 'Sir," he directed Poppa who stumbled about, wringing his hands, "help me right this wagon so we can take him home and get the doctor."

"Help Larkin, Poppa, Hurry."

Poppa seemed to understand, then, and throwing his arms in the air, he rushed to join Larkin who was doing all he could to heft the wagon away from the tree and back onto all four wheels.

Uncle Samuel's body was so battered and bloody the only thing recognizable was his size and short tattered beard. Clare knelt next to him at the side of the road and tore a strip of petticoat to sop at the blood flowing from numerous cuts on his face. There was faint movement in his chest and Clare gave a thankful prayer that he was still alive. "We must get him to Dr. Plummer, quickly."

It seemed an eternity passed before the wagon was righted and Nabby led about in the direction of home. Clare climbed swiftly into the back of the wagon to aid Larkin. He gently lifted a moaning Samuel and maneuvering carefully, laid him in the wagon. Tears streamed from Poppa's eyes as he stood holding Nabby, speaking softly to the mare.

Kneeling on the floor of the wagon by Uncle Samuel's crumpled, blood and dirt-covered form, Clare ripped another chunk from her petticoat and began to sop at the blood flowing from a deep gash on his neck.

Larkin stripped off his shirt and gave it to her. "Cover him." Poppa started to get into the wagon to drive, but Larkin motioned him toward the other side. "I'll drive. Sir." Poppa nodded, wiped his eyes on his sleeve as he circled the wagon and climbed up next to Larkin. He kept his forlorn gaze fastened on Samuel as

Larkin took the lilies and clicked his tongue for Nabby to move on.

Poppa was talking, continuing the sad mumble that Clare thought would echo in her heart forever. "I killed him. It's my fault. I killed my brother Samuel."

"No, Poppa, no. Samuel is alive. Everything is going to be all right. We'll take him home where Momma and Aunt Polly can see to him and we'll send for Dr. Plummer. Uncle Samuel will be all right."

Larkin darted a look back at her, his face grim and doubtful at her pronouncement, but he nodded.

Clare leaned forward to listen above the rattle of the wagon as her father told what happened. "Samuel—he was in a hurry, said I was too slow. He shoved me away from hitching up, yelled at me to get away. He was climbing over the crossbar when he got caught in the whiffletree. He cursed the mare. He was rough, he shouldn't have been so mean to her. She's young yet, and skittish. Nabby got scared, took off running before Samuel could get free—"

Clare hardly needed to hear more. She knew of Samuel's impatience, his hot temper. Poppa was much better with horses, gentle and patient. The time he'd gotten hurt, a bad-tempered horse reacted when a rat raced under its feet. The horse's lightning kick struck Poppa in the head. This time, it was Samuel's mishandling that caused the trouble.

"When Nabby started to run," Poppa was saying, "and Samuel's 1-legs caught in the whiffletree, I tried to catch Nabby. But I stumbled on a root and pitched to the ground." Fresh tears filled his eyes as he told Clare over his shoulder, "We were hitching up under the big maple in the yard. In the shade. I jumped right up but by then—by then, Nabby was running, dragging poor Samuel who was screaming, screaming, scaring Nabby more. But Samuel was right. Ayuh, I'm clumsy. I'm slow. And now I've killed my own brother."

"No, Poppa, no. It was an accident. It wasn't your doing." Clare scooted to wrap her arms around him, her wet cheek against his back. Everyone knew of Samuel's impatience, his fiery temper, but she also knew from past experience that the target for this terrible accident would be Poppa. He knew it too, and was already taking the blame on himself.

But if anyone was to blame it was she, for sneaking away to meet her darling Larkin, when Poppa needed her.

She sat mute, riddled with guilt and worry that Uncle Samuel might die. If she could only erase the whole day and start over. Go with Poppa as she should have done. And yet, Larkin was everything to her. Everything.

Clare swayed on her knees next to her uncle's battered and bloody form as Larkin guided the wagon carefully but swiftly along the uneven road. Under her hand, Samuel's chest lifted, but the frighteningly longer periods between his raspy breaths made her own heart quake. Clare leaned low over him, her voice catching in her throat, "Uncle Samuel! Stay with us. We're going for help. Aunt Polly's waiting. Don't leave us Uncle Samuel, please—"

They'd gone about a mile when Samuel opened his eyes, looked at her and took a shuddering breath, the life ebbing out of his face. Frantic, praying herself mistaken, she leaned close, hoping to feel his breath on her cheek. She touched the side of his neck to feel a pulse. Nothing. Finally, she drew back and for a long while could only stare in heartbroken disbelief at his open, unseeing eyes. "No—!" she whimpered. She closed his eyelids as her own eyes filled.

Uncle Samuel had been a difficult man, but honest, hardworking, respected. The family would not be the same without him. His loss was going to be enormous and heartbreaking for Aunt Polly and their children. Clare tried to find her voice to tell Larkin there was no longer a need to hurry, no need to take so much care in driving the bumpy road, but she failed. Her tears flowed and pooled around her mouth. She sat back, wiping her eyes on her bloodied sleeve. She finally gave way to soft sobs. Larkin and Poppa turned to look. She shook her head, choking, "He's gone."

Poppa stared at Samuel's still form and moved as though to climb into the back of the wagon next to Clare. Then he turned back, groaning, and with his head in his hands he doubled over, moaning, "What'd I do? What've I done?"

"Shh, Poppa, shh." Clare crept forward. "You did nothing wrong, Poppa. Uncle Samuel should have let you handle Nabby, you're wonderful with horses and you would've been fine. Samuel shouldn't have lost his temper—" Her shoulder brushed Larkin's and he turned to look at her, his expression solemn, and deeply caring.

"I'm sorry, Cla—Miss Hobb. I'm so sorry for your loss, Mr. Hobb—" His eyes took in Clare's tears, the blood on her hands and clothes. "Would you like me to stop, Cla—Miss Hobb. Are you all right?" He looked desperate to comfort her, to take her in his arms.

"I'm alright," she whispered, straightening her shoulders. She nodded toward the group coming around a curve of the hill road.

Uncle Edward, portly and with deep concern marring his handsome face, led the way on horseback. Riding alongside came Uncle Simon, thin, agitated. Their wives, Juliette and Li via followed behind on foot a while later. Then Clare's sisters, Alice, and Hallie, trotted up, skirts in hand, and pushing by them, her young brother, Oakley.

Her tall, angular grandmother was there, arm hooked through Eugenie's as they hurried, their faces pale with worry. Racing at the edges were Clare's cousins and some half dozen workers from the mills. Of course word of the accident would spread swiftly at Hobb's Mills and tasks would be abandoned. Someone would have heard Samuel's and Poppa's shouts, could even have seen the runaway happen but wasn't close enough to help.

Stricken voices carried on the wind as the wagon closed the distance. Then the springtime afternoon grew deathly quiet. Clare closed her eyes and prayed as she'd never prayed before, that this was a dream, a terrible, terrible nightmare. But she knew this was no dream.

Chapter Three

HER MOTHER'S RELIEF WAS EVIDENT AT SIGHT OF POPPA sitting whole and sound next to Larkin. In deference to the one who had been hurt, Momma clapped her hand over her mouth, swallowed her cry of alleviation.

Clare reached out to grasp Poppa's shoulder, her eyes on the approaching group. "Poppa, you didn't kill poor Uncle Samuel. It was an accident. Remember that Poppa. You wouldn't hurt your brother."

Folks spilled around them as Larkin slowed the wagon. A row of stunned white faces peered in at Samuel's bloodied body.

"It's Samuel, blame it all!" Edward exclaimed. "He's breathing, isn't he? We sent a mill hand to fetch Doctor Plummer."

"I'm sorry," Larkin told him, "but Samuel passed. It was a bad runaway. We got the wagon and mare stopped, but not in time. Samuel's legs were caught in the whiffletree and he was—was— This is a rough road, as you all know. A lot of rock and boulders."

"Pounded to death," someone muttered.

"Coulda' been mangled by a bear, torn up as he looks," another offered darkly.

Aunt Polly arrived and gripped the side of the wagon, eyes on her dead husband, and she began to wail, "Samuel, oh, Samuel. Dear God—Samuel!" Her eyes rolled back in her head. As she crumpled, Grandmother Hobb and Eugenie caught her.

Larkin, looking grave, gave the women a few minutes to help a near lifeless Polly into the wagon next to her husband's body, then continued on down the road.

"What in thunder did you do, Frank?" Edward shouted as he rode alongside the clattering wagon, his horse tossing its head at the blood smell. "You were given a simple job and now this!"

Simon joined him, disbelieving and furious as he glared at Clare's father who sat slumped, and grief-stricken beside Larkin. "Samuel killed!" It couldn't have been clearer that Simon felt the wrong brother lived.

"What happened wasn't Poppa's fault," Clare stood up in the wagon, swaying, her voice quivery. Shock from the tragedy, grief at the loss, anger at her uncles, was overwhelming. She sat down again quickly. In any regard, no one seemed to have heard her, or cared to listen to what she had to say.

"Runaways happen," Larkin spoke in a tight voice to the angry men keeping pace with the wagon. "You all know that. Today was a tragic accident, but Frank did nothing to cause it and he did his best to stop it."

Clare was about to further remind them of Samuel's impatience, tell about his mistreatment of both Poppa and the mare, Nabby, but the sight of Aunt Polly, her eyes glazed with disbelief as she wept over her husband's body, stilled her tongue.

In numb silence, then, the wagon and crowd moved on, finally reaching the stone-fenced lane to Homestead House. The sun shone brightly but Clare felt cold. The wind sighed mournfully in the grove back of the house, the big maple on the front lawn seemed to weep in the wind.

Larkin drew the wagon to a halt close to the front verandah. Edward and Simon dismounted and hurried to lift Samuel's body from the wagon. The clutch of womenfolk rushed ahead into the house to make ready, others helped Aunt Polly down. Poppa got out of the wagon his expression unutterably sad. He stumbled to the maple tree, dropped to the ground, and sat there, exiled by his living brothers' attitude.

Consumed with guilt that she'd been with Larkin instead of helping Poppa with his delivery, Clare pushed Larkin's hands away when he came to assist her from the wagon. He seemed to understand. He nodded and moved away, his expression forlorn.

Her dress was soaked with blood and the smell of it in the warm sunshine made her nauseous. She staggered a bit when her feet touched ground. Alice, hurrying to her side, asked, "Are you all right, Clare?" She took her hand. "Oh, sister, it must have been awful, coming on the accident, seeing what happened. Momma said you'd gone to the far pasture to look for lambs. I'll help you wash up and change your clothes. This is so sad— Poor Aunt Polly." She stared after their aunt who stumbled her way into the house. "And Grandmother. Samuel was her oldest and she depended on him so much. We all did."

"Yes," Clare responded, while her conscience wanted to shout to everyone within hearing that what happened was her fault, not Poppa's. She went to him, leaned down to take his face in her hands. "Remember what I said, Poppa. You didn't do this. No matter what Uncle Edward and Uncle Simon say to you, this terrible accident was not your fault."

From what seemed a million miles away, she could hear Larkin explaining again, to the fragment of crowd remaining in the yard, what happened. It was an accidental runaway, he insisted firmly, that no one, no one, could have stopped.

She looked gratefully toward Larkin over her shoulder, and saw that his eyes were on her. Someone had given him a clean shirt to replace his that had covered Samuel and he was tucking the shirt into his trousers. He started toward her, but she turned back quickly and rushed into the house, tears for another sort of loss stinging her eyes.

————

INSIDE, Alice caught her elbow and Clare allowed her to lead her upstairs. "If you'll get me a clean dress, Alice, the old blue one will do, I need to go back to Poppa." No telling what they would do to him. From the moment the horse kicked him in the head leaving Poppa mentally infirm, he was a useless burden in his brothers' view. Now that he was considered responsible for Samuel's death —she could hardly bear to think how he'd be treated.

Her hands shook as she washed up at the marble-topped washstand in her room. She dried her face, smothering her tears for a moment in Momma's embroidered linen towel, before she went to change her soiled dress. On her way downstairs, Clare passed a window in the hallway. She saw Larkin in the yard below preparing to leave. She waited for a few minutes on the stair landing, awash in guilt, arms wrapped around her body to ease her aching heart, then, when he was striding down the lane toward home, she continued her way downstairs.

A corner of the kitchen was curtained off and behind it the women were preparing Samuel's body for his lying in. Clare hurried by, a lump in her throat.

Poppa was still under the maple tree but standing backed against the huge trunk now and he wasn't alone. Facing him in an accusing semicircle that included Uncle Edward and Uncle Simon and some neighbors, he was being grilled over and over about what took place.

Poppa brokenly repeated the same details he had told her and Larkin—that Samuel felt he, Frank, was too slow hitching up. That Samuel took over and yelled at the young mare and struck her. Frightened, the mare bolted, catching Samuel's legs in the whiffletree. Poppa tried to catch Nabby, but tripped on a tree root and by the time he was on his feet, the runaway was impossible to catch.

"Samuel wouldn't have had to help out in the first place if you weren't such a bungling idiot, if he could have counted on you to do things proper," Edward maintained, his face red with anger, eyes glazed with shock and grief.

"Most of the time we have to do your work and our own," Simon added through clenched teeth. His eyes on Poppa were so accusatory and filled with disdain that dare, watching, recoiled. Simon continued, "And now even that wasn't enough, now Samuel is dead. Samuel! The best of us. Lord help us all with what you've done, Frank."

Fury like acid roiled in Clare's throat. They knew perfectly well about Samuel's impatience, his roughness at times with animals. What Uncle Edward and Uncle Simon objected to was the fact that their simpleminded brother survived, while the strong one, the family leader, lay a mass of broken bones and stilled heart on a table in the kitchen.

They weren't seeking truth, they were afflicting punishment. From their tone, their every word, their gestures, they wanted Poppa to be certain how much they blamed him for being alive.

Her poor father! Clare's fury mounted and she was about to intervene and never mind the consequences when Momma appeared at her side and touched her arm. "Wait, dove."

The deep frown that creased her mother's forehead, the anger carefully concealed behind her eyes, told that she had also over-heard the verbal abuse against Poppa. Momma was too much a lady, though, and too submissive by nature, to voice the objections she was no doubt feeling.

"Polly is resting," Eugenie quietly told the men. "We have the linen cloth ready for—for Samuel's coffin if you men will fetch one of the ready-made coffins from the sawmill. Your mother has made the parlor ready. She has asked that one of you take word of our loss down to the village so that the bells can toll Samuel's passing. Frank, my dear," her voice firmed, "you've been through a lot today. Please come inside. You need rest."

"Yes," Clare said, and before her uncles could say anything more, she rushed forward and grabbed her father's arm, pulling him along. "Come, Poppa."

A pall of grief lay heavy over the rest of that afternoon as the pine coffin was brought and lined with fine linen that had been woven at the mill. Samuel's remains were laid out and his coffin placed in the parlor where Grandmother Hobb took a nearby chair and sat the rest of the day, lips moving in silent prayer. Aunt Polly had been put to bed and was being cared for by the other women. They moved softly to and from her room, hearing her grief, wiping her tears, plying her with medicinal tea to calm her.

As Clare tended her share of early evening chores, from down in the village church bells tolled, announcing Samuel's passing. At the house again, she helped to prepare a light supper because the living had to eat, no matter how steeped in sorrow.

There was little conversation around the table at the evening meal. Poppa could have been diseased or a criminal from the looks cast his way, the avoidance of touching him, or including him in what conversation there was. He sat like a pale ghost curled into itself. Clare could hardly swallow for the pain she felt for him.

In the hours following the tragedy, her uncles and aunts had come to accept the details of what happened, but they couldn't excuse Poppa. Regardless of what actually took place, to their minds, if Poppa was more competent and not slow-witted, the accident would never have happened.

It was a relief when the meal was finally finished, each family retiring to their own quarters, Edward and his family to their cottage on the banks of Swift River opposite the mills, Simon and Livia to their small house near the orchard. Aunt Polly asked to be helped to her own house on the east knoll above the sheep pasture. After saying goodnight to Grandmother Hobb, Eugenie, Frank, and their children moved in a body up the winding stairs to their chambers.

"You don't have to talk about it, Poppa, if you don't want to anymore," Clare told him gently when their family settled in their sitting room upstairs. But he needed his own family, especially, to understand what happened and so he told the story again, in a sad, weary voice.

"Samuel was—mad as thunder at me!" His fingers picked at a loose thread in his trousers. "Said I wasn't hitching fast to please him." His chin lifted and he gestured with his hand to make his point, "I was taking my time because-because we all know that young mare is skittish. Samuel shoved me out of the way, knocked me to the ground, to do the job, himself."

Momma caught Poppa's hand and held it tight. He looked from her to Clare and back again to his wife. His lips quivered, "Ayuh, he scared that mare, handling her so rough. Nabby bolted before Samuel—screaming like a banshee—could get free of the whiffle-tree. I got up to help and—and tripped on that big maple tree root. By then the mare was 'way off up the road. Samuel, Samuel, he..." Poppa covered his eyes and tears squeezed between his fingers.

Clare's own eyes were swimming. "Oh, Poppa, I'm so sorry."

"It's terribly sad what happened to Samuel, but you're not to blame, Frank!" Eugenie caught him in her arms as he rocked back and forth in his chair. "It is not your fault! We all know that Samuel has—that he had a hot temper and little patience."

"We believe you, Poppa," Clare knelt by her parents, her head on Poppa's knee. "You couldn't help this terrible thing happening." *But I might've, if I hadn't let my foolish heart, my obsession with Larkin, rule over good sense. If I hadn't sneaked away against family rides to be with Larkin instead of helping Poppa, the tragedy today could have been avoided.*

She went to bed that night exhausted but too upset to sleep except in small snatches. At times she stared into the dark, tears dampening her cheeks. She told herself that if she could just wake up, this nightmare would vanish like a mist on Sandwich Mountain when the sun climbed.

As painful as any were her thoughts of Larkin and how her feelings for him had caused such a tragedy to happen. Her mind pulled away, clinging to a more pleasant time, to the day last year when she saw Larkin for the first time. For the rest of her life she would remember that day as if it had only just happened.

With a shopping list from her Aunts and Momma in hand, she'd ridden along with Poppa to Sandwich Village. Behind them in the wagon were several one-hundred-pound bags of flour for the general store.

"I'll help you, Poppa," Clare said, jumping down as soon as he'd drawn the team to a halt in the narrow street in front of the market.

"Too heavy for you, daughter. Go on inside and do your trading. This I can do myself."

She had persisted and in the process a bag of flour slipped away from them both to explode at her feet and send flour flying. She was coated from hemline to eyebrow.

A male chuckle from in back of her brought Clare's glance swiftly around. A rough-hewn, handsome farmer stood there, sturdy as a white pine. The outline of his shoulders strained again the fabric of his homespun shirt. But it was his slate gray eyes, smoldering interest and amusement that captured her full attention. He looked to be only a few years older than she but he must be new to the neighborhood, she'd never seen him before.

She was suddenly angered. The nervy dog, to laugh at her predicament! She batted flour coated-lashes at him. "We're not a circus for your entertainment! Go on about your business, Mr.— whoever you are."

Poppa was hefting another bag down from the load, scolding himself for clumsiness. "Poppa, wait—"

"A snow angel is what you look like." Their onlooker was still laughing, his tan hands resting on his hips as he ogled her.

"Nonsense." She gave up trying to help Poppa and turned on the stranger. Under the flour her cheeks flamed. "Would you just go away?" Because he'd started toward them, his stride masculine and in command.

"I can help."

"You're not needed, as you can see." She nodded, breathless and thankful, toward the storekeeper who'd come out, assessed what happened, and shaking his head, had begun to assist the unloading.

"An extra set of hands will make the task go quicker." And the stranger ignored her. He nodded a friendly grin at Poppa, and proceeded to help unload to the last bag of flour. Clare cleaned up the mess on the sidewalk with a broom and dustpan the clucking storekeeper's wife provided. Unable to help herself, Clare stole glances at the wide-shouldered young farmer, noted that he hefted the flour to his shoulder like it was no more than dandelion blossoms.

"I'm Larkin Wade." He caught her staring and he smiled. He brushed off his shirt-front and held out his hand.

She looked up at him. Her heart thudded in her breast as though it were a bird about to take wing. As much as she wanted to rebuke him, it was hard to stay angry at a man so handsome, who had shared the unloading chore so readily with Poppa. She swallowed her pride, and brushed at the flour on her skirts. "Thank you." Her floury fingers met his and the touch was electric. It was a moment before she could tell him, "I—I'm Clare Hobb. I—suppose I am a funny sight."

"Beg pardon but you're a mighty pretty one," he said softly, "and I'm guessing you're plumb beautiful when you're not coated with flour." With that he tipped his hat, accepted her father's thanks, and set off across the street, saying over his shoulder, "I hope we meet again. Miss Clare Hobb."

As do I, her subconscious echoed, to her shock. *Heavenly days,* she scolded herself, *mind your thoughts!*

Surprisingly, on the way home that day, Poppa could tell her things about Larkin Wade, besides the obvious that she could see for herself: that he was handsome, tall and strong, and a man of good humor. "The young fella came to these parts a month or two ago." Poppa told her. "Took up the old Taylor farm."

She knew about the Taylor place a few miles up Young Mountain road. She asked, "Can he make a living off of it?" She remembered that the elderly Taylors had let the place go in their filial years, barely scratched enough for sustenance and to keep themselves warm in winter.

Poppa didn't reply, his mind seemed to have skipped from the subject.

"Just him? Has the fellow no family?" she pressed, then felt a blush rising in her cheeks when she found herself hoping that Larkin Wade wasn't attached.

Words suddenly spilled from Poppa, "There's just the woman who raised him, Mabel Wade and — a young boy, Nick." He nodded. "Came from Portsmouth. Harder life there than on the farm."

"You know a lot about them. How—?"

He clicked his tongue to hurry the team faster and seemed to have dropped the subject.

Clare asked, "How does it happen you know so much about the Wade family, Poppa? Tell me, please. Think, now."

His lips moved as he tried to pull thoughts from the cotton of his mind. He licked his lips as he struggled for words. "They were friends. Your Momma and Mabel Wade. When they were girls growing up."

Clare was astounded. "What? Really? The woman who raised this—Larkin Wade—was once Momma's friend? When Momma was a child at Gilford Village?"

"Ayuh. Sundays they went to church together." He smiled at a far distant memory. "Mabel Taylor was a jolly young girl, fine at playing the organ. Eugenie was shy—but by the faith, she could sing like a nightingale, and can still! Master fine. They were the best of friends."

"Good friends? But why haven't I heard about Mrs. Wade?" she'd asked the day of the flour incident. "Does Momma know she's back?"

"She knows. They met for a visit in the village one time, maybe two."

"But—Momma's never said a word."

Clare was aware that Momma's own mother died when Eugenie was a tot, and that her father, Doc Forbush, didn't remarry. That he was a distant, busy man and Eugenie, growing up, saw little of him. "Go on, Poppa, please."

For a moment he pulled at his ear. "Your mother's friend, Mabel, married real young. She moved with her husband to-to Portsmouth. If I remember, they were married a sad short time." Poppa nodded, "Ayuh, he was drowned by the bursting of a mill pond. Wasn't a full year into their marriage."

After a silence, absorbing all she was hearing, Clare asked, "And Momma didn't see Mabel, Mrs. Wade, again until this year?"

"Ayuh. When Mabel brought her family back to Sandwich, to claim the land left to her by the Taylors."

"But if Momma and Mrs. Wade were such good friends-"

Poppa shushed her with a shake of his head, "The way of our folks is sometimes hard to collate. Don't mean no harm."

It saddened her to realize what he meant, "hi other words, now that Momma and her friend are grown women and from different stations in life, it would be improper for them to behave as equals, as the good friends they once were?"

There was silence and then he said, "Don't think on it, Clarie, does no good."

"Sorry, Poppa, but I have to think about this. I find it so hard to understand, it's grossly unfair! If I was Momma, I wouldn't stand for it. The rules in this family are just too strict. I myself, sometimes feel I must ask permission even to breathe."

Not that the Hobb family was alone in the way they viewed society. Most in the community saw it unfitting for the higher classes to mix with the lower.

Clare had known that her shy, sheltered mother joined the large Hobb clan when she married Poppa at age eighteen. Previous to that Eugenie's chief companion was her father's strict but kindly younger sister, Aunt Zilpha. Clare hadn't heard a whisper about Mabel Wade until now, from Poppa.

He was unfortunately right considering how society would view an association between the two women, one from the aristocratic Hobb clan, the other a common laborer's widow. Poppa knew how his brothers would react to such a friendship. And their wives, Clare thought, would keel over in apoplexy if Momma invited Mrs. Wade to tea at Homestead House.

She sighed, her heart heavy. Gentle Momma wouldn't have the backbone to stand up to them and invite her friend and not care a whit what others thought. They wouldn't heed her wishes if she did speak out. She might as well save her breath to cool her porridge. As it came about later of course, it was permissible for Eugenie to have Mabel to Homestead House to work in the kitchen.

Then came the huge picnic at Hobb's Mills last summer. For this annual event the entire community and from miles around were invited, to thank them for their business at the mills. Clare and Larkin had seen one another briefly after the flour incident; once or twice in the village and occasionally when Larkin drove Ma Wade in their wagon to Homestead House to work.

Larkin and Clare's attraction to one another, ignited the day of the spilled flour, grew. The day of the picnic they spent an hour talking, getting better acquainted. In the evening they danced several dances together under the scowling glare of her Uncles—Samuel, Edward, and Simon. Clare's Aunts looked on, horrified. Momma spoke quietly to Clare, begging her not to upset the family. Poppa, bless his dear, simple heart, didn't notice anything amiss.

Larkin had asked permission to call on Clare. But her uncles allowed to Larkin that even to ask he had overstepped the bounds of what was proper toward a young lady of Clare's station. They ordered him to not come near her, anymore that night or in the future.

Sometimes Clare hated her uncles for being so obsessed with Puritan values and custom that they saw any example of change or going against the grain as original sin.

Clare had never been so humiliated and angry as when her uncles rejected Larkin, disregarding her opinion and wishes. She'd declared to no avail that Larkin was the most decent, wonderful person she'd ever met. She was furious that they looked down their noses at Larkin, as if he were less than nothing, rather than the honest, good-hearted, hardworking farmer that he was.

Young swains had been weeded from her life before, by her uncles, who'd found the men unsuitable for one reason or another. Finally, the field was narrowed to the one man they wanted for her: the aged but wealthy and politically-minded doctor. Never mind that she had no romantic feelings toward him, her uncles saw Doctor Plummer as the perfect match for her, an ideal addition to the family circle.

She vowed, after getting to know Larkin, that she'd follow her heart and let the devil take the hindmost. She would see him in secret, although both disliked hiding the fact of their affections for one another.

If only they could have foreseen the tragedy of this day. She turned into her pillow to muffle her sobs. What was she to do? Confess to Momma and Poppa that this was all her fault? What then?

Chapter Four

CLARE TOSSED IN HER BED, ASKING HERSELF OVER AND OVER: should she go to Momma and Poppa and tell them that she was to blame for what happened? That she was with her forbidden lover when she could have been helping Poppa?

No one, other than Larkin, knew why she was along to bring Uncle Samuel's body home. It was accepted that she'd been out looking for orphan lambs and came upon the scene. There would be terrible scandal if she told. Her poor parents already had more heartache than they could scarcely bear.

She stared into the dark until her eyes ached, finally coming to a resolution, *I can't tell them.*

In exchange for keeping the secret she would make up for this terrible day by devoting herself to her family. From this time on, she would make every effort possible to shield Poppa from her uncles' abuse, their misjudgment and ill-treatment of him. Somehow, she'd make things better.

Aunt Polly was right; it was time Clare was more responsible. No more whiling away the hours reading Emily Dickinson's poems, or vanishing from chores to follow winding lanes simply to see where they might lead. Behind her now must be the pleasantries of exploring wood paths, abandoned cellar-holes, and houses nearly hidden by tangled roses—imagining folk who might have lived there.

Although it equaled a decision to never take another breath, she would put an end to her love affair with Larkin, that never should have begun in the first place. Tears dampened her pillow. Those brief sweet fevered days were finished but would stay in her heart. For her family's sake, she prayed for the strength to go through with her plan.

Next day, aching with weariness after a night of little sleep, Clare moved through her daily tasks in a state of numbness. In addition to her usual chores, there were preparations for Uncle Samuel's funeral. All of the women and girls fell to doing their part. The huge house was scrubbed and polished top to bottom. Roasts were put in the oven, cakes and breads were stirred and baked to feed the crowd who would gather at Homestead House after the funeral.

Clare was relieved to be too busy to think. And then, as she was passing through the huge kitchen, she heard Momma say, "Mabel Wade would be such a help, maybe we should send word for the young man, Larkin, to bring her here to give us a hand."

At mention of his name, Clare trembled with emotion. Life was so damnably unfair. Tears welled in her eyes and she buried an urge to kick and scream. In Mabel Wade's kindly presence, she might break down altogether. Weaken in her decision to keep her secret. Give up on the promise she'd made to herself to forget Larkin for her family's sake. She took deep breaths until she was strong enough to speak.

"Momma, we don't need Mrs. Wade. Look, we're nearly finished. It's good for all of us, don't you think, to work out sorrow making things nice to honor Uncle Samuel?" She swallowed the tightness in her throat.

Momma wiped her hands on her apron and nodded with a sad smile, "You're right, dove." She went back to kneading a fresh batch of bread dough. "We can hardly labor enough, to show our respect for all that Samuel was to this family."

The other women in the room, who'd been listening, assumed a renewed and healthy proportion of self-righteousness and tackled their own work with more verve despite their sadness.

Clare breathed a sigh of relief. It was a rare occasion for her aunts to give account to anything she said.

SAMUEL'S FUNERAL drew one of the largest gatherings seen at Sandwich in years. Under sparkling sunshine, Larkin stood next to Ma and Nick, several paces behind the main crowd in the graveyard. His glance traveled discreetly again and again to where Clare stood with her family on the opposite side of the open grave.

· He had delivered Ma's gift of food to Homestead House yesterday but Clare had been busy elsewhere in the house. He hadn't seen or spoken to her since the runaway. Now, despite dark circles under her eyes and an expression of sad regret, she was very beautiful. He ached to stand beside her, to take her hand and whisper words of comfort. He silently cursed the ruling that kept secret they were sweethearts.

Immediately following the preacher's closing words, Larkin took Ma's elbow and with Nick trailing, led his family forward to offer their sympathy to Mrs. Polly Hobb, now Samuel's widow, and to the others.

Polly was so grief-stricken, her face bloated and red from crying, Larkin doubted she even recognized them as she thanked them for their kindness.

Clare's uncles were perfunctory, quickly dismissing him after thanking him again for bringing Samuel's body home.

Eugenie, eyes brimming with tears, caught Mabel's hands. "Thank you for the basket of applesauce doughnuts you sent over. They were delicious. Bless you all for coming." She hugged Larkin and Nick and then dashed away to the waiting carriage.

Larkin wasn't surprised that he and Ma weren't invited to the funeral day dinner. It didn't bother him so much for himself as for Ma. He'd learned recently that Clare's mother and Ma were once close, girlhood companions. Now, society's rules separated them. Still, he had to have a word with Clare, just a word.

He hurried, reaching her before she climbed into the carriage next to her mother. "I'm so sorry, Miss Hobb, about your loss. If we can do anything, Ma or me, please let us know."

She didn't look at him, although her gloved hand touched his fingers. Her chin trembled, "Thank you."

His gaze followed their departing rig, his heart yearning for just one small backward glance from Clare. She didn't turn. They were not supposed to know one another well and she was guarding their secret. If only he could comfort her, in whatever way she might need him.

Larkin exercised patience in the days and weeks that followed. He expected that Clare would give some signal that her time of mourning for her uncle was finished. She might even appear at their rock. He went to their meeting place looking for her every chance he got. A terrible loneliness assailed him when each time there was no sign of her.

It was six weeks after the tragedy when Larkin spotted Clare in front of the store where she'd spilled flour that day they first met. She was dressed in somber gray, her face hidden in the shadows of her bonnet. "Clare," he called, "Clare wait." He ran to catch up before she entered the store.

"I'm very busy," she said quietly, without looking at him. "Good day, Larkin." She started again for the store's entrance.

"Clare!" The anguish in his voice halted her in her tracks. "For God's sake, you've surely got a minute to spare for—for a friend. We need to talk."

She turned, tears glistening in her beautiful eyes. She whispered, "Please go away, please." She looked small, tortured, desperate to be rid of him.

He put his palms up, backed away a few steps, and spoke softly, "All right, I don't want to get you into trouble, sweetheart. You don't want to be seen with me here on the street. I understand. But Clare, you've got to meet me at the Rock so we can talk. Promise me you'll come."

"I can't." After a painful eternity, her eyes met his. Her voice was ragged with emotion, "I can't see you anymore. Our meetings, what we were—that's all finished."

If she had knifed him, it couldn't have hurt more. He waited until a woman, market basket on her arm and staring, walked by them and entered the store.

He kept his voice low, "You can't mean that, Clare. I'm sorry if I've rushed you. I know how hard it must be on your family to lose Samuel. I can be patient as long as it takes. But please don't say you can't ever see me again."

"But it's true. This is very difficult for me. I beg you to understand my situation, Larkin. Uncle Samuel would be alive today if

I'd gone with Poppa, helped him to hitch up and make his delivery, instead of sneaking away to meet you."

Heat filled his face. "Blame me if you need to, but don't punish yourself for what was pure accident."

"I don't blame you, and I'm not punishing anyone. I have to think of my family now. I've so much to make up to them for, and at present they need my full attention." She nodded to a gentleman tipping his hat to her as he passed by. Her smile was quivery, "Good day, Mr. Coolidge."

"Miss Hobb, Larkin. Good day."

"Mr. Coolidge," Larkin responded absentmindedly.

It was all he could do not to shout at Clare, *"Nonsense! I need you. You need me."* As terrible as the tragedy was, she couldn't possibly set aside what they meant to each other. He was about to make the strongest argument in him, that their love was the most important thing on God's green earth, when she left him standing and entered the store. The summery day turned flat, empty.

He wanted to go after her, shake her, make her see reason and agree to meet him at their rock. With great effort, he turned and walked away. God knew that what happened wasn't her fault, although she believed that it was, and she could have prevented the tragedy. In time she would understand that her uncle's death wasn't her doing. The two of them could go on from there.

Because loving Clare was something that would be part of him if he lived another hundred years.

———

THE MIDSUMMER DAY was heating up to a near scorcher, dare, wearing her oldest, most faded dress, stood on the threshold of the henhouse looking in, wrinkling her nose from the smell, a wheelbarrow at her knees and a shovel gripped in her hand.

This was Poppa's chore she was about to put her hand to, but he'd been called from this job to repair the broken well sweep which Aunt Polly swore he'd not repaired properly an earlier time. Her own household tasks and needlework could wait.

Although her aunts and uncles had sometimes been unkind to Poppa before Samuel's tragedy, now they were downright cruel. They sought any excuse to accuse him of not doing his share of work about the farm and mills, heaped more tasks on him than any human could possibly keep up with, and now deliberately lumped on him the lowliest, most unpleasant tasks normally given to a transient handyman desperate for work. As if Poppa could no longer be trusted with the real workings of the mills and farm!

As much as she could, Clare made herself a buffer between her uncles and their torment of Poppa. Few would know today that she, not Poppa, cleaned the henhouse so that he could rush on to yet another task when finished with the well sweep.

Once again, her young brother had sneaked away to go fishing with Nick Wade. The boys were becoming fast friends, slipping off to be together. The way she and Larkin used to do. She missed those times with Larkin so much it was as though half her soul had been ripped away.

Several times in the last month or so, Larkin had sent secret messages by way of Nick and Oakley asking her to meet him. At first, she'd written back that she simply could not and would he be kind enough to leave things be?

Later notes she didn't reply to at all, although it hurt to ignore him.

She had no such problem dissuading elderly, stout, Doctor Plummer's attentions. Twice he'd come to call on her at Hobb's Mills. She pleaded a headache on one occasion. On another she insisted Alice tell him that she was abed with her monthly. He had pills that could help her, he'd told Alice, but Clare refused to have him in her room, insisting that all she needed was peace and quiet to feel better.

She sighed, remembering. Soon, she supposed, Uncle Edward and Uncle Simon would insist that she comply with Doctor Plummer's efforts to court her. Thus far, the family's period of mourning had shielded her from actually socializing with the doctor, or anyone else for that matter.

Mumbling epithets against her uncles and life in general with each shovelful, Clare scooped piles of speckled chicken droppings from under long rows of roosts and into the wheelbarrow. It was hot and close inside the henhouse and her clothing was soon wet with perspiration, her hair streamed in her face, the foul odor had her near to gagging. Accompanying her sputtering disgust was the contented clucking of hens from outside in the sunny chicken-yard.

She poked her head out the back door and said to them, "Go ahead, be happy, but you're still going to end up in a dumpling stew!" It seemed a lifetime had passed since the days she slipped away to be alone with Larkin. Hard work like today's helped put him from her mind, but only briefly. At night when her mind relaxed, he stole back into her thoughts, her dreams. He was once again her Larkin, her deepest love, and joy filled her soul. Then came the morning, and the hard necessity of returning him to the shadows of her heart.

She had seen him a few times in the village, and although she hated doing so she ducked from sight before he could spot her. Once when she walked with Alice and Hallie to church, they met Larkin face to face on the road. She made out that he was no more than a mild acquaintance, and hurried on. Behaving so toward Larkin nearly killed her, but she'd stick with her bargain because she must.

Unless, by some miracle, she could somehow smooth the relationships between her uncles and Poppa. She might then resume her relationship with Larkin. If he still wanted her after how she was forced to treat him these days.

She doubted though, that her uncles would ever change.

Uncle Edward had revered his older brother, Samuel, surely loved him, but life in Samuel's shadow hadn't been easy. Since the tragedy, Uncle Edward had slipped into Samuel's shoes as family leader, a role he had surely craved for years. Outwardly more easy-going and affable than Samuel had been, Edward enjoyed power and recognition more. Since Samuel's death, he seemed bent on keeping Poppa tight under his thumb.

Uncle Simon was even more impatient, and complained that Poppa's mistakes, no matter how trifling, cost them money, too much money. They were so terribly unfair.

Clare scooped at the chicken droppings, her nose twitching from the odor, which reminded her that Simon, the more suave of her uncles, perfumed his mustache to please Aunt Livia, his much younger wife. She shook her head in disgust.

It also required money to keep Livia happy and Uncle Simon meant Hobb's Mills to profit as much as possible. By nature a worrier, it concerned him that they could fail without Samuel to oversee the operations. Rumor had it that Simon, in keeping the books, occasionally took a little extra for his beloved Livia and no one complained about that.

When the henhouse was clean, Clare took fresh straw and filled each nest that lined the wall, then sprinkled the straw with lice powder to keep infestation down. She was almost finished, feeling unbelievably dirty and smelly, when Hallie stepped into the henhouse, an egg basket over her arm.

Hallie, a new yellow bow fashioned by Aunt Livia in her hair, gasped. "Clare! What are you—?"

"Never mind, just never mind," Clare ordered, brushing at her filthy skirts. "I've already gathered the eggs, they were in the baskets outside the door in the hall. Didn't you see them?"

"I thought there might be more. You look terrible, and phew," she held her nose. "Why would you—?"

"Poppa's very busy, Hallie. I took this chore for him and helped out, that's all. Now, please, just forget it. There's no need to mention this to anyone."

Momma knew, and hated that Clare must tend such lowly work in the barns and shed, but dreaded more that Poppa would be ill-treated if the work went undone.

"Doctor Plummer was at the house this afternoon."

"He was? Someone's sick? Hurt?"

"He came to see you. Aunt Livia says you are very lucky that he thinks of you as a potential bride. Maybe he was going to ask for your hand today. But we couldn't find where you'd gone and the doctor returned to the village."

Clare hid a smile, immensely relieved that she'd missed him.

"If he could see you, I don't think Doctor Plummer would want you even for a maid of all work."

"Such a pity, too." She made a mocking face, then said seriously, "Hallie, dear, you know what fussbudgets our aunts can be about what is proper for a young woman and what isn't. So I beg you to keep it our secret that I was cleaning the henhouse when Doctor Plummer called. Sometimes a person has to do what they have to do even if it's not ladylike. I'm going to take a bam before suppertime so make sure everyone stays out of the washroom. And would you please stop staring!"

THE TENSION at Hobb's Mills didn't let up; if anything, it worsened. When a late summer storm left the flour mill turbine clogged with debris, Poppa was blamed for not clearing it out soon enough, which led to a break down and loss of time and production.

Aunt Livia's favorite chestnut mare threw a shoe and fault fell on Poppa for not noting ahead of time that it might happen. Livia ranted for a week that because of Poppa, the precious creature could have been lamed.

He didn't sharpen scythes and saws properly. Any task not done to perfection he was ordered to do over again. If Poppa did a job well, and much of his work was fine, it was ignored or made light of. All that autumn, her uncles' and aunts' treatment of Poppa would send a healthy-minded person over the brink! Clare was convinced. She had to wonder if that was their intention?

It was hard not to hate her uncles and their wives, hard not to throw up her hands at it all and run to Larkin, the man she loved and couldn't forget no matter how hard she tried. It would be so easy to admit that life without him was near unbearable. But letting him know that would give him hope, which for now she would not be able to fulfill.

———

SANDWICH VILLAGE RESEMBLED a Currier and Ives holiday lithograph come to life when, a few days before Christmas, Clare went with Poppa by horse-drawn sleigh to deliver a few small orders for bolts of cloth, and bags of flour. She would also complete errands for Momma and the Aunts.

"Wait for me after you're finished in the tobacco shop, Poppa." But he was already off across the snow-packed street without answering. Clare frowned ruefully, then shrugged. He'd been out of tobacco for days and smoking his pipe was one of the few things that gave him peace.

With Momma's list in hand, Clare hurried into the general store. She hummed to herself, it was hard to resist the Christmas spirit pervading the town. It took almost an hour of deliberation to make her selections and to give a few minutes to the occasional friend who came in and wanted to express holiday greetings and chat.

The winter afternoon was dimming and snow fell softly when she stepped from the store into the sharp cold. On the street-comer, a group caroled, *Joy To The World.*

All that faded when she noted the heavy-coated figure next to their sleigh talking to Poppa as he fed their horse a handful of oats. Larkin. Her pulse skittered crazily.

"Merry Christmas, Miss Hobb." He touched his hat.

"Merry Christmas, Mr. Wade." The formality was ridiculous, but so much had changed. Even before the tragedy, their intimacy was a secret to most, including Poppa who stood waiting, smiling, his nose above his beard red from the cold.

Larkin leaped to aid her into the sleigh. "Let me help." He tugged at the soft robe to cover her. His gaze was tender, soft as a caress. "Cold out. You don't want to take a chill."

She pulled the robe from his grasp. "No, one doesn't want to do that. Thank you." His nearness and touch, after so terribly long, made her senses spin. She tried to shut out all awareness of him as he shook hands with Poppa and they stood talking for a few moments about winter work.

"You're trying to sell your place I hear," Poppa said as he climbed into the sleigh and took up the reins with a jingle of harness bells.

"Ayuh. Had an offer the other day but the man wanted me to practically give him the place. Can't do that. I'll hold out as long as I can."

"I hate to be rude," Clare said breathlessly, "but we need to be going, Poppa." If they sat there another minute she'd be leaping into Larkin's arms, to cling to him forever and let the devil take the hindmost. "Good day, L-Mr. Wade. Please give our holiday wishes to your family."

He stepped back, frowning. But he tipped his hat and said, "Our holiday wishes to your family, too."

Clare, her cheeks flaming against the cold, nodded and they glided along the street with harness bells tinkling.

She didn't wish Larkin ill-fortune in his attempts to sell out, but it was comforting to know he remained nearby even though out-of-bounds to her. An occasional glimpse of him was balm to her aching heart and wouldn't hurt, providing she stayed the course of her intentions as long as was necessary.

She would cherish the image of him today, feel the touch of his hand as he covered her with the robe—the sound of his voice as he wished her a happy holiday—for a long time. And one could never tell when their situation might change through some miracle or other. *Merry Christmas, Larkin, I love you so...*

It was a few days after Christmas, the sort of cozy evening Clare liked. She sat reading her book before her family's sitting-room fire. Oakley and Hallie lay on the floor chattering as they put together a puzzle. Momma sewed, Poppa dozed in his big chair. At a knock on the door to their private quarters, Momma rose to answer it.

Uncle Edward directed his words to Clare, looking up from her book. "Clare, Doctor Plummer is waiting downstairs to see you." Edward's expression brooked no disagreement.

Clare's stomach turned over. She bit back a protest that being courted by Doctor Plummer was pointless. Unfortunately, a few days previously, she'd promised Momma she'd give the good doctor a chance. They would spend a few evenings together, get better acquainted personally. Then, if Clare still wanted no future with the doctor, Momma and Clare would make that clear to Edward and Simon and the others, hopefully without raising further ire against Poppa's family.

Closing her book, Clare spoke as graciously as possible, "Tell Doctor Plummer I'll be down. I'd like to change, first, though." She buried a sigh and went to her room, putting off going downstairs by brushing her hair for several minutes, and then putting on a different dress. Her uncles' recent ultimatum that she welcome the doctor, treat him with the good manners a Hobb showed any guest, felt akin to a prison sentence. But it was that, or add further to the resentment building against the "burdensome branch" of the Hobbs.

Downstairs in the main parlor, Clare and Doctor Plummer played checkers. When his pudgy hand attempted to cover hers, she moved her hand quickly, smiled, and asked about winter activities down in the village. "I hear the library has stocked some new books? I've read *Jane Eyre* and *The Tale Of Two Cities*, several times each. I can hardly wait to read The *Portrait Of A Lady* by Henry James, I hear it's quite good."

"You don't want to weaken your brain by reading such trash, my dear," he appeared genuinely shocked. "Those books are fiction!"

She sat to attention and seized this opportunity. "But I love to read, especially fiction! I love it! And how does one decide what's trash and what is not, without judging a book for themselves?" She hopped her checker over several of his and smiled at him sweetly, "Do you have time to read for pleasure, Doctor? I know how busy you are."

"Medical journals," he clacked stoutly, "medical journals. Political papers."

"Of course."

It seemed forever before they finished the game, and then the doctor asked, "How about a little music, Miss Hobb? Would you play the organ for me, dear?" He nodded toward the organ that sat against the opposite wall, draped with a fringed burgundy cloth.

She tried to beg off, "I'd love to, Doctor, but I play very poorly." It was the truth, she had little gift for music. On the other hand, Alice was quite musically talented but never touched the instrument anymore. Hallie would like to play, but no one seemed to have the time to teach her.

"But you'll do your best for me, won't you?" Doctor Plummer was asking.

She shrugged in resignation and went to sit at the organ. She began, her fingers lightly stroking the keys and her feet pumping the pedals. She was inept, really quite horrible, but the doctor didn't seem to mind. He stood at her shoulder, singing out in a rich baritone as she played, *The Flying Trapeze,* and then, *I'll Take You Home Again, Kathleen.*

"Sing with me," he urged after a few minutes, with a rattle of his false teeth, "I know you have a sweet voice, from hearing you talk." They sang several duets. His voice was much better than hers, and he obviously loved to sing. His favorite was, O *Promise Me,* and after three renditions of the same song, Clare could have wept from boredom.

After a while, he took her hand from the keys and kissed her fingers. She pulled her hand away, stood up, and moved away from him in discomfort. Why did he always have to stand so close, his belly practically against her?

"As I warned you, I'm not skilled at playing die organ and it's been ages since I've even tried. I apologize for playing so poorly."

"Doesn't matter, dear, for now it doesn't matter. I'd love to see that you have lessons." His expression was adoring, "We could have a future, joyfully filled with music."

"Doctor Plummer, I really don't think—"

Before she could turn away, he reached for her, his breath a mix of whiskey and rotted food as he attempted to kiss her.

Clare turned her face just in time, and moved from his grasp, saying with a quick smile, "My sister Alice made a batch of delicious ginger cookies today. Please make yourself comfortable there on the sofa, doctor, and I'll bring you some cookies and tea." She ignored his frown of disappointment, and flew to the kitchen. How many evenings like this must she endure, before the elderly doctor recognized how little they had in common? Before the others accepted that she would not marry Doctor Plummer under any circumstance?

Due to his busy medical practice, and involvement in politics, the doctor's visits were spaced far apart that winter, and she was eternally grateful. Because her uncles were against strong drink, and thinking it might help her cause, she pointed out to them that the doctor was usually on the verge of inebriation when he did call on her. She was chastised for not concentrating on the doctor's many fine qualities, for making a to-do about this small manly flaw.

Demon rum, or no, they wanted Plummer in the family, and she was the offering.

Chapter Five

April, 1886

THANKFUL TO BE OUTSIDE FOR A CHANGE, CLARE WALKED down to the riverside gristmill for a bag of fresh ground meal. Sunlight streamed through the trees along the river, birds sang in the blackberry bushes.

As she neared the mill she spotted Uncle Edward and Uncle Simon behind stacks of bags on the platform. Edward spoke Poppa's name, Frank, more loudly than the rest of what he was saying, followed by a derisive laugh. What now? She slipped nearer, crouched behind a bush, and strained to listen above the crushing, grinding drone of the mill stone from within.

"We have to do something about Frank," Edward was telling Simon, somberly. "The welfare of Hobb's Mills is in my hands, yet I can't get Mother to see that Frank is destroying us, that his mistakes have us on the down grade." With her eyes intent on their shadows falling across the mill wall, Clare frowned and continued to listen, catching snatches of their conversation.

Simon agreed, "It gravels me that because he's Mother's favorite, she won't hear a word against him. Maintains that he's as important to the running of Hobb's Mills as he ever was. Which is pure nonsense!"

Edward chuckled without warmth, "Poor imbecile. Best job for

him would be to stick his feet in the dirt, plant himself for a scare-
crow to keep birds out of the crops. Be more help than harm, that
way." He concluded, "We've got to take the matter in hand, face
the truth of his uselessness whether Mother sees it or not."

A chill traveled Clare's spine. What on earth did they have in
mind?

"He'll never do an honest good day's work again," Simon
growled, "which means double the work and trouble for everybody
else while he's molly-coddled."

Clare's heart ached for Poppa. She was torn between covering
her ears and running away, and stepping out to shout at them what
cruel liars they were, to talk so about her father. But she couldn't
move.

"—there was that time I sent him to clean the beaver dam from
the river above the flour mill, remember?" Edward said. "The
beaver's tangled mess was clogging the flow."

"I remember," Simon recalled in disgust, "that instead of
getting to work to save us time and money, Frank sat down on the
bank to watch the creatures, the weak-brained fool! After what
happened to Sam, a man wonders what Frank will bring down on
us next?"

"You're wrong!" Clare exploded from hiding. She gathered her
skirts in her free hand and raced up the steps to the platform, her
voice raised so they wouldn't miss a single word, "Poppa only
watched those beaver for a moment. He sat down to take his boot
off and shake out a sharp stick. And Samuel—"

"This is none of your business, girl," Edward's eyes were wide
in amazement at her audacity, butting into a private conversation
between her male elders. "Go on about your duties now." He
waved as though she were a child or a bothersome gnat. His conde-
scending attitude was typical but annoyed her particularly today
and she stood her ground.

"I won't go. Poppa is my business, he's my father. And it's time
the two of you forgave him for what happened to Uncle Samuel.
Not that Poppa was at fault any more than Samuel himself! Uncle
Samuel tortured that horse, caused it to run—"

"Mind your tongue, Miss!" Edward's good looks vanished as
his face swelled like a toad's. "I'll stand for no back talk from a
young snip!" He glowered at her when she didn't budge. He

advanced and shook his finger at her. "Well then, if you want the truth we'll give it: We have only your father's story for what happened to Samuel. I pity your Poppa, Clare, he was a good man once. But I ask you to remember that his brains have been scrambled and for too long now he's just not accountable."

His words brought her unbearable pain and it was hard to breathe. Before she could protest that their heavy-handedness was much of Poppa's problem, Simon was speaking, "As far as the beaver incident, it was your father's job to keep the river clear of debris so the water wheel didn't get clogged. He failed at that simple task—like so many others. The debris had built up far more than should've been allowed from the early spring rainstorms, not to mention the beaver dam. An' he still sits down to take a twig from his boot? We lost time grinding at the mill and time is money! A young woman, of course, never thinks of practical matters."

"I do! And you're too hard on him, both of you." Clare's eyes flashed. "All Poppa needs is a little patience and caring and he'd do his work just fine."

"Fine?" Edward's hands lifted as though he might throttle her. "If Frank was doing his work fine, Samuel would be alive, dammit! Are you blind, girl? Your father acts normal some of the time but we all know he's not. He is a feeble-minded burden, a dangerous one. None of us can turn our back on that."

"He's your brother, your blood kin," she reminded with tears stinging her eyes as she backed away. "Poppa's not at fault for what happened to him. And he does the best he can."

"Not enough," Edward said, smoothing his anger. His voice was grave, "Because of your father's—handicap, Samuel isn't here to look out for his family, for poor Polly and the children. Not here to do for the rest of us like Samuel always did."

Simon threw in, "Don't have to tell you, young lady, that your father hasn't been able to do his share, take care of his own as a man should, in years. If it wasn't for your grandmother's generosity, the lot of you would be living at the poorhouse."

She gasped, resisted the urge to cover her ears, to stomp her feet and scream. To throw herself at them and pound them with her fists.

Edward continued, "Your Uncle Simon and I are concerned for the welfare of each and every one at Hobb's Mills. Lord knows what this all is going to come to, but it's a worry, we grant you, keeping Hobb's Mills profitable so that it provides for so many. Clearly, you don't understand that we have more to consider than your father's well-being alone. Eventually, he may have to be—" he didn't finish, but exchanged a quick look with Simon. "We've work to do, young lady," he smiled in fatherly fashion, reached to pat her shoulder, "and I'm sure you have tasks needing your attention." He turned on a heel and with Simon following, moved toward the deep interiors of the noisy mill.

An icy hand gripped Clare's heart as she watched her uncles go. What had Edward been about to say? Surely they wouldn't try to have Poppa committed? Taken from his own family? If they had any such plan, Grandmother Hobb wouldn't allow it, and personally, she'd fight tooth and nail any such thing happening.

A few minutes later, she found one of their hired fellows to provide her with the bag of meal she'd come for. Bidding the man good day, she stepped out of the cool mill into the sunshine, her mind churning with turmoil over the situation between Poppa and her uncles.

At first, she was too shaken from her angry exchange with Edward and Simon to pay heed to the tall shadow crossing her path. She looked up, and her eyes met Larkin's intense gaze. A few feet away his horse was tied to the mill's hitchrail. The music of water splashing over the mill's water wheel filled the void of silence between them.

She fought a nearly overwhelming desire to throw herself into his arms. Tell him everything, and beg his help in ending this terrible situation. Instead, she tried to move around him, her heart too full to speak. He blocked her way. She looked up, and finding her voice, insisted, "Let me by."

His slate gray eyes taking her in were troubled, his normally kindly mouth, grim. She fought remembering what kissing that mouth was like. Her heart raced uncontrollably as she tried again to move around him. He caught her arm. Hadn't she had enough trouble for today? She tried to wrest her arm from his grasp.

"I was hoping I might see you, Clare," he said huskily. "It's been a long time." The truth was, he looked for her everywhere he went. Today, coming for some flour for Ma, he'd gotten lucky. Except for the shadows under Clare's eyes, her expression of worry and sadness, she was more beautiful than ever and he wanted to just look at her and look at her.

"It's race to see you, Larkin. Now, I really must go."

She didn't meet his eyes. Would have walked away without another word. As though he were practically a stranger, and never a sweetheart. He had heard rumors that Doctor Plummer had his eyes on Clare as a prospective bride. Surely she wouldn't care for a man old enough to be her grandfather!

"I'm not your enemy, Clare. Please, let's talk."

She flushed and said, "I must be going. I'm expected at home. Please let me by."

"Don't do this, Clare, don't hurry off like I'm nothing but air." His hand on her arm was firm yet gentle. He drew her toward the trees where the river rippled quietly over the rocks. Sighing, she let him lead her. "Privacy," he stated. "We need privacy and we need to talk."

"I've been busy," she said when they halted in the shade, out of sight of the mill. "I've tried to explain that to you before but you refuse to understand. My family needs me now." *There are things happening at Hobb's Mills that you don't know, that I'd be ashamed to tell you.*

He nodded, resisting the urge to snatch her into his arms, bum his lips across hers to wake her from this sad withdrawn state, melt away her decision that they were finished. "You've not even fifteen minutes to spare, to come to the Rock so we can talk and mend what's happened to us, allow me to hold you?"

"Don't, Larkin."

"I'm only trying to understand," he insisted. "If you knew how much I miss you, how much I love—"

"Please don't say it, L-Larkin, I beg you. It hurts too much, because...." her voice died.

"I know, your family needs you. I need you, too, Clare. You behave as though how we feel about one another can be tossed aside and ignored. I don't agree with that one bit. I'll love you to the day I die and I know damn well you love me, too. Say you love me, because you know it's true!"

Looking down at her, he watched myriad emotions play across her face: regret, alarm, sadness—affection. For a second he thought she might even discard her outward ruse of disinterest. His hope deflated when her defensive manner returned. "Please, Larkin, let's not talk about this anymore." She spoke sharply and tried again to pull away from him but he couldn't let her go.

"I don't want to force you, but what's happening is about as clear as mud to me. I think I deserve a few words with you at the least. In the village when we both happen to be there, you hardly look up when I speak. Or you duck and hide. I'm lucky to get a nod from you and I don't remember the last time you smiled."

Momentarily distracted by her beauty, he nearly lost his train of thought. "What's really the matter, Clare? Your Uncle Samuel died tragically, and that's very sad, I don't deny it. My heart goes out to you in your feelings. But there's more to this—this avoiding me—than your Uncle's death. You've dropped me like a hot potato. I beg you to tell me what this is really about."

"It's as I've tried to tell you before, I shouldn't have been with you that day. Because I was. Uncle Samuel died." She looked away from him. "Everything is changed, Larkin, and it can't be helped." She stood trembling, and finally looked up at him, her eyes shiny with tears.

"What's changed, that can't be fixed?" he asked softly. He attempted to pull her into his arms. She pushed him away with her bag of meal.

"What can't be fixed is that I can't bring my Uncle Samuel back to life! I'm the one who could have made the right choice that day, to help my father. Because I didn't, Samuel died. Everything's gone wrong." Things she never wanted to tell him poured from her lips, "My father is being treated wretchedly by his brothers and their wives. They blame him for Samuel's death and I'm too much of a coward to tell them the truth, that what happened is my fault."

"Clare, my darling—"

"No, don't touch me. You asked, and I'm trying to tell you." Tears of fury stung her eyes. "They browbeat Poppa constantly to punish him. They humiliate him, and I'm sure they'd prefer simply to be rid of him. I have to stand by Poppa in these troubles, take care of him and my family, don't you see? Even if I chose, there is no time for-for us, nor could I possibly take the chance of such a tragedy happening again. Now you know. Please let's just leave it that."

"I've seen some of how your father is treated by his family. I respect what you're wanting to do, Clare. I feel the same about taking care of Ma and Nick. But please don't shut me out in the bargain."

He caught her slim shoulders in his hands. "The tragedy happened and can't be changed, it's true. But you and I belong together. Let's face what comes, together. I want to take care of you." His fingers wrapped around her chin and forced her to look at him. "I will help you care for your family. We can be— married." This wasn't how he'd planned to propose marriage but the words spilled from his heart and he was glad they were finally out.

She hesitated, surprise in her eyes and a whisper of joy in her faint smile before her expression became blank again, her feelings buried. She shook her head. "Our marrying is not an answer and isn't possible in any event."

"Damn it, Clare! Save me a little pride, please! I'm about to throw myself at your feet and grovel, beg like a pure fool because I love you so! Or—" he hesitated, his frown deepening as he let her go. "Maybe you agree with your kin that I'm not worthy of you? That Doctor Plummer could provide for you far better? If that's how you feel, I can't blame you, because for now it's true enough. I'm a near penniless farmer but that won't be forever."

A good dozen men had come in past months to view his farm with a prospect of buying it. None had. He had one or two offers, laughably low, that he'd been tempted to take. But he'd held on, not selling, because the next prospect to come might want the property enough to pay a fair price.

Unexpectedly, placing her parcel on the ground, she grabbed his hand, then quickly let it go as though it bunted. She squeezed her fists at her side. "You're more than worthy in my eyes, Larkin, so please don't believe that. My uncles are ignorant about many things and about you more than any other." She withdrew a delicate handkerchief from the ruffle of her sleeve and wiped her eyes. "I care for you, Larkin, more than I can ever say. But I have my family to think of—particularly considering that I've brought this terrible thing on them. I could never leave them. They depend on me."

He caught her shoulders again and shook her gently, his heart in his eyes, insistent, "Marry me and I'll take care of the lot of you!"

She didn't answer. She didn't have to. The truth of it was,

trying to wrest a living off his farm of rocks, he could scarcely take care of himself, Ma, and the boy, let alone a wife, her parents and siblings. What did he have to give to a girl and her family used to having the best of everything? He let her go. She retrieved her bundle and walked away from him, across the road and up the knoll toward Homestead House gleaming richly in the warm spring sunshine.

———

FOR DAYS FOLLOWING their meeting at the mill, Clare's mind was haunted by Larkin's face, his expression of disbelief and heart-shattering disappointment at what she'd had to tell him. Of course he'd find it hard to understand why she must deny him. A person would have to be in her shoes to truly recognize the facts: that the bargain she'd made with herself to give him up for her family's sake, was the only recourse possible. That doing so tore at her heart as much as it hurt him. She'd read once that time healed broken hearts. At the moment she doubted it to the depths of her soul.

To the best of her ability, she had "swept up the heart and put away love," but could she succeed at it as the poet Emily Dickinson had done?

Events continued to prove she had no choice but the one she'd made. The warmth and respect shown her father and mother in the years before Poppa's head injury, by his brothers and their families, had completely dissipated. At every opportunity, Frank, Eugenie, and their children were made to feel like outsiders and no longer a viable part of Hobb's Mills. In spite of a warm spring, everywhere there was an emotional chill and feeling of impending doom.

There were days when Clare felt she couldn't bear another moment, but was hard put to find any answer other than to be a buffer, when she could, between Poppa and his kin's ill-treatment of him. She encouraged Momma and her siblings to keep their chin up and to pray that the ill-feelings swirling about Hobb's Mills toward them would eventually fade. Samuel's family found it hard to forgive and it was taking a long time. Good, happy days were bound to return to this life, this place, they all loved.

CLARE WAS in the summer kitchen with the rest of the Hobb's Mills females helping to preserve raspberries.

"It's time you helped with the berries," Aunt Livia said to Clare half-teasing, half-resentful. Her eyes were like amber glass. "Where were you this morning when we were out picking?" Her manner said she already knew but wanted Clare to say it for everyone else to hear.

"Clare was shoveling out the cow shed," Hallie spoke up. "She does chores like that a lot, when she thinks nobody will catch her at it. I think she likes the animal barns."

Clare glared at Hallie who simply shrugged and popped a red raspberry into her mouth.

The women as a group stared at Clare. Aunt Polly's face, above her high-necked black widow's weeds—which after a year she could pack away but didn't—puckered in shock and distaste. "Shoveling out the cow shed? Why-ever-more? Wasn't that your father's job? I heard Edward giving him orders—"

"I didn't mind. Poppa was busy elsewhere."

"Oh, Clare, think of it," Aunt Juliette's narrow chin dipped as she chided in her soft voice, "there's women's work and there's men's tasks. It's not seemly for you to do barn work. So dirty, so—." She shook her head with the honest horror she felt.

"I hope," Aunt Polly, said, her eyes rolling toward the ceiling, as she stirred a steaming pot of raspberry jam, "that Doctor Plummer doesn't get wind of such doings." Perspiring in her black dress, she grabbed a towel and patted her face.

"Oh, for heaven's sake!" Clare turned on them all. "I'm here, all of a piece, the same person I ever was except for a small blister on my thumb. I'm not ruined. Shoveling manure didn't hurt me, it's honest work that has to be done."

It was as if all the air had been sucked from the room in one unified gasp when she said manure. Aunt Polly clutched the edge of the preserving table. "You would use that word? I never—!"

Momma was equally displeased. "Clare, love, you must not use coarse language. What's come over you? Apologize to your aunts and cousins this minute, and never use that word again!"

"All right, I'm sorry. I apologize. But if—" she smiled around tightly at each one, "it's necessary for me in future to shovel-whatever you want it called—I'll simply have to do it. And to any of you who'd like some variety from endless dishwashing, making beds, matching countless stockings on wash day, polishing lamp globes over and over, making berry preserves —I recommend a bit of barn work. The cows, the chickens, the pigs, are appreciative as much— or more—than humans!"

Others in the room looked askance while normally sober Alice covered a smile with her berry stained hand.

Aunt Polly was furious. "You would make such silly remarks, you, whose addlepated father's blundering sent my husband to his grave! How dare you!"

Momma gasped and Clare felt as though she'd been stoned. She licked her lips and said through a dry throat, "I'm sorry, Aunt Polly if I offended you, but Poppa—"

"No 'buts'." The hostility in Polly's eyes scalded. "Your father is the one who should have been doing the barn work. However, when does he ever do as he should? He's trouble, dangerous, and if something isn't done about him..." she didn't finish.

"Uncle Frank could go completely crazy, attack one of us women!" Livia, the pampered aristocrat, shivered and hugged herself. Her eyes were wide, her voice just above a whisper, "Don't you all worry about that? I do!"

Eugenie, stricken, finally found her voice. "Livia! Polly, what are you saying?"

"I'm saying that Frank should be put away, that's what! Taken down to Concord where they put other crazies!" Polly sniffed, "We'd all be better off."

Livia nodded agreement fiercely. Aunt Juliette looked uncomfortable but didn't speak in Poppa's defense, either.

"Better off? Crazies?" Eugenie was pale and looked like she might faint. "My poor husband! You really think—?"

Clare stepped around Momma and faced Aunt Polly, and Livia. "My father isn't insane! He's only a little confused at times due to his old head injury. Aunt Polly, are you sure it isn't that you want to hurt Poppa, hurt Momma, and their children because of what happened to Uncle Samuel?

"We're all terribly sorry about Uncle Samuel's death, but you have no cause to abuse my father the way you've all been doing."

She directed her final word to Livia who had turned her back on Clare, pretending not to listen, "Poppa would never hurt another soul, especially a member of his own family."

Grandmother Hobb banged a wooden spoon on the table to get their attention. She was very pale, but her eyes flashed anger. "There will be no more talk of sending Frank to Concord. I won't have it, do you hear? I'm quite aware of what's been happening around here these past months, the blame that's been heaped on Frank for Samuel's accident, a tragedy Sam brought on himself through foolish anger. I've lost one son, and I won't lose another. We are Hobbs, all of us, and we will respect and care for each other —right here at Hobb's Mills."

The women went back to their assorted tasks with the berries, chastised and outwardly minding Grandmother Hobb's orders.

But Clare overheard Aunt Livia hiss to Juliette, "Frank is her favorite, and the old woman chooses to be blind to his mental failings. Of course he should be put away and Simon says he will be, before long. What if Frank goes on an insane rampage and kills one of us like old man Hoit killed Anna Dow? Remember, they found her choked to death in Peaslee's pasture? Frank's not right in the head, after all."

"Oh, I don't believe he'd ever hurt any of us except by accident," Aunt Juliette whispered back. "But—but maybe he should be put away. For his own good, just in case. Safe Harbor For The Feebleminded, down to Concord, is a nice place, I'm told. It's crowded, I hear, so we might not get him in right away." She added, as though it was important to the decision, "They make nice baskets and brooms, those folks at Safe Harbor. Baskets and brooms better than some of our craftsmen right here in the village make."

Livia's pretty nose twitched, "Somehow, we have to help Grandmother Hobb see that it would be the best thing to put him there."

Never, Clare thought, never. But she was too frightened to put her thoughts into words. Surely, Poppa's own brothers would not put him in an institution? But from all evidence, they were at least considering the plan. And what exactly did they envision for her and Momma, Alice, Hallie, and Oakley? Would they be exiled from Hobb's Mills? Put out to work elsewhere? Taken to

Portsmouth or Concord or Manchester and turned out on the street to manage however they might? Would they end up in the poorhouse?

Clare brought her runaway imagination into check. Of course that wasn't Edward and Samuel's intention. They might hold hard feelings toward Poppa, and because of it ridicule, criticize, and underestimate him, but they would never stoop to anything so dastardly toward their own blood kin as putting him in that institution when it wasn't really necessary. Would they?

Chapter Six

"Sir?" Larkin scratched his jaw, stunned at the gentleman's offer. After months trying to sell his property and receiving lukewarm interest, he'd about given up. Now this genial, finely-dressed fellow from New York was offering to buy his farm and pay him ten times more than it could be worth! *The man is a fool. Or was this a dream and I'm the fool?*

They stood in the cottage yard, the visitor's hired horse and buggy waiting by the barn. For most of the day they had examined the property together, in and out of the barn, shed, and chicken house; strolling up the hill fields and back down.

Mr. Seeley, the prospective buyer, had breathed deeply of the scented air and over and over exclaimed about the magnificent views, the convenience to the lakes and streams. Larkin agreed to the beauty of the countryside, but couldn't the mail see for himself how difficult it would be to farm the rocky acreage?

"Would you repeat your offer, Mr. Seeley?" He'd hear it one more time before his conscience forced him to blurt out the property's faults—poor soil, scant pasturage, the rocks that seemed to breed more rocks.

Seeley chuckled and repeated his offer. "Five thousand dollars. All right, six if you're going to give me a hard time. I've looked over much of this pristine area of New Hampshire. Heard about your farm being for sale when I was looking at another property near Alton Bay. If you'll sell it to me for six thousand I will have made a very good bargain."

Six thousand dollars wasn't great wealth, although it was an outrageous sum to pay for the property, much more than Larkin ever thought he'd come by. It would be funds enough for a new start and better than he had. Maybe, he thought, out West. Start all over with Clare at his side.

He was not alone in wanting to look elsewhere for a livelihood. It seemed like every other week a family from those parts set out for the West and more fertile farmland. Others went off to the industrial mills of southern New England cities, for better pay than could be had from hardscrabble hill farming.

If he was ever to realize his dreams, he must put this money where it would mean something and have a chance to grow. That is if the man was still foolish enough to buy after he told him the truth.

"Mr. Seeley, you must want to know why I'm wanting to sell." He felt the offer slipping away as he continued, "I got to warn you, this property isn't as fine as it looks. It's not—"

Seeley held up a hand, "I know exactly what I'm buying, Mr. Wade. I can see that you're concerned you'd be taking a man's money for a pig in a poke. You'd be right to feel you're cheating me, if I was thinking of fanning this property."

"But if you're not going to farm—?" There was timber on the higher slopes of the property, spruce and hemlock, that could be made into lumber. Even that, though, wouldn't be profitable for a man paying so much for the land.

Mr. Seeley's eyes were sparkling as he looked about, ignoring Larkin's question for the moment. "If I'm not rushing you, how soon might I take over?"

"Uh—um, s-soon," Larkin blustered, still in shock, "whenever it suits you." He followed Seeley as he strolled the larger hillside field one more time, seeming to mark off measurements in his mind.

"I'll have to tell my family," Larkin said to Seeley's back. "We'll need to decide what we want to do, where we want to go. I'll need a little time to sell whatever farm stock we won't need for the new start." His eyes took in a small flock of sheep further up the slope, back down at three cows grazing behind the stone barn. Ma would likely want to take her chickens, and her piglets.

Seeley turned and nodded in satisfaction. "Two weeks? Three?" He rubbed his palms together. "I'd like to get my workers up here as soon as I can, get as much of the hotel built this summer as possible."

"Hotel?" Larkin stared at Mr. Seeley and wondered again if the man was out of his mind or at the least, ribbing him? His farm was sure no city, not even a village. A hotel in the middle of nothing?

"Indeed, a hotel. A grand hotel, one-hundred rooms, I think. Like those in the White Mountain country north of here. Like Profile House, in Franconia Notch. You know about that one?"

Larkin shrugged, he didn't.

"Wild, beautiful country up there. Profile House entertains guests from all over the United States and Europe, clientele the likes of the Vanderbilt families and Ulysses S. Grant. But I like what I see right here. I heard that a branch railroad into Sandwich is hoped for, is that true?"

"True." He'd heard those hopes himself, but doubted the railroad would ever come.

"Doesn't really matter," Seeley said, as though he read Larkin's mind. "The coach ride from Wolfeboro to Sandwich is so beautiful, I don't believe folks will mind not traveling by train the last few miles."

He shook his head and smiled at Larkin, "No sir, Mr. Wade, I wouldn't attempt a day trying to get a profit from your land by farming! However, it's perfect for a resort hotel catering to wealthy folk who want to escape now and then from crowded, bustling city life to a quaint rural area."

"Are you sure?"

"I am. People from Boston, New York, Chicago, would see all this," he waved his arm, "as paradise. It's peaceful, the scenery magnificent. City folk hunger for beauty such as this. I would put in riding stables, arrange wagon ventures to the lakes for swimming, boating, fishing. In winter there would be sleigh rides and ice skating. And in the fall —can you imagine what city dwellers whose view is nothing but big buildings would think of New Hampshire's fall colors? Oh, they'll come, they'll come."

Listening, Larkin saw the reasonableness of the plan. He might have tried it himself, had he thought of it, but in the end he wouldn't have had the funds necessary to launch such an undertaking. A hotel of one-hundred rooms, riding stables and all.

"—saw the quaint mills down there," the man was saying, motioning toward Hobb's Mills in the river vale a few miles distant. "Do you think the mills might be for sale? The hotel could make its own flour, linen, wool, lumber. I think vacationers would like that added charm."

"I'm sure, Mr. Seeley, that Hobb's Mills can't be bought. The Hobb families have owned it for generations and are settled in pretty fair." His thoughts turned to Clare, wondering with burning curiosity what this change in his luck might mean to the two of them?

He hadn't given up, had made several more attempts to see Clare following her pronouncement that day at the mill that they were finished and he must accept it. She wouldn't budge. On each occasion she had barely spoken to him. Her manner almost angry, as though she regretted that they'd ever met.

If she truly meant to never have any more to do with him, it would be torture to remain in Sandwich. Life here would be unbearable if he was not allowed to see her, touch her, feel the warmth of her smile and affection. He would ask her again to marry him. go West with him. He wouldn't let himself think that her answer would still be no when he told her of his newfound fortune.

"Will you stay to supper?" Larkin asked, after he and Seeley had gone to the house for a cup of coffee at Ma's kitchen table.

"I'd be pleased to. Is that baked beans I smell from the oven?"

"Ayuh," Ma said pridefully. "An' there's fresh greens wilted in vinegar and sugar. We got brown bread, and berry pie."

In the end, Mr. Seeley, well-to-do New Yorker, also spent the night. By lamplight in the Wade's humble kitchen, he and Larkin discussed details of Larkin's moving out, and Seeley's construction crew moving onto the land to commence building.

Next morning after breakfast they set off together to complete their transaction at the bank in Sandwich village. Following that, they visited the tavern and toasted the event, both delighted with the deal they'd made. Numerous friends clapped Larkin on the shoulder in congratulations and no little envy. They listened with doubt, though, to Mr. Seeley's prediction that New Hampshire was on its way to being a playground state, his claim that most residents' income would one day come from the pockets of vacationers!

They were more inclined to agree with Larkin's view, that a man wanting to make a good new life was wise to go out West.

Larkin felt better that day than he had since Samuel Hobb's death, and Clare's spurning him right after. Surely she would see reason now.

———

WORD SPREAD like wildfire that Larkin Wade had sold his farm and the new owner meant to build a large fancy hotel to cater to rich vacationers.

Nick came to Hobb's Mills and shared the news with young Oakley, adding that the Wades would be departing for the West within a week or two. Oakley, envious of Nick's opportunity to become a cowboy, could talk of little else.

When Clare heard, she was devastated and set out for a long walk through the orchard and fields to recover. Larkin was leaving, he was going out West. Her senses spun dizzily and it was hard to breathe from the knowledge she was about to truly lose him. He could meet and marry another where he was going.

She'd known that his property had been for sale and that there was a possibility he would leave. But she hadn't accepted that it would actually happen. Her heart had chosen to believe that he'd always be a short way up Young Mountain road, available should her situation change.

As she walked, she was barely aware her surroundings, the song of birds in the orchard, the fragrance of sun-warmed grass under her feet. One plan and then another came to mind and was discarded. The fact remained that she could not cut her ties with Larkin entirely. Never. She came to the road that led to the Wade farm and she began to run. She knew what she could do, and still help her family.

He was in their shed, sorting tools, his ruggedly male back to her through the open door. "Larkin," she said softly, "I heard your good news."

He came outside into the bright sunlight, staring at her as though seeing a beloved ghost. When he finally shook off his surprise, he moved to take her in his arms then looked down at his dirty shirt and changed his mind. "I was about to clean up and come to Hobb's Mills to see you," he told her. "I was coming to your door and this time nobody was going to turn me away."

"I've come to ask a favor," she told him. His mussed hair and the smudge of grease on his tan cheekbone didn't hurt his handsomeness one bit.

He grinned, "Anything, Clare, you know that."

She paced for a moment then asked pointedly, "When you find your property out West and get settled, would you look for land there for my family? For Momma and Poppa, my sisters and my brother, and me? Then send us word?"

He looked puzzled and shrugged. "Of course I could do that but it's not necessary. You know what I want for us, Clare. We can be married and you can come along as my wife."

She frowned. The silence stretched between them, broken only by a woodpecker at work on the shed roof, a breeze soughing through nearby trees.

"I'm honored by your offer, Larkin, but I can't accept. I can't leave my family and I won't burden you with their care. I ask you just this one favor: to look for land for me and my family as well as for yourselves." She stood firm as a rock.

Making a sound deep in his throat, he shook his head and turned his back on her, his hands on his hips. Then he turned to face her again.

"Dammit, Clare! In just a little while I was going to come find you and ask you again to marry me." His eyes gleamed. "Nobody on earth was going to stop me from finding you at Hobb's Mills and making my proposal on bended knee, in front of all your snobby folk if I had to."

"You mustn't—" she shook her head, a defensive shine in her eyes.

He persisted, "I thought, a minute ago when I looked up and saw you, that that's why you came to me—to admit we belong together, should go West together." He reached for her but seeing how his words had disturbed her, his hands dropped to his sides.

Yet he couldn't let it go at that. "Please don't refuse me, Clare. Come away with me—"

A knot ached in her throat and it was hard for her to speak in light of his determination, his love. "I'm sorry, Larkin," she said huskily, "but that's not why I came today. My situation hasn't changed except that my family needs me even more than when I last saw you. I can't abandon them." If she walked away from her family now, if she were not available to protect and fight for them, Poppa would surely be committed.

"You're heaven to me, Clare, I love you! And you're asking me to be just a landseeker for you, not your husband? Let's go to the preacher tomorrow."

"We can't."

He ignored her and plunged on, "Ma will come help you and your folks pack up for the trip West. I'm having a look at Kansas. We'll find good land together, as man and wife, with your folks and mine." His strong tan jaw set and his look was determined. "I'm not poor anymore, Clare. I'm not wealthy, either, but I'm not poor. I got money enough from sale of the farm to make a very good start out West. I want to take care of you and your family. It will work out, I know that it will."

He was completely serious and she loved him all the more for it, but she couldn't let him do this. She shook her head. "No. I've thought this out carefully. I won't burden you with my troubles, with care of my family. You deserve the new start without additional charges. I only ask that if you come across good farmable land, free or at a very small price, that you please let me know. I must find a way to get Poppa and Momma away from Hobb's Mills before—" She stopped, chagrined at having said too much.

"Before what?" His brow furrowed. He moved toward her, heart rending tenderness and concern in his gaze. "Before—what, Clare?"

She looked away so that he couldn't see the regret she was feeling, her anger at the unfairness of her position. "It's complicated, and unpleasant to speak about."

If she told him the truth, that her uncles might try to have Poppa committed to a mental institution, and that she, Momma, and her siblings were being treated like outcasts in their own home,

Larkin would be angered enough to do something rash— like stay here to protect her and not follow his dream in the West.

The way her uncles felt about Larkin, his intervention could make things even worse, for her family and for Larkin. She cared too much for him to risk ruining his chances.

"I feel I'm asking a big enough favor as it is, Larkin, if you will just do this one thing for me, please, and not ask questions."

"Are you being threatened, Clare? I have to know. Are you or your family in danger of some kind?"

"Nothing like that. It's just that—we may not be able to make our home at Hobb's Mills very much longer. My uncles worry, with the economy failing as it is in these parts, that the mills can't continue to support so many of us. Maybe—in that respect—it's time for us to go. I admit, also, that the bad feelings my uncles hold toward Poppa have extended to the rest of us. To Momma and me, to my brother and sisters. But I'm not in danger, Larkin, truly. And even the unpleasantness could pass in good time."

"If anything bad ever happened to you—" anger sparked in his eyes, "I'd have to hurt someone in return, even your uncles! They are such fools to blame your father for Samuel's death! And no one has the right to make life so unpleasant for you and your folks at Hobb's Mills that you feel you must leave. Hobb's Mills is your home as much as anyone's. You should be allowed to stay as long as you please, stay until the day you marry me."

She blinked back tears. "Thank you, Larkin. I appreciate how you feel. But let's not speak of marrying when nothing can come of it."

He still looked angry, but his voice was soft, "If you change your mind about going with Ma and me, there's time. You and your family can join our traveling party. We don't have to marry if you're so against it. We won't be leaving for another week yet. Think about it, Clare. I want you with me."

She sighed, wanting to go with him as he asked, more than anything, but it just wasn't possible. "I promise to think about it, Larkin. But when the time comes for leaving Hobb's Mills, it won't be easy to uproot my family.

"In spite of the ill-feelings toward us just now, we all love Sandwich. As you say, it's our home, the only home we've ever known. Any other life would be strange to us, and maybe even more difficult. It's possible I won't be able to convince Momma and the others to leave, ever. Circumstances at home would have to be very much worse. I'd have to have a definite destination to offer. A better and safer place, or I don't think any of them, except Oakley —who'd give anything to be with Nick— would go. And they can't manage without me, I'm convinced of that."

"I'll find land for you, Clare, as soon as I get there. So fast it will make your head swim. You won't have to spend a day longer than necessary here in New Hampshire. You're going to be with me, in Kansas."

A smile broke on her face. "Thank you, Larkin."

"Thank you for asking the favor."

In a couple swift motions, he whipped off his dirty shirt and tossed it on the ground. He pulled her close, wrapped her in the blanket of his love, kissed her hard. His heart, beneath his bare skin, thudded as one against hers that beat furiously below the thin fabric of her dress.

Clare's breath caught, his mouth on hers throbbed with a passionate message. He whispered her name. She clung to him, her mouth ravenous for his. This was wrong, when they had no future as man and wife, but she couldn't help herself. But maybe, just this once—

"Larkin," she whispered urgently, "is there somewhere private —?" she was too embarrassed to finish.

"Oh, my love," he groaned, "do you mean—what I think?" He looked at her intently, as he considered her invitation. In the next moment, regret was in his eyes. "I want to make love to you more than anything else on earth, Clare. It's all I can do to hold myself back. But if you won't marry me tomorrow and come with me, then I won't risk leaving you with child—to face alone the shame that'd cause you."

Her emotions whirled and skidded. Clear-headed reason returned and with it a maelstrom of disappointment, humiliation, shock. What had she been thinking? The trouble was, she hadn't, she'd let desire carry her away. Of course he was right.

She removed her hot, teary cheek from his chest. Eyes down and feeling utterly miserable, she whispered, "I'm sorry, Larkin, that things have to be the way they are. Truly sorry. But my family must come first right now, and possibly for a very long time. I can't marry you, I can't go with you."

"It'll be different someday." His voice was rough and tender at the same time. "Wait and see."

He pulled her back into his arms and she felt a strange numb comfort.

Chapter Seven

_____

IT WAS HARD NOT TO BE DISAPPOINTED WHEN A LETTER DIDN'T arrive from Larkin those first weeks after his departure. But then, Clare reasoned, it would take time for him to reach Kansas. Possibly a very long time to locate land for himself, and for them. She must be patient and keep herself busy while she waited to hear, not let her mind go imagining terrible things.

——

"I BEG YOUR PARDON, Doctor Plummer, what did you say?"

The robust doctor was paying a social call, had shared the midday meal with the entire clan at Hobb's Mills, smoked with the men in the library afterward, and now sat with Clare in the parlor. She was exhausted from responding to his attempts to converse with her, ashamed she couldn't keep her mind on what he was saying.

"I said, 'that hotel being built up Young's Mountain Road is going to be the grandest structure in these parts, don't you think?'" His teeth clattered as he spoke, and the alcohol on his breath, typically strong, was nauseating.

"It's appears the hotel will be very grand when it's finished."

"That Wade fellow who owned the property took his money and ran to the West, Fin told." His fat jowls bounced; "Wise thing to do, I suppose. At the same time, I'm beginning to agree with that New York gentleman who is building the hotel— that catering to visitors from other states is going change the face of New Hampshire, will be a good thing for us all."

This reminder of Larkin—it was September and she still hadn't had a single word from him—was almost more painful than Clare could bear. For sure she could not put up with her guest another minute. "I—I'm truly sorry, Doctor Plummer. We women spent a long hot morning in the kitchen, preserving apple butter and I'm very tired. I apologize for being such poor company."

"I'm to blame," he said cordially, teeth clacking. "I've overstayed until well past candle lighting." He used the old-fashioned term although lamps, not candles, had been in use at Homestead House for ages. He hoisted his huge form up from the sofa. "It's obvious you have other things on your mind and have had a full day. It's I who should apologize and take my leave. Will you walk with me to the gate, Clare? I came by foot today, I've put on a few pounds and felt the walk would be good for me."

"Of course, Doctor." She stood eagerly, yet awash with guilt at how much she wanted him out of her sight. Sooner or later his talk would rum serious about the two of them. This evening she was not up to the game-playing that would hold him off.

The air had turned crisply cool following a warm afternoon. Leaves rustled down from the big maple tree in the front yard. The smell of ripening fruit wafted toward them from the orchard as they made their way down the lane through twilight shadows.

It was a night Clare might have enjoyed being out in, given other circumstances.

At the gate, the doctor turned to her, his eyes glittering in the twilight gloom as he took her hand in his pudgy one. She was instantly on guard, instinct telling her that he had more on his mind than saying goodnight, and he was determined to have his say. She resisted the urge to turn and flee, waited courteously. She would let him down kindly if possible, but her answer, long graven on her mind, would be a firm no.

"You're very lovely to this old fellow's eyes, Clare. You're intelligent, sweet, well-mannered. An ideal young woman who'll eventually get over her penchant for imaginative misbehavior at times."

Her mouth dropped in surprise. Misbehavior? It had been ages since she'd felt free to walk the hills, gather flowers, climb a tree, slip off to meet the young man she loved.

Did he know about me and Larkin in the past? No, he meant my other passions —for long walks, watching birds, picking flowers. Pleasures I 've had to set aside due to obligations, not because I 've outgrown the things I like most.

She waited for him to go on, more than ready with her reply if he'd just get to it.

"I'm sure your uncles have relayed my fondness for you, revealed my intentions toward you?"

"Yes, doctor, they have, but—"

"I would consider it a great honor if you'd consent to be my wife, Clare." He continued before she could respond, "I believe I have much to offer as a husband. I'm far from poor, I have prospects in government, I would not be against having children with you, if you want them."

"Wait Doctor, please—!" Have children with him? She flushed to the roots of her hair, looked at her toes. She was a farm girl and had some clear ideas how offspring came about. She couldn't imagine herself with Doctor Plummer doing that.

She blurted the truth. "I have no interest in marrying anyone at this time, Doctor Plummer, I must make that very clear. Please don't take offense." She spoke earnestly, "I'm honored that you've asked for my hand in marriage. I'm sure there are many women in Sandwich who'd welcome the chance to share life with such a man as you, truly! But I must decline." She thought of lonely Alice, but she wouldn't wish this curmudgeon on her dear sister.

In the fading light, she watched his face sag into wrinkles of disappointment. "Are you sure, Clare?" he clattered, "I can give you a little more time to think about my proposal of marriage if you wish it?"

"That won't be necessary."

"You have no interest in being my wife?"

"I'm sorry, no." None, none, none.

He gripped her hand and then with no warning he hauled her against his stomach. "A kiss then, just a kiss," he lisped and clattered, "I miss—loving a woman—so much."

Clare struggled to free herself, "Doctor Plummer, please! What are you doing?"

He was very strong and wouldn't let her go. "C'mon, don't resist me." His mouth slopped all over her face and then he began to drag her behind the stone wall that lined the lane.

"Doctor Plummer, stop! Please!" She twisted in his imprisoning arms. His clattered endearments, "so sweet, must have you... lovely girl," sent chills of fear along her spine. His strong breath made her sick.

"Dearest girl, please understand. I want you so. I must—" One hand came up to graze her face and throat. "You are so beautiful, so young." His fingers tried to get inside her bodice, the sound of a button popping was loud in the evening stillness. "Your skin feels like flower petals. Mmm, so smooth."

"Stop it!" She jerked back fiercely but he clutched her in the vise of his arms.

"Don't fight me sweet one. If we just—now, now, lay down girl!" he ordered, forcing her backward onto the grassy lawn. He dropped on top of her, his weight driving the air from her lungs. He panted in her ear, "You'll marry me, be glad to, when you're no longer a virgin. You'll be happy as my wife. You'll see."

She was riven with shock at his words and then she began to fight him ferociously. "Doctor Plummer, you've had too much to drink!" She freed her right arm and as he tried to kiss her she drove her elbow into his nose. He howled and clutched at his face. She rolled away and leaped to her feet.

His nose was bleeding when he staggered to his feet. Several dreadful seconds ticked by. He seemed dazed as he looked at her in the gloom, her rumpled clothing and the dark bits of grass in her hair. She was panting hard, her furious sobs sounding like a hurt kitten.

"Oh, my goodness. What have I done? Miss Hobb, will you forgive me? I got carried away. Are you all right? I didn't mean to do this, I swear." He drew out a handkerchief and mopped his nose.

"You had no right!" she told him hotly, brushing her skirts and pushing her hair from her eyes. To think that he believed she'd be glad to marry him if he took her virginity! At the moment, if she had a club, she'd beat him senseless with it.

"No, I didn't have a right. I've never done anything like this before. But you're so appealing and— Please, Miss Hobb, it won't happen again. I'm a good man, a good doctor. I beg you, don't speak of this to anyone. I'll do anything, if you'll just keep this our unfortunate secret. Please, don't tell—"

"I'd be too ashamed to tell anyone! All I ask of you is to behave yourself, and leave me alone. Completely. Do you understand, Doctor Plummer?"

"I'm a lonely old fellow. Miss Hobb," he shook his head, "but of course that's no excuse for my behavior tonight. I won't bother you again, I promise."

She felt sick to her stomach. "Please, just go." She waited, shaking, and didn't feel safe until he was weaving away toward the village.

The instant he was out of sight, she sat on the ground, shivering uncontrollably. Tears were hot on her face as she rocked back and forth, her arms locked around her knees. "Oh, Larkin," she whispered, "Larkin. Why didn't I find a way to go with you? I have to get away from here. Why, oh why haven't you written, so I can come wherever you are?"

She sat there for a long time, needing strength to stand, to go up to the house and pretend that what had just happened never occurred. Finally, she dried her tears on her sleeve and with a heavy sigh got to her feet, walking slowly. Moments later she climbed the steps of the verandah and stumbled to sit in one of the wicker chairs, her head in her hands.

It was hard to believe what had just happened. But her quivering insides, the pain in her elbow and her back, her humiliation, were proof enough that it had taken place. She whispered a small prayer of thanks that she'd escaped from the doctor in time.

A few minutes later, Momma came out to the porch, carrying a pretty, softly glowing lamp. She placed the lamp on a small wicker table and took the chair next to Clare.

"Doctor Plummer asked for your hand?"

Clare stiffened, but spoke in as normal a voice as possible, "Yes, Momma, he did, but I turned him down."

Momma frowned, but she nodded. "Your decision won't sit well with the family, as you likely realize, dear. But you have a right to do your own choosing, and I wouldn't ask you to do otherwise."

Clare left her chair to kneel in front of her mother, and hug her. "Thank you, Momma, thank you for understanding. I can handle the others." Not easily, though, it was just one more trouble added to the rest.

As she returned to her chair, Clare wondered if marrying Doctor Plummer, bringing such a highly regarded man of means into the family, would have made things better for Momma and Poppa, eased the tension against them? It was possible her uncles planned to foist Clare and her family into Plummer's hands as a means to be rid of them. As Momma said, they weren't going to like it one bit that she'd turned him down, run him off as it were.

If she was another sort of woman, she might've agreed to marry Doctor Plummer. Spend a few months as his wife, then divorce him, take his money, and do as she pleased. She had too much conscience for such a move, unfortunately. Even to the pawing old doctor, she couldn't be that cruel.

The better plan, one she could carry out and keep her self-respect, would be to take her family from here and move west. Maybe she was foolish to believe she'd see Larkin again. He hadn't written in all this time. But she couldn't have married the old doctor in any event, not even as a way to solve her family's problems. She'd save herself for Larkin—in case there was eventually a chance for them.

"It's a beautiful evening, isn't it?" her mother broke the silence in a while. "Dove, you're missing a button." Momma strained to see in the light from the lamp.

"I think it came off in the laundry and I didn't notice," Clare mumbled. "I'll repair it tomorrow. Yes, it's a very lovely evening," she sighed, glad to give her attention to other matters. "I don't expect any place is as beautiful as here in the fall. Everywhere you look these days, the leaves on trees are the colors of rubies and gold." For a while they were quiet. "Momma," Clare reached to take her hand, "have you ever thought of leaving Hobb's Mills, of living somewhere else?"

Momma frowned. "My goodness, no, why do you ask?"

"I just wondered, if, when you and Poppa were first married, you might have considered striking out on your own, seeking 'new vistas', so to speak?"

"It never crossed my mind to live anywhere else, and why would I want to? I have everything I've ever wanted, right here at Hobb's Mills. Your Poppa, my children, Grandmother Hobb who has always been so kind to me. This place is in your father's blood, he was born here and he could never adapt to anywhere else."

"But there's so much trouble between Poppa and his brothers."

"Oh, some of the family can be difficult at times," Momma agreed, speaking casually although her face showed deep concern. "But that's to be expected in any family. You take those moments with a grain of salt and keep your mind on the good times, the blessings you have. Now, you, Clare, if you were to meet and fall in love with a young mail who wanted to take you away, why I'd just have to convince him that the both of you would be better off right here," she waved a hand toward the darkness in the yard, "right here at Hobb's Mills."

Clare smiled sadly to herself. It was as she suspected. If they were ever to leave Hobb's Mills, it was going to take gigantic effort to convince her family. "Why are Uncle Edward and Uncle Simon so harsh with Poppa?" she blurted, "He's not responsible for what happened to his mind, and he loved Samuel as much as they did."

Minutes passed and she was afraid her mother wasn't going to reply. Finally, she answered and her voice was faint, "They are afraid of your father."

Clare sat up straight. "What do you mean? He wouldn't hurt anyone."

"Not that. Something else," she hesitated, deliberating if she should say more or not. "They believe that Grandmother Hobb is too softhearted about your fa titer's—weakness. The mills aren't as profitable as they once were, what with so many folks leaving the country. But to my mind, our mills and the farm has always had ups and downs, and always will."

"I'm sure you're correct."

Momma continued, sounding regretful, "It's your uncles' concern that because Poppa is not as able to care for his own family as they are able to care for theirs, that Grandmother Hobb, when she dies, will leave a larger portion of Hobb's Mills to your Poppa, than to them." She added quickly, "I wouldn't want that, either. I'd want your grandmother to be equally fair with all her kin. Still, it's her right to do as she pleases. In the end, she may do what they fear."

Clare whispered, "—so that's it. I felt there was more behind

Edward and Simon being so critical of Poppa. Greed. They don't want Poppa to inherit."

"I'm afraid so, but please, Clare, don't mention a word of this to anyone. There's trouble enough." Her voice quivered, "Hard feelings about Samuel's tragedy are so slow to die down. No need to add to them about a matter that may never come to pass."

It was like Momma to want to forget, to pretend nothing was wrong. Clare, on the other hand, sensed imminent danger ahead, a worsening of their family situation that would have to be faced square on and resolved.

Chapter Eight

January, 1887

LARKIN'S SECOND WINTER BLEW IN ACROSS THE KANSAS plains. Over the past many months he'd written several letters to Clare, telling her where he was and to let her know that luck was with him, that she should come. There hadn't been a single response.

Although his determination to find land right away hadn't panned out exactly as he hoped, a few months after his arrival he'd found the place he wanted. One thousand acres of rolling prairie, a stoutly built, though plain, farmhouse, and outbuildings. A few head of cattle were thrown into the deal. He'd worked himself near to death since then, to make ready for Clare's arrival. As promised, he found properties he thought would suit her family.

With every post, his hopes ran high that he'd hear from her— that whatever problems preventing her from writing back were solved, and she was on her way. Or he pictured that she would just show up on the next train, bag and baggage without writing ahead, her reasons her own. He thought of her night and day, his spirits plunging when weeks passed and there wasn't an answering letter, when there was no sign of her arrival.

Now, he piled more wood on the flickering flames in the parlor fireplace and took a nearby chair, his head in his hands. In the kitchen, Ma hummed to herself as she cooked up a chicken stew. She was the salt of the earth, such a help to him—with encouragement, great meals, keeping the house clean. Nick was out somewhere sledding with other boys from the nearby town of Sweetbrier.

As he sat there, Larkin asked himself a dozen questions and in turn rejected the answers he came up with. Had Clare changed her mind altogether about coming west? He supposed it was possible, she loved her home place, Hobb's Mills, dearly. Did she love it enough to stay where her uncles were so strict, and cruel to her father? Were her mother and father refusing to budge? Maybe she had decided Doctor Plummer was the better deal and she had married him. Wouldn't she still write and tell him if she'd had a change of heart?

Were his letters getting lost somewhere along the way?

It was possible that her uncles were keeping his letters from her, but that didn't make a lot of sense if they wanted to be rid of Clare's family. Wouldn't they be glad to send them off to Kansas? Not into his keeping necessarily, they had little regard for him, but just out of their way? If Clare wasn't receiving his letters, she wouldn't know how to reach him.

He would write again, but this time he would send his letter to her in care of the owner of die store where Clare and Larkin met, and he'd request the storekeeper, Mr. Aldrich, to give the letter to Clare personally. He was a fool for not thinking of this sooner.

If she wasn't here by spring, he was heading back to New Hampshire to get her. Bring her home with him to the Kansas Flint Hills. He raked his hands through his hair and went to get his writing paper, ink, and pen, revived with fresh hope.

————

CLARE LAY in bed on a late February day recovering from a severe bout of sore throat and fevers. Frost laced the window and a fire crackled in the fireplace of this room she shared with Alice. She was glad winter was about over, spring made the worst of situations seem better. And this past year, with Larkin vanished to the West, had been the most difficult of her life.

Hallie entered the room, head down reading the Bloomingdale's mail order catalogue she carried open in her hands.

Clare rasped, "The mail came?"

Hallie nodded absentmindedly. "This Bloomingdale's catalogue came for Aunt Livia. Momma asked Aunt if I could bring it
up to you to look at." She stood there, still turning pages and
studying them. "Here's a 'Princess of Wales adjustable bustle'. I
wonder if Momma would let me have that?"

"She may," Clare coughed, covering her mouth with a hanky,
"you could ask." A second bout of coughing ripped through her
chest and when it was over, she gasped for air. "Hallie, was there a
letter for me?" It had been a very long time since Larkin had gone
west, saying he'd find property for her right away. Was it more difficult to find land than he'd expected?

Hallie shook her head. "Uncle Simon is the only one who got
letters. Business, I suppose, orders and payments for the mills."
Her eyes were glued to the page. "Would you look at this Cash-
mere shawl, it's beautiful!" Her mouth opened wide in astonish-
ment, "Oh, my goodness. They are asking fifteen dollars for it!
Well," she surmised, "Uncle Simon would probably buy it for Livia
if she asked, he adores her."

Yes and yes, Clare thought, wiping her sore, red nose.

"Do you want to look at this?"

"Not right now. Keep it until you're finished."

Hallie dropped into a chair and pored over the book, mumbling
to herself, "I'd love to have this locket, just dearly love to have it."

Clare's thoughts remained with Larkin and the fact she'd not
heard from him in all this time, nearly a year and a half. Had something terrible happened to him on the way west or after he arrived
in Kansas? If so, wouldn't Ma Wade or Nick get word to her? Ma
Wade had known that they cared very much for one another, were
in love. She would understand that Clare would want to know,
even bad news. Unless a tragedy had befallen all three and there
was no one left to write to her?

She sighed raggedly, hated her feelings of helplessness as her
mind traveled back over events of the past months. Grandmother
Hobb, weakening with advanced age, had fallen and broken her
arm in November, and later, bedridden, she'd developed pneumo-
nia. For many weeks, fearing she might die, the entire family's

attention was focused on healing Grandmother and she was now recovering.

Poppa, during that time, had pretty much been left alone except for minor incidents. On one occasion, Aunt Livia claimed that Poppa had frightened her women friends she was entertaining at an afternoon tea. He had walked by her house; she claimed he stared through the window, and in a 'totally mad manner' had ogled the ladies. If Livia went for a walk, she viewed his presence anywhere in sight as a threat. Uncle Simon ordered Poppa to stay away from Livia, or else. Poor Poppa.

Clare feared that her uncles were biding their time, just watching and hoping for Poppa to make the move that would allow them to put him away in the Safe Harbor Institution. It was wearing on her, being the constant bulwark, but she couldn't let down her defense. Momma, also, did what she could to keep Poppa from trouble, making Oakley help his father so jobs would be completed on time, so there would be fewer mistakes.

———

ONE EARLY SUMMER DAY, when Clare was on her feet again, Oakley's gangly form came slamming into the kitchen at Homestead House. His hazel eyes were wild, his wheat-colored hair flyaway. "Fire!" he shouted. "Everybody, the sawmill's burning!"

Clare ran out the door. She gasped at the scene down the hill. Crimson flames and smoke roiled from the mill. The huge pile of sawdust waste on the offside of the mill from the river had also caught. Everything in sight could burn to the ground if the fire wasn't stopped.

Ignoring demands that women and children stay back, she joined the bucket brigade dipping bucketfuls of water from the river and passing them along to be dashed on the flames. Strident voices of terror punctuated the afternoon, the fire hissed and roared. She spotted Poppa repeatedly try to join the line and help, only to be shoved roughly aside, and even struck, by Uncle Edward. "Leave him alone!" she shouted. And then, "Poppa, come get in line in front of me. Here, take the bucket," she handed it to him, splashing, "pass it along."

There were ashes in Poppa's hair, soot on his face, and his eyes glittered with stark terror. She knew, deep inside, that he had something to do with the fire, and if he hadn't had, directly, someone was going to blame him for it anyway.

It wouldn't matter that sawmill fires were common and could start in a half dozen different ways. Lumber and sawdust waste were rich with volatile pitch and resin. A single spark from friction of the wooden shafts moving the up and down sash gang saws, powered by turbines, could set off a fire of immense proportions. A careless worker could cause a fire if not careful with the ash from his pipe, or cigar. Which was why smoking was strictly forbidden at the mill.

A worker, or someone from outside the mill, who held a grudge against the well-off Hobb family, could easily torch the sawdust unseen, with intent to destroy.

Clare worked on with the others, grabbing a filled bucket, passing it to the next until her arms screamed with pain. But there was no slowing down, no giving up. Her hair came undone and blew in her face, flying cinders burned her face, her hands. A steady ache settled in the middle of her back. Up and down the line, people shouted to move faster, the fire was growing, everything in sight could go up in flames.

An eternity passed before the fire was contained and the mill a smoldering black skeleton. The sawdust pile that to start with had been as high as a shed, was a huge, steaming circle of burned ground.

The chain of workers fell out of line, many dropping where they were to rest. The women who'd watched hurried back up the hill to make sandwiches and lemonade to feed the firefighters. Clare stayed, every muscle in her body aching from tension and long activity. She was wet to the skin, her hands were blistered from handling hundreds of wooden buckets of water. The skin of her face burned.

"Go to the house where you belong, Clare," Uncle Edward ordered, his expression grim.

"How did the fire start?" she asked him. Might as well get it over with.

"Do you have to ask?" he questioned, with a cold hard look at Poppa who was helping to stamp out the last sparks that flared where the waste pile had been.

IN THE EARLY dawn three days after the fire, a sound from outside woke Clare. She'd slept in fits and starts the nights since the fire. Ointment eased the mild burns on her face and hands, there was nothing to ease her conviction that someone, probably Poppa, was going to pay dearly for the fire.

Oddly, her uncles, cold-faced, refused to speak of the fire except to say that it was costly and that the mill would have to be rebuilt. Poppa wasn't mentioned in relation to what happened. Which was far more frightening than their usual ranting about him. Clare was riven with worry day and night.

She hurried to the window. Momentarily stunned, shock quickly yielded to deep fright and uncontrollable fury. Down below in the drive, Edward half-lifted Poppa into a hitched buggy. Assisted him, because Poppa's ankles were strapped together with a string of leather to keep him from running off! Like a prisoner! If she wasn't seeing it with her own eyes she would never have believed it.

Damn them, they were going to do it! Without a word of discussion, with no chance for him to tell his family goodbye, nothing.

She whirled and shook Alice awake in her bed. "Get Momma and come," she shouted through a tight throat. "They are trying to take Poppa away." Alice looked at her in disbelief, and then, her face rigid with alarm, threw back her blankets. Clare yanked a wrapper over her nightgown and raced outside in her bare feet.

Poppa sat in the buggy, submissive, his head down, barely turning to look at Clare when she called out to him. She clutched her wrapper with one hand, with the other she yanked Poppa's small satchel from the buggy and threw it to the ground. Never in her life had she been so angry, so desperate. She freed his ankles while Edward, seated beside him with reins in hand, blustered that she was interfering.

"You'll be sorry, girl!"

"Get out of the buggy, Poppa. Come with me. No one is taking you to Concord."

Poppa looked at her, mixed emotions and confusion in his face as he pulled away from her to stay where he was. "Edward says I started the fire with my pipe. It was my fault and someone could have died." He licked his lips. "I have to go now. I don't want to leave. Don't want to leave my Eugenie, my children, but they say I have to, that I could hurt my own loved ones, if I stay. Edward is right. I'm dumb and no good."

Tears spanged in her eyes. "Poppa that's nonsense, you'd never hurt us, or anyone else. Your mind is a bit slow, that's all. Maybe you forgot you weren't supposed to smoke in the mill. And maybe you had nothing to do with the fire at all. Anyone could have done it and we'd never know the truth."

Uncle Edward darted a frenzied, angry look at Clare, clicked his tongue at the driving mare, and once more tried to leave.

Clare ran around the rig and snatched the lines from Edward's hands. "You let my father go, right now! You're not taking him anywhere! I'll throw myself under the wheels of this buggy if I have to, but Poppa stays with me!"

"Don't be foolish, girl. We've put this off long enough." In spite of the fury in his eyes, Edward forced his voice low, effusing patience. "We want what's best for Frank, too, can't you see that? hi Safe Harbor Mental Institution he'll be taken care of, he won't be doing harm to himself or to anyone else. This is hard for you, for your mother—" he nodded to where Eugenie, in a white nightgown and flyaway robe, and Alice, came running from the house. "I understand that, but the decision has been made and your father agrees. The matter is final."

"It's no such thing! Poppa belongs with his family, not in a mental institution." She looked past Edward to her father, "Poppa, get out of this buggy, this minute." Her mind moved fast and she implored Edward, both hands gripping his arm that held the reins, running alongside the buggy starting to roll, "We were going, anyway, Uncle Edward, in just a few weeks. All of us, Momma, Poppa, my brother and sisters and I. We won't be in your way. We were leaving Hobb's Mills for good. It's what we want. Truly."

Edward's eyes narrowed in study as he looked down at her distraught and determined face. Shaking his head with doubt, he nevertheless drew back on the reins, stopping the buggy. "Going where?" he was blunt. "And how can you go, survive someplace else, with no man to look out for you other than your disabled Pa?"

"Kansas, if it's any of your concern! It's all been decided," she lied. "Grandmother will let us have a team and wagon and provisions. We'll be away from here by sunset, if you'll let my father go, let me take him."

Others had hurried outside at the commotion, some dressed, others in their nightclothes.

"All right," Edward wrapped the reins around the buggy's brake handle, "we'll discuss the matter if you're serious about taking Frank away from here."

"No, Edward, stay where you are." Simon bustled forward. "There's no use for more talk. We've made the right decision. This is for Frank's good, for the good of all of us. We've contacted Safe Harbor and they're expecting him. They've had a waiting list but they can take him now. It's all settled."

Livia's small booted feet trotted alongside Simon and she held his arm. They had risen early, coming down to Homestead House to make sure that Edward executed their careful plan.

"You should have married Doctor Plummer and saved yourself this situation," Livia coyly told Clare. "If you all had moved in with Doctor Plummer, he could have kept an eye on your father and he wouldn't need to be taken to the crazy house."

"Maybe you should have married Doctor Plummer, yourself, Livia! You'd be high society as wife of the upcoming governor and wouldn't you like that! Or—maybe you're the one should be put away with crazy people. I'm not sure of the health of your mind." Fact of the matter, it seemed to Clare that the worst sort of acts in life were often done by so-called sane people, not the mentally deficient.

"Keep quiet everyone," Edward ordered. "I believe Clare when she says they are making plans to leave here. You'll be taking on a lot of trouble, girl," he addressed Clare as he climbed from the buggy, "but if it's what you and your family really want, then I say, go ahead and make the effort. You have my blessing."

Poppa's family made a circle around him as he climbed from the buggy, Eugenie, weeping, put her arms around him. "Oh, love, oh Frank."

Simon patted Livia's arm to console her as they followed the others into the house. "There, dear," he kept saying, "there dear, I'll take care of you."

Polly was in the kitchen, starting breakfast with Juliette's help.

Hearing the explanation of what happened, a deep frown settled into Polly's face, her mouth was a tight hard line. "We'll see! We'll just see what Frank and Eugenie and their children do. I'll believe they are leaving when I see it with my own eyes! Shouldn't have all come to this. Frank should have been put away right after that horse kicked him and left him an idiot. I'd have my Samuel today." She glared at Clare, her parents and siblings. "We'll just see," she muttered.

Juliette looked miserable as she broke eggs into a bowl. But she said nothing.

In the parlor of Grandmother Hobb's quarters a short while later, Clare sat down facing her grandmother to ask her help. Edward and Simon had wanted to be present, but Grandmother had ordered them out of the room, she would speak with Clare first and hear her side of the story.

"We need a wagon and team, Grandmother. Some provisions and a little money. I've promised that we would be gone by sunset today. It was the only way they would let me have Poppa. If I hadn't stopped them, Edward and Poppa would be well on the way by now to Concord and that awful place where they keep the feebleminded."

Grandmother's face was grave and still pale from her lingering illness. "The fools! They'd not attempt this if I was on my feet, they wouldn't dare!"

"Things have been difficult for a long time anyway, Grandmother. We'll be better off in Kansas, away from Uncle Edward and Simon, and the others. Poppa will get better, I think, when he's not being harassed by their constant demands and complaints."

"It saddens me, though, oh, how it saddens me. We're family and we should stay a family. But I'm not blind, and I know my foolish sons and their wives have made life here very hard for you and your parents. I never thought it would come to this, but I suppose it's best you do go. Kansas, you say? Isn't that where the Wade family has gone? Mabel is a fine woman."

"I believe the Wades went to Kansas. I haven't heard for sure. Kansas is just one consideration. We could go to Indiana, or Missouri. I've heard there are farming opportunities in those states, too. We can support ourselves on a small farm, and perhaps I can take other work, too. I'll talk it over with Momma and

Poppa before we set out. If you will give us the means to travel on, I'm sure I can do the rest."

They'd get by, somehow. Hadn't her great-great grandparents, Nathaniel and Mary Hobb, arrived in the Sandwich area in 1768 on horseback with their household goods, all their worldly possessions, hauled behind them on a sled? Look what they'd accomplished.

"You're a wonderful young woman, Clare, and I have undying respect and admiration for you. I'll give you what you need for the trip, but you won't be traveling by team and wagon nor will you leave by sunset today."

"What do mean?"

"You'll take the time you need to get ready and you'll go in comfort by train. I'll see it arranged. We'll hire a boxcar or two to carry your most urgent needs to survive in the new country; a wagon, horses, a cow and a few chickens, tools, household goods."

"That's so kind of you, Grandmother!"

"Decide on your destination, let me approve your final plans." Tears filled her faded eyes, her pale lips quivered. "It breaks my heart to do this, to send you away from your home. I only pray that with time your uncles will regain some good sense, cease harboring ill-will toward your father, and you all can come back where you belong."

Choked with tears, Clare hugged her grandmother. "Thank you so much for this. We'll miss you dreadfully, Grandmother. And I, too, pray that someday we can return."

A bustle of activity commenced that same day as Clare and her family decided what they needed to take and what could be left behind.

Upstairs in their quarters, Clare lamented for the third time in the past hour that she wished she knew where in Kansas the Wades had gone. "It's helpful when adjusting to new surroundings and customs to know someone who is already familiar with the place," she said to Momma who was taking things from her wardrobe to pack in a large trunk. "But I suppose it's also important, from now on, that we learn to think and act on our own and not depend on others. Isn't that one of the reasons for leaving Hobb's Mills? Of course it is," she answered herself when Momma didn't reply.

They had decided to buy tickets as far as Kansas City, spend time there before deciding on a final destination. Clare was packing a small case with combs, brushes, and soaps when she felt her mother watching her.

"What is it, am I forgetting something?" She went on with her task. "I'm sure I've packed enough handkerchiefs." She turned to smile at Momma and found her standing very still with a dress draped over her arm and making no move to put the garment in the trunk at her feet. She wore the strangest expression Clare had ever seen on her mother's face.

"Momma? What's the matter?" Her mother broke into sudden tears and nervously patted at her apron pocket.

"Clare, can you forgive me?"

"For what, Momma?" Clare dropped a bar of lavender soap into the small chest and alarmed, went to her.

"Larkin Wade's letters." She seemed to drag the words from the bottom of her soul.

Clare's breath caught, her heart thundered. "Larkin's letters? What do you mean, his letters?"

Chapter Nine

Momma reached into the deep pocket of her apron and pulled out a sheaf of perhaps six or eight letters tied with green ribbon and held them out.

Clare's hand shook as she took the packet. "You? You, Momma? What have you done? I've had letters but you kept them from me—?" she looked at the dates on the letters, eight of them, from Larkin. The first had been posted soon after he left, while still in New Hampshire. One had been sent to her in care of Mr. Aldrich at the Sandwich general store. "You've had these all this time?"

"I'm sorry, dove," her mother was weeping to the point she could scarcely speak. "I know it was wrong of me. But I knew that you were in love with that young man. The boy, Nick, had seen you two together. He told Oakley that you and Larkin were meeting secretly. Oakley told Hallie and of course Hallie ran to me with the news as fast as she could. When Larkin Wade left these parts I prayed that would be the end of it. When his letters started to come, I had Oakley or Hallie, one or the other, intercept them and bring them to me. The last one was given to me by Mr. Aldrich at the store. You were sick abed at the time and I'd gone to town to trade. He gave it to me, saying the letter might cheer you up. But I kept it."

"Oh, Momma, why?"

"Not to hurt you, darling, truly. I—I was afraid you'd be rash and go to your young man. You seemed so unhappy after he'd gone. I was terrified that you'd leave us and join him in Kansas. Or that you'd want us to give up our home here and go, too."

"Momma, I would never have gone without all of you, or without your approval. And now you surely understand that leaving Hobb's Mills is the only choice we have, don't you?"

"I—I wish we didn't have to go. It frightens me so to think of starting over in some strange place. But Grandmother Hobb has advised me. We had a long talk, and she believes it's the only way to keep Frank out of the asylum."

Clare, her knees weak, went to sit on Momma's bed, the letters gripped in her hand. Most of them had been posted from a town in Kansas called Sweetbrier, so Larkin had found a place to stay, was by now likely settled in.

Her heart climbed into her throat as she opened the first of the Sweetbrier letters and scanned it, telling Momma. "Larkin says there is land for us and fine prospects. Oh, thank you, Momma, for not destroying these letters." She held them to her lips, tears of joy filling her eyes.

She went to put her arms around her mother. "Don't cry now, please. I forgive you. We have so much to do. Here, Momma," she handed her a handkerchief, "dry your tears and smile for me. There you are. We all need to put on a good face. We're going to Sweetbrier, Kansas!" They wouldn't be blundering off into the unknown like a bunch of dumb sheep. Sweetbrier, Kansas. Old friends to welcome them when they arrived. Larkin.

He would be a familiar face from home, she mustn't allow herself to look forward to seeing him in any other light than that. It was bad enough, that at night when her guard was down, she could think of nothing but Larkin. Everything came back to torture her then: his voice, his touch, the way he looked at her. Their hungry kisses. The ecstasy of being held against his strong body.

Everything she couldn't have.

Most nights she was possessed of an aching longing that could only be shaken off by morning's light and a long day of hard work.

Grandmother insisted to the rest of the family that Frank and his family would leave when they were properly ready and not a moment before.

In the next few days they continued preparations, choosing household goods, tools, and stock animals to take. As Clare worked, fragments of Larkin's letters flitted through her mind, butterflies of delight, causing her great excitement at the prospect of seeing him again, and peace of mind that her family was doing the right thing.

"I cussed myself roundly for agreeing to leave you behind when I wasn't more than fifty miles on the road," he had written in the first letter which he posted while still in New Hampshire. "I worry about you, my beautiful Clare, and wish you'd told me more of your circumstance which sounded fair dire to these ears. If only I could have convinced you to marry me, then and there. ANYTHING short of kidnaping you and causing you to hate me. I know we would be happy. Will be happy. I miss you so...

A few months after his arrival in Kansas he had written, "This land I've found may be the next thing to paradise. I have bought 1,000 acres at $2.00 per acre from a sad fellow who couldn't wait to sell out. Poor gent's wife took up with another man, a wagon freighter headed back east to Ohio. I couldn't share my own story—too private, although my heart surely broke as much as his when you told me you wouldn't marry me that day I asked you to come with me. I intend to change your mind, darling Clare, you can count on that."

"Clare, is anything badly wrong?" Larkin wrote with urgency in his most recent letter. "Have you changed your mind about leaving Hobb's Mills and your troubles there? I can't understand why there has been no word from you. I'm sure you and your family would like this place.

"Sweetbrier is a thriving village in Rolling Prairie township. The hamlet has neat homes and pretty yards. Signs abound of the local folks' pride and ambition. There are two each of stores and blacksmith shops, a lumber yard, grain elevator, drug store, harness and shoe store. A school and a church.

"As this is a major shipping point for cattle and wheat, the tracks of the Katy railroad—that's the Missouri, Kansas, and Texas line, has a depot on the southern end of town. If you come by train, you will likely take the New York Central line as far as St. Louis. From there you'll take the MK & T, also called the Katy, west to Junction City, Kansas and then south from there to arrive right on Front Street in Sweetbrier."

The last lines of the letter stated, "If I do not get a reply to this letter in a reasonable time, I'm coming back to New Hampshire to get you."

dare lost no time sending him a wire saying that she and her family were making preparations to come. Everything else they would discuss when she arrived.

The fact that Momma—who'd never do anything that would hurt another, especially her own daughter—had hid Larkin's letters from Clare, was proof enough how much her family needed her.

Uncle Edward was right, as much as she disliked admitting it, that moving her family to Kansas, dealing with Poppa's mental problems in particular, wasn't going to be easy. But she'd do anything to escape the torment her uncles and their wives heaped on Poppa. And to be near Larkin again, in any capacity, was worth whatever problems lay ahead.

———

UNDER A WARM SUN, Larkin stood in the Sweetbrier implement yard talking with the owner, an older, friendly fellow who wanted to sell the business to him. The owner had plans to move to the Pacific Northwest so he and his wife could live near their children. From the day Larkin decided to come to Kansas, he'd been careful with his money, waiting until he found a good farm he could afford, working hard to make his first crops pay, buying a valuable young bull so he'd have top-grade beef to sell in the future. Now he debated buying into the implement yard. There wasn't a lot of money left from the sale of his New Hampshire farm, but his Kansas farm was beginning to pay off already and the implement yard seemed like a good idea.

Along with the farm, the yard could provide a comfortable future for him and Clare when the time came they could get married.

He'd not had a word from her, although each trip to town he checked at the telegraph office across the street, and at the post office. His next stop today.

"This business will make you money, Wade," the dealer was saying as he mopped perspiration from his forehead with a blue bandanna.

"I know that it would, but I don't want to cut myself short. I've invested a lot of money fast," he frowned, "maybe faster than I should."

"Time for this is perfect, Wade. Folks are tired of planting and harvesting the old way, everything slow and by hand. They want machinery to make their labor easier, and to triple their profits. Tobias Proctor said he'd go partners with you. If I made the deal sweeter, would you buy, then?"

"Deal's sweet enough, and you're right about the timing being good." He hesitated. "Proctor came and talked to me about going halves." Tobias Proctor was a widower with two small children to raise. He was a good man and Larkin liked him a lot.

He was about to reach for the dealer's hand to shake on an agreement when he heard his name, "Wade, hey Wade!" shouted from across the street.

Across the way, the telegrapher, a thin, mustached fellow by the name of Nyle, stood out front of the small telegraph office next to the train depot. He waved a piece of paper.

"What say?" Larkin yelled back.

"Telegram, Wade! Think it might be the one you been waitin' for."

"Hold on a minute," Larkin told the implement dealer and strode to meet the telegrapher halfway. He scanned the paper and then let out a whoop. The wire was from Clare saying that she and her family were coming to Sweetbrier. He'd see her again, in a matter of days! He tipped the telegrapher every coin in his pockets, stood in the middle of the dusty street and read the telegraph over and over. It didn't tell him much, other than that she was coming to Kansas. It was enough.

Clare was coming, and nothing on God's green earth was going to stop him from making her his wife and giving her everything he could to make her happy.

Ma was going to be excited at news about the Hobbs. Nick would be, too. The boy had said several times since they'd arrived that he wished Oakley, Clare's young brother, could be there in Kansas to "cowboy" with him.

With little trouble, Larkin, Ma, and Nick had taken to this country. Might not be so easy for Clare and her family. They were a hardworking bunch, but they were also used to the best of everything. Kansas was as different from New Hampshire as night was from day. What if Clare hated it and wanted to go right back home?

That's what happened to the fellow who sold him the farm. His wife hated Kansas and left with another man. But of course Clare wouldn't do anything like that. Clare loved him, he knew it in his soul.

He was positive she'd have married him long before now, run away to do it if she had to, except that she was beholden to her family. Making herself pay for what she felt she did wrong, meeting him that day instead of going with her father and then her uncle getting killed.

Shoving worries aside, he told the implement dealer he'd be back later to discuss their agreement. A short while after that he got his horse from the livery and rode toward his farm. When he got there and shared his news, Ma was as tickled as he knew she'd be.

"I'm so glad they're comin'!" she told Larkin, eyes flashing happily as she poured him a cup of coffee. She shook her head, her smile replaced with a touch of sadness, and anger. "I saw for myself before we left Sandwich, besides what you told me, how bad Eugenie and Frank and their children were bein' treated. Like they was less than them others at Hobb's Mills. I don't hold with folks behavin' toward their own kin that way. It's not right. Frank can't help that he's simple, a lot of folks are. But you treat such folks kindly, if you got any decency in you at all."

She filled her own cup and sat down. "Eugenie is one of the sweetest women I've ever met, although she's delicate, has been from the time she was a girl. Don't know what that dear woman will think of Kansas, I reckon it will take time for her to adjust. Life ain't the same here as back there in New Hampshire. Now that Clare, she'll do all right. She's got backbone. Her sister, Alice, that quiet one you never hardly hear a peep from, might get along here all right, but I got high doubts about that youngest girl, Hallie. Spoiled, she is."

Nick came in, dusty and smelling of the barn. He was told the news as Ma served them cake. Nick chortled, "Oakley is goin' to be so glad to see that we're livin' smack dab in the middle of the Wild

West. We're goin' to have us a good time, ridin', and ropin' cattle, an' all!"

"Wild West?" Larkin laughed. "You might be right, this is ranch country, though I'm not sure it's that wild anymore. Anyhow, we're going to do all we can to make the Hobb family feel at home. Right?"

"Right!" Nick said with a grin, wolfing his cake.

"Well, of course we're goin' to make them feel to home," Ma exclaimed, "an' I better get to cookin' so there's plenty of food ready when they come. Got to set this house to rights, too. Shoo, boys, shoo right on out of here!"

"Sure, Ma." Larkin gave her a peck on the cheek, grabbed Nick's shoulder and hustled him outside ahead of him.

As he headed for the barn, Larkin whistled a tune that he remembered from the day he first spent time with Clare, at a summer-time picnic. Kitty O'Neil, wasn't that the name of it? He'd danced with her that evening, and once he'd held her in his arms he'd known it was something he wanted to do for the rest of his natural life.

THE TRAIN GROUND TO A STOP, wheels screeching. "Where are we?" Hallie asked with a pout, peering out the window at a clump of humble buildings, at clusters of people on the depot platform.

"Somewhere in Ohio, I think," Clare answered. "West of Columbus."

Poppa and Hallie weaved their way up the crowded aisle, intent on stretching their legs. "Don't wander far," Clare called after them, "we have only thirty minutes before we have to be back on this train."

She said to Momma and Alice as they joined the throng in the aisle, "If the two of you will go to the depot restaurant to get us some food, I'll walk back to the freight cars and check on Oakley, and our stock."

Within minutes, she was helping Oakley fetch water for their animals from the tank by the tracks.

Much too quickly, the iron beast, their home until they reached Kansas, began to roar and hiss. The conductor walked up and down the depot platform shouting, "Aboard, all aboard. Last call, all aboard!"

Clouds of steam rolled past the open door of the cattle car where inside, Clare and Oakley tended their chores. Hens clucked in their crates over cracked corn, their cow, Belle, tied in the comer, let out a loud mooo. The horse, Dan, drank from his bucket of water.

"You're doing a good job, Oakley, I'm proud of you," she told her brother in a rush. "I know it can't be too comfortable back here where it's crowded and stuffy—compared to the passenger car." The freight car held everything they now owned, their livestock and the feed for them, their wagon, furniture, pots, pans, dishes. "But it's a big help to have you here to watch out for our animals and household goods. It can't be more than a few days until we reach Kansas. I think we have enough feed for our stock to last, don't you?"

"Sure, there's enough feed." He kicked a bale of hay next to bags of oats and one of cracked com. "You better get going, Clare, or you'll be riding with me an' Belle an' the pigs. An' stop worrying."

"I'll be glad when I can stop worrying!" she said ruefully. "For now, it's my job. They say that a car left untended could be robbed. That reprobates could slip into the car at one stop and out at another, taking much of what we own with them. You're a safe-guard to that happening, and I want you to know it's appreciated."

Poppa had wanted to ride in the cattle car with Oakley, prefer-ring that to close contact with strangers, but Momma, uneasy at this venture they were undergoing, felt better with Poppa at her side.

"Goodbye, then, until our next stop." She hugged Oakley, who waved her out of the car. Back on the cindery ground, she hurried along the line of freight cars toward the passenger cars. She prayed the rest of her family had completed their missions and were back on board.

Clare was still several yards away from her own car when an altercation erupted up ahead. Folks starting to board waved their arms, shouted and stirred around like a disturbed hornet's nest. With horror, she spotted Poppa in the middle of the trouble.

She ran the rest of the way. A man gripped Poppa's arm with

one hand and drew his other fist back to hit Poppa. "Let it go!" the fellow shouted. "Drop it now or I drop you!"

"Stop it, this instant!" Clare rushed to Poppa's side and got between him and the red-faced giant. "You won't hit my father. I demand to know what's happening here." From the corner of her eye she saw Hallie, squeezed back into the group of onlookers as though she were one of them, a stranger to Poppa.

"He's trying to steal my wife's carpet bag," the man blustered, "come picked it up right in front of our eyes, and he won't put it down." He spewed a fountain of brown tobacco juice that just missed the hem of Clare's dress.

Clare frowned. Then she saw that Poppa held tightly to a reddish carpet bag that was almost, but not quite, identical to one of her mother's. "Oh, Poppa, that isn't Momma's," she told him quickly. He looked at her dumbfounded.

From the time they left Sandwich, Poppa had wanted to be in charge, to take responsibility for his family. Even to carrying their money. It broke Clare's heart to deny him. At home in Sandwich everyone knew him and wouldn't dream of cheating him. A stranger, sensing her father's fallibility, might take advantage. Momma, the only other adult, was only too happy to let Clare be in charge.

"There's been a mistake," she told the man and then addressed his frightened wife, "Ma'am, your bag looks like one my mother carries and Poppa picked it up thinking it was hers. All this shouting has confused him. He's not—he's made a mistake, that's all. Here, Poppa, give the bag to me so I can give it back to these nice folks."

She pointed, "See, there comes Momma and Alice." Momma hurried along carrying sacks of food, her face was twisted with worry. Alice had her hand on her arm and was saying something to calm her. Clare told her father, "Alice has Momma's red bag, Poppa. See?"

Poppa looked, and then seemed to shrivel with shame. "Sorry," he told the woman. "Sorry." He held out the bag.

"Better keep an eye on him," the giant said. "I just about hit him into seven Sundays. He could get hurt, pickin' up other folks' belongins' that away." This time Clare stepped out of danger of the brown stream that flew from his mouth.

The train whistle pierced the air, pistons began to grind and cars to bang. The giant wiped his mouth on his sleeve and hustled his wife toward the steps of the passenger car. "Get on the train, Annie Lou."

The rest of the crowd surged past Clare and her family to board. A snickering teenage boy looked back at Poppa and chanted, "Up the ladder, and down the tree. You're a bigger fool than me!"

Clare boarded last. She was barely on board before the train shuddered and lurched forward, almost throwing her off her feet before she scooted onto the seat next to Hallie.

She asked, her mouth an inch from Hailie's ear, "Why didn't you do something? You were standing watching and not lifting a finger to help Poppa, to explain the problem to those folks. If I hadn't come in time, that man would have broken Poppa's neck, and you would have just stood there and let him."

"I didn't want people to know," she answered in a near toneless voice, nose in the air.

"Know what?"

"That Poppa is relation, that he's my father." She cut a glance at Clare. "And before you start scolding I want to remind you that I didn't want to leave New Hampshire, either. Why'd we have to leave, anyhow? I liked it there. Hobb's Mills was our home." Her face puckered in an unattractive frown.

Clare glared at her younger sister. "None of us wanted to leave Sandwich, but may I remind you that because of what happened to Uncle Samuel we were all being punished daily, especially our poor Poppa. They were about to — Oh, Hallie, you know we couldn't stay."

"You all could have gone. You could've left me there. Aunt Livia would've let me live with her. I didn't need to come on this wretched trip."

"Yes, you did need to come along. We're your family. And I'm not so sure Aunt Livia would have welcomed you as much as you think."

At their leave-taking, Clare remembered, Livia had been incensed because Grandmother Hobb had given Eugenie a very old tea set that had belonged to Nathan and Mary Hobb, Poppa's grandparents.

Obsessed with the perceived injustice, Livia had utterly ignored tearful Hallie who didn't want to leave the aunt she so admired.

"Poppa can't help the state of his mind, but all of us can help him to be better. I'm ashamed of you, Hallie, for not coming to his defense back there. And I'm telling you now, before we go another mile, if you don't stop behaving like Livia, I'm going to—going to—I don't know what I'm going to do, but you will regret your actions I guarantee."

Hallie sniffed and pulled herself further away, her expression dark as she stared out the window at the farms and pastures passing by.

Clare sighed. "I don't like talking to you this way, Hallie," she told her softly, "but we have to help one another every minute if this family is to survive."

"What do you care?" Hallie glared. "You're making us move to Kansas so you can go off with that Larkin Wade. Then it'll be up to Momma and me, and Alice, and Oakley, to make sure Poppa doesn't do stupid things. You won't be bothered anymore."

Clare's cheeks burned. "Where did you get that idea? That's totally untrue. I'm taking us to Kansas because—oh, never mind, Hallie." It was useless to argue with the girl, who plainly sided with their aunts and uncles against her own family. Perhaps life in Kansas would change her, although some people never changed.

"Please remember what I told you, Hallie." Swaying with the motion of the train, Clare returned to her seat beside Alice.

Alice had done more than her part in preparing for the trip, but otherwise had had little to say. Once underway, she helped Momma and Poppa off the train, and on again at their many stops. She'd brought books to read for Hallie and Oakley. Even so, Clare had no idea what her older sister really thought about this trip. It was Alice's way to not talk very much about anything. Clare asked her opinion now, hoping for conversation to pass the long hours of travel.

"Well," Alice took a moment to consider, "I honestly don't know if leaving Hobb's Mills was the right thing to do. Momma is frightened of this journey, what we might be getting into, in Kansas. Everything so strange."

"You're right," Clare sighed, "but I couldn't see anything else we could do. Remaining at Hobb's Mills was impossible." She might have married Doctor Plummer, but that was a step she simply couldn't take. "Kansas, where we already have friends, seemed the best answer."

The truth was, Clare had felt a deep sense of peace, of being set free from hell, from the moment they boarded the train back home at Wolfboro. The feeling increased with every click-clacking mile away from New Hampshire. All the stops and starts at numerous burgs through Massachusetts, New York, and now Ohio were only minor irritants. They were on the move west.

Along with calm, she felt her confidence restored, reveled in expectation of better things to come for all of them. And what did they have to lose, anyway?

Not that there hadn't been pain, leaving Hobb's Mills. Clare faced the murky window, barely noticing her reflection, her mind on the day they departed.

Grandmother, always a very strong soul before her recent illnesses, had nearly crumpled to see them go. She was the only one who really seemed to mind their leaving.

Uncle Simon, the money hawk, was very disturbed over the amount of funds that Grandmother Hobb provided them. Never mind that it was barely enough for the trip, and a small start in their new life. His attitude was appalling. Then there was his wife Livia's unkindness to Hallie, brushing off her affection because the tea set she wanted was going to Kansas with Eugenie.

At the end, Aunt Juliette, who always had more heart than the others but was too timid to show it, had cried, falling into Momma's arms, apologizing for not being a better 'sister'.

Widowed Aunt Polly stood back with her children, silent, arms tightly folded over her bosom and clearly glad to have them out of her sight.

Clare made a small sound of distress in her throat, remembering.

"What, what's the matter?" Alice asked.

"Nothing, really. I was just remembering Uncle Edward's behavior the day we left."

"I thought he was kind, considerate."

Clare rolled her eyes. "It did look that way."

Uncle Edward had effused good will from the moment what to do about Poppa was taken off his shoulders. He disgusted Clare and she was barely able to accept his overblown wishes of godspeed.

Memories and feelings tumbled one over another. It seemed a lifetime had passed since the sweet, carefree days when she slipped away to meet Larkin at their private place by the Rock. She was a different person, then. Happy, a bit airy-minded perhaps. Well, no more. Life was demanding that she use every bit of courage and resourcefulness she could draw from herself. Part and parcel of that was seeing to her family's welfare.

It would be difficult to be near Larkin, and not resume their love affair, but her family must come first as long as they needed her. She was sorry to use Larkin, asking his help to find them a new place, but at the time she hadn't known what else to do and she had had to act on the spur of the moment.

The gentle swaying of the train made her sleepy. She leaned her head back, closed her eyes, and listened to the iron wheels, saying, "going to Larkin, going to Larkin, going to Larkin."

Chapter Ten

In Danville, Illinois, a problem with the engine required a night's layover at a small hotel not far from the New York Central tracks. After a supper of steak, gravy, and fried potatoes in the dingy dining room, Clare and her family retired to their room.

It was crowded, with two beds to be shared between the six of them. As soon as Hallie began to grumble, Clare offered to entertain her family by reciting an Emily Dickinson poem about trains, called, "I Like To See It Lap The Miles" but no one seemed interested. "All right then," she said, "let's have Poppa tell us stories to help us go to sleep. Tell us some of the stories you used to tell us, Poppa, when we were little."

Alice coaxed quietly, "Do, Poppa. I'd like to hear about the lost girl and the big dog that saved her life."

"Tell us about the terrible Willey slide," Oakley said, beaming with excitement.

Hallie seemed to have forgotten for the moment that she was on the outs with the rest of them. "Do you remember the story about the ferocious red cow? Tell that one, first, Poppa."

"Give your father a chance, children," Eugenie chided, looking pleased that they had asked. "Don't hurry him and he'll tell your stories. You can do this for the children, can't you, Frank?" She patted his hand.

"Ayuh. Think I can." He licked his lips and sat up straighter. He looked at Hallie, "There was this old woman," he began. "Her man bought her a cow, a really mean old red cow with sharp horns."

Hallie chimed in, "The old woman kept the red cow tied to a tree. When the woman went out to milk, the cow would lower her horns and take after that poor woman."

Poppa continued, "Well, the woman was smarter than the cow. Round that tree she'd go, the red cow right after her. Round and round they'd go until the rope was all used up."

They were all laughing hard as Hallie finished, "The red cow could go no further and she was well tied. The woman sat down on her stool, milked the cow, and took the milk to the house to feed her children."

"Ayuh," Poppa smiled. "She was one smart woman."

"The little girl that was lost, Poppa, tell that one," Alice urged softly.

"Was back in June of 1873 near the village of Warren," Poppa began. "Little Sarah, only three years old, wandered into the woods looking for berries. She got lost. Searchers from many villages went out looking for her. On the fourth day, they found Sarah's footprints in the mud by a stream."

Clare, Alice, Oakley, and Hallie whispered in unison, "All around her footprints were the tracks of a bear. 'She's been killed,' the searchers thought, 'she was eaten by the bear. Might as well give up the search.'"

Hallie stretched out her arms, "Sarah's mother begged them, 'don't stop looking, please.'"

Poppa continued, "The searchers were about to, though, when a man named Heath dreamed about Sarah, three times, in one night. In his dream, he said, Sarah was under a big pine tree and was being guarded by a bear. The pine tree was by a path that crossed a brook."

"May I tell the rest?" Momma asked. When everyone nodded vigorously, she said, "All right, then. Sarah was found right where Heath said she would be. She was sleeping under the pine tree and bear tracks were all around her. She was carried home. She told her mother and father, 'a big black furry dog stayed with me every night and kept me warm.' Nobody wanted to tell her that the big black dog was a bear."

"Is that a true story?" Oakley wanted to know although Poppa had answered that it was every time he told it.

"True as gospel."

Momma said, "When she was grown, Sarah wrote down what she remembered of that night in the woods when the 'big dog' saved her. The searchers wrote their stories about it, too. It's positive truth as far as we've ever known."

"The Willey slide, tell about that now, Poppa," Oakley said, although his eyelids were getting heavy.

Momma pressed a delicate hand on Poppa's arm. "We don't need to hear everything about that terrible tragedy. Tell it quick, Poppa, leave out the worst."

Oakley's face was ringed with disappointment but he knew better than to complain or he might not hear it at all.

"It was the summer of 1826," Poppa said. "The sky was full of black clouds, a storm was coming over Crawford Notch. The Saco river began rising in the dark of night, higher than it ever had before. Right up to the Willey house the river rose, sure to carry it away."

For a moment Poppa looked confused and seemed to lose his train of thought, then he continued, "The Willey family and their two hired men thought they would drown if they stayed in the house. They took shelter from the storm at the foot of the mountain at the back of the house. But then a great slide came down through Crawford Notch. The Willey family and their hired men were all buried alive and they died in the mud. There was an arm sticking out of the logs and mud here, a foot there, the top of a head and—"

"That's all we need to hear, Frank," Momma cautioned him. "It was a terrible thing most folks in New Hampshire will never forget."

They were all silent for a moment, then Oakley said, "A notch is not a notch out West." Hallie's nose wrinkled, "What did you say?"

"I said a notch isn't a notch." He yawned. "Out West the low place between mountainsides is called a canyon. Sometimes the writer calls it a ravine or a valley. But never a notch."

"How do you know?" Hallie demanded.

"I know because Nick Wade let me read two of his dime novels, Deadwood Dick and Jesse James. There wasn't a notch in either of those stories but there were lots of canyons and ravines."

In the silence that followed this bit of information, Oakley fell asleep—and missed Momma's shocked expression that he had read those lurid tales of blood and thunder.

———

WHEN THEY CROSSED the Mississippi River, Clare and her family joined other passengers at the windows for a view of the longest river in the world. Clare was fascinated, remembering lessons in geography. She laughed when Oakley exclaimed, "Now we're in the Wild West!"

Soon after, in St. Louis, there was another forced layover for a night, the cause known only to the powers operating the train. Clare wondered irritably if they'd ever set foot on Kansas soil! She stood at their hotel window and looked out at the starry night above the street lamps, and thought of Larkin.

Which was a mistake. She was going to be so busy getting her family settled in Kansas, and finding a way to support them, there would be no time for matters of the heart.

Larkin might try to change her mind about that. But she could hold strong when she must.

———

CLARE HAD ALLOWED Oakley to ride with them in the passenger car this last leg of their trip from Junction City, Kansas, to the town of Sweetbrier, but she was beginning to think it was a mistake.

"Prairie dog!" Hallie stated for the thirtieth time, her face just inches from Oakley's where they sat together.

"Chicken!" he argued, "it was chicken, you dumb bunny."

Clare leaned across the aisle, glaring at them. "Will you two please stop bickering!" she whispered. "Other passengers are ready to throw you off the train."

Hallie stuck out her tongue at Oakley, he put his thumbs in his ears and waggled his fingers at her but at least they were silent for the moment.

Hallie had to be starving, which no doubt contributed to her foul mood.

At a dusty little train stop not long after they crossed the border into Kansas, the family had settled in at a long board table in a dingy, fly-infested restaurant. Oakley had said the meal they were served was prairie dog. According to stories he'd read, prairie dog was an Indian delicacy which was also much loved by outlaws and other "filthy riff-raff."

He related the information soberly, seriously.

Hallie had believed him and wouldn't touch her food. In time, Oakley, choking with laughter, admitted he was joshing. By then Hallie would in no sense admit she'd been fooled, that the meal might in fact have been chicken. The chicken/prairie dog harangue had gone on too long and Clare was about to lose patience.

"Read the books Alice brought for you," she told them now. "Or take a nap. If you'll just be nice, you'll see how quickly the time will pass and we can get off this train for good."

She reflected that the trip could have been much worse than it was turning out to be. With all that, Clare was anxious to have solid earth under feet again and not a rocking train.

———

"Sweetbrier," the conductor announced, swaying with the movement of the train as he strode up and down the aisle. "Next stop, Sweetbrier. Rolling Prairie township."

The knowledge that she was this close to Larkin sent Clare's heart racing. Would he be different? More than a year had passed. Sometimes a new place altered a person's thinking, their ways, what they wanted out of life. How they felt about someone...

"This can't be where we stop, where we're supposed to live!" Hallie wailed as she pressed her face to the window. "No mountains. No fences. No trees. Just a lot of nothing! With big ol empty sky over the top!" A few of the passengers chuckled and others nodded agreement.

Clare frowned mildly at Hallie. Personally, she rather liked what she saw. The hot golden landscape, rolling away to a blue horizon on both sides of the tracks, had its own special beauty. On her left a dust devil raced alongside the train toward the lump of a town ahead. She started as the train shrilly whistled its approach. A few minutes later, with a grinding of pistons and steam billowing past the windows, they chugged into the small dusty town. They came to a jerking stop in front of a weathered depot. The weary passengers sat for a few seconds without moving, like rabbits frozen under the eye of a salivating dog.

"We're here," Alice sighed quietly, from her seat next to Clare.

"Yes." She was glad that they were all getting off the train together, that Oakley wasn't still cooped in the cattle car. Her brother, seated next to Hallie on one of the bench seats up ahead, squirmed with excitement. Across the aisle, Poppa had fallen asleep next to Momma.

"Yep, it's Sweetbrier," Oakley exclaimed, stretching his neck to see. "Name's right there on the depot. See the sign, Hallie, just over the heads of the folks waiting? Oh, and there's Nick. He's taller, but that's him!" He laughed and made a face through the window at Nick Wade who was jumping up and down, grinning and waving his hat. Nick looked to be inches taller, and a true westerner by the way he was dressed.

"Mercy," Momma said as she peered out the window, her hand to her aching forehead. "Kansas is very different from Sandwich, isn't it?" Poppa, next to Momma, snored softly.

Alice spoke up, "I see Mabel Wade. She's standing right behind Nick, next to the man in the brown suit." She pointed out Mabel among the folks who waited on the rough board platform. Mabel wore a broad smile of expectancy.

Clare looked and her heart squeezed in painful disappointment. Where was Larkin? He wasn't with Ma Wade and Nick.

"Praise the fathers, we're not completely alone in this wilderness," Momma sighed. "It will be good to see Mabel and her family."

"We're going to be fine," Clare said, biting her lip as she took in the dozen or so shabby, false-fronted buildings on the west side of the tracks. Momma was right. Could anything be so different from the picturesque villages and mountains of New Hampshire?

Getting used to this place was going to require strong effort from the whole family. Her glance again swept the half dozen or so folks waiting on the station platform. Why wasn't he there to greet them? He'd sent Ma Wade and Nick, but evidently didn't care enough to meet them himself. Her disappointment changed to resentment, even as she told herself it shouldn't matter. Romantic involvement with him wasn't part of her future, anyway.

"Wake up, Poppa," she stood and leaned over him, pressing his shoulder. "We're here."

Poppa jerked, "Hmm, wh—?" He stared up at Clare with a wild, bewildered expression.

"We're here," she said again, gently, "in Sweetbrier, Kansas."

He jerked to a sitting position and glanced with alarm out the windows on one side of the train, and then the other. Deep wrinkles of worry settled in his face above his long beard. He licked his lips nervously, and shuddered, "I don't know this place. Where are we?" He leaned to study the people waiting on the platform. "I don't see Edward!" his voice was frantic. He twisted his ear. "Where is Simon? Where is everyone? They'll need us!" He moaned and rocked, "We're in trouble, we're in bad trouble, now."

"We're not in trouble, Poppa," Clare assured him, caressing his shoulder. "We're in Kansas. Remember, that's where we've been traveling to for more than a week now. Edward and Simon are back at Hobb's Mills."

"Where we ought to be," Hallie muttered under her breath. "If we'd only—"

Clare quieted her with a fierce glare. She took her father's arm. "C'mon, Poppa. Let's get off the train. We're finally here. No more need for Oakley to be penned up in the car with the cattle. No more lurching and jerking and clanging doors when we try to sleep. No more bad food at strange station stops." Of course, whatever lay ahead could be just as bad, or worse, and if not—would certainly be different. "C'mon," she coaxed. "We're at our new home."

Oakley was already scrambling to get off the train. Alice helped Momma to her feet. They were all glassy-eyed, rumpled, and sagging with fatigue from the long trip. Clare ordered, "Hallie —please stop frowning like that and help me carry our things."

The small family group, used to New England summers, recoiled as one when they stepped off the train into a blast of searing mid-western heat.

"Eugenie! Frank!" Mabel Wade hurried forward. She clasped Momma to her bosom tightly. "Dear Eugenie, I'm so glad you're here." She then urged, "All of you, come over here with me into the shade while we wait for your baggage to be unloaded."

Clare was the next to be wrapped in Mabel's embrace, then Alice and Hallie. Past Hallie's shoulder Clare saw Larkin loping toward them. So...he did come! For a few seconds, it was more than the wind and heat that took her breath away. He looked taller than she remembered, tanner, and incredibly handsome. Her Larkin.

His eyes hardly left Clare's face as he shook Poppa's hand, welcomed Momma, Alice, and Hallie, and clapped Oakley's shoulder. "Clare," he said finally, the one word speaking volumes.

Alice slid a quiet, knowing half-smile at Clare.

"Yes," Clare answered, "we're finally here." She placed a hand on her bosom to quiet its stupendous rise and fall under the delicate corded silk of her blue traveling suit.

"I wanted to be here waiting with Ma and Nick, but I had a customer at my implement yard over yonder. He's a cranky old fanner or I'd have told him he could just wait for his corn planter til after I met you all."

"Implement yard?" She looked in the direction he indicated and saw across the way, beyond a homely building facing the street with a large sign over the door—PROCTOR AND WADE, FARM MACHINERY—a spreading acre or two of machinery, some new and bright-colored with paint, some older. "I thought you farmed." Clare's breathing inched slowly toward normalcy.

"I do. I run a herd of cattle—not a real big herd at present. I raise wheat. Just finished cutting the wheat crop, it's curing in the fields now. A few days ago I bought into the Sweetbrier implement yard where my partner and I sell plows, harrows, drills, windmills, saddles, barbed wire—you name it. If we don't have it, we order it for our customer. Every sort of implement and tool a farmer or rancher might need."

"Goodness!" He had come up in the world since his arrival in Kansas. "The town is small, but I suppose a number of ranchers and farmers travel in from the surrounding area to trade?" Sweet heaven, had his shoulders always been this broad, his eyes this sharp slate gray? For sure he was much tanner, his cheekbones stood out like the features of a god.

"They do. They come to Sweetbrier to trade from the whole of Rolling Prairie and beyond. Wheat and cattle are startin' to show real good profit in these parts. My partner, Tobias Proctor, and I, are real busy supplying equipment to the ranchers and farmers. 'Course, I'm working on my ranch most of the time, and Tobias manages the implement yard. I'm there only in an emergency when he can't be." He explained, "Tobias is a widower with two little children and one of them has been sick with summer complaint. He found a neighbor to look after his little girl, Beth, this afternoon, so I could come on and meet you folks."

His glance followed Clare's as she viewed the town which sat mainly on the west side of the tracks, random clusters of humble homes. Drab business establishments lined dusty Main street, and again along Front street facing the tracks. Following an instant's chagrin, he chuckled, "Sweetbrier is not so backward as it looks. There's a civic group led by the mayor chomping at the bit to make improvements. It'll change and get lots better with time."

She nodded. Truth to tell, it was a pretty miserable looking place, but what choice did they have? To her mind, Sweetbrier could use a great deal of improvement.

"Come, let's get your things. I'm sure you're all tired." He smiled at her family grouped behind her. "Ma has a great supper waiting for us out at the ranch. She's been making up beds for everybody."

"Beds?" Under the same roof with Larkin? "Oh, my, no, we can't put you to all that trouble." Clare swallowed a throatful of arguments against the plan. She nodded toward a tall drab structure on the other side of the street. Reading the hotel sign hanging from the second story gallery, she said, "We can stay there, at the Hilldale Hotel." On the hotel's long porch, below the sign, two men sat forward in their rockers, their eyes intent on the goings on at the depot. Larkin waved at them and they waved back.

"You can't stay there," he said.

"Of course we can. It can't be any worse than other hotels where we've put up on our way here. We'll be staying at the hotel until we can find a place of our own. Are there stock-pens close?" She was positive that there was, she could smell the odor on the wind from the south.

"Sure, there's corrals and fenced pastures southeast of the tracks that belong to the railroad. Cattle and hogs are held there before they're shipped."

"Good. For a small fee, we can leave our animals there until we're established, I'm sure." At the question on his face she told him, "We've brought two cows and our team of horses, some chickens and a pig. We brought a wagon and tools. I'm sure we can find a place to store our household goods until we find a house. Who should we speak to about putting up our stock in the railroad's corrals?"

"That'd be the mayor, Alfred Fuller, who is also the station agent, or his sidekick, Dinger Toledo, who manages the stockyards for Fuller. But talking to either one isn't necessary, because you're coming to our place," Larkin was adamant. "Ma and me won't take no for an answer."

His gaze held her so strongly it seemed impossible to move in any direction other man the one he chose. Which only served to raise her ire. Didn't he know she couldn't be anywhere that near him, without stirring old fires of her feelings for him? She tore her gaze away to see what the others wanted.

Mabel was looking at Momma with a mix of eagerness and caution. The two women's fortunes had reversed drastically. Would Eugenie hang on to the old standard that she was above Mabel socially and couldn't mingle with her on common ground? Would the offer of hospitality be seen as charity, Eugenie too proud to accept?

Momma hesitated and all eyes were on her. Her thinking was reflected in her face, the lift of her chin, her smile. This was a new place, with no doubt new patterns of society in effect. Edward and Simon and their wives were thousands of miles away, not present to protest her decisions, or repudiate what she really wished to do."

"I'd like to go home with Mabel, and thank you, dear, for your hospitality." Momma took Mabel's hand. "Frank, that's fine with you, isn't it?" He nodded, willing to do whatever Eugenie wanted."

"I still think the hotel—" Clare protested. Under the same roof with Larkin would have her emotions all a-tangle. Her resolve to keep distance between them would melt like snow in July and who knew how she'd behave then?

"I'm tired of dingy old hotels," Hallie said. "They are so wretched."

"Spending time in a house again would be nice after this long week," Alice concurred.

"I'm going with Nick," Oakley declared with a big grin at his friend.

Clare maintained in desperation, "I really don't believe we should intrude on you folks, make extra work for you. We can go to the hotel."

"You're outvoted, Clare," Larkin's grin sent her heart into a triple-time beat, "but I'm sure you'll find our ranch comfortable enough."

Comfort was not what worried her. Around her, the group waited for her response, anxious to be doing something. "Oh, all right," she finally gave in. "We'll come, but just for tonight. Tomorrow we will look for a place of our own, or move to the hotel until we find one."

Larkin nodded in satisfaction, his eyes watching her so intently her face flamed anew. He told her, "I have several properties in mind that I want you to see."

He caught Poppa's shoulder in his tan grasp. "Now, if Mr. Hobb and the boys will come with me, we gents will unload your animals and furniture from the railroad cars, and get ready to bring them out to the ranch. You womenfolk go on ahead." He motioned to a wagon and team tied under a tree out front of his implement yard and next to a watering trough. "Our place is only seven miles from town, you'll be there and out of this hot sun before you know it."

Mabel had Eugenie's arm and was already leading her to the wagon, talking a mile a minute. Alice nodded toward the two women. Clare smiled privately at Alice, the two young women silently communicating that at least this thing between Momma and her friend was a good start to their new life. The rest they'd tackle as need be.

Heaven knows what I'm going to do about Larkin, though, Clare thought. She'd expected to be situated miles from him. It was a danger to all her plans being in the same room with him, at his table, close enough to touch.

"Kansas ain't so sorry as it looks to you, Eugenie," Mabel was saying with concern as they rattled along a dusty rutted trail from town and out onto the prairie. "Takes some getting used to, is all. The weather can be a trial at times, we had a drought last summer, but the snow this past winter has made the winter wheat crop real fine. There's good people here. There's others a body wishes would just move on, but I think that's true of any place you live, don't you think?"

Momma was looking down at her feet.

Mabel's plump face, moist with perspiration, turned crimson with embarrassment that she might be poking her nose where it didn't belong, but she had to say it, "It's plumb unfair, Eugenie, that you had to leave Hobb's Mills, if leavin' wasn't what you wanted in your heart. A change this big—it's gotta be hard for you. I s'pect your folks back there, when it comes down to it, are goin' to miss all of you mightily."

"We had to go," Momma said, without elaborating that they'd been forced out of their home because of Poppa's mental problems and what his brothers and their wives wanted to do about him. "There were so many of us there. Someone had to make a new start," she said gamely. "It turned out that Frank and I and our children are the ones to do that."

"We're the hard-luck branch of the family," Hallie said dourly from her place in the back of the wagon. "But if we'd just stayed...." her voice died away and she looked forlornly out across the prairie.

Mabel clucked her tongue. "I have to say I'm surprised at how things have turned out for you folks. None of it makes a lick of sense to me. But I'm awful glad you're here, now. Your comin' to Kansas may be the best thing for you. Like it's turned out to be for Larkin, Nick, and me. I sure enough hope so, and I want to do anything I can to help you folks get along out here."

We'll do fine. What New Hampshire lacked and Kansas has, is Larkin Wade. Clare blushed to the roots of her hair for having the thought and she silently reprimanded herself.

"I have to admit I was afraid to come," Eugenie said, "I've always thought of the West as being wilderness, over-run with wild beasts and scalp-taking Indians."

Mabel laughed. "That might have been a fit description years back, but not anymore. We got the Katy railroad through town for travelin' where we want to go and for bringin' goods—whatever our hearts desire—in, and shippin' our wheat and cattle out. Our mayor, despite that he's a queer duck, is bound and determined to make Sweetbrier a clean and pretty town."

She clucked her tongue for the team to move a little faster and smiled widely. "My boys, Larkin and Nick, have done real good for us since we come here. Larkin works hard dawn to dark, the tasks of two or three men. I worry about him over that, sometimes. He works awful hard. But he's a smart one, too. He studies his plans careful before he puts a penny into them, like our ranch, and the implement yard. I'm so proud of him I could near burst."

Clare smiled to herself, she'd always known what Larkin was capable of, it was others lacking good sense, particularly her uncles, who couldn't see the correct measure of him.

"And you should be proud of him," Eugenie replied. "Farming in New Hampshire is hard work, and often not profitable. The mills have always been the main source of income for the Hobb families."

Mabel asked, "What about that hotel the New Yorker gentleman was goin' to build on the land Larkin sold him? Did that come to pass, or not?"

"Indeed it did." Eugenie was silent a moment, thoughtful. Using her hands, she said, "To know what it looks like you need to picture a castle, like a picture from a fairytale book. A white castle with more than one hundred rooms."

"No!" Mabel exclaimed. "On our old land, a castle?" She laughed, as though a castle was too outrageous to imagine.

Momma nodded. "City folk seem to love it there. It's claimed the hotel has a billiard hall, a bowling alley, a music room, and a barber shop. The dining room is one of the largest in New England, and serves fine meals. They say the menu offers eleven entrees, twelve vegetable dishes, fourteen relishes, six kinds of pie and twelve other desserts."

"My, six kinds of pie! Twelve other desserts!" Mabel exclaimed.

"The hotel imports wines from all over the world," Clare chimed in, "and brandies and ales and sherries. All the things rich people seem to require."

Momma touched Mabel's arm. "Some say that Seeley's hotel and others like it are a sign of the future, that New Hampshire will forget trying to farm and will become a mecca for tourist folk. Seems strange, but that's what they predict."

"I can see it," Mabel nodded. "Ain't more beautiful country anywhere. But for us ordinary folk to make a livin', you need more than pretty mountains and streams. An' totsy wines," she mimicked with a chuckle, lifting the pinky finger on her hand holding the reins.

All of them laughed except Hallie who said haughtily, "Aunt Livia and Uncle Simon went to supper at Seeley's hotel and they said it was very elegant."

Clare looked at her. *And some of us will simply have to do without elegant dining and accept things as they are.*

All around them, golden-prairie swept away like ocean waves to meet a deep blue sky. It was pretty country in its own way, Clare thought. Whether she and her family could make a profitable, good new life here remained to be seen.

She sneaked a look back over her shoulder, wondering how long it might be before Larkin, Poppa, and the boys arrived in the other wagons with their belongings and herding the animals.

Chapter Eleven

"WHAT A BEAUTIFUL HOUSE, MABEL!" MOMMA EXCLAIMED
when they finally drew the wagon to a halt before a soft-silvered,
two-story frame house with a wide porch. Pink hollyhocks bloomed
at the corners of the porch and white leghorn chickens scratched
and clucked contentedly in the side-yard.

"Well, it's comfortable, and I do love it. Larkin was so proud to
provide me this house. I never thought I'd have anything so fine,
comin' to this country, but I'm real content, just real content."

Two calico kittens came stretching inquisitively from under
the front porch and Hallie squealed with delight. She scrambled
from the wagon and went to pick them up and pet them.

Clare was glad to see Hallie's sulk evaporating for the time
being. With deep curiosity, Clare followed the others as Mabel
showed them around inside the house. The kitchen was sunny and
clean, the dining room large enough for a farm family and a haying
crew to sit down to eat all at once, Mabel proudly pointed out. She
led them to the sitting room.

When she pointed out Larkin's chair, and the stack of farm
papers on the table next to it where he did his studyin', Clare
secretly let her fingers graze the back of the chair. His. He sat here,
to pore over his papers and learn all he could about farming prac-
tices on the prairie. Trying so hard to better himself. She admired
him for so many things, his ambition not the least among them. His

handsome looks, sensual appeal, good humor and kindness, of course topped his qualities.

Mabel brought them glasses of cool ginger tea. "Now I want you all to rest," she told Eugenie, Alice, and Clare. "You've had a long trip and you have to be plumb wore out. I'll finish gettin' the meal ready. We're havin' cold sliced veal loaf, sour cream potato salad, buttermilk rolls and watermelon preserves. Spring greens— I cook 'em til they're just tender, then add some sliced boiled egg and crisp bacon. Rhubarb pie, and amber pie. Them men will be here before we hardly know it."

Clare's mouth watered at the description of Mabel's meal.

"We'll help," Eugenie responded. "Tell us what you'd like us to do."

"We had enough sitting on the train," Alice said, quietly but earnest. "It will feel good to be in a kitchen again."

"Show me your dish cupboard," Clare said, "and I'll set the table."

Mabel smiled around at all of them. "It's so good to have you ladies here!"

Supper was a pleasant affair, although Clare was so conscious of Larkin, seated across the table from her, she could hardly eat. He seemed almost to loom, sun-browned and muscled with that twinkle of good humor in his eyes. It pleased her to note that he ate with the appetite of a working man who enjoyed food and appreciated the work that went into preparing it. "You've outdone yourself. Ma," he complimented more than once, and later, "this rhubarb pie is plumb tasty."

"Is the rhubarb pie not to your likin', Clare?" Mabel asked kindly. "If you'd rather have a slice of amber pie—I make it with strawberry jam, sweet cream and eggs—I'd like to get it for you."

"Everything is delicious, Mrs. Wade, truly. I guess the long trip has affected my appetite. I have a lot on my mind—we have so much to do to get settled here."

Poppa moved in his chair to sit up straight. He turned to Mable and said softly, "This jam pie—this amber pie you call it, Mabel, is the best pie I've ever tasted." He looked pleased that he'd gotten out what he'd wanted to say. He rarely spoke up at all, other than to his immediate family.

"Thank you, Frank," Mabel smiled at him.

"Y-y-you'll teach my Eugenie how to make it? She's a fine cook, too, master fine." He reached to pat his wife's hand and she smiled back at him.

It was a wonderful moment and it lifted Clare's spirits. Poppa had his ups and downs, good days and bad, and probably always would. But there was a very good chance Poppa would be much more like his old self here in Kansas, away from the pressures of his domineering brothers.

"You have an organ in the parlor," Alice spoke quietly to Mabel. "Do you play?"

"Larkin bought the organ for me, as a house gift when we moved in. It had been years since I got to play one, and I had to teach myself all over again. Yes, I love to sit down at that organ when there's time, and just let troubles of the day fly away. Remember, Eugenie, when you used to sing and I played the organ at church, when we were just girls? What good times, those were—"

"They were good times, Mabel," Momma smiled. "You were the dearest friend a quiet lonely little goose like me could have, back then. And," she said quickly, "I'm happy we're still friends after all this time."

"If you girls would like to play," Mabel's glance took in Alice, Clare, and Hallie, "you're welcome to, anytime."

"Thanks," Clare answered. "I certainly could improve." She remembered playing the organ for the doctor, and how disastrously that brief relationship ended.

"I'd love to learn to play," Hallie said, "if you'll teach me, Mrs. Wade?"

"Same as done," Mabel answered.

After supper, Larkin came into the kitchen where the women were clearing the table. "Clare, would you go for a walk with me?"

She looked at him, standing much too close, and felt a heat throughout her body. She tried to answer him, it was on the tip of her tongue to say no. Before she could find a polite way to refuse, he continued, "We need to talk about some important matters, about the land I'd like you folks to have. Frank said that I should talk to you about it."

"Go ahead," Mabel waved a dish towel at them. "Eugenie and I can finish up in here."

Back at Sandwich, a young couple who weren't promised to each other might be allowed to attend group parties together, or church, but walking out without a chaperone, with dark about to descend, was a different matter. Sneaking to be together was the answer for some, of course.

Clare waited for her mother to show subtle disapproval, to make some gentle, gracious excuse that would let Clare off the hook, but Momma seemed more interested in the red geranium blooming on Mabel's windowsill than her daughter's honor.

Clare sighed. What was she thinking, anyway? Larkin wanted to talk about matters that desperately needed her attention: like a place for the Hobb family to live, a means for them to survive! He didn't have seduction on his mind. Necessarily.

"All right."

He reached for her arm to lead her outside but she moved away. Her heart held too many delectable memories, ached with too many yearnings. If he touched her in the least, she'd forget every intelligent decision she'd ever made. Her family's survival would be in strong question, and she'd be a quivering blob of emotion.

Outside in the purple twilight, grasshoppers sailed away from their footsteps. At one side of the house was a large bam, smoke house and corn-crib. They strolled past Mabel's kitchen garden and a young orchard of cherry and apple trees.

Ahead of them wheat stood in blotches of gold shocks, across a broad expanse of darkening fields meeting a purple and yellow skyline. In the pastures to the right, cattle grouped in the shade of a copse of trees, others grazed.

"I don't know how you do it all!" Clare exclaimed. "This is incredible, Larkin, but such a big place to keep up with."

He laughed, pleased that she was impressed. "I have a hired man who has a room back yonder in the barn. I hire other help when I need it. A lot of the work, such as cutting and threshing the wheat, gets done with the help of neighbors. Farmers and ranchers hereabouts know that harvesting wheat, or rounding up cattle to ship, is done faster and cheaper when we join up, work for one another, to get the job done."

"You've done very well for yourself."

"I was lucky to get this place how I did. I had cash to buy the ranch, otherwise it would have cost me several dollars more per acre. The owner wanted to get out, bad. His wife had left him. A drought meant the crops already in weren't going to pay off much. It wasn't a lot, but I shared with the original owner the earnings from that first harvest after I took over, and from the increase of cattle I sold, as we agreed. The profit I make from now on is mine."

Clare told him with honesty, "We don't have the investment that you had, to put into a farm. I was still hoping to find free land that Poppa and Momma and I might homestead. Make the improvements required until we could hold title. One-hundred-sixty acres would be a lot to manage, but we could try, the family all working together."

"As far as I know there are no free homestead lands left in eastern Kansas, they've all been claimed in the past twenty years or so. There is free land, still, 'way out in western Kansas, but that's a hard country. No trees to build houses from, folks have to live in a dugout, or a soddy made of sod bricks. Water is scarce, has to be hauled by team and wagon, by the barrel, from a creek or spring if there is one. No close neighbors to help in times of need."

"That doesn't sound very encouraging."

"Well, it's true. Which is why I didn't look further than Rolling Prairie here in Eastern Kansas. It's best that your family buy a place hereabouts, Clare. The soil is rich, the ground level enough for either plowing or working cattle. If hail ruins your wheat or your corn, you still have your cattle. We raise hogs, oats, barley, sheep, poultry, bees—anything that is profitable. If calamity hits, we've got something else to depend on. Neighbors don't live so far off from one another, either. There are three farms, a few hundred acres each, that I want to show you."

"But we—"

He continued, "One is owned by a widow who wants to return back East to her people. Another is owned by a shiftless fellow who just doesn't want to work hard enough to make his place pay. The other belongs to an absentee owner, who prefers living in Kansas City."

"We don't have enough money to buy a farm like you're describing, Larkin. We'll have to find something much smaller—our funds are very limited." Too embarrassed to look at him, her chin trembled. "My Uncle Simon—the rest of the family at Hobb's

Mills, decided we needed only enough to make a small start, and after that it would be up to us how well we fared."

He shook his head in disbelief, muttered some unflattering terms about Simon, then told her, "Clare, I can help with some financial backing. Be glad to!"

She turned on him with a look hard enough to stop a wagon flying downhill.

His hands came up. "All right, all right. You've been taken down aplenty by how your kin has treated you, forcing you out of where you legitimately belong. You want to do this on your own and keep what pride they've left you. I understand, Clare. But I'm here to help you when you want me to."

Her eyes filled with tears. "Thank you. If you will just help us locate a small property that we can pay for ourselves, my family will be fine. I intend to find work to help out." She could write home and ask for more money, but she knew without a doubt that any such request would be censored by Simon, who'd be against any financial dealings not directly profitable for Hobb's Mills. Come what may, the unlucky branch of the Hobb family must manage on their own, must make their own good luck. She had that to prove to her confounded uncles!

"Clare—" Larkin's voice was deep, sympathetic. The descending dark was velvet around them.

She wiped her eyes. "I'm all right, I really am. It's getting late. We'd best start back."

"Clare," he said again, with so much emotion it was like a wave crashing over her, drowning her in feelings she'd for so long tried to keep buried. Suddenly she was in his arms, gripping him as tightly as he held her. Their lips met in starvation, a burning fever. "Larkin," she whimpered. "I've missed you so."

He raised his mouth from hers, and for a few seconds gazed into her eyes. Shadows curled protectively around them, shutting off everything but the two of them. "Clare, you're so beautiful, I know I've got no right to you, but I want you more than anything else in the world."

She wanted to protest but couldn't as Larkin kissed her more deeply, fiercely. She tried to halt the dizzying current racing through her, and failed. She ached for fulfillment of his lovemaking, wanted to sob her anger that she couldn't stay in the arms of this man she loved, forever and ever. Put aside concern for her family, pay no never mind to how they fared or what might happen to them. She burned a final kiss on his lips and took several stumbling steps backward, and breathed deep.

"No, Larkin, please. Let's not do this, not now." Her face, her whole body, was on fire. She couldn't look at him for fear he would see in her eyes how much she loved him, wanted him. Wanted to forget everything but him.

"When?" his voice was raw with passion. "Clare, I've missed you so."

I've missed you, so much at times I thought I'd die. "I don't know when, if ever." Her voice broke, "At—at the moment I'm tied to my family. Surely you see that, can see how much they need me? My own life, my personal wishes simply have to wait." She walked several paces away, had to take care or she'd be back in his arms in spite of herself.

"Your personal desires include me?"

"Larkin, please don't."

"I'll take that to mean yes. If you can wait, then I will, too."

"That's not fair to you."

"Anything is fair to me if it includes you."

"We have to get back to the house, the others will worry."

"One more minute." He pulled her to him, and weakening, she allowed it.

She'd have these last few kisses to treasure, although she couldn't let this happen again. In another moment, fighting the emotions tearing her apart, she pulled away. "We have to get back!" She hurried ahead, her heart aching with desire, and with regret that her life couldn't be personally ordained as she'd like it to be.

At the house, Mabel was a warm wonderful hostess as she showed where each one would sleep. Clare and her sisters would have the spare room, three abed. Momma and Poppa would have Larkin's room. Clare was thankful that Larkin would sleep in the barn with Nick and Oakley. "Warm night," he said, "we don't need blankets."

NEXT MORNING FOLLOWING BREAKFAST, Clare and Larkin set out in his wagon to see the properties he'd selected to show her. "I'm taking you from your work," she apologized.

"It's no bother. My hired man and Nick can take care of chores on the ranch for the few hours I'll be away. Of course, in a week or two when the wheat is cured and ready to thresh, I'll be real busy. I wanted to do this, Clare."

For the next hour and more they drove around the countryside, Larkin showing her the properties he'd picked. In each case they would serve the Hobb family well enough, but were too expensive —out of reach unless the family took on a huge mortgage—an unwise, if not impossible, step.

"Isn't there anything else? A small piece of land that wouldn't require so much money to buy it? For now, we just need a roof over our heads, a garden spot, and pasture for our animals. I'd like us to be closer to town where it will be easy for Momma and Poppa to do their trading. I'd like to get work, there, too."

Larkin heaved a sigh. "There's a place on the edge of town, twenty acres, a ramshackle house and barn. It belonged to an elderly widow, Mrs. McCrum, who wasn't able to keep the place up. She died a month or two ago. The land agent who loaned her money over time owns the place now and he has it for sale fairly cheap."

"Show me."

"But the place really isn't right for you. I shouldn't have mentioned it."

"Show it to me, please."

His mouth set in a grim line but he drove them back toward town. They were almost there when he turned the team off the main road and drew the horses to a halt before a decrepit house and barn surrounded by fields of thistle and other weeds. "There it is." His tone made clear his low opinion of the property.

Clare hid her own dismay.

The unpainted house was salvaged from complete ugliness by bright sunshine spilling over it. The front portion of the homely structure was single story, with a long sloping roof over the left side and a shorter steep roof opposite. There was one door and a window. A two-story addition was attached crossways to the back of the smaller section of the house. A chimney rose in the center like an unhealthy weed.

The silence was filled with the clank and squeal of a windmill situated in the backyard, partway to the barn. A hot wind stirred up a powdery dust and shushed through the leaves of the trees by the house.

"What're you doing?" Larkin caught her arm when Clare started to climb from the wagon. "Surely you've seen enough? The place is awful."

She shook her arm free. "I want to see inside the house, see if there are enough rooms. I want to look inside the barn. What are those pathetic trees in the grove by the house?"

"Cottonwoods," he growled, and climbed from the wagon to follow her.

She opened the creaking door of the house, recoiled from the smell, and then went on in. "My, but it will take work." They wandered through the rooms. While in the kitchen, a russet bird flew in where a windowpane was broken, then out again. "It's big enough," Clare said, after they'd crept up the rickety stairs to view the rooms on the second floor.

Outside again, they wandered through the outbuildings, each needing a good shoveling out. and repair. "What's this?" Clare asked later, walking in bright sunshine toward a cave nearly hidden in a clump of dusty lilac bushes. "Of course," she answered herself, "it's a root cellar. Very handy." A cardinal sang "whata-cheer-cheer-cheer," from the lilac shrub then took sudden wing, a flash of red, as they approached.

Clare and Larkin stood together on the bank of a sluggish creek that ribboned through the property. "Water is low," Larkin noted, "and the creek will practically dry up before summer's over."

"Still, it is a creek, and quite pleasant, really. Look at the wild rosebushes growing along the banks. Pretty."

"I reckon. They are wild sweetbrier roses, you see 'em a lot around here. Guess that's where the town got its name."

As they turned back, Clare stumbled and Larkin caught her, holding her longer than necessary. Her heart beat fast, she tried to pretend nothing out of the ordinary had happened, talked fast about the property as she moved away. "Fixing up this place is a challenge, but I feel up to it, and my family will be, too, with a little prodding. I would like to talk to the man who owns it."

"No, Clare."

"Yes, this property will do fine if the price is right," she told him stoutly, although Hallie's favorite word, wretched, actually came to mind.

"I could help you find another place, Clare. There's no hurry. Take your time. I can lend you money if you need and—"

She waved him silent. "I want to talk to the land agent before discussing the matter with Momma and Poppa. I'd like to see the town, too, if you'll show me." She would need to look for work to help support them, regardless of what property they settled on. Others in the family might find outside work of some kind, too.

"Dammit, Clare, you deserve better than this. I saw how you and your family lived in New Hampshire. I remember!"

"I remember, too, perfectly. But that's behind us now. If you can't show me the town right now, I can drive myself in, later."

"That won't be necessary." *I'd do anything in the world for you, Clare. Don't you know that?*

A short while later, in town, Clare made a tentative deal with the land agent. Right after, Larkin said, "I want to show you the implement yard I own with my partner, Tobias Proctor." They located the kindly-faced giant in the shack that served as the two men's office and store.

"Just got this shipment of horse gear in today," Tobias turned from hanging halters and bridles on the plain board walls. For whatever reason, he gave Clare a long look, then nodded cheerfully as though coming to some kind of agreement. He clasped both of her hands in his, "Nice to meet you, Miss Hobb."

"And I you, Mr. Proctor."

One by one, Larkin walked Clare to the various places of business: general store, hardware store, shoe store, drug store, and hat shop, and introduced her to the merchants. They were plain and friendly people for the most part, and clearly showed their respect for Larkin. Clare crossed her fingers that she'd remember their names when she again met them on the street or in the stores when she came in to town to trade or ask for work.

Clearly, it was important to Larkin that she meet and like his friends. Luckily, today she was meeting just a fraction of the four hundred population of Sweetbrier.

They were walking past the hotel, side by side and very close because the boardwalk was narrow, when a man came bustling out and down off the hotel porch. He saw Larkin and Clare and pulled up short. He tipped his hat and bowed to Clare and spoke a greeting to Larkin.

"Clare, I'd like you to meet the mayor of Sweetbrier, Mr. A.E. Fuller."

"Alfred," the mayor quickly corrected.

"Ayuh. Mayor Fuller, Alfred. As I might've told you, Clare, Mr. Fuller is also manager of the Sweetbrier Railroad Station. He oversees the shipping out of cattle and grain. He takes care of folks departing town on our two trains a day, as well as taking care of incoming folks and freight. Miss Hobb came in on the afternoon train yesterday."

"Indeed! I saw her arrive," the mayor hooked his cane over his arm, doffed his pearl gray derby, and caught Clare's hand. His eyes glittered appraisal behind gold rimmed spectacles. "One can hardly miss noting the arrival of such a beauty in our little town. If I hadn't been so busy settling the station books, I'd have rushed to welcome you then, Miss Hobb."

"Thank you, Mr. Fuller."

"You're most welcome, dear." There was a speck of dried food in his thick moustache as his lips smothered her fingers a trifle too long. She drew her hand away. "It's nice to meet you."

"And you, my dear." He pulled out his pocket watch. "Need to be going, train will be coming down that track any time. Hope you'll be happy in our town, Miss Hobb. Anything you need, you may call on me." Even as he spoke, they could hear the distant wail of the train.

"Thank you, I will."

As Clare and Larkin continued along the street, he told her, "The mayor, as you'll leant in time, is a stuffed shirt, very full of himself. He doesn't like me, much."

"Why wouldn't he like you?"

"He fancies himself someday being the Lord of a bonanza farm, like a couple fellas are running up in the Dakotas. George Cass, president of the Northern Pacific Railway, and Ben Cheney, a prominent part-owner of an express company joined up to buy eighteen sections up there from the railroad company. Those men are his heroes. Alfred Fuller owns a few shares in the Katy railroad, the Missouri, Kansas, and Texas, which you'd think makes him Jay Gould from how he's puffed up about it. He expected to buy the land I'm on, but the owner never did plan to sell to him because he plain and simple didn't like Fuller, plus the good mayor didn't have cash in hand and I did. Mayor Fuller is convinced I somehow cheated him out of the property he had his eye on."

"Is he a good leader for the town? The community must like him, to vote him mayor."

"There's two sides to that. Fuller has friends in high places, or so he claims. One of them, a rich railroad man, so he says, has promised to build Sweetbrier a big fancy courthouse and more if they would change Sweetbrier's name to his, which is Conroy. That promise to the voters got Fuller elected. The 'friend' has never shown, and the promise never materialized. But there are kindhearted, simple folk, who believe in the mayor and haven't given up on the courthouse he's guaranteed. They are sure it will happen, 'when complicated details' are finally worked out."

"He seemed a bit pretentious to me."

"Oh, he's that all right, and probably a thief to boot, but that's another story."

The conversation ended as they approached a trio of sun-bonneted women with market baskets over their arms. Larkin introduced Mabel's friends, Muriel Fayne, tall and rather austere, and jolly, ruddy-faced Carrie Spencer, who, with her husband, owned the farm bordering Larkin's on the west. Finally, the circuit minister's wife, Liddy Goodlander, whose shy, retiring manner reminded Clare of her sister, Alice.

Later, Larkin asked if they might stop at the blacksmith shop where he needed to ask about a wheel he'd left there to get new spokes.

"Of course." Clare liked the ringing sounds, the hot smells of metal, and horses of a blacksmith shop. She would always link them to Poppa and his wonderful skills.

The smith, Sam Dorsey, was a short, burly, bald fellow, his friendly face and clothes, especially his leather apron, were covered with soot. Clare shook his hand, anyway. There was a chance Mr. Dorsey might give her father work in the future, over-look Poppa's mental shortcomings in light of how good he was at smithing.

They were trailing back along main street when a feminine voice called Larkin's name. "Yoohoo! Larkin. Yoohoo, Larkin Wade!"

"Someone's calling you." Clare shaded her eyes against the sun and saw a young woman approaching them along the plank walk. She was beautiful, raven-haired, with a curvaceous figure in a bright red calico dress. As she neared, she had eyes only for Larkin.

"Myra, how are you? Clare, this is Myra Tibbets, she works at the post office. Myra, meet Clare Hobb. Clare and her family came in on the train yesterday. They are old friends of ours from New Hampshire. The Hobbs are looking to buy the Widow McCrum's old place."

Myra's perfect nose wrinkled in a frown. "That awful rundown house? Well, I suppose it could be fixed kinda decent." She took Clare's hand in hers, her smile welcoming. "Sorry, didn't mean to discourage you. I hope you and your husband will be very happy here in Sweetbrier."

"I'm not discouraged. I intend to like it here, in fact I already do. And—I'm not married. No husband. I moved here with my mother and father, my sisters and brother."

Myra was surprised, and her smile cooled. Her smoke-colored eyes found Larkin's hand on Clare's elbow. If she could have slain Clare with a glance, it would have happened then. She recovered, giving Larkin her attention with a winsome smile. "You're coming to the basket social Saturday night, aren't you?" She added with a giggle, "As soon as I've decided how to decorate my basket, I'll give you some hints so you'll know that it's mine. Remember my fried chicken?" she asked him, as though it were a major conspiracy.

"I remember. It was nice to see you Myra, but we have to be goin'."

"Of course." Wiggling her fingers in farewell, she said, "It's time I got back to the post office, too." She told Clare, "I work for my uncle who has the O.K. General store. 'Dealers in country produce, housekeeping goods, fine teas'. The post office is in back of the store, past the pickle barrels. Bye Larkin." She added after a hesitation, "Nice meeting you, Clara."

"Nice meeting you, too, Myra. You may call me Clare, that's my name."

Myra shrugged. The fabric was pulled tight around her very curvaceous backside as she gathered her skirts in a fist and hurried back the way she'd come.

Larkin was watching her go but Clare, her throat drying, couldn't read his expression for sure. A man would have to be blind, though, not to see Myra's beauty. Her very sensual feminine appeal.

"Is Myra a good friend?" she asked Larkin as they headed back to the wagon.

"Just a friend. I see her around at picnics, and dances. I got her box by accident at a social this spring. She's a good cook. Makes a fine apple pie."

She probably uses too much nutmeg; a lot of cooks spoil the cinnamony flavor of apple pie loading it with nutmeg.

"And fried chicken?"

"Very good fried chicken."

Well, Clare thought, *your 'just a friend' is besotted with you! Totally in love. I'm sure you're aware of it, too, Mr. Larkin Wade.* She quelled a sudden rise of jealousy. Larkin was not hers, they no longer had romantic ties and wasn't she fighting to keep it that way? What young woman wouldn't be attracted to him? She resisted the urge to look at him, feast her eyes on how truly handsome he was. She must keep her mind on business, on details of buying the little farm and setting it to rights so her family would have a decent place to live, a means to survive.

It didn't hurt, though, to hope that Larkin would skip the Saturday night basket social.

Chapter Twelve

"Now," Clare warned her family as they piled less than spiritedly into their wagon at the Wade ranch, "you're not to expect too much from the property I've found for us."

Following the hefty breakfast of pancakes and ham Mabel cooked for them, her family had been all too content to stay where they were enjoying Mabel's company. Luckily, Larkin had to be out early counting cattle and later preparing for a crew of threshers for his wheat, or she might have been tempted to linger, herself.

She helped Momma into the wagon. Poppa looked confused, but when he saw that the rest of them were climbing into the wagon, he joined them. Alice gave him a hand up.

"The house is small and a bit rundown." Clare took up the reins and clucked to Hector and Dan, their driving team. "The barn will need some repair. But there is a pretty little creek on the property, plus a good well, and twenty acres of land where we can graze our livestock. Next spring, we can put in a garden. Maybe in time we can add to the land, with more acreage for wheat and cattle."

It wouldn't be as nice a place as Larkin's ranch, or as profitable as his implement yard in town, but she believed the property could in time provide for them adequately.

They would be self-sufficient, with no need to depend on others. They wouldn't need to beg from their relatives at Hobb's

Mills. Most especially they would not be asking for further help from Larkin. He'd done them a large favor advising them about Kansas property, giving them a pleasant place to stay their first nights here, but more than that wasn't necessary. She was no beggar-woman with no will to help her own. She was still a Hobb, though one considerably down on her luck. And who knew but what one day she and Larkin would have their chance, together? Maybe she could bring that about sooner than late.

They made the five mile trip west from the Wade farm in near silence. Foreseeing her family's response to the property she'd picked for them, Clare gnawed the inside of her cheek in dread. They would simply have to understand that this was the best she could do.

Windswept white clouds rode the wide blue sky over the property as they approached. Hauling back on the reins, Clare brought them to a rattling dusty stop before the unpainted house. "This is it," she said. Her family sat in stunned silence. The windmill off to the right of the house sang in the wind. About them, dried brown weeds rattled and whispered loneliness.

Hallie stood up in the wagon, hands on her hips and outrage in her eyes. "It's a shack. Why are doing this to us, Clare?"

"I'm not doing this to you, I'm doing it for you. This little farm is all we can afford just now." Thanks to penny-pinching Uncle Simon.

"What kind of trees are those next to the house?" Poppa asked, leaning over the side of the wagon for a better look at the small grove of spindly trees, leaves turning like silver coins in the wind. "They don't look healthy to me."

"According to Larkin they are a type of Cottonwood tree that grows here in Kansas," Clare answered. "They look—how they are supposed to look. We can be thankful they shade the house." She turned to her younger sister, "Hallie, we can fix a swing for you in one of the trees."

"I'm not a child," the girl stormed, jumping down from the wagon.

Then grow up! Clare wanted to tell her, instead she kept silent and with a sigh climbed from the wagon and then helped her mother down. Poppa and Oakley set off to explore the barn with its sieve-like roof while Clare led Momma, Alice, and Hallie into the house. Dust seemed to rise with each step. The stagnant air reeked of abandonment and droppings from unnamed creatures.

"These two small front rooms can be our kitchen and pantry," Clare said, leading the way. "This part is the original house, the two-story addition was built on later. Come, I'll show you." She led them through a door on the left into a much larger room dominated by a large, pot-bellied stove and stone chimney behind it. "This could be our main living area. Not exactly a parlor, but it will do."

There was dust everywhere, debris in the corners of the room, evidence of varmint's nests. Clare's spirits sagged, seeing it through her family's eyes. She realized now that she had glossed over in her mind the worst details of the house yesterday, seeing it with Larkin, because she'd known how important it was to find a place, any place, that her family could call their own.

"That stairway doesn't look safe," Alice said, pointing to the narrow rickety steps leading upward at the far end of the living room.

"No, it doesn't," Clare agreed, "but we can fix it." One by one they crept up the stairs carefully, to view the two and a half rooms on the second floor. The ceilings were so low one could barely stand erect. A homemade rope bed looked ready for collapse in one room, a filthy quilt rotted on it. Clare looked at Momma, who hadn't spoken since they had entered the house. Her eyes held a sad, pained expression and she held a lace handkerchief delicately to her face.

"It's going to be all right, Momma, it really will." Clare gave her a hug. "You'll see, a good clean up and lots of fresh paint will help the house wonderfully."

Momma's eyes were shiny with tears. She nodded and her lips quivered when she said, "I—I suppose you're right. I just can't seem to forget that we had every comfort at Homestead House. Hobb's Mills was so beautiful. It was our home, and I loved it so, from the moment your father made me his wife and took me there to live. It was our home."

Hallie seized the opportunity to reissue her complaint, "We should never have left. I told you so. I told all of you! It was wrong to come here. I'll write to Aunt Livia and tell her about this wretched place. She'll want us to catch the next train back to Hobb's Mills."

"I wouldn't count on that, Hallie." Except for the fact that Grandmother's beautiful Bavarian tea set went with them, Livia was more than glad to be rid of their family.

Clare grabbed her sister's slender shoulders and fought to keep her temper in check. She spoke as calmly and kindly as she could, "Hobb's Mills is beautiful, it was our home. Every need we had mere was richly filled. But please don't forget that because of Poppa's mental troubles, because of what happened to Uncle Samuel, we became outcasts at Hobb's Mills. It really wasn't our home anymore and we nearly lost Poppa to an institution. If you'll just remember—if we all try and remember—coming to Kansas is what saved Poppa, what saved our family. Now, it's time to make the best of what we have—where we are—and try to put Hobb's Mills from our minds!"

"Yes, Clare-love, you're right." Momma dabbed at her eyes with her lace handkerchief and lifted her chin. "Pining to be at Hobb's Mills is useless. We have Poppa with us and that's more important than anything."

"We're sorry for complaining," Alice said, slipping her arm around Clare's waist. "And," she said, looking around, "it's not as though we've never had common chores to do. We have had, and we worked hard. We can clean this little house, move our own things in, and it will do nicely. Won't it Hallie?"

Hallie didn't answer. Instead, with a deep frown, she kicked at a small pile of debris. A rat sprang out and raced away, leaving Hallie screaming and stomping her feet.

In a moment, they were all laughing, even Hallie, as she wiped away tears of sudden fright.

———

LARKIN HAD BEEN certain that once Clare showed the Widow McCrum's place to her family, that would be the end of it because they'd refuse to live there. He was shocked, that same night at the supper table, when she announced that she was going through with buying the property.

"It will take hard work, but we'll have it livable in no time," she said enthusiastically as she spooned delicately into her persimmon pudding.

He had counted on keeping her at his ranch for weeks and maybe months. In the back of his mind he had hoped that when she didn't find property equal to what they had in Sandwich, she would give up her stubborn mission to provide for her family, and marry him. Join her family with his, right here on the ranch. Well, he was a fool for wishing any such thing to happen anytime soon.

———

"ARE you sure about the McCrum place, Clare?" He'd convinced her to sit with him on the front porch after supper clean up, but she kept a foot of space between them on the porch swing. "The McCrum house is so small and rundown. The barn roof has holes like a sieve. The fences are falling down. You and your family aren't used to living like—that."

"Like poor folk?" her chin jutted proudly. "Well, that's what we are for the time being, and I intend that we will make the best of it." At last she told him in full detail how close Poppa's brothers had come to putting him in an institution, and how leaving for Kansas was all that prevented it. "We'll be fine and we appreciate what you've done for us. We won't burden you further."

"You're no burden!" he protested. "Clare, if you and I—" He leaned close, his lips inches from her inviting mouth, his own remembering too well how hers felt and tasted. He wanted her so much.

She put up a hand to stop him and leaning back she looked at him squarely. Although her chin quivered, she told him firmly, "There is no 'you and F Larkin. I told you that before you left New Hampshire and again the other night. What we were—is over."

His voice rasped, "You let me kiss you the other night." And she'd been jealous of Myra when he introduced them. He'd pretended not to see it, but her jealousy was clear as day and it had given him pleasure to his core.

"That was a mistake. It won't happen again."

His smile tightened as he struggled for patience. "All right, forget about us. Just don't be in a rush to buy the McCrum farm. Take your time til you find something better, I'm sure a place you'll like will turn up. And I swear," he lifted his palms, "I'll not bother you." *At least I won't until the time is right. And when that time* comes, my proud Miss Hobb, I'm going to prove to you just how much I love you, how much you love me.

They were silent for a time, while out in the darkening evening locusts sang. "I'm glad you came to Kansas, Clare," Larkin said finally. "I was afraid that old rich Doctor Plummer might talk you into marrying him." She made a strange little sound of protest. He waited for her to say something more and when she didn't he continued, "Doctor Plummer could've done fine by you, taken care of you and your family probably better than all of you had at Hobb's Mills."

"I would never have married him!" She looked suddenly ill, there in the dusky evening, and she started to shake. She covered her face with her hands. Then she dropped them and tried to appear that she was herself, and fine. She failed. Shiny tears welled in her eyes.

"Did something happen back there, with Doctor Plummer?

"She had told no one, was haunted at times by memory of Doctor Plummer's pawing hands, what he had almost done to her. She told Larkin now, a simple description of what happened that she hoped didn't sound as awful as the actual experience had been.

He swore under his breath. "I would've killed him, if I'd been there. Him being an important doctor wouldn't have made a whit of difference!"

"He was drunk. He didn't know what he was doing."

"He knew! And he should have been pounded for even trying!"

"It doesn't matter, now." She was silent a moment. "I think my turning down Doctor Plummer's proposal of marriage was one of the things my aunts and uncles held against me, against our family. It was the last straw. We had to go."

"I'd never let anyone hurt you."

"I know that. But I can take care of myself. I did that night."

He could sense that she was about to call an end to the evening and excuse herself to go inside. But he couldn't let her go. Not yet. Even as he felt her fighting it, there had been a closeness between them in their conversations tonight. He wanted it to continue as long as he could get her to stay outside here with him.

"I've never told you about myself, all of it anyway. Would you like to hear how I came to be with Ma Wade and Nick? I know you know they aren't blood family, although Ma has been the only mother I've ever known."

She hesitated, as though she might turn him down, and then she said, "Yes, go ahead. We've talked enough about my problems. I'd love to change the subject."

Their times together back in New Hampshire had been rare, and sweet, and far too brief for lengthy conversations. She knew little of his past. He began, now, "It took Ma a long time and asking a lot of folks questions before she found out how and why I happened to be shoved into her care when I was a brand-new infant."

"Tell me everything," Clare urged softly, her hand a feather on his arm.

"According to what Ma was told, the man who fathered me was educated, well-off, and a prominent Portsmouth judge. But as years went on he had himself a drinking problem. He dallied with a young orphan girl of strong peasant stock, an immigrant from Scotland. I was the result."

"Go on."

"The girl who gave birth to me was plenty scared, and shamed. She was hardly more than a child herself. The judge refused to help her. I was just a few days old when she handed me off to Ma." A frown creased his brow. "She just shoved a market basket with me in it at Ma. Hardly said anything more than, 'take care of my baby'."

Clare's throat filled, and she nodded. Her gaze was glued to his face, cherishing every feature. She ached to touch him, hold him, but she thought better of it, for fear they'd go too far. Empathy could so easily turn to passion. She held her hands tightly together in her lap and waited for him to continue.

"The girl ran away before Ma could catch up to her. Ma was told that the girl stowed away on a ship headed to Scotland. Nobody ever heard her from after."

"Nothing?"

"No." He hesitated, "but I used to dream about her, what she was like, and that someday she'd come back and find me. She didn't of course."

"What about the judge who fathered you, did you ever meet him?"

"Ayuh." The memory was so painful, so infuriated him, he hated to tell her about it. But finally, he said huskily, "Ma never gave up trying to find out all of my story. She wanted me to have a history to be proud of, to know my father. When I was about seven years old, she took me to meet the judge. He wanted nothing to do with us and he treated Ma like dirt. Her such a kind, wonderful woman to take me in and treat me like her own! I hated him."

She covered his hand with hers in consolation. He traced her knuckles with his thumb. "I didn't treat her much better, myself."

"What do you mean? That can't be true! You'd never treat Ma Wade badly."

"It is true. It didn't do much for my pride, knowing that if I'd been a kitten I'd have been bagged and thrown into the sea to drown. If I'd been a puppy, I would have been knocked in the head to die. Instead, I was just shoved into a market basket for someone else to worry about."

He swallowed the bitter taste in his mouth, wiped the back of his hand across his eyes and looked down at Clare. "I mistrusted adults, even Ma. I rebelled against her love and teaching, ran wild from the age of eleven to almost twenty, got into all kinds of trouble. There were women," he said, adding when he read the question in her eyes, "But none who really mattered. They were wild and lonely like me and for a week or two we made each other feel a little better. Somehow, I managed to stay out of prison. Ma never gave up on me, and she finally won me over. Truth is, she saved my life." A grin tilted the corner of his mouth, "Suddenly, I was a bad boy gone good."

Clare grasped his hand tight. "I think your real mother loved you very much. She must have known from Ma Wade's appearance that she was a kind soul, and would be good to you."

"I came to realize that, as I got older and wiser. But when I was a boy I was sure my real mother would find me and life with her would be some kind of damn golden fantasy. There was a note—" he fell silent.

"A note? Please tell me." From the expression on his face, it had been very important to him.

"When I was running wild, and just a little older than Nick and Oakley are now, but still a boy, I found a piece of paper blowing in the gutter along the street in Portsmouth. Don't know why I picked it up except it was a time when I was at my lowest. There was writing on the paper." He looked at her and she waited, seeing how difficult this was for him to talk about. "'Love endures all things' is what it said." He grinned, embarrassed. "I got the cock-eyed notion that my real mother had written it to me and fate destined me to find it."

"Oh, Larkin!" Tears burned her eyes.

"I feel like an idiot, talking about it now," he said, clearing his throat. "The note was probably written for someone's sweetheart, but back then I didn't take it that way."

"Of course not. You'd been abandoned, and that hurt. Did you keep the note?"

"Ayuh. I was a fool over that note. Never could throw it away. It's in a trunk, somewhere in my belongings." He scratched his jaw and gave her a penetrating look. "I still believe what the note says, Clare, that love endures all things. I believe it most when I think of you and me. I've felt that from the day we met."

She couldn't breathe. She started to stand but he pulled her back down, saying hoarsely, "That's not the end of the story. I haven't got to the part where we moved to Sandwich."

His touch was turning her to melted butter, her resistance vapor thin. She swallowed and said, "All right. You came with Ma and Nick to Sandwich. Go on."

"Ma talked a lot about going back to find the old property she'd inherited. I wasn't as ready for that as she was. It was strange, but my visit to the judge's courtroom, the 'halls of justice', simmered a burning ambition in me for quite a while. I decided I'd be a lawyer, or even a judge. A far better one than the old reprobate who was my father had been! I studied, read bushels of books about law. Those dreams were passing fancies. I was meant to be a farmer, a rancher. I love the land."

"What became of the judge? Did you ever hear from him after you saw him as a child?"

He sighed, "Not a word. Although he was in the news and subject of a lot of talk. He was eventually disbarred from the judge's bench, due to his failings brought on by alcohol. He lost everything, a fine mansion and fortune. He died a penniless, broken old man. I still intend to show the cold-hearted old cuss up, but by following my own path working with the land."

"You will, Larkin, you will. You've made a fine start here in Kansas. Ma Wade is so proud of you, she can hardly stop talking about how you plan carefully, spend wisely, and work very hard."

It's you I want to be proud of me, you I want in my life. It was all he could do not to sweep her into his arms, carry her off into the shadows of the hayfield and make love to her. Any such move would only send her farther away, as long as she had her mind made up that they could not be sweethearts. He said on a deep sigh of reluctance, "It has gotten late and I've probably worn your ears off. You'll want to turn in."

"I do have to go in, but I appreciate very much hearing your story, Larkin." She hesitated, thinking of his start in life compared to her own very comfortable one and how far he'd come... Driven by impulse she couldn't fight, she leaned forward and pressed her lips to his mouth in a soft, lingering kiss. "Larkin Wade, you're the most wonderful person I've ever met." She gathered her skirts and fled inside.

His eyes followed her and his feelings soared. He wouldn't want a woman who was any less proud, any less dedicated to the ones she felt responsible for, but Lord, the wait was hard. He wanted her now. No woman would ever be right for him but Clare. God help him to not continue his life as a bachelor forever, dammit!

Chapter Thirteen

It took Clare and her family a full half-day to get moved to the McCrum property. With Clare doing the driving, she and Momma, Alice and Hallie, went in the wagon carrying their household goods—kitchen stove, tables and chairs, beds, pots and pans and other utensils, bedding and linens. Oakley and Poppa drove a wagon borrowed from Larkin and loaded with their crate of clucking hens, their pig, plow and other tools, and with Belle and Bertha, their cows, tied on behind.

In short order, the women tackled the house with brooms, and a bushel basket to carry out debris; with mops, and strong yellow soap while Poppa and Oakley cleaned the bam and chicken coop, with an eye on the root cellar to be restored later. In the house, beds were set-up in the bedrooms and covered with clean sheets and quilts. When the cupboards were thoroughly cleansed downstairs in the kitchen area, Momma's cream china dishes with a pink rose pattern were unpacked and put away. Greased paper was fastened over the broken window until the glass could be replaced. That night, they ate a cold supper from a picnic basket Mabel sent with them.

Bright and early next morning, Clare tackled setting up the kitchen stove, then set to cleaning the living room heating stove, getting ashes and soot on her arms and face and in her hair.

"If we had some paint, and painted the walls right away, we'd all feel better about our new house," she told the others.

Momma turned from where she peeled potatoes at the work table. "At home at Hobb's Mills we made our own paint. We called it milk paint, because we made it of milk, whatever pigment we wanted to color it, linseed oil, eggs, and animal glue or wax."

"We don't have some of those ingredients, or we'd try your recipe, Momma," Clare said, wiping an arm across her brow and leaving more soot. "Alice can walk into town and if the price isn't too dear, she can buy a couple buckets of paint at the hardware store. We'd be able to paint the walls this afternoon."

"No, no, I can't go," Alice turned from where she scrubbed at layers of ancient filth on the door and said with a frown, her voice thinned with uneasiness. "I don't know anyone there. I really don't want to go."

"We need paint, Alice, and I can't go," Clare said patiently. "I'm filthy and I don't want to wash up until I've finished with the dirty work. Everyone else is just as dirty, or busy. You're the cleanest, you'd just need to take off your apron." She wouldn't dare send Hallie, who if she had the chance would likely sneak onto the next eastbound train and they'd never see her again. "Please, Alice, you may pick whatever color you choose, how's that?"

"We'll need more soap, too." Momma decried, "I never saw a house let go so badly."

Hallie was sitting on the floor, an injured pigeon in her lap. It had flown in through an open window upstairs and injured a wing trying to get out again. "This pigeon is going to be my pet," she announced. "I'm naming her Merrylou."

"Do you know for sure she's a she?" Clare asked over her shoulder.

"Doesn't matter," Hallie said stubbornly. "She's still my Merry bird. She will get better and then she will carry messages from me all the way to New Hampshire and Aunt Livia."

Clare pressed her palm to her forehead, leaving a streak of dirt, and prayed for patience. She bit back what she would like to say and prepared to unroll the living room carpet. Hallie might never get over her unhappiness at leaving Sandwich, and what Clare was going to do about it she had no idea.

Alice, feeling ill from nerves, washed her face and hands in a pan of water on a bench they'd placed for that purpose by the back door. She smoothed her dark hair and her hand shook as she adjusted her spectacles. She wished Clare was taking care of this errand into town, not she. Being alone with strangers made her terribly uncomfortable.

From the time she'd been torn asunder from her love affair with Everett and banished to live for more than a year with aging Aunt Zilpha, she'd felt a terrible lacking in herself. A flaw others would surely detect if she allowed them to get too close. Staying in the shadows, hiding away, plain and unnoticed was much her preference. Dealing with people other than family and small children unnerved her, made her heart beat so fast she felt she would explode and die.

Except for leaving Momma and Poppa, causing them and her siblings to worry, there were many times she would have preferred death, to living without the love of her life. She hadn't spoken of their cousin Everett in years. Not a word. No one besides herself knew that she still pined for him, especially at night when she was at rest, her mind free, her heart lonely. She couldn't stop wishing that she was the one he took as his wife, to love her, give her children, and a life worth living.

Her family's insistence that she complete this errand felt like a hand in the middle of her back, pushing, pushing, as she made the walk into town. Early summer heat lay over the clusters of buildings and dusty streets. Few people were moving about and for that she was glad. She located the hardware store, CAHILL'S—HARDWARE OF ALL KINDS, three doors down on the left side of Main street, where Clare said she would find it.

Alice took a deep breath, and went inside where it was slightly cooler. She stood blinking to get used to the darker atmosphere after the brightness of the sun, and studied the shelves of goods—small tools, hammers and bits, rolls of canvas, and below the shelves—barrels of nails and such. She swallowed a dryness in her throat, and whirled when a woman's voice spoke behind her.

"Hello, Miss, is there something I can help you find?" The tall, rawboned woman smiled.

Alice did her best to relax. "Thank you. Yes, I'm in need of a gallon of white paint. No, no, not white. I believe I'd like yellow. Lemon yellow. No, lighter than lemon, yellow like sunshine."

The hardware lady chuckled. "My, well, yes, I think I can get you that color paint. Sunshine yellow, or near to it." She led the way toward the back of the store, saying over her shoulder, "I'm Mrs. Cahill, but most folks call me Eva. My husband, Gully, owns the hardware. He's gone on the train to Junction City to buy some wrenches and axe handles. Our stock has gotten low on both."

Alice was trying to think of a reply when a sharp sound, the crack of a gun, sounded from the other side of the wall, making her jump. She cringed, and watched for Mrs. Cahill to react and tell her what to do. Should they hide behind the counter? Or run outside? Go for help? But the woman wasn't fazed and continued to search the shelves of paint. Alice moistened her lips, hugged herself tightly to still the nerve bumps chasing up and down her arms.

"Umm, Mrs. Cahill, wasn't that a gunshot just now? It was close, just on the other side of that wall, sounded like. Didn't you hear it?" As she spoke, another shot cracked and again she flinched.

"Oh sure, I heard. That's just good-for-nothing Dinger Toledo at the cafe next door. When he's not workin' over to the stockyards, he holds down a chair at the restaurant, jawin' with whoever else comes in. When the durn fool gets bored with conversation, he takes out his pistol and shoots flies off the ceiling. Happens a lot. I don't pay it no mind."

"B-but someone could be hurt."

"I dunno about that, Dinger's a good shot. Stupid Eye-talian wastes a lot of ammunition, though."

And some people thought Poppa was peculiar! Alice shook her head in bewilderment. She didn't know who was more curious, Mr. Toledo for blasting flies off the ceiling, or Mrs. Cahill for paying the matter so little mind.

Eva Cahill found the paint and carried the two buckets up to the front counter. "I don't believe I've seen you around Sweetbrier before, Miss. Are you new to the community?"

Alice was still shaky and her throat was dry as toast. "Y-yes." She chewed her lips. "I moved here with my—my family. My name is Alice Hobb. It's—nice to meet you, Mrs. Cahill." Her thin hand zig-zagged forward to meet Eva Cahill's large bony fingers. "We have taken the—McCrum farm."

"My," Mrs. Cahill clucked, "you're going to need a lot of paint!

Are you sure two buckets is enough? Poor old Annabelle McCrum was too frail to keep up her property much. Neighbors did what they could, don't you know, but they had their own farms to look after. She'd usually run them off, anyway. She was too poor to pay, and she hated charity. So the place just went to rack and ruin."

Alice nodded. She knew about pride observing her stubborn sister, Clare. She dug into her drawstring purse for coins to pay for the paint. "Thank you very much, Mrs. Cahill. It was nice meeting you. I'll be going—my family is waiting for the paint."

"Where did you say you're from?" Mrs. Cahill called just as Alice reached the door, a bucket of paint in each hand.

"New Hampshire. Sandwich, New Hampshire."

"Never heard of it, the Sandwich part. Thought a sandwich was a piece of meat between two pieces of bread." Eva Cahill laughed at her own joke.

Alice hesitated, turned and smiled timidly. "Sandwich is also the name of the township where my family and I lived. Named for the Earl Of Sandwich, of Great Britain. He was a friend of New Hampshire's governor, a long time back. Bread and meat put together, the Earl of Sandwich's favorite food, was named after him, I'm told. A sandwich." It had been ages since Alice had carried on a conversation of this length with a perfect stranger, and she was surprised to find herself actually enjoying it.

Still, she was glad to have the errand taken care of and a few minutes later, passing the general store, she remembered to buy the bars of soap Momma wanted. Thanking the elderly gentleman who waited on her, she put the soap in her drawstring bag tied at her waist, picked up a bucket of paint in each hand, and heaving a sigh of relief, left the store.

It was a drudgy little town, she thought, as she strolled along, the sun prickling her back through her dress. Sweetbrier was a nice name, but was perfectly awful to look at compared to Sandwich Village. Still, she was glad to be here and not there.

There wasn't a soul in the whole countryside around Sandwich who wasn't aware that Everett had jilted her because he didn't think enough of her to stand up to Uncle Samuel. Instead, he'd let her be shamed while he went on to find happiness with another. She was pitied for being the plain spinster she was.

With effort, she pushed sad memories from her mind.

She was well on her way when she heard whimpering sobs that seemed to come out of thin air. She halted and looked about her intently as the sobs increased.

Finally, behind a boulder several yards to her right, she spotted a thatch of blonde hair, just showing above the top of the rock. The child's cries grew louder. Alice put her paint down on the ground and hurried. On the other side of the big boulder a little girl in blue calico held her bare and bloodied foot in her lap. Her little face was scrunched with pain, tears making streaks down her dusty cheeks.

"My goodness! What happened?" Alice dropped to her knees next to the child.

"I—I tried to jump off the rock an' my—my toes caught and—and I stubbed them bad. My ankle hurts. I think I busted my leg."

Alice ran her fingers over the child's legs and ankles. "No, no, I don't believe you've broken anything. But your poor, torn little toes. Here, I have a hanky we can wrap them with."

As Alice worked over the small dirty foot, the child's sobs subsided. "You're a nice lady."

Alice looked at her for a long moment. "Thank you! What's your name, darling?"

"Beth. Beth Proctor."

"Well, Beth, do you think you can stand with my help?" Alice assisted Beth to her feet. The girl stood wobbling, wincing with pain.

"Where do you live, Beth? I'll help you to your home. I'll leave my paint here and come back for it later. Come now, which way?" She put her arm around the small girl. "Lean on me as much as you need to."

"I have to go back to the implement yard. That's where my Pa is. He told me not to wander off. But I saw a little brown rabbit and I tried to follow. Then I jumped off the rock. Pa's gonna be worried."

"We'll get you back to the implement yard, then, and ease his mind."

With Beth hobbling and Alice holding onto her, they made their way back into town and along Front Street.

"Pa!" Beth called as they neared the implement yard where a big broad-shouldered fellow was walking toward a shack with a sign over the door that said Office. "I busted my leg, near to, anyhow."

"Bethie, what on God's green earth happened?"

He rushed forward and knelt in front of Beth. Alice released her, wanted to tell him that the child was all right but she couldn't find her voice.

Beth made a face of terrible pain. "I jumped off a big rock and stubbed my toes. I think they might be busted. They liked to come right off my foot," she whimpered. "They hurt so bad I couldn't walk. This nice lady helped me."

He looked then at Alice and their eyes met, hers shy, his curious. Even though he'd never seen her before, he felt an immediate connection, a familiarity with her. He got slowly to his feet. She was plain, and wearing a shy, almost frightened smile. Beneath the thin gray fabric covering her bosom, he'd swear he could see her heart palpitating. When he realized he'd been staring at a very private part of the woman's anatomy, his glance flew upward to her face.

She didn't seem to have noticed his slip in manners, or she was ignoring it if she did. There was a shadowed sadness in her pretty blue eyes that made him feel protective toward her, in a way he hadn't felt toward a woman since his darling JoEllen died. He held out his hand, "Tobias Proctor. You've already met my daughter, Beth, here. My boy. Will, is around here somewhere."

The big bearded fellow had the warmest, kindest brown eyes Alice had ever seen. It was hard to speak, to sound normal, "My name is Alice Hobb. You must be a partner to Larkin Wade?"

"Sure am! You know Larkin?"

"We—my family, are from New Hampshire, the same area Larkin came here from."

"I met your sister!" he exclaimed. "Clare, correct? Very pretty girl. Friend of Larkin's."

"Ayuh, Clare's very pretty." *And no doubt she'll become Larkin's wife if our family ever learns to get by without her propping us up.*

He hesitated, wondering if he would be overstepping bounds of propriety for what he was about to ask a young woman he'd barely met. He plunged ahead, "Look, Miss Hobb, I'd like to repay you for helping Beth. We're about to head home for some supper. Would you join us?"

Alice's mouth went dry. "No, no thank you. I couldn't. My own family is waiting. I left my buckets of paint back by the side of the road." She motioned over her shoulder in the direction she'd come.

"Another time, then. Say, can we give you a ride home? I feel we do owe you something."

"No, please, you owe me nothing. I must be going." She whirled about, stumbling away with her glance on the ground in front of her.

"It was nice to meet you, Miss Hobb. I hope you'll enjoy living here in Kansas."

She nodded and turned briefly to wave. "Goodbye, Beth. Mr. Proctor."

Further down the road, past where she'd found Beth, she lifted her chin and looked squarely ahead. The paint buckets swung from her hands, her stride became long and carefree. She wasn't sure what just happened, meeting Mr. Proctor. Perhaps nothing, really. But for some reason, on this very strange day, she felt as though she was starting to come alive, to waken after years of near unconsciousness. Tobias Proctor. She liked his name.

Chapter Fourteen

THE SOUP MOMMA WAS MAKING FROM FRESH VEGETABLES and ham Mabel insisted they take smelled heavenly.

"I'm so hungry I could eat a bear." dare dropped into a chair for a brief rest in their freshly scrubbed little kitchen. She leaned forward, elbows propped on the table and her chin in hand.

Momma looked over her shoulder with an amused frown as she stirred the soup. "Now dove, you know you wouldn't eat a bear."

"No, not really. I'll settle for the soup. It smells wonderful."

Hallie was making biscuits at the other end of the table, fussing over them like works of art. The biscuits had begun to rise in the warmth of sunshine pouring through the window.

Clare smiled, "Lovely work you're doing with the biscuits, Hallie, they'll be perfect with the soup."

Alice came through the door. "Sorry I'm late." She set her buckets of paint down.

"We were beginning to worry," Momma said.

Alice's cheeks were flushed, and she wore a faint smile as though she looked inward at something pleasant.

Clare mused, dropping her hand from her chin, "Alice, did something happen while you were in Sweetbrier?"

"No, not really." Her glance focused on the paint as she lined the buckets up neatly by the wall. "I helped a child, that's all. She'd stubbed her little toes badly. I was on my way home when I found her crying and unable to walk."

"I see." Clare silenced further questions in her mind, she didn't want to push Alice into her typical reticence.

"What did you do with the little girl?" Hallie closed the oven door on the biscuits and turned in interest. "Where is she now?"

"I wrapped her bloody toes and I took her back to her family. She'll be fine. She's very sweet."

Clare marveled privately that a simple trip into town and giving aid to a child could bring about this moment, this rare alteration in Alice's regressive manner.

In the years following the end of Alice's love affair with their cousin, she had shown very little joy in life. Although outwardly kind and polite, and hardworking, she had consistently worn a quiet sadness about her like a cloak. She showed no interest in fixing up to look pretty or feminine. She got upset at others' attempts at matchmaking, wanted only to be left alone.

If helping a child was all it took to turn Alice around from being so quiet and withdrawn, Clare hoped every child in the neighborhood would need a touch of help from her sister!

The days following were long and work-filled. Clare helped her mother and sisters paint the walls, sew new curtains, and arrange their few pieces of New England-style furniture in the small prairie house. It was a near-miraculous transformation to Clare's mind, but Hallie despaired that it would ever be a "decent" place to live.

———

NICK LOUNGED on the back of the small sorrel horse he'd ridden to the Hobb farm, waiting for Clare's answer. The hot July winds pushed at her skirts as she stood in the yard at the foot of the windmill, where Nick had watered his mount at the trough. Larkin and Mabel had sent Nick to invite the Hobbs to their ranch for a wheat threshing party, to help with the work, but as importantly, the pleasure of getting together with neighbors and friends.

"Of course, Nick, we'd love to come. It will be a chance for us to repay you folks for all you've done for us since we came here to Sweetbrier." Threshing was a busy time, Larkin would hardly notice she was there. She'd be equally busy preparing the meals and cleaning up after. It would be good for Momma, for all of them, to meet their neighbors. Clare pushed a damp curl behind her ear, and smiled. "We'll be there at first light. Tell Mabel—your grandmother, we'll bring a cake or two."

He grinned, "Grandma's already bakin' up a storm for the hungry threshers, but I've never known there to be too many cakes. Not for me, anyhow. Oakley around? I'll say howdy to him before I get back."

"You'll find him and Poppa cutting thistle out of the far pasture. I suspect they'll be more than glad to leave that chore and help with the threshing."

Mabel's kitchen next day was steamy and crowded with women and girls in their aprons. At the table by the big stove, Alice floured bowls of chicken parts and passed them to Clare to fry. Momma snapped string beans and Hallie washed small new potatoes to cook with the beans. Roasts and hams already cooked filled one table, loaves of bread, fresh-baked pies and cakes covered another. The chatter of the women accompanied the muted humming and ringing of the threshing machinery and shouts of the workers coming through the open kitchen windows from the golden fields outside.

Every now and then, Clare glanced out the window at the workers shrouded in dust as they fed sheaves of wheat into the steam-powered thresher where the grain was separated from the straw. The straw was carried away on an elevator attachment with conveyor belts and deposited into a stack on the ground, the grain falling into a winnowing rack where the chaff was shaken or blown free. Clean grain poured out through a channel at the bottom of the machine into bags, to be loaded onto wagons and delivered to the depot in Sweetbrier. The air was filled with flying chaff and dust and covered the workers until they were hardly recognizable one from the other. Even so, each time she looked, Clare's eyes of their own accord could pick out Larkin from the others. His tall, dust-covered figure, dark sweat-stains down the back of his shirt, his hat pulled low to shut out the glare of the sun, was unmistakable as he hustled at his work. Her heart would pick up a beat.

When the sun was noon high, the tired crew ambled to the

backyard pump where they washed up. They sagged onto the benches at the tables the women had set up in the shade.

Clare took secret delight in seeing that Larkin had extra servings from the deep dish of fried tomatoes, which he seemed to particularly like, and homemade cottage cheese cold from Mabel's springhouse. She kept his tin drinking cup filled with "switchel" made from vinegar and ginger, with spring water. All the workers relished the drink, and cold buttermilk, on this hot, tiring day.

It was enough for Clare to be the recipient of his white-toothed grin of thanks, the touch of his hand grazing hers as he held out his cup.

When a bit a golden chaff fell from his tousled hair onto her arm, Clare privately gathered the chaff between thumb and forefinger—and for no intelligent reason she could fathom-tucked it souvenir-like, down in her apron pocket.

She could almost pretend, during those three days threshing at the Wade ranch, that she and Larkin were there as a couple. A harmless pretense, since she kept it to herself.

For days, lines of loaded wheat wagons streamed by the Hobb place from several large ranches, rolling up dust in gritty clouds behind them as they headed for the Katy train station and shipment out from Sweetbrier.

"There goes another load," Poppa would beam with pleasure and exclaim at the distant sound of the train's whistle. Ear cocked to listen, he was like a child joyful at the sound of a new toy.

"Then, you're liking to live here in Kansas, Poppa?" Clare asked him.

"Ayuh, I am. This place is master fine, master fine."

One day, a group of women came to call at the small Hobb dwelling. A few of the women they'd already met at the Wade ranch, or around town. Myra Tibbets—who Clare was sure had designs on Larkin—was one of them. Another of the group had brought an apple cider cake with baked on meringue frosting, to welcome the newcomers.

Eva Cahill, from the hardware, announced they were there to invite Momma, Alice, and Clare to join the Ladies Sweetbrier Betterment Club. Clare was in the kitchen, stirring up the fire in the stove to make a fresh pot of coffee to go with the cider cake, when one woman's voice rose above the other female chatter in the next room.

Clare slipped into the front room to listen, standing because there wasn't enough chairs for everyone. Myra, in ruffled pink, watched her, sizing her. Myra's smoky-eyes then roved the simply furnished room with something like contempt. She tossed her raven-dark hair when she again looked at Clare, and smiled sweetly.

Larkin surely couldn't care for such a person, beautiful though she was, Clare thought, swallowing resentment.

"I don't like soundin' small-minded and unkind," Mrs. Cahill was saying, "but Mayor Fuller is about eatin' us out of house and home. He shows up at our store about closin' time, makes out he has town business to discuss with Gully, and Gully ends up invitin' him home with us to supper. I have children at home to feed, and it's not like Alfred is payin' me the way he does Liddy."

Larkin had told Clare, the day he introduced her to the circuit minister's wife, that the mayor took his meals two or three times a week at Mrs. Liddy Goodlander's table. The pay helped supplement the minister's meager income from preaching to his various flocks around the countryside.

The rest of the time, the mayor freeloaded at other homes, according to Larkin, and loved to organize socials where the women provided bountiful tables of food. Mayor Fuller lived at the hotel, didn't like paying for the meals there or at the cafe, if he could get them free somewhere else.

Carrie Spencer, plump, pansy-eyed, spoke up, "Reverend Goodlander is gone from home so much of the time, you must like having a man of the mayor's caliber call on you a few times a week, Liddy. Don't that make you feel safer?"

Liddy flushed. "I-I really haven't looked at it that way. My husband has his work that calls him away. My boy, Gordy is home with me. I quite accept how things are."

"I'm honored to have him at my table when he's not at Liddy's!" Mrs. Fayne's chin lifted in hauteur. "He's the mayor, after all. He appreciates even the simplest meal."

"Well, of course he does, Muriel, because he doesn't have to pay for it!" Eva Cahill turned to the Hobb women, "I'll say it if no one else will, our dear mayor is a tightfisted skinflint."

Muriel looked aghast and reproachfully told the roomful of women, "I think Mayor Fuller is a wonderful man. He likes a clean and pretty town. He got us those new plank sidewalks, don't forget. It was his suggestion that the business folk plant geraniums in their window-boxes. He does his best to make sure Marshal Seavers stays sober when he's on duty. Mayor Fuller got us a stout stone jail built to house the rowdies that come to Sweetbrier at cattle shipping time. We all know he pesters the merchants to keep the streets clean of horse-droppings. We ladies have him to thank that our hems don't drag through constant filth when we're out and about."

Myra said, her hand resting prettily on her bosom, "I like Mayor Fuller's manners, he's so refined. He's never come right out and boasted, but he's dropped hints that he comes from a well-to-do Kansas City family."

"Hogwash." Mrs. Cahill waved that off. "My Gully says that Alfred Fuller's father was a simple farmer, an apple grower who made a living selling apples, cider, and vinegar, in northeast Kansas. Near some small town, I don't remember the name."

"Oh, no, that's just gossip, I'm sure," Myra looked furious at the rebuttal. She sat forward, "There's money in his family background, anyone can see he's quality." Her tone, the expression on her face, said that she could recognize quality even if the others couldn't.

Muriel Fayne sniffed, "Regardless of where he came from, he's our mayor, an office that should be shown due respect."

"He's a moodier," Mrs. Cahill said in disgust.

Momma was looking stricken as though the room might go up in flames. Ladies in Sandwich never talked like this. Clare chewed her lip not to laugh out loud. She was quite enjoying the show, although she felt sorry for Momma.

"Well, even if he is something of a moodier," Muriel argued, "he shows his appreciation at being our guest. Why, just last week, he praised my gooseberry pie to the skies! Plain old gooseberry pie. You'd have thought it was ambrosia."

"Does anyone know if we're any closer to having our new courthouse?" Mrs. Cahill asked dourly. "I'm not gettin' any younger, waitin' to see it built."

No one seemed to have the answer about the courthouse, and talk about the mayor dwindled away. Conversations over the cake and coffee were calmer. The new fabrics just in at the drygoods store were discussed. Concerns over school-age children running wild about town during the summer also came up.

An hour and a half later, the Hobb women saw their guests off with a promise to attend future meetings of the Sweetbrier Betterment Club if at all possible. They would try to come up with suggestions for keeping town children off the street when they could be at activities more constructive. Too bad they didn't have long days of farm chores to do, like the rural children had.

"Alice, have you ever thought of teaching school?" Clare asked that night at the supper table. "You're wonderful with children, you'd make a fine teacher."

Everyone looked at Alice. "I—I have thought about it. But, I— I'd have to meet—be part of the community, deal with the children's parents. I'm not sure I'd be good at that."

"Stuff and nonsense." Clare sipped her glass of milk and then smiled warmly. "If you'd give yourself a chance and make up your mind to it, you'd be perfect, Alice. Tell you what, if the Sweetbrier school already has teachers, we can find out if there's a close-by country school for you. Wouldn't you like to teach?"

"I'd have to think about it. I suppose we could use the money, couldn't we?"

"Definitely. I'm going to see if there's some sort of work I can do in town, now that we've finished settling in. I'd consider teaching, but you'd make a much better one. You have more patience and a wonderful way with little ones."

The remainder of the money they brought with them would last but a few more weeks at best. It would be fortunate if both Alice and she found paying jobs. Already they'd made arrangements to sell butter and eggs in town, and occasionally fresh baked goods such as they had made at home at Hobb's Mills.

Poppa cleared his throat and his eyes were sharp, "Might's well be me to go out to work. I can tell you, my daughters won't labor for others just because we come to a new place. No, they won't."

Clare smiled and reached to pat his hand. Poppa had days when he was remarkably his old self and this was one.

Away from the heavy-handedness of his brothers, he'd have more such periods, she was convinced. She was proud of how hard he'd worked in the wheat harvest for Larkin, and on their own place these first weeks. Poppa and Oakley had spent days chopping thistle out of their fields. They'd mended the fences and got the root cellar ready for the storage of winter vegetables. Mabel insisted she was going to have tons more than she needed.

Lately, the two men of the family were up at dawn each day to work on the barn roof while it was coolest.

"You have a lot to do here, Poppa. It's kind of you to want to look out for Alice and me, but we wouldn't mind working for someone else." She thought again of their need for money, that would be dire by wintertime. "Let us try first to find proper work, and if we don't find anything, you can look."

"I am a very good blacksmith. I could work for the smith in Sweetbrier. My womenfolk can stay here at home safe. Do their knitting and tatting and making things pretty."

"If Sam Dorsey, the smith, needs the help, of course you'd be right for the job." It was important to encourage Poppa. She'd already thought he might work as helper at the blacksmith shop and earn extra income.

At the same time, she was leery how others might treat him for his mental confusion which could still crop up when he was over-whelmed by too many orders, too many things coming at him like lightning. The calmer his life, the better he managed. She'd like to see him satisfied with working their farm, tackling the chores and the seasons in their time, but if he insisted on seeking work in town, she would back him up. In many ways, it was important for him to always be the head of the house.

———

"WHY ARE you getting all dressed up?" Hallie wanted to know right after breakfast cleanup one morning. "Are you going to see him?"

"Now, Hallie, don't pry," Momma said from where she finished wiping and putting away dishes.

"Who do you mean by him?" Clare knew, but pretended indifference.

"Larkin Wade, that's who."

Clare had long since forgiven Momma for withholding Larkin's letters, but her mother couldn't hear his name without a look of guilty regret. Clare went over and gave her mother's shoulder a squeeze and Momma smiled her gratitude.

Hallie chattered on, "I've seen you whenever we go over to Mrs. Wade's to visit. You're constantly at the windows looking to see where he's at, your face all long and sad." Hallie let her jaw droop and pulled her eyes down at the corners.

Clare couldn't help laughing and she made a face back at Hallie. As hard as she tried to hide her emotions concerning Larkin from everyone, and herself in particular, she supposed that at times her deep-in-the-heart feelings surfaced and showed.

"For your information, my dear little sister, I'm going into Sweetbrier to ask for work."

"How do I look?" She twirled to give Hallie and Momma the full effect of her blue-striped lawn suit, pale blue suede gloves, and the flower-bedecked toque perched stylishly on her head.

"Beautiful enough to win the hearts of a dozen gentlemen," Alice said, coming into the room from where she'd been making beds.

"Thank you, but I'm after work, not hearts." The heart of only one gentleman was all she'd ever care about and out of necessity that had to be shelved.

Walking to town, Clare pondered Alice's uncharacteristic remark about "winning the hearts of gentlemen." Was Alice having romantic thoughts of her own these days?

Clare suspected something was afoot with Alice, a secret that Alice was keeping to herself. Lately, it was easier to get Alice to run an errand in town. On market day she spent a lot of the time playing tag and talking with the child, Beth. When they baked apple tarts to sell to the grocer, Alice always saved one back to give to Beth. Come to think of it, last time that happened, Alice gave Beth three tarts, and Beth ran to the implement yard with one of them for her brother, Will, and the third for her father. Did Alice fancy the burly Mr. Proctor, Larkin's partner at the implement yard?

Clare made a vow to keep her eyes open and find out! In the same second, she felt a twinge of jealousy. Alice was free to pursue a romance, if she so wanted. Clare, for the time being, was not Her family leaned on her heavily, for every important decision and ruling as well as a major portion of labor. They would need her income to survive, providing she found work today.

As she walked along, she sang softly the words to the popular song, Whispering Hope:

"Soft as the voice of an angel
Breathing a lesson unheard
Hope with her gentle persuasion
Whispers her comforting words."

Alice Hawthorne had written the song; Momma said she'd named her eldest child for the songwriter Alice.

Taking one side of Main street and then the other, Clare stopped in each establishment with friendly greeting and to ask for work. The cafe and dry-goods store were family run and needed no extra help. The owner of the drugstore managed his small amount of business himself. The butcher could not afford her. Or so they claimed.

She stopped in at the office of the SWEETBRIER INDE-PENDENT and bought a copy of the weekly newspaper from the editor, who introduced himself as James Myers. He stood back, young and myopic but peacock proud as she scanned the sheets of his paper.

"There are no jobs for women listed?" She sniffed in weary disgust, "But you print column after column of ads to take our money, if we had any: Doctor Barker's Blood Thinner, Orange Wine Stomach Bitters, Ague Pills, Liver Pills, Positive Rheumatic Cure." She shook her head, took a moment to scan an article about the Betterment Club which reported that members had called on Mrs. Eugenie Hobb and daughters, Alice, Clare, and Hallie, to welcome the new residents to the fair city of Sweetbrier.

"But no work?" she complained. "What's a woman to do if she needs work?"

Editor Myers was still sputtering, "But-but-but—" when she bade him good day and returned to the street.

Her feelings of industry and enthusiasm began to wane as the morning wore on without success in her quest for employment. She hadn't really expected to find an ad for help in the Independent. In a small town like this where everyone knew everyone else there wouldn't be a need to pay for an ad. Need of extra help would pass word of mouth and be filled. The knowledge didn't help her disappointment although she felt guilty for being rude to the editor.

The day was heating up viciously and perspiration trickled down her face from under her flowery hat. Her feet hurt, she had worn her best shoes, which she hadn't had on since long before they left New Hampshire. She should have known better.

Passing the implement yard, her eyes covertly sought sign of Larkin should he be in town, but there was only Mr. Proctor and two other men, standing and talking in a field of machinery.

At the O.K. General store, she was told by Myra's kindly uncle that Myra was all the help he needed, that Myra was the post-mistress but also helped wait on customers if the store got busy. Midway back in the store, Myra sat on a high stool behind a counter, engrossed in a magazine with a colorful cover. In back of her, rows of pigeonhole boxes against the wall marked the post-office.

Larkin hadn't gone to that box social the first Saturday night after the Hobb's arrival in Kansas when they were his guests. Perhaps Clare had no right to be glad about that, but she was.

"Hello Myra."

Myra's head snapped up, she closed the magazine, rolled it up, and shoved it into a pigeonhole behind her. "Yes?"

Clare reached into her pocket and brought out her letter addressed to her grandmother in New Hampshire. "I'd like to mail this, please. And while I'm here, is there any mail for me?"

"Were you expecting a letter?" Myra's envious glance was practically glued to Clare's hat. "From somebody special?" She smiled confidentially. "A fella?"

Clare smiled back. "No fella. I thought there might be a letter for my family from New Hampshire."

She supposed it was useless to hope that Uncle Simon's heart had softened by now and that he might have sent them money. Hallie had written and posted two or three letters to Aunt Livia, so it was surely known by all at Hobb's Mills the needy condition of Momma and Poppa's family in Kansas. If Simon had relented, Clare could spend more time at home getting their farm in opera-tion, rather than seeking outside work.

Myra, comely in blue calico, briefly checked the pigeonhole boxes. She shook her head, "Like I thought. You don't have nothing. No mail." Her eyes, with a glint of jealousy, returned to Clare's attire. Her tongue traced her rosy lips. "Law!" she exclaimed, "but your hat is the most beautiful I've ever seen in my life!" She hurtled around the counter for a closer look, and jabbed a finger to touch the feathers and flowers.

Discomfited by Myra's abruptness, Clare retreated a step. "Thank you. My Aunt Livia back in New Hampshire designed the hat. I thought it a bit flamboyant at first, but I've come to like it and at the very least it keeps one's head covered from the sun."

Myra's dark eyes narrowed. She stood with arms crossed, the fabric of her dress stretched tight across her burgeoning breasts, "You live out at that awful old McCrum place but you can put on the dog in that outfit? Don't add up to me!"

Clare's cheeks burned. She wished now that she had chosen a plainer hat, an older dress. But her family history was no business of Myra's even if it would give her a better understanding of why they lived as they did. She said a bit defiantly, "We're fixing the place up to be quite homey."

"I reckon you don't plan to stay in Sweetbrier long, though, do you? You'll be going back to where you come from, New Hampshire you said it was?" Myra's, chin lifted, waited to have her hopes confirmed.

"I expect to possibly live the rest of my life right here. How about you?"

Myra sniffed, and returned behind the counter. She looked toward the front windows of the store. "I have the good sense to leave here in a minute, if I could, if I had the money some people have. Only excitement in this town is when the cowboys bring their cattle to the railroad depot for shipping east. They stir things up some. Now, if I marry a good-looking rancher from here, I won't mind staying."

Clare felt a jolt of concern. Did Myra have Larkin in mind as the rancher she hoped to marry?

Myra was chattering on, dreamily, "He'll be able to take me on trips to Denver, and Kansas City, and maybe even Europe sometimes. I'd buy me some fine clothes." Her snippety expression added, *Lots finer than yours!*

Clare fended off jealousy. "I hope you get your wish," she smiled quietly. *As long as it has nothing to do with Larkin.*

She had no proof that Myra was after him as a prospective husband. Plus, she couldn't conceive the possibility of their marrying and she would be foolish to concern herself with the image even briefly. She had plenty of other worries, without adding to them. "I really must go. I have several errands and I'm keeping you from your work."

As Clare started for the door, Myra reminded behind her, "I'd go on back East if I was you."

Clare turned in time to catch a look of hatred on Myra's face. A dark look quickly exchanged for an artificially bright smile.

But you're not me. Clare refrained from making the retort aloud. She might not be in a position to marry Larkin herself, but Myra was decidedly wrong for him!

Chapter Fifteen

CLARE'S MIND WAS STILL ON HER EXASPERATING conversation with Myra when she reached the east end of Main Street and the Hilldale Hotel.

"Hello, Mayor Fuller," she said as she nearly ran into him, about to cross the street to the depot.

"Miss Hobb, lovely to see you!" He tipped his hat and hurried on, mumbling something about a load of filthy hogs needing to be weighed for shipping out and that fool, Dinger Toledo, would need him to see the job was done right.

Clare shook her head. He surely was a curious fellow, considering all she'd heard about him from Larkin, and recently from the women members of the Betterment Club who'd come to call. She dismissed the mayor from her thoughts and climbed the wooden steps to the hotel porch.

A fellow, likely Marshal Seavers considering the badge pinned to his vest, was half-asleep in the shade of a leafy, dusty vine, growing along the side of the porch. His chair was tipped back and his feet propped on the rail. To her "Good day," he sleepily touched his high-crowned hat. Larkin had told her that Sweetbrier was a peaceful town for the most part. The exception being when a wilder element of cowboys off the ranches raced their horses up and down main street, got into drunken brawls, and destroyed property. Fortunately, shipping season was brief and happened but twice a year.

Clare nodded politely at the marshal and crossed the porch, firm in her resolve to secure employment at this last opportunity.

They must hire her! She breathed deep, worked on a relaxed smile, and altered through one of the double doors opening inward.

The lobby smelled of stale tobacco, faintly of fried potatoes and other, stronger odors she preferred not to guess at. Flies circled in the center of the room. There were three or four fat worn chairs, and a scattering of small, battered tables. Potted palms in the corners needed dusting or watering, or maybe both. Through an open door to her left Clare could see a parlor room where a dandified fellow was plucking out a tune that sounded like it might be O, Susanna.

The red-haired clerk behind the registration desk asked, "May I help you, Miss?" His mustache was youthfully sparse and his Adam's apple bobbed in his throat as he asked, "Do you need a room?"

"No, thank you. I'm here to seek employment."

He looked surprised, his glance studying her from head to toe. Then he took a few steps off to the side to a half-opened door and called in, "Mr. Daly, a lady here to see you."

There was a loud "harrumph," the creaking springs of a daybed as someone got to their feet. "Huh? Wh—?"

"Sorry to wake you from your nap, Mr. Daly, but the lady—"

"I heard you, Tom, I heard you! I'm comin'."

Clare remembered Mr. Daly from the day they were introduced, when she and Larkin were making a survey of the town. She hoped he'd remember her. She smiled expectantly as he came from his office, his cane tapping on the plank floor with each step. He was a small fellow, slender and balding. His face was badly scarred and so was his hand gripping his cane. Two fingers on his right hand were missing. He looked at her with curiosity. "Didn't we meet sometime?"

"Yes, Mr. Daly. We were introduced a few weeks ago by my friend, Larkin Wade." She stepped around a brown-stained cuspidor and gave him her hand.

"Uh, um, yes. I remember now. How can I help you? Tom, can't you give the lady a room, whatever she wants?" He frowned at the young man. "I apologize for my addlepated clerk, Miss."

"Oh, no, no, he did nothing wrong. I'm here to ask for work, Mr. Daly, not a room."

He studied her for a moment, then shook his head. He turned on his heel and waved her off. "You're too fine for hotel work, Miss. Keeping this place up is drudgery you'd not even guess at. Better look elsewhere. Or go back where you came from and live the life of a lady, as any fool can see you were born to do."

In any other circumstance, she would agree with him one hundred percent that this work wasn't for her, but she was desperate. "Wait, Mr. Daly, please—!" But he'd already returned to his office and closed the door behind him. Probably to return to his nap. At the desk, Tom, the clerk, shrugged helplessly.

"Can you tell me something about the work that goes on here?" she asked in a thin voice. "And is Mr. Daly always so shortsighted? I can't believe that he wouldn't even hear me out. I could explain that I'm no stranger to hard work, I could prove it to him."

The clerk grinned crookedly. "John Daly is all right. Mostly he treats his help real good." He lowered his voice, "Pain makes him a little crabby sometimes. He was caught in a mine explosion in Colorado years back and that's what crippled him. He doesn't complain, he says that was his lucky day. For one thing, he survived the explosion. For another, the other miners took up a collection for him. He took that money, and some he earned later from selling sausages from a butcher shop he owned, and he bought this hotel."

"I see. How many employees does the hotel have?" She prayed they could use one more, that somehow she could change John Daly's mind about her.

"Well, there's Mattie Britton, she's the cook. We got two maids, Flora and Jewell who besides cleaning rooms and doing laundry serve in the dining room. The cook and Flora live upstairs in attic rooms on the third floor. So do I. Mr. Daly is here only part of the time. He comes in to balance the books, see that the hotel is running the way it should."

He came around the desk and looking over his shoulder worriedly in the direction of the office, he said in a lowered tone, "Plain truth is, I wish Mr. Daly had hired you." His eyes fastened on a dusty potted fern nearby and color filled his face. "You see,

Jewell is my sweetheart and she—" his voice sank nearly out of hearing, "—she's with child."

"You're the father?" For a second she was mortified that she'd spoken her thoughts aloud, had asked a question that was none of her business.

"Yes. Jewell and me intend to get married, and she wants to stay home with the baby when it comes. I worry about her working here, she don't feel well a lot of the time. The turpentine and other stuff she and Flora sometimes clean with, makes her sick to her stomach."

"Why don't you explain that to Mr. Daly? If he's as nice as you say, I'm sure he'd understand."

"I can't. Not just yet. He has strong rules against any fooling around among the help. He'd fire me on the spot if he knew what I've done. I have to have my job here, so I can take care of Jewell and the baby." "Tom," she touched his arm, "I'm going to help you!"

"Oh, no, please don't rouse Mr. Daly, I beg you, Miss, don't tell him."

"I'm not going to rouse him, and I'm not going to tell him your problem. That part is up to you. But I'll be back, to take your Jewell's place. In the long run, I think Mr. Daly will understand."

The clerk look baffled, but relieved to see her leave without stirring up further what was already a big problem.

———

TWO DAYS LATER, Clare stopped in the middle of doing laundry at tubs they'd set up in the back yard at home, heating the water over an open fire. "I'm sorry, but you all will have to finish," she told her sisters. "Momma, you've done enough today, why don't you lie down. I'm going into town." She brushed at her damp apron and started for the lane. Her eyes hurt from smoke from the fire. She was sweaty in her faded everyday skirt and shirtwaist, felt unclean from handling dirty clothes, and her straggling hair was tied under a scarf. Perfect.

Hallie froze as she helped Alice wring rinse water from a sheet and asked after her, "Clare, what are you doing? Aren't you going to change, first? You can't go anywhere looking like that!"

"But I am going, just like this."

Momma and her sisters dropped their work to rush across the yard after her.

"At least take off your soiled apron!" Alice insisted.

"Get your hat, your gloves," Momma pleaded. "She won't listen," she said to Alice and Hallie, her hands in the air, "she's not listening to one word we're saying. Has she gone daft?"

"Somehow, I think she knows exactly what she's doing," Alice said, "but I'll be plagued if I know what it is."

Clare turned at the end of the lane where it met the main road and waved back at them. "I'll be back soon," she called, "I'll explain then."

Tom Grant, the clerk, didn't know her when she returned to the hotel, nor did Mr. Daly when she requested to see him. When she told Daly she was there for work, and explained who she was, the hotel owner laughed so hard Clare was afraid he'd fall before he made it to one of the chairs in the lobby.

"All right. Miss, you have the job." He shook his head, and wiped his eyes on a large handkerchief. "I'll be breaking my word— but we need people with real spirit around here."

"What do you mean 'you'll be breaking your word'? Has someone asked you not to hire me? I don't understand—"

"You want the job or not?"

"I want it."

"Then it's settled. You can start work tomorrow. Tom, show the lady around the hotel before she leaves today. I'd do it myself but this chair is mighty comfortable. Go on, now. Anybody wants a room, I'll take care of registering them."

"Thank you, Mr. Daly." Clare followed Tom into the dining room to the right of the lobby, the doorway a few steps from John Daly's office. "We can seat fifty to a hundred people, when there's a special occasion in town, like a wedding," Tom explained to Clare.

There were numerous tables, each covered with a dingy white cloth and centered by a small coal oil lamp. At mid-day, there were only a few diners having tea and coffee. Clare recognized Carrie Spencer and her farmer-husband, neighbors of Larkin's. Praying Carrie wouldn't see her in her state of dishabille, Clare ducked back from sight.

She followed close on Tom's heels to a large kitchen where a stout woman in faded calico and a broad white apron was rolling out pie crust at a work table.

"This is Mrs. Britton, Hattie Britton," Tom said, "but we just call her Cook, or Cookie. Cook, this is—what's your name again?"

"Clare. Clare Hobb."

"Clare is our new maid," Tom said. He explained how Clare had fooled Mr. Daly into hiring her by changing the way she dressed. The three of them laughed.

"Normally, I don't leave home looking like this but I need the job, badly."

Hattie wiped floury hands on her apron and took Clare's hand in her plump fingers. "Ah, fiddlesticks, you look fine. Sometimes we got to do what we got to do. I'm pleased to meet you, Miss Hobb. Anything you need, just let me know. Pantry's right there. Shelves on the left hold the cleaning-rags, furniture-oil and soaps. Upstairs in the hall you'll find a cupboard full of clean sheets, towels and other linens. Laundry is done out back of the hotel."

"I'll show her. And she doesn't start work until tomorrow." Tom snatched a cinnamon and sugar coated slice of apple from the pie dish waiting for a top crust. Cook slapped his hand, but smiled.

Clare met the maids, at work upstairs cleaning the sparsely furnished rooms, and decided she liked both of them. Jewell, Tom's sweetheart, was a peaked blonde with cornflower-blue eyes and a timorous smile. She was very young, and thin except for her stomach mounding under her soiled apron.

Flora was dark and middle-aged. Her enormous brown eyes were warm and friendly. She moved to take Clare's hand and in doing so, caught her foot on the chamber pot she'd moved from under the bed. It tipped over, spreading dark liquid across the carpet. The smell was overpowering. Clare backed away, trying not to gag, to behave normally but almost deciding in that minute she couldn't possibly take the job.

One thing she hadn't considered was that she would be emptying stranger's chamber pots. Daily.

"Sorry," Flora mumbled and leaped into action to right the chamber pot and grab up soiled towels by the door to sop with. "I'm so sorry."

"It's all right. Accidents happen. I'm very glad to meet you, Flora." Clare fled the room, the hotel. Outside, she drew fresh air into her lungs. What had she'd gotten herself into?

Unfortunately, work at the hotel was her last chance to help her family financially. She had to take the job.

Gradually over the next few days Clare grew accustomed to work at the hotel. In the end, her tasks were not that different from those she did at home. With the murmuring sounds of summer coming through the open windows, she swept and dusted the rooms. Washed the bed linens and hung them on the lines behind the hotel to dry. Changed the sheets once a week. She helped in the kitchen and served in the dining room at mealtime. And kept up a constant fight swatting flies.

Sometimes she had to take over Jewell's tasks when the young woman suffered a serious bout of morning sickness, but Clare didn't mind. Instead, she wondered if someday she might be in that condition herself, expecting a child?

The four elderly, permanent residents at the hotel were sweet, but they loved to chat and it was sometimes hard to get away from them to do her work.

Drummers came in on the train with their sample cases to show the goods they wanted to supply to local merchants. She enjoyed the amusing stories these traveling salesman told about life on the road, away from Sweetbrier, but had to draw the line when their flirting became too serious and they offered to "take her away from all this."

The one real enigma was Alfred Fuller, the mayor, who had a permanent room at the hotel. While all the other rooms were furnished sparsely with only a bed, a single chair, bureau and lamp, his was crowded with fine furniture. Expensive knick-knacks were everywhere.

It made Fuller nervous if Clare, or one of the other maids, spent more time than he felt necessary to clean his room and he hovered during the cleaning. On one occasion he had come up unexpectedly behind Clare as she dusted, frightening her. When she protested, he said he was only there to ask that she take care handling his things. They were valuable, his inheritance, he said, and meant a great deal to him.

"I hope I can trust you not to snoop," he had said to her as she finished cleaning that day.

Clare was too insulted to find words to reply to him. He had smiled and waited for her to exit the room. He had his own lock and key, and always locked his door upon leaving.

A few days after that, Clare was dusting the lobby furniture when Tom, behind the registration desk, addressed the mayor as he was about to leave the hotel. "Sir, your rent?" he called softly after him. "I need to talk to you about that." He added, "you're late again. Sir."

"Don't nag me, man," the mayor turned on him angrily. "If I don't pay on time, it's because I'm busy."

"I know, sir, but the boss—"

"Is my friend, and he understands. I could get you fired, you know. I'm sure John wouldn't like it if he knew a pimple-faced clerk constantly harassed the guests for money."

Tom turned crimson, his eyes flashed anger as he kept his tone polite, "I'm sorry, sir, but you're behind in your rent two months going on three. I'm just doing my job. You're supposed to pay if you're going to live here."

Looking like he might explode, the mayor turned back, pulled out a wallet, drew out a few bills and threw them on the counter. "Now, leave me alone. I have more important business to attend to than paying for a lousy room in this flea-bitten hotel. I'll be glad when I can move out of this place for good."

"Yessir, thank you, sir."

The mayor slammed from the hotel and Tom muttered darkly, "Goddamned skinflint jackass!" He saw Clare trying to smother a smile and he apologized, "Sorry for swearing in your presence, Clare, but that man really gets my dander up."

"I understand. I've seen skinflints before, but none like Mayor Fuller."

"He's the worst. On top of not wanting to pay for anything he doesn't have to, there's rumors he's a petty thief. Unfortunately, he's slick, and nobody's been able to prove anything when stuff comes up missing after he's been around."

"He has beautiful art objects and furniture in his room."

"Yeh," Tom scoffed, "he says it's stuff he "inherited from family'. Every now and then something fancy comes in for him on the train, usually after he's made a trip out to the city. If it's heavy, like a table or large trunk, he makes me help him haul it to his room. One of these days he's not going to be able to get through the room to his bed. Or somebody he's stealing from will come and see him off to jail."

"I admit he seems odd. I've heard about his dishonesty. But some folks here claim to like him a lot, they believe that he's an honest and good official." She was remembering how certain members of the women's Betterment Club defended him.

"Yep," Tom said drily, "there's fools everywhere. Or folks too nice to recognize a bad egg when the smell is right there."

Finished with the dusting, Clare turned to wiping down the front windows. Across the street was the implement yard. This was one of the busiest seasons for Larkin on his ranch where he was now cutting hay, but she couldn't help hoping for a glimpse of him.

He was seldom there, although one afternoon she saw Alice, with a market basket on her arm, at the implement yard talking with Tobias and his children.

––––––––––

CLARE HAD BEEN WORKING at the hotel a week and a half when Larkin came storming into the hotel dining room as she was helping to serve the noon meal. He caught her arm and pulled her aside.

"Why, in the name of sweet reason are you working in this place? I just heard about it this morning, one of my hands had supper here last night and told me."

"Oh, good, he dined on our special then, fresh greens, catfish filets, and buttermilk biscuits with strawberry sauce." Seeing that light-hearted banter would get her nowhere, she turned serious, "I work here because I need to, and I want to, and please let go of my arm."

"You don't have to work here, Clare. I've said I'll take care of you, and your family. Now go on in there to John's office," he pointed, "and tell him you're quitting, right now."

She looked at him in shock. "I can't do that, and I won't. And you can't tell me what to do, Larkin Wade!"

He stood there, his face crimson with anger under his dark tan.

Finally, seeing she was not about to budge, he threw up his hands. "You're so stubborn. You rile me to my core, Clare, more than you have any idea, and you have for a damn long time!" His bootheels were like gunshots, as he crossed the floor and out of the hotel.

Clare looked after him in hurt and confusion, quickly replaced by fury. So it was him! She had suspected that Larkin had told the merchants in town to turn her down when she asked for work. Now she was positive. How dare he? If he'd stayed around one more minute, she'd have had it out with him for betraying her behind her back. Luckily John Daly had broken his word, and she had the work and salary she needed.

Larkin was a fool to think for a minute that she'd give up, be his charity case. She had too much New England pride for that, and he should know it. Not to mention that her family couldn't do without her, and she personally owed them, for reasons she'd long kept secret. She loved Larkin and always would, in the deepest part of her heart. But he couldn't rule her. She wouldn't be turned into a meek, dependent mouse when she wasn't that sort at all. Someday, her situation might be different. For now, she had to lead her life in the way she felt was best.

She kept an eagle eye on the implement yard after that, just waiting for the day Larkin would show up there and she could give him a piece of her mind for what he'd tried to do.

Finally, the day came. It was early morning and she was cleaning an upstairs room when she looked down on the implement yard and saw him drawing his blood bay to a halt near the business office and dismounting. She tossed the stack of sheets and blankets she was holding helter-skelter onto the bed and squared her shoulders.

"I'll be back in a minute," she said as she dashed past a gape-mouthed Flora in the hallway. "Cover for me if you have to."

Chapter Sixteen

CLARE DASHED DOWN THE STAIRS. AS SHE CROSSED THE LOBBY, she collided with Myra bringing the hotel's mail. Letters and a magazine went flying. "Sorry." Clare stooped, quickly gathered the mail and shoved it back into an astonished Myra's hands. "Sorry, Myra," she repeated and flung the hotel door open into the sizzling morning, prepared to confront Larkin. She stopped short.

Poppa had appeared out of nowhere and across the way in the implement yard he stood talking with Larkin. Larkin's tall figure towered over Poppa's stooped form and his hand rested on her father's shoulder. She couldn't see Larkin's face clearly in the shadows of his broad-brimmed hat, but she sensed that he was smiling as he talked. The two of them started toward the blacksmith shop located just beyond the implement yard on the same side of the street; Poppa walked with confident ease.

Even so, she had to have this out with Larkin. Clare hurried down the steps, clutching her skirt in her hands. Her progress slowed once again as she started to cross the street. She halted, her lip caught between her teeth.

Maybe this wasn't the best time to give Larkin a piece of her mind for trying to block her efforts to find work. If his aim this morning was to help Poppa get a job at the blacksmith shop, and take that load from her, fine. It didn't change the fact she'd also found work, despite his efforts to ruin her chances!

She turned back, a half-smile on her face as she looked over her shoulder at Poppa and Larkin disappearing together into the dim interior beyond the wide open doors of the blacksmith shop. The scene warmed her heart. She'd give Larkin a good talking to, later. Right now if she meant to keep her job, she'd better hurry and finish doing up those beds. Jewell was sick again, poor girl.

She asked Tom, as she entered the lobby, "Is Myra angry with me? I gave her quite a bump, but I didn't mean to. She's left the mail and gone?"

"Nope. She's still here, in there." With a lewd grin, he nodded in the direction of the closed door to John's office.

"Oh!" A flush heated Clare's face. "Well, Myra often visits John. It doesn't necessarily mean—any tiling. So clean up your mind, Tom." She grabbed her skirts and hurried upstairs to the beds waiting to be made.

———

THE RARE TIMES when her work at the hotel was caught up and Clare took a break, she liked to head down the block to the blacksmith shop to check on Poppa. Sam Dorsey had hired him as a helper, to keep the fires going in the forge, to hold a temperamental horse when it was being shoed, and to sharpen tools at the grindstone in back. To sweep the floor and make deliveries. But Poppa was quickly proving his worth in shoeing horses himself and in his skills as a "jack-of-all-iron-trades."

From the past, Clare was well aware that Poppa could make axes, hoes, scythes, and plow blades expertly. He could repair anything made of iron.

"You love this work, don't you, Poppa?" she asked him one day, standing aside and watching as he hammered a red-hot piece of iron into a decorative door hinge. He gave the iron several ringing taps on the anvil before he answered.

He grinned, his teeth white in his sweaty, soot-stained face. "Ayuh, Clarie, I do."

"And the customers, how do they like your work?"

He frowned for a second. "Sometimes I get confused—when there's a lot to do and I'm taking Sam's place." He suddenly asked,

"Did you know Sam had to go to Council Grove on some business? That's where he is today."

He was suddenly puzzled and for a moment struggled to bring his mind back to what he'd been talking about. He continued, "When somebody wants me to hurry it up, get their job done, I get all turned around. I kinda forget everything, and I worry."

"If you can just relax and not worry, Poppa, I know you'll do fine."

"Ayuh, I will." He smiled. "Larkin's neighbor, Jim Spencer, said the new wagon wheel I built for him was the best job he ever saw." He hurried on excitedly, "A lady came in—I can't remember her name—and she wants me to make her a weathervane. She said I was rec-recommended as somebody who could do the job—just how she wants it."

"I'm so happy for you, Poppa."

"We have to thank Larkin, too. He told Sam Dorsey he should hire me."

"Yes, that was nice of Larkin."

"You should marry that boy, Clarie. They don't come any better than Larkin Wade. In all of Kansas," he spread his arms, "and all of Sandwich back home, there's no better than Larkin."

His pronouncement took her breath away. Unfortunately, deep down, on the subject of Larkin's fine qualities, she agreed. "For pity sake, I can't marry Larkin. I have all I can do working at the hotel and at home. Anyway, I'm quite peeved at him. I'm sure he's the one who went around town telling each and every merchant to turn me down if I came asking for a job. He shouldn't have done that."

"He loves you, he wants to take care of you."

"I realize that, but he can't order my life as though I have no mind or will of my own. You've never yelled at Momma and pointed your finger and told her to get cracking what you wanted her to do. You're just not like that. I want a man like you, Poppa."

He looked shocked, disbelieving that she would say such a foolish thing. He clapped his hand over his mouth, walked over to an overturned barrel, sat down and stared at her. "Like me?" he dropped his hand to his lap. "Oh, Clarie, you can't mean that! I'm —not right in the head, not—like a man's supposed to be. When I got hurt, it changed me. I'm different. I know it, and I don't like it.

It's not how I want to be." He said almost angrily, "You should thank God that Larkin's not like me, Clarie!"

"I remember, Poppa, how you were before that terrible injury to your head. Big and strong and handsome." Much like Larkin, actually. "You could do anything. You had the most wonderful sense of humor and made people laugh all the time with such funny stories. You're still that man, Poppa, and you always will be, to me. And when the time is right, I do want — a man just like you." And it would probably be Larkin, if he'd stop trying to force her into a mold of his own making, if he'd be patient until she could get her family established to the point they could take care of themselves.

He studied on what she said for a full minute, and then he said softly, his eyes bright with unshed tears, "I'm glad you remember, Clarie. I hope you never forget. I try to remember, too, and I try to be the way I was."

"You're doing a lot better here in Kansas to my mind, Poppa. You just keep it up."

He grabbed her arm. "And you, daughter, you give that boy a chance. I got this job, we got the farm and Oakley's taking care of most of the chores there real good. You need to be thinking of settling down with a husband, having children of your own."

Her throat tightened. She hugged him. "I'll take your advice, Poppa. When I can."

CLARE COULDN'T HAVE BEEN MORE pleased when comments began to drift to her about the good job Poppa was doing for Sam Dorsey. Not that it was all perfect. On one occasion, there was a mix-up of the customer's directions and that job, making the size nails he wanted, had to be done over. But the original nails Poppa made were then available to sell to another customer.

Ari incident with the mayor, Alfred Fuller, didn't turn out half so well. He raised a terrible row when he felt Poppa was too slow building a small iron enclosure he'd ordered made to protect a locust tree struggling to survive in the empty lot where the court-house would one day be built.

The truth was, Fuller was constantly looking over Poppa's

shoulder and complaining, slowing the work. In the end, although he accepted the iron work, Fuller said it wasn't what it should have been and he refused to pay for it out of city funds. Sam Dorsey had had to absorb the cost of the materials, and Poppa hadn't received pay for the many hours he spent on the job.

Clare was furious. "From what I've heard, the mayor doesn't only cheat people out of what he owes them, he's on occasion an outright thief," she fumed that night at the supper table, when Poppa, worried and repeating himself, related the incident.

"Clare, that's a terrible thing to say!" Momma admonished. "He's the mayor. Are you sure?"

"No," she admitted, "I'm not sure. I've only heard rumors that he's light-fingered. It's no rumor, though, that he's a moocher, getting everything free that he can. The whole town has seen that, although some folks, who like him a lot for their own reasons, actually don't mind."

For all Clare knew, Fuller's fine possessions might be inherited as he claimed so she decided against describing the intriguing contents of his room at the hotel.

"Just don't let the mayor get the better of you, Poppa. Don't allow him to cheat you again, when his unfairness is so uncalled for." Seeing Poppa's deep frown, she asked, "What is it?"

"There's been times," he said slowly, "times that the Mayor has asked questions about where Sam keeps his money at the shop. He says is it safe? Like that. He tries to see where we keep the money. It's hidden in Sam's office. I try to keep my eye on the office, when Sam's not there."

"Let's stop this right now!" Momma ordered. "Let's not get carried away. You two are surely wrong about this. I've met the mayor. He's polite and kind, a gentleman."

"I hope we are wrong," Clare said with a smile, and leaned to kiss her mother's cheek.

"I have news," Alice said softly.

Utensils clattered as everyone turned to hear. "Go ahead, Alice," Hallie urged, "what is it?"

"Tobias Proctor told me of a teaching position available at a small school about four miles west of here. I talked to the chairman of the school board, and I've been promised the job. I start in September. There will be about a dozen children from farm and ranch families out that way. It's called Popcorn School, though I'm not sure why they call it that."

Clare was thrilled. "You're right, this is very good news. You can take one of our horses to ride, especially when the weather's bad. It's closer for me to get to town, I can walk." She had come home so tired from work at the hotel that she had just now realized that Oakley wasn't present. "Where is Oakley? Has anyone called him to supper?"

Momma told her, "He's riding at the Wade's, helping to count and sort cattle for shipping. Nick came for him, said they needed the help. Those boys were so excited to be 'cowboys'. We couldn't have kept Oakley here for anything."

"Oh." She took several weary bites and said, "I suppose it's up to me and Alice to do Oakley's chores tonight then. Hallie can help Momma with the dishes. I'll be glad when I can fall into bed."

In the dusky interior of the barn, they'd milked quietly for several minutes when Alice spoke up, her tone soft and casual, "Tobias Proctor came by again today as I was hanging clothes on the line. He asked me—" she fell silent.

"Asked you what?" Clare continued to milk, burying her smile in the cow's flank.

"He was out this way delivering a new plow to a farmer who needed it to prepare his fields for winter wheat." Time ticked by as Alice said no more, and then finally continued, "Tobias has asked to come calling on me."

"I wondered when you would bring up the matter, and confess your affection for the father as well as for his children!" Clare's glance met Alice's and she grinned wickedly.

"Affection for Tobias?" Alice colored and her glance slid away. "It's nothing like that. He's just a friend."

"Sorry, but the look on your face says quite differently. You care for him, Alice, you know you do." Clare chuckled, "Dear sister, I'm so very happy for you!" She slid her milking stool backward and stood up, moving her frothing pail of milk away from the swishing cow's tail.

"All right, I do care for him," Alice admitted, stripping the last drops of milk from her cow's teats, her forehead against the cow's side. "But nothing will happen beyond that. We're friends, Tobias and I. I'm very fond of his children. But that's all there is."

"Because you're still in love with Cousin Everett?"

"Because I don't intend ever to be hurt again, not like that."

"But you'll give a love a chance, won't you?"

For a moment, Alice didn't answer. She stood up, holding her own pail of milk two-handed in front of her as she looked at Clare. "I don't know if I can," she admitted. "We'll have to see, won't we? And as far as love is concerned," she put down her pail and walked over to grasp Clare by the shoulders, "What about you and Larkin? You're wildly in love with him, you're perfect for one another, yet you keep him at arm's length. You know he loves you, that he's nearly killing himself with hard work to prove he's worthy of you. Why don't you give love a chance, dare, and stop behaving as though this family can't survive without your constant aid?"

Clare was taken aback, too frustrated and angry at first to speak. Then she found her voice, "That's not fair! Who had the gumption to make the decision that we leave New Hampshire? That, or watch Poppa be placed in an insane asylum! Which came very close to happening, I remind you. Who stood up to our pompous uncles and their rigid rules? Who brought us here to Kansas? We're starting to get by, yes, but our financial affairs are still touch and go. Your teaching job will be for only a few months of the year. Poppa could make a mistake at the blacksmith job any day and be fired. As kind as Mr. Dorsey is, his patience with Poppa could have its limits. I empty slop jars and launder soiled sheets to give this family food and shelter! Good grief, Alice, when would I have a chance to answer my heart, to give my love to Larkin as I'd like to? I made the bargain with myself to—" She stopped just short of confessing that it was her own irresponsibility, loving Larkin, that had set their family's troubles in motion in the first place. Tears were hot in her eyes as she grabbed her pail of milk and left the barn.

Behind her she heard Alice's soft, "Oh, sister, forgive me!"

Clare stopped where she was, put her pail down, and covered her face with her hands until she could regain control. Alice was not the one needing to be forgiven.

LEFT ALONE in the Hobb's tidy front room, Alice and Tobias sat across from one another, the silence between them as thick as a wall.

Why couldn't she speak to him more easily? He was kind enough to call on her. He wasn't handsome, exactly, but sitting there with his patient smile, his shoulders bulging in his dark suit and his hair combed neatly, he looked very good to her. Still, it was as though her tongue was glued to the roof of her mouth.

After what felt like a lifetime, she was able to tell him, "My family is pleased that I've been hired to teach at Popcorn School in the fall. I'm obliged that you told me about the position."

"That's nice. I knew you'd be perfect for the job."

"Your children, Will and Beth, go to the school in Sweetbrier, isn't that right?" She knew perfectly well that they did, but it was so difficult to think of things to talk about. The evening was going very badly. Tobias must be itching to leave and never come back.

"Yes. Beth is smart. She loves to read and do numbers. Will is pretty smart, too, but he likes to play."

"They are very nice children."

He shook his head and chuckled deep in his throat. "Oh, but they can be a handful at times." He sobered. "Especially since their mother died. We all miss her a lot."

"I'm sorry you lost your wife, and the children their mother."

"JoEllen was a wonderful woman, Alice, like you."

His words struck like a warm dart. Her heart filled from the look of affection in his brown eyes, but she could think of nothing to reply.

"Alice," he leaned toward her, his voice earnest, "the children and I would be honored if you would attend the harvest fair with us next week. Most everybody from around here takes in the fair. It's a chance to visit with other folks, have a good time away from all the hard work of summer. I think you'll like it. Will you go with me?"

She ran her tongue over her lips and smiled nervously. So he hadn't totally given up on her. "Y-yes, thank you for asking. I would like to go." She thought of something and plunged on, "The harvest fairs back in New Hampshire were very nice. As a child, I remember how much I wanted to taste the maple sugar and candy on display. Of course, there was maple sugar candy for sale, but that candy on display, competing for ribbons, looked so much more delicious." She took a quick breath. "My grandmother made beautiful baskets and they always won ribbons for being the finest."

"Maybe you'd like to enter some of the contests? Bring a cake or pie or a pretty you've sewn? The women get real serious competing for the ribbons they give out. I'll parade some of my new farm machinery. I reckon Larkin will be showing off some of his cattle, and samples of his grain crops."

"It sounds wonderful, and a lot like our fairs at home in Sandwich."

"That's sure a funny name for a town, or a village as folks call their towns back there. Sandwich reminds me that there'll be lots of good food at the fair. Sausages and kraut, candied apples on a stick, big ol' dill pickles, sorghum cookies, and enough sweet watermelon to reach from here down to the next county!"

They laughed, and a short while later, Tobias rose to leave. He took Alice's hand and, with her permission, kissed her cheek. "I'm right pleased that you're going to the fair with the children and me. Don't worry about nothing, you just come."

"I will, and I thank you." It was hard to breathe, but when Alice left the room to join the family, her eyes were shining.

———

LUCKILY, the harvest fair took place on Sunday, Clare's day off, and she could go. The fair was held in an open field in the bend of meandering Sweetbrier Creek a mile south of town and a half-mile east of the Hobb's small farm. The family, all except Alice, walked to the fair and then separated. Poppa and Oakley headed toward the pens of noisy livestock and Tobias's display of farm machinery.

Momma and Alice went off to see the displays of baked goods, the quilts and other needlework. Hallie, overcoming a brief spell of shyness, joined a group of young people running foot races for prizes.

Clare wandered alone through the noisy throngs. Alice, almost like Cinderella, had been transported to the fair with Tobias and his children, in his spanking new buggy drawn by a high-stepping team. She would envy Alice, if she wasn't so happy for her.

When she came to the huge penned bull, Clare couldn't

believe her eyes. The animal had male anatomy of unbelievable size. Clare looked, looked away, looked again. She turned blindly, and stumbled headlong into Larkin. "I'm sorry," she said, "I didn't see you."

"Fine looking critter, isn't he?"

Her face was hot as fire. "He's—he's your critter?"

"Yes. And he's daddy to a whole crop of pretty calves on my place."

"That's good. Did-did he take a ribbon here at the fair?"

"Ayuh. But Ma took it with her. She's all over the grounds, showing off that ribbon, and inviting folks to our other displays."

Clare nodded. Out of the blue she wished she was the one showing off the ribbon, and the displays from Larkin's ranch, as his wife. The pain was so acute, knowing it couldn't be, that she almost cried out. She took a deep breath to get herself in hand.

She recalled Alice saying that Clare should give love a chance. In this moment that had her so shaken, she wanted nothing so much as to do just that, with every fiber of her being. If she could be with Larkin every living day - take his meals to him in the field, warm his bed at night with their special love, share laughter and the daily conversations that a man and wife exchanged—it would be a dream come true.

Somehow, she had to see her family well taken care of, to the point they could forge ahead on their own, then there would be time for her and Larkin to rekindle their love. Fulfill the wonderful promise of the feelings they'd shared in New Hampshire, before the terrible accident. Unless—Larkin decided at some point not to wait for her.

Unnerved at the thought that she might have made a mistake from the beginning, putting him off, caused her stomach to clench tight. Her mind chased in dizzying circles. Of course she'd done the right thing—for everyone concerned. She'd saved Poppa from being institutionalized, was doing everything she could to keep her family together, away from Edward and Simon's harassment. She might have chosen anywhere for her family to rebuild their lives, but the truth of the matter was, she'd chosen Kansas so that she might be near Larkin. No matter what she'd told herself, or others about coming here, she wanted to be close at hand when the time for them was right.

He was looking down at her, his eyes studying her face with concern. "Is something wrong?" he asked huskily. "I'm sorry about that day in town, you know. I shouldn't have gotten angry with you. I was wrong. I've missed you."

His look was so galvanizing it made it hard for her to think. "We all need a break from work," he was saying, "it's been a scorcher, making hay, but thank God we're about done with that, and separating the cattle I'll have to sell. I'm sure you're glad to be away from the hotel for a while." With a slight frown, he added, "I was real surprised to hear that you were working there, as I guess you figured out."

Suddenly, resentment that he'd tried to prevent her getting a job was back in spades, flooding out all other feeling. "Yes, I suppose you were surprised. As hard as you tried to prevent that, it's a miracle I was hired. Thank goodness John Daly broke his word to you!" Didn't Larkin realize that if he'd succeeded, he'd be putting off that much longer any chance they had?

"I beg your pardon? Broke his word? What are you getting at?"

"You know exactly! You went to each and every one of your business friends and told them not to hire me. I believed their excuses when they turned me down. But you were the one behind it because you wanted me to fail. You planned for me to come dragging my family back to your door, like poor beggars!" He didn't know her well, if he didn't realize she'd have too much pride for that.

"That's nonsense. I wouldn't do a thing like that, even though it bothers the hell out of me to see you doing such work." He stared at her as though she'd surely lost her mind and what the hell was he to do?

Clare studied him for a long moment in confusion, then looked away. Larkin would never lie to her, she knew that better than anything. She began to feel foolish, ashamed that she had accused him. But if he wasn't the one John Daly broke his promise to when he hired her, who was?

She was looking off into space, not really focusing on anything when movement in her line of vision brought her around to see Myra in a tight-fitting jade-green dress, waving at them from where she stood by a small corral of squealing pigs.

Clare drew a sharp breath. Myra, of course. She'd wanted

Clare to return to New Hampshire, had known Clare was seeking work so she could stay in Sweetbrier.

Why hadn't she seen that Myra was the one John Daly meant he'd broken his promise to? Myra often brought the hotel's mail personally to John. And she stayed a while, sometimes with the office door closed behind her and John. But it was Larkin Myra really wanted, and who wouldn't, given the choice? And in the long run, what did it matter, who asked John not to hire Clare? She'd gotten the job. She'd been terrible to Larkin just now, over a trifle.

"I'm sorry, Larkin. It appears that I've made a mistake." She slanted a glance up at him and gasped at his expression.

His tan face was a thundercloud of frustration and anger. "Yes, you did. Don't you trust me, Clare? Do you have any idea how hard it is for me to wait until you're ready to come to me of your free will and be my wife, which we both know is meant to be? My God, what do you really think of me? I've tried from the moment we met to make myself the man you deserve, prove how much I love you. And all you can think about is why we have no right to be together."

"I've never thought of you as unworthy, Larkin. That's never been the reason! You're the finest person I've ever met, I've never believed less. And I said I was sorry."

But he gave no ground. "Forget it!" He turned on his heel and headed to where Myra waited by the pigs, motioning him over, her gaze feasting blatantly on him as he approached her. Myra's happy squeal rose above that of the pigs, "Larkin, have you seen the piglets? They are so sweet. Come see them with me!"

In shock, Clare watched him join Myra, saw Myra's arm loop through his. Pain filled her throat and tears stung her eyes. It was all she could do not to run after him, grab him. Hang on and never let him go. She cursed the pride that paralyzed her, keeping her feet planted where she was. For the first time she could recall he was truly angry with her and he'd made it abundantly clear that he was tired of trying to please her.

I've made a bigger mistake than simply accusing him of something he didn't do. I've given him to Myra. Eager, voluptuous, man-starved Myra, who will do anything to keep him. I'm a fool, a terrible fool!

Chapter Seventeen

A DAY THAT STARTED BADLY AT THE FAIR, SHOWED NO SIGN OF improving. Activities and sights Clare would typically enjoy, held no appeal whatsoever. A long table had been set up under a tent for shade. When she sat down to eat, before food she'd normally devour, she stared off into the white-hot distance and stirred and stirred with her fork, forgetting to eat.

A voice at the other end of the table penetrated her misery. "This is the best chicken and noodles I've ever eaten," Alfred Fuller was saying as he took a ladle from Liddy Goodlander's hand and helped himself, heaping his plate from the large iron pot, noodles slopping over the edge. "My third helping. Sorry for you folks missing out on this food for the Gods. Mrs. Goodlander, you're as good a cook as the finest chefs in Europe."

"Please," Liddy shook her head, trying to draw away as he moved to keep her by the table. "The dish is nothing."

"No, no, now don't be shy. Accept the praise you deserve, my dear." Fuller caught her arm to keep her and raised his voice, "Folks, I want you to meet the finest cook west of St. Louis. I sincerely mean it. Liddy Goodlander, take a bow."

"Thank you, Mayor Fuller, but I must go over there and tell my son Gordy to stop." She tried to pull away, her eyes on a group of boys wrestling in the grass several yards away.

"I tell you folks," the mayor continued to grip Liddy's arm as he droned on, "the good Reverend Goodlander misses out on a lot of mighty fine meals. If he knew how lucky he is, he'd stay home and let someone else do his preaching!" He guffawed, and several men joined him in the laughter.

Eva Cahill stood up from her place at the table nearby. "For pete's sake, Mayor, let the poor woman go. Can't you see you're embarrassin' her?"

He laughed again, shook his head, and released Liddy. Her face was scarlet as she rushed away. He looked after her, and the expression on his face wasn't one a man should have for another man's wife.

Clare felt sorry for Liddy, but she had her own problems. As the hours of the fair wore on, everywhere she looked there was Larkin and Myra together. Walking along eating candy apples, side by side viewing his grain samples in a row of baskets, laughing at a group of children as they raced after an escaped rooster.

Myra, in Clare's place beside Larkin. But it was her own fault for mistrusting Larkin, insulting him with the silly accusation that he'd tried to prevent her getting work.

Maybe it was her enormous headache that made her forget people's names as they stopped to talk to her. Her aching head that prevented her from following the simplest train of conversation.

Feeling numb all over, she stopped walking to watch Tobias's children, Beth and Will, as they took turns sitting on the seat of a bright green new corn planter, pretend lines in their hands as they urged a pretend team to keep moving. Tobias beamed at his children, Alice stood proudly at his side.

Alice looked prettier, happier, and more at ease than she had in a very long time, years in fact. The sight thrilled Clare, and helped to ease her unhappiness a trifle.

LARKIN SAT across from Myra on a blanket near his wagon, sipping lemonade from a tin cup. Spending hours with her hadn't been easy. It irritated him particularly at the moment that she insisted on feeding him a molasses cookie out of her hand, rubbing a loose raisin back and forth on his bottom lip. She giggled inanely as he brushed crumbs from his chin. He wished she wouldn't try so hard, but likely she sensed that she was losing his attention.

"It's so warm," she said, her full lips pouty. He watched her as she slowly unfastened the tiny buttons, one by one, at the throat of her dress. With her eyes on his face for his reaction, she coyly pushed the neckline open. "Ooh, that's better." She patted the top of her burgeoning breasts that glimmered with perspiration. He felt a stir of lust. She smiled to see that his gaze was fastened where she wanted it. He was seeing the start of what any man could tell would be a beautiful body when undressed.

"There now," she said. "Let's undo you, sweetie, so you can cool off." She reached for him, unfastened his shirt, slyly slid her hand inside and over his chest in slow circles. With her tongue between her teeth, she hummed seductively with the motions. Her eyes glittered.

Her fingers on his bare skin were hot. His lust, at the same time, strangely cooled. He was feeling snared like a fool rabbit. He didn't like the feeling, no matter how pretty the woman trying to trap him. Myra's seduction was too obvious and he was a fool if he gave in—when she was not the woman he wanted.

"You're right, it's a hot day," he said and took a long drink of lemonade. He eyed her over the top of his cup. She smiled, her expression daring him to resist her sensual advances.

Instead, in another minute, it was all he could do not to laugh. He didn't because he didn't want to hurt her feelings. Instead, he put down his cup and caught her fingers to stop their roving.

She leaned into him and whispered coyly, "Let's go for a walk over there in those woods, where it's cooler, Larkin, sweetie." The 'woods' she pointed to was a wild plumb thicket on the far side of the field. The most it offered was a smattering of shade, a little privacy from the fair. "We can find a nice place to sit and talk. Cool off before the dance tonight."

He couldn't help but wonder what they might talk about?

She had been chattering all day but hadn't really said much of anything. If he'd answered her once he'd answered her twenty times that yes, he liked her dress, yes, her new hair style was very pretty.

She'd told some mildly interesting stories about her work at the post office. Some comments she'd made about people he knew weren't really funny. The remarks she made about "crazy old Frank Hobb" coming in for the mail and then forgetting what he'd come for, infuriated him and he'd about walked away from her right then.

It wasn't gentlemanly of him to think it, but he was gravely doubtful, talk was what she had in mind, anyway, if they went over to the 'woods.'

"I ought to be going," he told her apologetically. "I'm plumb wore out from haying season. I'm afraid I'm not good company."

"Oh, yes you are, Larkin, sweetie, you're the best company a girl could have. Don't talk bad about yourself that way!"

He was about to protest again, to repeat his apologies, and leave, when he saw Clare talking with her sister Alice, and Tobias, and his ire rose again that she hadn't trusted him. That she'd think he'd pull a lowdown trick like jeopardizing her chance to get work. He loved Clare and she frustrated him to the limit. He'd just about reached the end of his tether with her and her standoffishness.

"Please, Larkin, please," Myra reached over and pulled at his hand. "Let's find some shade and talk. Pretty please?"

Clare was watching them with an open frown. Even from that distance, he could see her displeasure that he was with Myra. He clamped his jaw. He turned a cold smile on Myra, "What the hell," he said, "let's find some shade." His lanky form unfolded and he helped Myra to her feet.

Taking her elbow in his hand, they headed toward the plum thicket on the distant side of the grounds. Glancing over his shoulder, he saw Clare turn to the rest of her family who'd come to join the group watching Tobias's children clamoring over the machinery. She told them something, it appeared they were disagreeing. Clare ignored whatever they were telling her, and set off in fiery fit in the direction of town, and likely her work at the hotel.

Larkin grunted to himself. Well, she deserved to have blisters on her toes from the long walk in her pretty little shoes. Maybe the heat of the day would steam some of the nonsense from her head and she'd start to see reason.

Myra was tugging at him, giggling for him to hurry. She had his hand up under her arm, against the side of her breast; the fabric of her dress was thin, he could feel the heat of her skin through it.

It was cooler in the shade of the plum patch. Skipping along through the weeds and grass, Myra led him around to the opposite side of the thicket, out of sight of the fair. She faced him then, and began to run her fingers over his chest, his neck, his arms. She took his hands and tucked them around her waist.

"I liked how you looked at me back there," she said huskily. "I could see you like me. Would you like to kiss me?" Without waiting for his answer, she rose on her toes and pressed her mouth firmly to his. His arms tightened around her as she pushed herself into him.

He kissed her, kept kissing her for a full minute, his fingers tangling in her hair as he held her to him. The more he tried to get involved in what he was doing, the more he felt apart from it. He'd never experienced such a lack of feeling. He kissed her again, harder, and ran his hand down her side to the curve of her ample hip. Something inside him recoiled.

This wasn't the one he wanted to touch, to hold. This was wrong. Wrong. He was reminded suddenly how close he and Clare had come to making love during their secret meetings back home in New Hampshire. He'd wanted her desperately then but he'd wanted also to wait until she was ready. He wanted Clare then, he wanted her now.

"I'm sorry, Myra, but I can't do this." He stood her away from him, held her firmly when she tried to enter his arms again, and press her mouth to his. "No."

"Why not? You like me, don't you?" her voice was thick, her eyelids heavy. She squirmed close to him, only to be set back.

"I like you, Myra, but not—like this. I'm not right for you. There are other fellows who'd suit you a lot better. Let me walk you back to the fair."

"I don't want to go back to no silly fair!" she said, fear and fury in her voice. "I'm not ready to go back! I—I need you." She started to whimper, a sound that made him think of a sick lamb.

Larkin gave her his bandanna to wipe her teary eyes. "I shouldn't have kissed you. I feel like a lowdown skunk letting you think I—never mind. Please don't cry. I didn't mean to hurt your feelings. You're a good person, Myra. But for a lot of reasons, you and I just aren't right for one another."

"It isn't that I'm not right for you!" she stormed at him, "it's her that's got you blinded, making a fool of you. I don't know what you see in her. Her father is nutty. She lives in that rickety old place, chases bedbugs and empties slop jars for a living, but still acts uppity, like she's as good as anybody. How can you want someone like that?"

His lips tightened but he didn't reply. The reasons he could want someone like Clare would stack mountain high. But for right now, he'd had about all he could take of Myra, of Clare, of women in general. "I'll take you back to the fair. I'm tired and I'm not staying for the dance."

Her eyes narrowed and she looked at him as though he was scum. "You had your chance with me, Larkin Wade. A chance any man would give his eye teeth to have. When you get over her, I'll be waitin' for you. Or maybe I won't. Right now, I don't want you to touch me, I don't want you close to me, I don't want you walkin' me back nowhere. I'll get there by myself."

She flounced off, back across the field to where several knots of men were moving tables to arrange for a dance area.

For a long time, Larkin stood where he was in the shade of the thicket. He wondered how his personal life had become such a hell of a mess, at the same time he was making great headway on the ranch. Damned if it wasn't going to be a relief to get back to breaking his back working his cattle and then fall plowing! Women be-damned.

ALICE HAD COME to town to buy a few supplies for her new school. After stopping at the implement yard to pass time with Tobias and his children, she crossed to the hotel to see Clare.

As Clare arranged plates on the tables in the dining room, she followed, adding the utensils. "What's wrong, Clare, what's happened between you and Larkin? I—the family, was so surprised to see him at the fair with Myra Tibbetts."

"I don't own him."

"No, but you care very much for one another. Myra has a reputation as the town vamp. She flirts with nearly every fellow who crosses her path. The cowboys who come to town are her— her dessert. According to Tobias she has a — a close relationship with John Daly. Surely you've noticed that, working here?"

"She brings the hotel's mail, and sometimes she stays to visit with John."

"Visits?"

"Alice, I only work here and I'm very busy. I don't know what's going on. It's none of my business."

"Fine. As long as you don't let Myra walk off with the man you love. Fight for him, Clare!"

"Larkin is free to do as he likes, keep company with whomever he chooses." Hadn't she insisted there could be no romance between them, that other responsibilities, her family's survival, came first? She had no call to complain if he chose to keep company with someone else.

"You're hurting, I can see it." Alice caught her hands and held them.

Her eyes swam with tears and she sniffled, "I don't think I'll ever forget seeing him with Myra. It h-hurt so bad I thought I'd die. If he truly cared for me, he wouldn't have flaunted her off to that plum thicket—paying no mind that God and everybody looked on."

"Tobias said that you and Larkin had had words, that Larkin was upset, but his being with Myra didn't mean anything, really."

I hate him for that unfaithfulness to what we've long meant to each other, our young love of the past, our possible future. Aloud she said, "If Larkin is a big enough fool to pair with someone like Myra, let him! He deserves the wretched girl."

Alice gave a wry laugh and pulled her into a hug. "Larkin would never choose someone like Myra over you, Clare, unless he's pushed. You need to make peace with him, and don't wait too long."

If Larkin wanted to make peace with her, he knew where to find her, Clare thought stubbornly.

For the next several weeks following the fair, she looked for him to come to her, declare that his infatuation with Myra was a mistake and over with. But he didn't. Twice she saw him on the street, when she went on errands for the hotel. He tipped his hat politely to her, as he would to any other citizen, but he made no effort to speak with her.

———

FALL SHIPPING SEASON arrived and Sweetbrier's stockyards were a scene of bellowing beasts, dust, and heat as cattle were brought in from the area ranches. From dawn to dark, the "yips" and shouts of cowboys and the rattle of horns and thumping hoofs could be heard as cattle were weighed and herded up the loading chute into the cars for shipping east, while a chuffing engine waited.

A pall of dust hung over the town for days.

Clare had little time to think of anything but the immediate tasks before her as stock buyers, ranchers, and occasionally even a few cowboys, took rooms at the hotel, and ate their meals in the dining room.

The mayor and his stockyard partner, Dinger Toledo, a slight, swarthy fellow who smelled of the barn where he lived, came to supper some evenings as guests of out-of-town stock buyers. They sat smoking cigars and talking numbers over the meal. Fuller and Toledo, as they did business, reminded dare of feral cats in cream heaven.

Curiously, the farmers and ranchers, when they came in, more often wore worried, angry scowls and counted their coins out carefully for a meal. She couldn't help but feel that Fuller and his cohort, Toledo, and the out-of-towners, possibly, too, had something to do with tine poor farmers' distress. If she and Larkin were talking, she'd ask him about it, but unfortunately they were not.

After a long busy day at the hotel, she would be so tired she could barely drag herself home. Poppa often worked late at the blacksmith shop, too, when a cowboy came into town with a horse that had thrown a shoe, or a rancher needed repair on a buggy or wagon and couldn't wait til next day for the job to be done.

Clare and Poppa walked home together, to supper Momma kept hot for them no matter how late they were.

Under a cloudless October sky, Sweetbrier cooked for days in the unusual heat. Clare felt listless, miserable. As she went about her daily chores at the hotel, she now and then saw glimpses of Myra when she brought the mail, but Myra came less and less often. Probably because she was seeing Larkin, had lost interest in John.

The days grew shorter, the clouds and wind meaner. It was sometimes well after dark before Clare and Poppa started the long walk home. If she had a task that kept her late, he waited for her. If he had a job at the smithy that he couldn't leave, she waited for him.

They were almost home one November evening when Poppa stopped short in his tracks. A cold wind swirled around them. "I have to go back. I forgot to lock up Sam's money box. He had to go home early. Oh, I shoulda remembered it!"

She faced him in the thin moonlight, hunched in her coat, her cheeks chilled. "It's all right, Poppa, I'll go back with you. We'll hurry."

The street was quiet, buildings were dark shadows. Here and there lamplight spilled from a window. They let themselves into the darkened, cavernous shop still slightly warm from a few red coals in the forge. Hearing a sound coming from the direction of the small back room that served as Sam's office, Clare caught Poppa's arm and whispered, "Wait." Their breathing was loud in the darkness as they huddled close together.

"Put it back."

At the sound of the voice from the inky shadows, Alfred Fuller halted. Waited. Listened. Nothing. He laughed at himself. Normally he wasn't this nervous, hearing imaginary voices. He clutched the money box to his chest and melted toward the back door he'd pried open and left ajar for quick escape.

"Put it back." The order was stronger this time, threatening.

Damned if he would. He'd planned tonight for weeks. Kept his eyes open. Watched where the money was kept, in a box that once held Winesap brand chewing tobacco. Planned how he'd pin the robbery on the half-wit if necessary, whose voice he now recognized. There were a couple of drifters in town who could be blamed, if not the idiot. He cursed at the sound of a match being struck. "Don't light that accursed lantern!"

The match flickered out, another was struck. "Don't need a light to know it's you, Mayor. And that you're trying to steal boss's cash takings for the week."

With shock, Fuller realized Hobb had moved closer, now only a few feet away from him. It really didn't change anything. Fuller laughed again and took another step. Over his shoulder he said, "Who'd believe you, loony? I'd have to say it was you that stole the cash box, or a drifter who robbed Sam. I have too many friends who'd say it couldn't have been me."

"I'd have to swear it was you, Mayor, seeing as how I'm a very reliable witness. Like Poppa said, put the money back where you got it. You're a fool if you take one more step with the shop's money." Clare stepped out with the lantern she'd lighted.

The mayor threw his arm up over his eyes in the sudden light. "What are you doing here?" he rasped angrily.

"Poppa wanted to come back and—set some mouse traps. I decided to keep him company. But my goodness, we've caught a rat, instead."

There was a long silence from the mayor. He wanted the money desperately, but he didn't want jail time. Nor did he want the reputation he'd worked hard to build, destroyed. He had to be free to go after bigger fish.

"I wasn't going to rob Sam, that was just a joke," he said with a soft, placating chuckle, "Earlier today I saw where Frank stowed the money box in the office, stuffing it in a drawer under papers. Careless as a child. Somebody brain-sick wouldn't see that was pure neglectful. I only came here tonight to make sure the money is safe." He held the tobacco box in a death grip.

"Safe? With you?"

"Not at all, Miss. I was going to take it to the marshal's office for safe keeping, let Sam know in the morning the favor I'd done for him."

"That's quite a story."

"You can't prove otherwise, Miss Hobb. I was taking this box to Marshal Seavers, but now that you're here, I'll turn it over to you so that I won't be accused. If the money disappears, it'll be your doing, or your father's."

"Bring it over here and hand it to Poppa."

It was as though glue held the mayor's feet to the floor. Finally, he moved with great reluctance and handed the money box to Poppa. His face was contorted with anger in the half light, half shadow.

"Wait!" Clare ordered. "I want to make sure you didn't take anything from the box."

Fuller cursed under his breath, "You're mighty suspicious!"

"With reason, wouldn't you say? Open the box, Poppa. Is the money all there?"

He riffled through the bills, stirred coins, and made a rough count. "Ayuh, I'm fair certain it's all here."

"Good." They had thwarted the robbery and had the money. It would be their word against the mayor's if they accused him of attempting to steal it. A few folks might believe them, the majority would not. She said on a sigh, "I suppose you can go, Mayor. Try and behave yourself."

He was furious. "Both of you remember what you accused me of tonight! You could be real sorry for that, if you're not careful."

"We won't forget," Clare said coolly. "And I'll also not forget how you were ready to pin your thievery on my father, Mayor Fuller. Leave Poppa alone, or I'll be singing what I saw and heard here tonight like an anthem! You please remember that, and be warned!"

———

THANKSGIVING DAY, Clare walked wearily home after serving hotel guests their dinner and helping to clean up after. Clouds brewing in the sky matched her perplexed state of mind. If Myra wasn't the reason Larkin was staying away from her, then what was the reason? She'd been wrong to believe he'd tried to squelch her efforts to get work, and she was rude to accuse him. But it wasn't a major crime and it was blamed well time he got over it! Given their past relationship, didn't he at least owe her an occasional "hello, how are you?" Confound him.

The small Hobb house was filled with happy chatter, and the delicious smell of roasting hens and stuffing. Alice had invited Tobias and his children to share the meal that Momma, Alice, and Hallie had prepared. Clare was too tired, to despondent, to eat more than a little bit. "I'll have my slice of mince pie, later. If you'll excuse me, please, I'd like to go to my room for a while."

According to Momma, Larkin had invited his workers and their families to share their Thanksgiving dinner. Mabel had cooked for days, preparing.

Clare lay on her cot and stared at the ceiling, wondering why he didn't come and snatch her into his arms, tell her that he loved her like no other, that Myra was nothing to him. Because he no longer felt that way? She turned onto her stomach and stifled her sobs in her pillow.

———

AT THE HOTEL a few days before Christmas, Clare came downstairs from mopping floors, to find a fragrant cedar tree sitting just inside the door in a bucket of sand. "Who brought the tree?" she asked Tom as he finished registering a guest, a portly traveling salesman.

Tom handed the fellow the key to his room, picked up his pair of satchels to carry them upstairs. "Larkin Wade brought it in. Said he had a gully thick with them on his land. He thought the hotel could use the decoration and I told him it sure could."

Larkin had been here, and she'd missed him. "Did he say anything? Did he ask to see me?"

"Wade just said the tree was an extra is all." Tom continued on up the stairs with the salesman. "We're goin' to decorate it, aren't we?" he called back over his shoulder.

Although she didn't intend to, she sounded snarly when she answered, "Yes! We'll decorate the tree." With her emotions smarting, and needing a moment alone, she rushed to the big pantry off the kitchen and stood there, fighting tears.

After a bit, with an angry sigh, she began to pull scrap fabric from a large bag on a bottom shelf.

When they had a moment from other tasks, Flora, Jewell, and she were braiding new rugs for the guestrooms. The rugs had been Clare's idea and everyone complimented that the rugs were a warm, cozy improvement. Perhaps they could braid a small circular rug to go under the tree in the lobby. No, she'd rather have the tree set up in the dining room, where guests could enjoy it while they ate, and folks on the street could see the candle-lit tree from the windows.

With the decorating project in mind, her spirits began to rise.

A few days later, large crates of gifts came in on the train from Hobb's Mills, with a note from Grandmother wishing them all a Merry Christmas. There were beautifully knitted mittens and scarves, bolts of wool, two jugs of maple syrup, maple sugar candies, crocks of wild blueberry jam, a wheel of cheese encased in thick wax, and a new pair of boots for each member of the family.

After the initial excitement of opening and viewing the gifts subsided, a terrible melancholy settled over the family, spreading from one to the next like a contagion. Clare fought her own bout of homesickness for Hobb's Mills and Homestead House.

She wished with all her heart that the terrible accident that took Uncle Samuel's life had never happened. That the family had dealt more kindly with Poppa's mental failings, and that they had accepted Larkin as a suitable marriage prospect for her. She and Larkin might have been wed by now, and celebrating this Christmas with a small child of their own. They would have a cottage on Hobb's Mills land, or they'd live at his place up Young's Mountain Road. Or somewhere else in

Sandwich township. Anywhere with Larkin would have made her happy.

Unfortunately, the tragedy had taken place. And all their lives had changed. Life in Kansas must be dealt with.

Chapter Eighteen

It was early January. Dawn broke with pink ribbons across the eastern sky as Clare trudged through the snow from home to the hotel, alongside Poppa to his work at the blacksmith shop.

Two days before. Reverend Goodlander had married Tom and Jewell in a brief ceremony. The young couple had left on the next train out, heading for Willow Springs, Missouri, where Tom had folks, and where they wanted to have their child. They wouldn't be coming back.

Unusual for him, John Daly was waiting at the hotel when Clare entered by the back way, stomping snow from her boots.

He motioned her into his office and while she stood, beginning to warm from the close heat in the room, he told her, "Fortunately, hotel business in the dead of winter is lighter than other seasons, but I'm still going to have to ask for more help from you, Clare. Tom has left me in a real bad way. Jewell, too, but it's easier to find a maid than someone who can do a good job running the hotel. I've been wanting to take it easier, enjoy life a bit more. I'd like for you to take over as manager."

She allowed his words to sink in. "Manage the hotel? My goodness."

"You would take Tom's place behind the registration desk, and oversee general operations. Flora has said that her daughter,

Rebecca, would like to take Jewell's job and I agreed. In busy season, you can hire on others, part time help, if you need it. Of course, I won't burden you with these extra duties without fair pay. There'll be a substantial raise, if you agree." He leaned on his cane and waited for her answer.

His offer was like a late Christmas present. Money was always a worry in her quest to get her family established. She felt confident she could learn any managerial tasks she wasn't already familiar with. "I'd love to have the job, and thank you very much, Mr. Daly."

"Call me John." He dropped into a chair.

"Thank you, John. The pay for this new position will be a blessing for my family." She straightened her shoulders. "I suppose my first task in my new role is to see if Cook needs anything in the kitchen. If you'll excuse me..." It was all she could do not to dance her way from his office.

Later that morning, Clare hurried to visit Poppa at the blacksmith shop to tell him the good news about her new job. The snow was beginning to melt but there was enough on the ground to make walking treacherous. She watched her step carefully. Hearing shouting voices as she approached the blacksmith shop, she looked up.

Two boys about Oakley and Nick's age were pelting the blacksmith shop with snowballs, yelling and laughing. "Hey, lunatic, c'mon out. Don't hide. Ain't no use to stay in there, fool crazy man. You got no fire in the forge nohow!"

"What are you doing?" Clare was horrified. She hurried, slipping and sliding. "Stop it, this minute!"

They turned and saw her. After flinging a last snowball each at the shop, they laughed guiltily and fled in the opposite direction. "I know who you are, Gordy Goodlander, and I'm going to tell your mother!"

His steps slowed, but when the other boy, whom she didn't know, motioned, he ran on. Gordy could use more of his father's presence, she thought. Unfortunately, Reverend Goodlander was on the road three weeks out of every four, preaching the gospel to his scattered flocks, as well as conducting baptisms, weddings and funerals.

"Poppa, where are you?" she called, hurrying inside the shop and not spotting him right away. "Poppa?"

"Here, daughter." She saw him then, in the shadowy corner piling coal into a carrier. He came toward her and when he reached the light coming in through a window, she saw that there was blood on his face.

"Poppa, you're hurt! What on earth happened?" She went to him, touched his face. He had a cut over his eye. "Those boys did this?" she demanded to know. "Wait until I speak to their parents!"

"It's just a scratch. One of the snowballs must have had a stone in it. They didn't mean real harm."

"Well, their mischief certainly is out of hand. They need to be given a good scolding and then some hard work to keep them busy. What about your forge fire? They said it was out."

He nodded. "They sneaked in with buckets of snow and dumped it on the fire. I'm building it up again. There's a few coals left. No real harm done."

"Poppa, they hurt you!"

"They were just funning me. I fooled like this when I was a boy."

"Even so, they could have put your eye out or something. This can't happen again." She thought for a moment, "Poppa, have you been made fun of before today, here in Sweetbrier? Have others called you names?" She'd hoped to be away from all such, here in Kansas. A futile hope, possibly.

He shrugged. "Most Sweetbrier folks treat me fine. Now and then somebody calls me 'crazy man' or 'weak-brained fool.' I try not to let it bother me. I guess a body has a right to call me what they think fits."

"They have no such right!" She threw her arms around him. "You're a wonder, Poppa. The smartest, sweetest, kindest soul in Sweetbrier or anywhere else. If I catch those boys tormenting you again, or anyone else treating you badly, I'll make them truly sorry for their actions, I swear!"

Poppa rarely complained, but she'd heard from others that the mayor picked on her father for the slightest cause. At times it seemed out of simple mean-ness, such as the boys tormenting him tonight. But she'd guessed that Fuller held it against Poppa that he hadn't gotten away with the smithy's money that night.

She helped Poppa rebuild his fire in the forge and then told him, "I'm going to spend the next few nights at the hotel, Poppa. There's a lot to be done and I'll be able to work later. But I'd like to celebrate getting my job as manager. Could you explain to Momma? Tell her and the others that I'd like all of you to come in for supper at the hotel, my treat, to celebrate my new job."

"Ayuh, Clarie, we'll come. We're very proud of you."

Justly pleased with the affect, Clare seated her family at a long table by the dining room's front windows that looked out on fluffy banks of snow. A fire crackled cozily in the lobby fireplace, lamps glowed softly from each table, delightful aromas floated from Hattie's kitchen. And then a group of men entered the hotel.

Her heart leaped at sight of Larkin flanked by some of his friends—Tobias, Mr. Cahill from the hardware store, Myra's kindly uncle, Mr. Jackson, who ran the general store. The young editor of the newspaper, a pencil stuck above his ear. There were a couple of others whom she didn't know but judging by their dress and weather-worn faces they were farmers, or ranchers like Larkin.

A moment later the mayor entered, scowling hard enough to sour milk.

Larkin left the group and came to where she stood, trying to get her breath back.

"Hello, Clare."

"Larkin."

"My friends and I are having a little business meeting. Can you put us at that table back in the corner, please?"

"Of course."

"Good evening, Mrs. Hobb," he nodded, hat in hand, to Eugenie at the window table with her brood. He smiled at Poppa, "Frank, how are you? Alice, Hallie, Oakley, nice to see you all."

"This way," she said, her chin high to hide her ricocheting emotions. When the men were seated, she brought cups and saucers. The stoneware clattered in her shaking hands as she poured coffee. "The special tonight is chicken and dumplings, and your choice of peach or apple pie. Our waitress, Flora, will be serving you."

"How are you, Clare?" Larkin asked, cutting into her forced formality before she could turn away.

She looked at him for a long moment, tried to read his mind, see everything he'd been up to lately in one probing glance. And how are you and Myra? Whatever he was thinking wasn't obvious. She stood stiffly, pretending indifference. "I'm quite fine. Excuse me, but I need to get back to my family. They've come to town to have supper with me and we've much to talk about."

"Sure, Clare. Good to see you."

Eating later with her family, Clare did her best to avoid looking in Larkin's direction. Whatever was being discussed, Mayor Fuller was decidedly unhappy about it. Larkin kept telling him to calm down. Some of the other men in the group argued that they had to talk the matter out and get it settled. "Fair is fair," one man barked loudly. "Damn right!" another echoed.

"How are things at the farm?" Clare asked, making strong effort to focus on her family. "I miss being there and I'm really sorry not to be doing my share of the chores these past few days."

"There's not so much to do now, anyhow," Oakley told her. "Our Guernseys are bred, we'll have calves in the spring, maybe we'll be lucky and one of the cows will have twins. Larkin sent a couple of his friends and Nick over to help finish patching up the barn, so now our critters are out of the cold. Chickens are cooped out of the cold, too. We may run out of corn to feed them, and we'll be out of coal, too, if this cold weather doesn't change pretty durn quick."

"I'll have an order of coal sent out, and feed, too," she said, although her mind threatened to wander. Larkin had sent help to patch the barn with no word to her about it? Of course, interest in Myra wouldn't change the kindness he felt toward the Hobbs. They had a history together, from New Hampshire, and he'd always been a thoughtful man toward others. She forced her attention back to the family.

"Alice, how is school?"

"It seems to be my calling, I enjoy it very much. We've had a few days when some of the children couldn't make it to school through the snow. They are intelligent children, and seem to make up their missed lessons fast."

"Momma and I are making some new quilts," Hallie said. "It's really drafty in that old house. That's why we use up so much coal."

"Umm," Clare said by way of answer, and changed the subject. "I wanted you all here to discuss the news of my job. Poppa told you I'm now the manager at the Hilldale. That means a lot more responsibilities—I won't be able to be at home so much, but it also means I'll be earning more. That will help support the farm, pay for feed for our stock, and for seed to plant next spring."

"We can eat here free anytime we want?" Hallie wanted to know.

"Not exactly free, and not just anytime you want, but occasionally."

"I think it's a wonderful opportunity for you, Clare," Alice said. "If we ever need extra help on the farm, I'm sure some of my older students or some of our neighbors would pitch in."

"Good. And when a need comes up, we can return the favor."

Momma mused, frowning, "I don't know that it's proper for a woman to manage a business. I thought that your working here," she sighed as her glance scanned the dining room and out into the lobby, "would be only temporary."

"I agree, Momma, it's doubtless I, a young unattached woman, could take over the running of a hotel back home without setting off a dreadful scandal. But I behave properly, and I like being here in town where Poppa spends his time. Few folks back at Hobb's Mills would understand that life in the West is different for everyone. Much freer. It doesn't really matter what they would think, anyway, does it?"

Momma hesitated, her expression revealing that for the rest of her days she'd regret the necessity of her daughter having to do this, but she shook her head, "No, I suppose it doesn't matter. I'm sure you'll do the work very well, Clare. You always do fine at whatever you put your hand to."

"I don't like it either, that my girls have to work," Poppa said. "But I'm close where I can keep an eye on Clare. I can look out for her. Nobody ever better hurt my child."

Clare smiled. "Thank you, Poppa. Thank all of you."

Her family had finished their meal and long since departed when Larkin's business supper broke up. His companions one by one scraped their chairs back from the table and—letting in blasts of wintry cold—shuffled out. Larkin remained seated, elbows propped on the table and chin in hand, deep in thought.

"May I get you something? More dessert? Coffee?" Clare's manner had softened despite her wish to remain indifferent. "Was your supper meeting satisfactory?"

"The meal was delicious and I couldn't eat another bite." He raked his hand through his hair, and looked exasperated. "As far as the meeting—" he shook his head. "Alfred Fuller has gotten to be a problem and I'm afraid matters are going to get worse if he isn't stopped."

"A problem how?" She stood at his elbow, waiting to hear, wanting to share even this brief passing moment with him.

"He's been cheating the farmers and ranchers for some time, with Dinger's help, probably. He juggles the weight figures and charges more for freight than is actually owed, pocketing the difference. Tonight we asked him to step down from his job as station master. We can't outright fire him, he's an employee of the railroad, not the town. He's refused. So we've given him a warning to retire, or change his tactics, or we report him to the Missouri, Kansas and Texas railroad officials. Maybe he'll reform. If a farmer suffering losses he can't afford, doesn't shoot him first."

She told him how Fuller tried to steal Sam Dorsey's money from the blacksmith shop. "We didn't report him, because it would have been his word against ours, and we couldn't have provided any real proof."

"Which has been the problem with his stealing all along. He's slick. But enough of problems about the mayor."

She moved aside as he slowly got to his feet. He touched her arm lightly. "I need to talk to you, Clare."

He's going to tell me about him and Myra and I'd rather die than hear him say he cares for someone else. That I've put him off too long.

"You don't have to say anything." To her dismay, her voice broke. "I understand."

He looked puzzled, "But I haven't said what's on my mind. What is it that you think you understand?"

"You and Myra." It was all she could do to pretend she didn't mind. She fought for control as tears burned behind her eyes. She wished she could just evaporate, rather than hear him tell her the dreaded news.

"Me? Myra?"

"Weren't you about to say that you're courting her? That you plan to marry her?"

He burst into loud laughter. "Hell no! Oh, my God, no! Where did you get that fool idea?"

"For starters," she recovered enough to say in defiance, "you spent that day at the fair with her! You were together for hours. I saw you two go to that thicket and—" Hot-faced, she looked at her toes. "Everyone knows what Myra is like." Her glance leveled with his. "She's had her cap set for you all along. That's been clear to me from the day you introduced us, when I first arrived in Sweetbrier. While I—I had to care for my family."

He tied to speak but she plunged on, "Heaven knows you've ignored me like the plague for weeks now. I might as well be a stranger. I've had no choice but to believe that you're in love with Myra." She waved her arms in the air, "Or maybe, even someone else."

He growled something unintelligible and reached for her, but Clare moved a chair between them. Until this matter was cleared up she couldn't let him touch her.

"I wasn't ignoring you in the way you think. I just got angry at the whole damn world that we couldn't be together and I needed time to cool off. It's not hard to keep busy when you got a ranch to run. Even then, when I tried not to, I was thinking about you, all of the time. The more I tried not to, the more I could think of nothing else but you."

"Larkin-"

He held up a finger for her to be still. "Now, about Myra, she has had her cap on backwards where I'm concerned! I have no interest in Myra, in that way." His glance gentled, "Clare, I guarantee nothing happened that day in the woods except a kiss, which for me was dull as dishwater. I coulda' been kissing a tin plate! Just a kiss." His eyes gleamed as he looked down at her, and a smile quirked the corner of his mouth. "If it had been you with me that day, I'd have done a hell of a lot more, if you'd allowed it." *Invited me the way Myra was doing.*

His expression made her heart turn flip-flops and her face warm. "But—"

"Wait—I'm not finished. Another thing, Myra is going to marry John Daly."

"She's what? You're joking." Both hands caught the back of the chair as she stared at him.

"No, I'm not, joking. They've had a thing for one another for a long time. You must've seen—"

"Myra brings the hotel's mail. Maybe John goes to visit her. How would I know what their relationship is, what their plans are? I'm very busy and John hasn't mentioned plans to marry Myra. Are you sure?"

If Myra had finally snagged a prospective husband, she'd surely broadcast the fact all over town. Unless she was holding last minute hope of snaring Larkin? Clare tried to force her confused thoughts into order, with little success. She looked up, repeating, "You're sure John and Myra intend to marry?"

"John mentioned it to me privately, himself, a few days ago. Al Fuller told the rest of us tonight that Myra and John bought tickets and slipped away on the train this afternoon, headed for the county courthouse at Junction City. They didn't want to wait for Reverend Goodlander. Guess the word hasn't gotten out yet, but they'll likely come back a married couple after a short honeymoon. Everybody will be able to read about it in the paper, James Myers can't wait to write up their story."

Clare was still in shock. When the couple returned, Myra would be Mrs. John Daly. Clare's boss's wife. The prospect held a hint of complication for Clare, but that was nothing compared to the relief she felt knowing Larkin was still available. He cared for her as much as she did for him, he still loved her as she loved him. Her spirits soared and a smile tugged at her lips, "Umm, Larkin-"

"What?"

She moved the chair from between them. "Now that John has made me manager of the hotel, I have less leisure time than usual. But if I could get away, one afternoon or evening, could we go for a drive?" She took a step toward him. "Being stuck in town as much as I am, I miss the country. I'd like to do that, if you would."

He grabbed her and swung her off the floor. "If I would like it?" he boomed, a broad grin on his face, "Clare, that was exactly what I was going to ask you!"

He kissed her forehead, his eyes filled with rapture, as though trying to prove to himself that they were really here together, in one another's arms. His lips then touched hers lightly, still seeking proof that the moment was true. "I can finally court you, as I've always wanted?" he whispered against her hair.

"Like we've both always wanted."

Before he could kiss her again, Clare threw her arms around his neck and kissed him on the mouth, a long, back-home-in-New Hampshire by-their-rock kind of kiss.

He growled low in his throat, "Good Lord, Clare! My angel, my darling—"

He was devouring her with return kisses when close-by, someone cleared their throat. Clare opened one eye and peeked past his shoulder. "Oh my, Flora. Rachel."

Larkin sighed in disappointment and let her go.

Flora hid a smirk. Her pig-tailed, seventeen-year-old daughter, Rachel, was trying to get a good look around her mother at what Clare and Larkin we're doing. Flora waved a hand at the room, "We thought we'd better clear the dining room tables, get the supper dishes washed and put away, you know."

"Of course, Flora, of course." She stood away from Larkin, her cheeks scarlet, her whole being tingling. She waved the women into the room.

"I'll see you to the door," she told Larkin.

"This isn't finished," he whispered as his lips brushed her brow.

"Oh my no," she whispered back, "nothing of the sort."

Chapter Nineteen

CLARE WAS BEGINNING TO UNDERSTAND THAT A PERSON could set or change goals easily enough; she could make bargains with her heart and fight hard to keep that promise immutable. Yet not for a single day could she rum off her feelings—her deep love for the one man destined to be her mate.

Until the day she took her last breath and was placed in her grave, she could take on mountainous tasks for her family's sake, but Larkin was in her heart for all eternity. Because of their love, she owed him, owed herself, much more than she'd been giving.

It appeared he was going to allow her another chance and she thanked God for it.

Larkin came for her in a sleigh with red and gold trim, shiny runners, and hitched to a patient-looking gray. "Will you be warm enough?" he asked Clare, coming around to her side where he tucked the heavy robe around her.

"Very cozy." She smiled back at him from the depths of her fur-trimmed bonnet, thrilled to her core that the day had finally come when they could be together. After days of a heavy, blowing snow-fall, the weather had turned bright and clear. The sky was an eye-hurting blue, snow was a diamond blanket as far as the eye could see.

They glided a few yards along the snow and ice-rutted street when someone yelled behind them, "Wade! Hold on. Stop!"

Larkin drew back on the reins and looked over his shoulder.

Clare said, "It's the mayor."

"I see that. Wonder what the hell he wants." He climbed down and walked back to meet Fuller. Their breath made white puffs as they talked. Fuller made his way back toward the train station and Larkin returned to the sleigh.

"What is it?"

"Fuller sent a rider out to find out why yesterday's train hadn't arrived, thought the blizzard might be the cause. It was. The tram is stalled about eight miles north of Sweetbrier in snow drifted higher on the tracks than a man standing up. I guess the crew tried to dig out, hoped there'd be a thaw, but they're still stuck. Passengers are half frozen. Fuller wants me to round up some help and go bring those folks into town. I'm sorry, Clare, but it looks like our ride will have to wait for another time."

She nodded, pushed aside the disappointment that she saw reflected in his eyes. "Of course. Take me back to the hotel, I'll send warm blankets and hot coffee with you. Bring those poor people to the hotel. I'll have Cook prepare kettles of hot soup. We'll get rooms ready for as long as they need to stay over."

When Larkin returned to Sweetbrier hours later, the hotel's windows were steamed over from pots of oxtail soup simmering on top of the big kitchen range. Enormous pans of biscuits baked in the oven. A fire crackled merrily in the fireplace of every room.

Clare and her staff were everywhere, helping the shivering, blue-lipped passengers thaw their hands and feet in pans of water, serving them hot tea and coffee, keeping them wrapped in blankets. And later, Clare and her workers listened patiently to the refugees' teeth-chattering stories about the terrible ordeal.

John Daly and Myra had been on the stalled train, and Clare was not quite over her shock at that fact. Plus, she was beginning to be irritated by Myra's demands for Clare's undivided attention.

"Lay out my clothes," Myra ordered, as she sat, stripped naked on the edge of her bed following a hot bath. The large thick towel Clare had provided lay at her feet.

Clare threw her a blanket, "You might want to wrap up in this while I get your dress and undergarments."

"If you weren't so slow, I'd be dressed already. I had to wait forever for you to draw my bath."

"I'm sorry," Clare said through gritted teeth, "but there were twenty-two other passengers on the train. Everybody needed care. We're doing the best we can to heat hot water for baths for everyone. Larkin and his friends are taking care of the male passengers. My maids, and I, are doing everything possible to make the women passengers comfortable."

"You don't need to see to anyone but me. I'm your boss's wife, remember?"

"I'm well aware of your position, Myra." The new Mrs. Daly had reminded her of that fact ten times in the past hour. "I repeat my congratulations on your marriage. I hope you and John will have a long happy life together, truly. Now, may I bring you some soup up here to your room, or would you like to come downstairs where we'll be serving folks in the dining room?"

"What kind of soup?"

"Oxtail."

Myra made a face. "I hate oxtail soup. You'll have to bring me something else. I want oyster stew, and for dessert, a hot fruit compote. No, I'll have custard, a caramel custard. Can you do that? After all, John did make you the manager here, although I can't imagine why."

Clare was ready to boil over. "You'll have your oyster stew, and your custard, Myra, as soon as I've seen to the welfare of our other guests. As wife of the owner of this establishment, I'm sure you'd want me to do that?" She didn't wait for Myra's answer but instead whirled out of the room.

She reached the kitchen, her jaw set and smarting from the exchange with Myra. The silly woman certainly had a high-flown image of herself! As Clare passed the partially-opened door to the pantry, a hand reached out and grabbed her wrist. She swallowed a squeal of alarm when she recognized the tan, long-fingered hand, and whispered, "Larkin, what on earth are you doing in the pantry?"

"Come on in and find out," he said softly. "We're supposed to be courting, remember?"

"I remember, but in the pantry?"

He pulled her into the small room that smelled of apples, pickle vinegar—and lavender drying in bunches from the ceiling.

"Now that we're official, I'll be kissing you anywhere and anytime, I get the chance. All right?"

"More than all right. I'm so glad it's you who yanked me in here." She ran her hands over his chest, stroked his firm jaw with her finger. "The new Mrs. Daly has been driving me nearly out of my mind with her demands. We can hide in here for only a few seconds, though. I must see that she has her special request for oyster stew and a caramel pudding. Now that she's the boss's wife, she has no patience toward a lowly employee like me."

"The new Mrs. Daly can wait." He kissed her long and hard.

"Just what I was thinking," Clare said, gasping for breath before they kissed again.

———

"I CAME HERE today to ask you something, Alice, but first I want to tell you some things about me, that you ought to know." Tobias had left Beth and Will in the care of a neighbor and had broken through heavy snow to make sure Alice and her family were all right, and if they needed anything. Those matters seen to, he and Alice now sat before the fire, talking privately.

"I feel I know you very well, Tobias. I've seen how you treat customers and how you operate your business. You're a fine father to your children. Everyone in Sweetbrier speaks well of you, likes you, as do I. You needn't tell me anything more than I can see for myself."

"Would you hush, sweetheart, and let me talk?"

Her face wanned, she smiled shyly and nodded for him to go ahead.

"I'm not a native Kansan, I was born in New York," he told her. "My parents died of a disease, influenza I think it was, that spread like wildfire through the tenement house where we lived. I had nobody to go to after they died, and I lived a crude, dark life on the streets. I begged for food, stole when I had to, slept in stinking alleys."

"You don't have to tell me this, Tobias. Un-unless you want to, of course."

"I want to. I want you to know that I came west to Kansas on an orphan train. I've never talked about it before, because I'm not proud of it, but I want to talk about it now."

"I've heard of the orphan trains. Social workers in the cities gathered children off the rough streets and sent them west by the trainload, to family's who would take them in, and provide the children with a healthier way of life."

"Right. When I got to Kansas, I was picked by folks who wanted my labors on their farm more than they wanted an orphan as part of their family. But that was all right, I survived and I learned a lot. But I told JoEllen a made up story—that I was born of wealthy parents, on a cotton plantation in Missouri. A pure lie."

"But why not tell her the truth?" Alice frowned in puzzlement. "Your beginnings were beyond your control, your life as a child was forced on you."

"Because I wanted to be something other than what I was, make myself look good to her."

"I'm sure you needn't have done that, I believe she would have understood and not minded the truth."

"You hit the nail on the head, Alice. You're a lot like her, I know now she would have understood, that it wouldn't have changed her mind about me. I don't want any secrets, anymore, however. Especially not between you and me. As I get older, I recognize that I am who I am and it's foolish to pretend what ain't so. And plumb tiring. Jo Ellen used to wear me out getting me to talk about the plantation life I never lived a day of."

Alice hid a smile behind her hand, and told him earnestly, "There's no shame to your beginnings, Tobias, none. You were a child and couldn't help what happened." She sat forward. "Goodness, I see so many positive things about your life that I hardly know where to start." She counted on her fingers, "If not for that orphan train, and the social workers who put you on it, you could be dead. Or—due to the way you were forced to provide for yourself in New York City—you could have ended up a criminal, possibly living out your life in a jail cell." She ticked off on another finger, smiling gently at him, "Instead you're a respected businessman here in Sweetbrier. And from what you've told me, you had a good life with JoEllen. Finally, you're a wonderful father, the best."

"I try to be. I love my children. Maybe because of my own

childhood, being a family is mighty important to me." He hesitated, then asked, "I look all right to you, then, Alice?" Only a little nervous, he came to drop to a knee before her. "You'll agree to marry me?" He took her hand in his. "That's what I came here today to ask you. Will you be my wife? My children's mother? I love you, Alice, more than I ever thought I could love another woman. Please say yes."

"Oh, Tobias, I don't know-"

"You don't want to?" He sat back on his heels, frowning.

"It isn't that. I'd love to be your wife, Tobias, and I've hoped you'd ask me. But I've considered the matter—in case you asked—and I've come to the conclusion that our marrying would be terribly unfair to Clare. She's put Larkin off for so long, and she loves him deeply. It just doesn't seem right. All she's ever done is take care of us, it's really her turn."

"Now listen to me, Alice, dear. I was with the bunch that went out and brought in those folks from the train stuck in a snow bank. We took them to the hotel to thaw them out, feed them and put them up, as you probably know. Well, I went looking for Larkin to ask if there was anything else he needed me for." He shoulders shook with quiet laughter. "I come onto Larkin and Clare in the kitchen pantry, and what they was doing," he shook his head, "I don't think they ought to put off marrying! Fact is, I think we ought to talk to them two, about having a double wedding. Them, and us. That's the other thing that was on my mind tonight."

Alice's eyes dazzled and a pink dot came to each cheek, but she couldn't speak.

Tobias stood, drew her to her feet and very properly asked, "May I kiss you, Alice?"

"Yes," she whispered breathlessly, and closed her eyes, "you may, Tobias."

"Well, then," he lowered his lips to hers. He kissed her a second time, and a third, but stopped suddenly when she began to cry. He drew back, could only stare as tears flooded her cheeks and she tried furiously to wipe them away.

"Alice! Did I do something wrong?" He thumbed at her tears, leaned close to look into her face with affection. "Darlin' what's the matter?"

"It—it's just that it feels so good to be held, and kissed. I thought it would never happen to me again, after I was separated from a boy I loved. And here you are, the most wonderful man under the heavens, wanting to marry me! I'm happy, Tobias. I'm crying because I'm happy."

"Hell, that's a relief!" he tossed his head back and laughed. "You had me plumb worried, Alice!"

———

CLARE WAS sure she had cause to worry. John Daly had asked her into his office, saying that he needed to have a private talk with her. In Myra's new role she'd bossed Clare relentlessly, demanding changes at the hotel that Clare, as manager, couldn't agree with. Raising the room rate and painting the building geranium pink were but two of many demands dare was resisting.

John took the chair at his desk, the hotel financial record book open before him. Clare waited to hear the worst, that he was about take away her job as hotel manager to please Myra. On that day passengers were rescued from the train stalled in the snow, Myra had wanted Clare fired for kissing Larkin in the pantry. They'd kissed many times that evening, whenever an opportunity arose; Myra caught them once, and Tobias had another time, although he slipped away without telling anyone, until Alice.

"What is it, Mr. Daly?" Clare broke the silence. "Is something the matter?" Protest was on the tip of her tongue—she liked her job and had done the best she could. Kissing Larkin might have been improper, but it hadn't done any harm. The snowy day of the rescue had been a wonderful new start for them.

Daly motioned her to a chair but she was too worried to sit. She paced, praying that she was mistaken, that she was not about to be tossed out onto the street with no other means of earning money. Her mind chased frantically after other ideas of work and came up empty. What would she do? The bulk of the family income came from her toils. Alice and Tobias wanted to marry and she encouraged it with a whole heart. She and Alice had talked of possibly having a double wedding, if details could be worked out. But now, this.

Her mind leaped to attention when she realized what John Daly was telling her.

"I'm going to fulfill my wife, Myra's, longtime dream. I'm taking her to Denver to live."

"To live?"

"She's always wanted to move to a bigger town. I'm ready for the change, myself. Her old life here, her—friendliness with the cowboys that come to town—well, our marriage will be better off away from Sweetbrier."

Clare nodded, for the moment not knowing how to reply or how John's plans might affect her.

"Even in the short time you've been here, the hotel has done better in your hands, Clare. It's cleaner, more efficiently run, the books are in fine shape. My wife would like to believe that she has something to do with the improvement, but I know where the due belongs. I'd like to sell you the hotel, Clare, at a fair price, if you're interested."

She dropped into the chair, so surprised at his offer that she could only stare into his kindly eyes. "Sell? To me?" A frown knitted her brow, "Oh, Mr. Daly, I appreciate the offer—and ordinarily I'd be interested. But I have no money. Not sufficient funds in hand, anyway." She thought it over, her mind beginning to buzz with possibilities. "If you could give me time to come up with your price we might work this out. I'd need to have a talk with my family."

"Like I said, I would make you a fair deal. I'm friends with McCann, the banker up at Junction City. I believe he'd loan you the money. I'd put in a good word for you."

The rest of that day passed in a whirlwind of excitement for Clare, as she envisioned what ownership of the Hilldale Hotel could mean to the Hobb family's future. If handled properly, a very nice income was possible. She'd like to post fliers advertising the hotel in other train stations. She would advertise in newspapers in the area, that the hotel was the perfect spot for weddings, all sorts of celebrations. She might even have the building freshly painted, but not pink.

At home that same evening, she made a pot of coffee, saw that her family was gathered around the kitchen table and served slices of dried peach pie Alice had made. She told them of John's offer.

She poured a dash of cream onto her pie and picked up her fork. "This is a wonderful opportunity for us. As owners of the hotel, we'd be better off financially, all around. Of course, buying the hotel will require a cash down payment. My question is," she looked in turn at Momma, Poppa, Alice,

Oakley, and Hallie, "should we write Grandmother Hobb and ask her for the money?" She went on quickly, "Of course you all realize that Simon would likely argue against it, even if Grandmother Hobb was in favor."

"He would deny us," Alice said bluntly, "and I'd rather we didn't ask him for a thing. We should find another way. Spare ourselves the humiliation of being turned down by our own kin."

Momma agreed, soft-voiced and sad, "We didn't get much help from home before, I doubt they'd grant it, now. I say we either turn down Mr. Daly's offer, or find a way to accept without help from home. Maybe a friend, Larkin Wade, would laid us the money? He seems to be doing so well. Mabel said just the other day that his winter wheat is going to make a bumper crop come next summer."

"That's true, he is doing well." Mention of Larkin nearly diverted Clare's thoughts from the matter at hand. She got back on path, "But Larkin expects to put his profit back into his ranch, hiring more help as he expands, for one thing. I'm against leaning on our friends, in any regard."

"Daughter, you are right. We will do this on our own!" Poppa slapped his palm onto the table, "We will buy this hotel that our Clare runs so well. Yes, I vote yes!"

"We don't need nobody else's help!" Oakley agreed, Adam's apple bobbing in his throat at his excitement. "We're doin' all right here on our farm, plus I earn extra money when I help out over at Wade's ranch during roundup and branding. I could do chores at the hotel sometimes, if you need me, Clare."

She smiled at him. Oakley was truly growing up. In just the past months his voice had deepened, becoming more masculine. Fine facial hair sprouted above his top lip.

"I don't think we should buy any old hotel," Hallie spoke up with a long-suffering sigh. "I think we should all go home to Hobb's Mills!"

With barely a glance at Hallie, Clare said, "Going back is not part of this discussion. Now, Mr. Daly believes we can borrow from the Junction City Bank and he's promised to put in a good word for me. I vote that we borrow just enough cash to make the down payment. We don't want to put ourselves too far into debt. If the hotel is run properly, the income from it should pay operating expenses, payment to the bank for the small loan, plus possibly a little profit most months. Profit is greater in some seasons than others, like when ranchers and their cowhands are in town, of course. What we earn should add up nicely in time. There are improvements I'd like to make at the hotel but the way John talked, he may make some of those himself as part of the deal." If she could just have screens put on the windows to keep flies out, she'd be blissfully happy.

"You'd be doing most of the work of running the hotel," Alice commented with concern, laying her fork aside. "The rest of us could help out only occasionally."

"Don't worry about that. There will be little change in my duties, from manager to owner. The chief difference is that income from operating the hotel will be ours, after costs."

Alice ventured, nodding slowly, "If something unforeseen comes up and we can't make a payment to the bank from hotel income, I'd be happy to help out from my teaching salary. Maybe we could take a little from our farm profit, if need be?"

"There's the money Poppa is earning as a blacksmith," Oakley put in, "and Larkin pays me well when I work with Nick over at their place."

"Then we're all in agreement that we buy the hotel?" Except from a sullen Hallie, the "yaaays" were resounding.

———

LARKIN WAS LESS than enthusiastic when she told him the news. He'd come into Sweetbrier on business with Tobias. Afterward, he stopped at the hotel for his noon meal, arriving on a cold blast of air from outside, and with snowflakes dotting his hat and the broad shoulders of his coat. He'd finished his steak and she poured him a fresh cup of coffee, then sat down across from him at their corner table in back.

"You're going to buy this place? Take on full responsibility?" His eyes were stormy and he shook his head. "Clare, I thought we'd come to an understanding, that finally we were going to be together, that we could set a wedding date. Tobias said that you and Alice were even thinking about having a double wedding."

"We are going to be together, Larkin! We can set a wedding date. And I think it would be grand to have our ceremony the same time as Alice's and Tobias's."

He looked doubtful, but asked on a hopeful note, "Owning the hotel won't change anything for you and me?"

"No, Larkin. I will never, ever let anything come between us again. I'm sorry I've put you off for so long, put us aside, but I had to do it. Poppa's family was so cruel to him for what happened to Uncle Samuel. Matters were getting worse and worse back at Hobb's Mills and I'm the one who started the trouble by not being where I should have been."

"You were with me," he said flatly. "One of the happiest days of my life, up until the runaway happened."

"I had to make amends to my family by taking care of them."

"I don't fault you for that and never did. What you've done for your family was right and honorable. But I love you, Clare, and waiting for you to finish taking care of everybody else first, has been hard as hell." He sat back from the table, his chair balanced on the two back legs. "To be honest, I've reached the end of my tether. I don't see how I can wait any longer. I want us to marry, to have young ones. A life of our own."

"I want the same. And it can happen, now. Can't you see, Larkin, the hotel and the farm will put my family's affairs on firmer footing. Oakley and Hallie are growing up, getting to be an age to help more and more, both at the farm and at the hotel. Alice and Tobias will help when they can. Poppa is doing so much better in Kansas and Momma is slowly adjusting to life here. As much as she ever will. I'll need to oversee operation of the hotel, but if you still want me, I'll be your wife. I'll live with you at the ranch."

"If I still want you—! You're the only thing I've ever wanted this much!" His chair thudded back into place and his hands clasped hers across the table. "I've got to kiss you, Clare. Is it all right to do it here—" his gaze scanned the ten or twelve others diners in the room, "or do we have to go to the pantry?"

Clare stood, and smiled at him, her eyes dancing in her flushed face. "I have very fond memories of that pantry." She took his hand.

Chapter Twenty

THE WOMEN WERE AT THE WADE RANCH, GATHERED AROUND
Mabel's table making plans for the double wedding scheduled for
Valentine's Day.

Clare and Alice were so happily engrossed in discussing possibilities for decorations, food, and the need for Reverend Goodlander to be contacted, that at first they didn't notice Mabel's
frown. Didn't recognize that she was signaling with her eyes for
them to look at their mother. Clare looked and her heart fell.
Although Momma made no sound, she couldn't have looked more
distressed, tears streamed from her eyes.

"For goodness sakes, Momma, why are you crying? What's
wrong?" Clare reached across the table to grasp her mother's hand.
Alice hurriedly went to kneel by Momma's chair and take her other
hand.

"Aren't you happy for us. Momma?" Alice asked, puzzled.

Momma looked stunned at the question and her blurry-eyed
glance darted from Alice to Clare and back again. "Oh, yes, I'm
very happy for you girls! It's not that. I couldn't be more pleased. I
couldn't ask for better husbands for my daughters than Larkin and
Tobias." She drew her handkerchief from her sleeve and dried her
eyes, only to have the tears start afresh.

"What then, Momma?" Clare asked, although she was beginning to suspect the problem. They were in Kansas, not at Hobb's

Mills, the home that Momma had loved so much. The home of her heart, where she'd like to see her daughters' weddings take place.

"From the time you girls were babies," Momma told them, crying softly, "I believed you would get married in the lovely old Sandwich church in the village. There would be weeks of parties at Hobb's Mills. When you were just tots, I was already picturing you coming down the stairs at Homestead House in your bridal gowns. It—it was such a beautiful dream. I had my heart set—but now, here in Kansas—"

Clare had had the same dream in her younger years, although it no longer mattered. She'd marry Larkin in a cow pasture, wearing an old ragged dress and with a single wildflower in her hand, just to be his wife, have him for her husband. But at the moment she hated the family back home for causing Momma this pain. When she could speak, she told Momma fervently, squeezing her hand, "We're going to make this wedding as beautiful as any we might have had at Sandwich, won't we Alice?"

"Every bit as beautiful!" Alice promised. "Momma, if we had stayed in New Hampshire, I wouldn't have met Tobias! Or his children. I love him so, I love them, they are about to be my very own family. My own miracle. I've never been so happy in my whole life. Think what I would have missed, if we hadn't come to Kansas."

Momma smiled and reached out to hug her older daughter. "That is so, Alice. I apologize for being a blubbering fool, over nothing, really."

Clare laughed. "Our double wedding ceremony will be a bit different from what it might have been back at Hobb's Mills, but who minds? We're marrying the finest men who ever lived and the community loves a party, no matter if it isn't terribly fancy. Isn't that right?"

"Indeed!" Mabel chuckled.

Alice stood up and uncharacteristically went up on her toes to dance around the room. "We will wear our very best dresses. We can remove silk flowers from our hats to make perfectly lovely bridal hairpieces. The church can be decorated with red and white crepe paper streamers, paper hearts and cupids."

Hallie, picturing the images Alice described, jumped to her feet and laughing gaily, took her older sister's hands, and danced with her. Although Hallie had been quiet until now, she couldn't contain the excitement and interest that had begun to show in her face from the moment the wedding plans were first announced. She was a female, after all, and what young girl didn't like weddings?

Larkin had told Clare that the Sweetbrier Church, served every third Sunday by Reverend Goodlander, had been built of old boards taken from a saloon that was torn down at White City. But Momma didn't need to know that.

"I'll make Marlborough Pudding, just like is served at weddings in New England," Mabel said. "It'll be new to some Kansas folks, but they'll love it. There's quite a good band from hereabouts, a fiddler, pianist, and a guitar player, who've played for other Sweetbrier doin's. We can hire them to give us music for the dancin'."

In another few moments, Momma's tears had dried. She was as excited as the rest and added her own suggestions, "It was a custom in Sandwich Village to bake a ring into the wedding cake as a symbol of bliss and happiness. The guest whose piece of cake contained the ring could look forward to a year of complete happiness."

"We can do that here, Momma," Clare told her, and Hallie, dropping into a chair, clapped her hands at the prospect.

"Do I get to be bridesmaid for both of you?" Hallie asked, sitting forward. "I've heard that if a bridesmaid sleeps with a piece of wedding cake under her pillow she will dream about her future husband."

"It's all right to dream, Hallie," Momma chided. "but marrying off two daughters at once is more than enough, thank you. I want you home with me for a while yet. Plenty of time before you think of marrying."

"I know, Momma. I just thought it would be quite the thing to sleep with wedding cake under my pillow." She giggled, and then possessed of another thought, asked her sisters, "Will you go on a honeymoon together, all four of you?" She began to jiggle in her chair, saying excitedly, "To Paris, maybe? Or London? I know, Florence, Italy! I've read about it and I'd love to go there."

Alice answered, "Tobias and I and the children will be going directly to his house after the wedding and the party following, to start our life together, and I can hardly wait."

Clare felt the same, but Larkin wanted to give her a wedding trip to Topeka. She might still talk him into staying right here at Sweetbrier. They could have their own suite at the hotel, but she supposed that wasn't a good idea—she'd be too handy to work or be asked to solve problems that came up. Mabel and Nick were here at the ranch and it would be difficult for her and Larkin to have a few days alone.

She told the other women, with a quiet smile, "Larkin talks of engaging rooms at the finest hotel in Topeka for our honeymoon. We'd see some plays, eat at the best restaurants. Dance." Make love.

In the end, Larkin and Clare both agreed they wanted to remain right there in Sweetbrier, anxious to begin their new life together, as Alice and Tobias would be doing. They could always go to Topeka later. Arrangements were made for Ma Wade and Nick to move to the hotel for a few days, to give Larkin and Clare privacy at the ranch.

The small church, modestly decorated with a Valentine theme, was packed with guests—ranch friends and acquaintances of Larkin's, residents from Clare's hotel, Sweetbrier merchants and their families, and nearly everyone else who lived in town or within driving distance.

Clare wore her best violet silk dress with white lace trim, Alice wore an elegant silver gray frock with a pale peach collar that reflected her radiant face. The two couples stood up front, one couple on each side of Reverend Goodlander, while Hallie, over by the organ, sang sweetly two songs, "Aura Lea" and "My Love Is Like A Red Red Rose."

Clare, facing Larkin, her hands in his, was overwhelmed by the enormity of this day, their wedding day. From now on their lives would be one. She wouldn't have to hide her love but could show it as her heart and soul had long demanded.

Lost in Larkin's warm gaze, his affectionate smile, she listened to Reverend Goodlander speak of devotion and honor, unity of family, the children their love would create...beautiful words.

Alice and Tobias repeated their vows first. Reverend Goodlander asked Tobias if he would take Alice to be his lawfully wedded wife, and the burly groom spoke loud and clear, sending a gentle titter around the room, "I do! As the Lord is my witness, I surely do!"

Then it was their turn and Larkin was saying softly, "I, Larkin, take thee, Clare, the light of my life, to be my wedded wife, to have and to hold, from this day forward, for better, for worse, for richer, for poorer, in sickness and in health, according to God's holy ordinance; and thereto I pledge thee the full measure of my love—all the days of our lives."

With tears sparkling in her eyes and a smile on her face, she mouthed, I love you, and then repeated her vows to him through an emotion-filled throat, finishing, "...all the days of our lives."

At the reception party held at the hotel, husband and wife at last, Clare nestled her face against Larkin's chest as they danced to the tunes played by the band.

"Happy?" he asked, his lips brushing her temple.

"Very, very happy. It was a beautiful ceremony, don't you think? Poppa was nervous, but he did a good job, didn't he, giving his two daughters away? Only one mistake, when he thought he was supposed to repeat the reverend. 'With the power vested in me-' Reverend Goodlander said, and Poppa repeated 'with the power vested in me.'"

Larkin's chest rumbled under her cheek as he chuckled. "Right away, though, your father recognized what he'd done, had a good laugh at himself."

Suddenly, Larkin stopped them dead on the dance floor. "What's that song they're playing?" He held her close and listened as the fiddler, foot tapping, led the guitar player and pianist in a rousing bit of music.

She looked up at him with a twinkle in her eye. "You should recognize the tune, you whistle it half the time. It's Kitty O'Neil. I requested it for you."

"Damn," he said softly, "it is. Thank you, wife."

"You're welcome, husband."

Three or four dances later, she asked, "Larkin, are you hungry?" she tilted her head toward the tables lining the room and loaded with food.

"Heck of a note," he shrugged, "but I don't know. I'm so out-of-my-mind happy we're finally married, I can't hardly think of anything else." He whispered then, his lips touching her ear, "all right, I am thinking of when we can leave here and head for die ranch. Ma has fixed my room up, her idea of a honeymoon chamber." He grinned wickedly, "Of course, that's not everything I'm thinking about."

Clare shook her head at his teasing. Flushing, she told him, "I didn't think it was."

They walked to the table set with the hotel's best china, along with Momma's dishes and crystal. At the opposite end, Reverend Goodlander conversed with Mayor Fuller and both men appeared to be upset.

Clare tried to pay them no mind, but it was hard not to overhear.

The reverend was saying, doing his best to keep his voice down, "All I'm asking, is that you take your meals elsewhere and not at our home, Mr. Fuller. Liddy is no longer comfortable providing your meals and she's asked me, to ask you, to understand and not come to our house again."

"I don't understand Liddy's objection," Mayor Fuller blustered. "I pay her generously for the meals she prepares for me. She's the one who suggested I take meals at your house in the first place, and help supplement your income."

"Actually, you don't pay her all that well. But there are other reasons that I won't go into now. This isn't the time or place." He threw an apologetic look in Clare and Larkin's direction. He finished quietly, speaking to Fuller, "My wife and I don't wish you ill will, we just ask that you not come again. That you find somewhere else to take your meals. Now, it's time I took Liddy and Gordy home. We'd like to spend some time together before I have to take to the road again."

Fuller glared after the minister, grabbed a plate, and heaped it high with sliced ham, bread, pickles, scalloped potatoes, and baked apples.

"Now that was an odd conversation," Clare murmured to Larkin when Fuller stalked off with his food.

"It was, but I think the minister handled it fine. You could tell it was a serious matter with him, but at the same time, he was careful not to spoil our wedding day."

"Nothing could spoil our wedding day, or this night!"

Later, as they drove home in Larkin's buggy, bundled to the

eyebrows, Clare sat back and looked up at the starry sky, feeling drunk with joy. She caught Larkin looking at her and in the mix of shadow and moonlight his eyes gleamed. Wordlessly, he took her hand and held it tight between them.

Clare had been in every part of the Wade ranch house but never in Larkin's room. It was larger than she expected, very clean, furnished with a masculine hand. This night there were feminine touches. Mabel had placed candles in exquisite holders, bouquets of silk flowers on the bureau and dresser. "This is your room?" she said inanely.

"Mine. Now ours." He walked over to a cherry red, floral decorated lamp with a gold plated base that sat on the bedside table. He lit it and it glowed softly. "The lamp is our wedding present from Ma. That and the mirror."

"They are beautiful. And very thoughtful of her." The mirror was a free-standing cheval style.

"Look in the mirror, Clare," he said huskily, "and see the beauty of you, that I see."

She looked, saw a young woman with passion-filled eyes, and an eager, trembling mouth. She spoke softly, on a catch of breath, "I'm not interested in myself, but in you. I love you, Larkin, I've always loved you so very, very much." Reaching for her neckline, feeling bold and shy at the same time, she began to unbutton the bodice of her wedding dress.

"Let me." He took over the unbuttoning, slowly fingering one button at a time, his fingertips grazing her rising bosom. She caught his face and brought his lips to hers, brushing his mouth with her lips and lightly with her tongue.

"God, Clare!" He returned her kisses, gently, sweetly, and then with fierce hunger. Her dress fell in a pile of violet silk and she stepped out of it.

"I love you, Larkin," Clare breathed between kisses, "love you, love you, love you." She peeled out of two petticoats.

"As I've loved you my darling," he helped with the fasteners of her corset cover and corset, "every hour and every day, from the first moment we met." He pulled her tighter, pressing his arousal tight against her.

Her breath caught, and her own desire flamed deep within her.

He motioned with his head at the bed behind them. "I'll be as gentle as I can, sweetheart." He asked in a rumble of impatience, "Do women always wear so many garments under their dress?"

Together, they managed to remove her stockings.

"Winter and summer," she answered with a giggle, "every blessed day."

"Well thank God they come off!" He nibbled at her ear, kissed the swell of her breasts above her chemise, crooned as he cupped her breasts in his hands. "It's been a long time, waiting for this night. I've been so hungry for you..."

"And I for you. Love me however you want to love me, Larkin. I've waited just as long." Off came her chemise and drawers and she stood naked before him.

He made a sound of revelation and his eyes flashed in delight. He whispered, "Just what I always dreamed of, only better, so much better. You're beautiful, Clare, you take my breath away."

A gentle wind outside their window accompanied their urgent breathing and each movement as they disrobed him. They reveled in the sight of each other for as long as it was bearable. Then, with a husky groan, Larkin lifted her in his arms and carried her to the bed. She slipped between the sun-dried sheets, watched him come to her, her own body possessed with wanting him.

Clare had never felt such bliss and abandon, as Larkin slid into bed beside her and took her into his arms. She met her husband's kisses and caresses with her own. When she could wait no longer, her body rose to be claimed and to give in return.

In rhythm with their lovemaking, the music from their wedding dance re-played in her mind, beautiful beyond all imagining. The pleasure of their love and the music was pure and explosive, climaxing in a grand crescendo.

After a while they rested, laughing softly in wonder at how it was to truly express their love as man and wife, how they had always known this night would be. They continued to kiss in sheer, starved delight, and then were ready for more.

"I've got to build us a house of our own," he said later. "So all our nights can be as private and wonderful as this."

She leaned over him and kissed his mouth. "Private until the patter of little feet arrive!" she reminded. "But oh, my darling, I'm glad this night is ours alone. The rest of the world can just take care of itself."

————

IT WAS STILL a joyous miracle to Clare, in the weeks following their wedding, that she could wake and find Larkin in bed beside her. A wonder that they could make love every night, legal and proper, and twice if they wanted.

It was a trifle embarrassing, but hardly a surprise, when in April, just two months after their wedding, she realized she was expecting a baby.

Content and the happiest she'd ever been in her life, Clare loved to drowsily open her eyes, see her husband dressing quietly in dawn shadows before going out to chores and trying not to wake her.

That their individual obligations kept them apart during the day only added to the anticipation and pleasure of spending time together at day's end.

When Clare couldn't be at the hotel, Rachel, Flora's daughter, replaced her at the hotel desk, registering guests and collecting payments. The young woman had turned out to be a smart and friendly addition to the staff, and she loved her work.

Occasionally, as the weeks passed, Clare and Ma bumped elbows as they ran the household together at the ranch, but it was no never mind, they laughed, apologized, and went on about their business.

Clare could have lived with her mother-in-law indefinitely, but Larkin insisted they have their own home, for their family. Ma Wade and Nick would live in the older house.

It was four months after their wedding, a beautiful sunny June morning, when Clare prepared for her drive to town and her duties at the hotel. She surmised that the meringue of billowy clouds on the far horizon might indicate a coming storm, or not. It was difficult to tell about the weather in Kansas. One just watched and kept guard for any possibility.

Still on their property a quarter mile west, their new home was rising. Clare drew the buggy to a halt in the dusty road out front, feeling especially content to watch for a few minutes the carpenters hammering and sawing her house into shape. Larkin and she had chosen the conservative design together. It would be a white two-story, with a pillared porch and balcony above with a bit of ornament woodwork on the eaves, and window alcoves, but not too fancy.

It was easy to picture a whole flock of their children playing in the yard and she smiled to herself. There would be a swing in that elm tree right there by the house. She'd plant a matrimony vine to shade the porch. Til they were very old, happily ever after, Larkin and she would sit on the porch in matching rockers at sunset and watch night come gently over their ranch, their world.

A distant rumble of thunder broke into her reverie. She sighed, then clicked her tongue. Her driving mare set off at a gentle lope. The clouds were darkening, the air grown humid and close. In the field off the road, their horses trotted back and forth restlessly, sensing the storm. Gusts of wind stirred the dust in the road; a few fat raindrops made dark circles as they splatted.

Might as well make a quick side trip on the way to town to check on Momma and Poppa, she decided, her eyes on the dark clouds. Her family was managing better than she'd expected without her, but worrying was a habit slow to break.

The wind practically threw Clare into the house when she arrived.

"I can only stay a minute," she told Momma who was clearing away breakfast dishes. "Where's Poppa and Oakley, out in the barn? Didn't they plan to cut wild hay today? It'll be dangerous out there, what with the storm, they'd better put off cutting hay until tomorrow."

"Poppa had to go into town before daybreak to the blacksmith shop. Mayor Fuller has an important job for him to do. That man is so impatient! Oakley's out at the barn finishing the choring."

"The chickens should be kept penned, until the storm's over. The other livestock will be better off in the barn, too."

"Oakley knows, he'll see to it."

"Where's Hallie? She should be helping you here in the kitchen, Momma."

"Now, Clare, there's no need for you to tell us what we have to do. The way you're constantly after us, you'd think we have sawdust for brains and can't think for ourselves. You have yourself to think about, and Larkin."

"Sorry, Momma. I just wondered about Hallie."

"Well, stop worrying. Hallie is upstairs making beds. We were going to do the wash today, but I'm not sure it's safe to be outside. The thunder and lightning is far off now, but that could change in a minute. Kansas storms, it seems to me, just don't know when to quit."

Clare laughed, "I think you're right about that. And I'd better be on my way or I'll be caught out in it before I reach the hotel." She hesitated at the door, "Has Alice been here to the farm, lately? I hardly ever see her, she's so busy with her new family." Clare's plan was to let Alice be the first in the family to hear that she expected a baby. Larkin, of course, already knew, his excitement at the prospect as great as Clare's.

"Alice was here two days ago, telling us how she's fixing up her house. Tobias insists she buy anything new that she wants, curtains, dishes, even a sewing machine. She's making new clothes for the children. I don't think I ever saw a happier, more content woman in my life. Well, you are, too, Clare. I just never thought it would be like this for Alice, after the incident with Everett, Samuel's boy. She loves Tobias and his children, and they love her."

Clare nodded. "She just glows, the times I do see her. We can all be thankful for Tobias, making this wonderful change to her life." She took a few steps back across the room and kissed Momma's cheek. "I'm happy for all of us. And now I really have to go!"

"Be careful driving in this storm, Clare."

"I will." She headed outside into a humid morning turned dark as night.

Chapter Twenty-One

THE STORM STRUCK SWEETBRIER FULL FORCE JUST AS CLARE arrived at the hotel. Thunder rumbled, lightning zig-zagged across the sky, and it started to rain. She pulled her rig into the hotel shed, unhitched, grained her mare, made sure there was plenty of water in the trough, and then hurried inside the hotel.

In the kitchen, she whipped off her damp shawl and hung it by the door. "Whatever you're cooking, Hattie, it smells delicious!"

Hattie, at her work table shelling peas, turned with a broad smile, "Pot roast, brown gravy, and them fat noodles." She motioned to where streamers of snowy noodles dried on a rack at the opposite end of the table. "Farmers come into town say that's their favorite meal when they eat here with us."

"Beef and noodles are Larkin's favorite, certainly. Anything I should get you from the market?"

"Been there already. I ran out of flour from making the noodles. Bought some lemon extract while I was there. Dessert today will be lemon pie."

"Sounds delicious! You're a wonderful cook, Hattie, and very good for business. I want you to know that. And if you need anything, let me know."

Hattie pushed straggles of gray hair out of her eyes. "If I do need somethin', I'll go myself, or send Rachel. No need for you to go back out in this messy weather."

Clare laughed, "Not only are you a good cook, you're a bit bossy!"

In the lobby, Clare asked Rachel, "How are things this morning?"

"Two of the drummers who came last week checked out this morning after breakfast. They said they'd wait at the saloon til time for the train. The drummer who came day before yesterday took his sample cases and said he believed he'd hire a rig and go on down to White City today. He didn't check out, he'll be stayin' here tonight."

"Good. Did Mayor Fuller catch up with paying for his room? He's two months in arrears."

"He came down for breakfast and then went out. Didn't ask him for the rent, he kind of gives me the willies."

"Blast his hide!" Clare used a very useful expression she'd learned since coming to Kansas. "He knows his rent is past due, I'll wring it out of him one way or another."

"Do you want me to go help mother clean the rooms?"

"Yes, Rachel, please, if you will. Is that a new dress? Very pretty. And I like your hair the new way, with your pigtails put up in a coronet. You look very grown up."

"Mother let me buy the dress with my pay from here at the hotel. She said I look grownup, too. And Mrs. Wade, next time the mayor comes in, I'll ask for the rent. I'll just be ready to duck if he gets mad."

Clare laughed, "You don't have to deal with him, I will. It's my job."

Later, she sat at her desk in the lobby, going over her record books. It was hard not to flinch, and be distracted, at each horrendous clap of thunder. As a child, she always believed thunder was a giant in the sky emptying his potatoes into a house-size bin. Kansas storms were greater than she remembered in New England, and this one sounded unbelievably ferocious.

Moments later she thought she heard the ringing of a bell between rumbles. She listened to see if the sound came from the direction of the doctor's house but it was too noisy outside to pick up the sound again. Mrs. Williams, the doctor's wife, used the bell to let the doctor know a patient needed to see him, rang it to bring Doctor Williams from wherever he was about town. Clare frowned, feeling increasingly uneasy as she returned to her work. Quite often, the bell was for a patient who needed a boil lanced, or a tooth pulled. On a day like this a need for Doc Williams could be for a more desperate cause. She rose and closed the record book.

"Hattie," she called into the kitchen, "I'm going out for a minute." She called up the stairway, "Rachel, would you keep an eye on the front desk for me?",

Hattie came bustling from the kitchen, "'Course we can mind things here, but you oughtn't to go out in a storm like this, Mrs. Wade! Why don't you wait til it lets up?"

"I'll be all right and I'll hurry back." She tied on her bonnet, threw her damp shawl over her shoulders. "I thought I heard the doctor's bell and I want to make sure there's no emergency. Someone might need help, might need shelter here at the hotel."

"We'll watch for you."

She reached the door at the same moment it slammed open in her face. Eva Cahill from the hardware store stood there, white as a sheet, her eyes dark with horror.

"What is it?" Clare pulled her inside and closed the door against the wind and rain. "What's happened? I thought I heard the doctor's bell. Is someone hurt from the storm?"

Eva nodded, her lips moved but nothing came out.

"What has happened, Eva? Please tell me! Who got hurt?"

"It was him, over to the implement yard," Eva mumbled. "Poor man got struck by lightning! Doc couldn't do a tiling for him and he's dead. I thought you should know, seeing how he's family."

"Who?" Clare grabbed Eva's arms and shook her. "Tobias? Larkin?" Larkin planned to come to town today but not until this afternoon. Had he come in early? "Who, Eva? Tell me!" she demanded, again, "who got struck by lightning? Who was killed?" Unable to wait, she released the frightened, tongue-tied woman, yanked the door open and raced toward the implement yard.

Eva followed, regaining her voice to a near shout as she caught up and ran alongside Clare, "Why, it's Tobias, we're fair sure. Poor fella hardly looks like himself, though. Hair scorched off. Skin's burnt the color of an Indian. Bones are all broke up inside from the lightning slamming him into a big old threshing machine he had sittin' there. Doc got there real quick but it was too late."

Oh, my God, poor Tobias. Poor Alice! This couldn't be

happening. Alice and Tobias had only begun their life together, were so happy. She prayed for there to be a mistake. Alice, after so many unhappy years had found true love. It couldn't be over so soon.

Clare slowed her steps, calling to Eva, "Alice? Does Alice know?" Whoever carried word to her, if they had, must be gentle. "Has she been sent for?" The words were hardly out when she spotted Alice melting into the crowd gathering in the implement yard. The children weren't with her, had evidently been told to stay safe at home.

Pushing her way into the rain-drenched group, Clare moved close by Alice. "Sister." She placed an arm around Alice's weaving form, held on tight. Alice, whimpering, held her hands down toward Tobias's terribly still form, his discolored, barely recognizable face. Clare's voice was thick with emotion, "I'm so sorry, Alice, I'm so sorry."

"Move back, everyone," the doctor ordered, and kneeling, he began to wrap Tobias in a sheet for carrying him away.

Alice tore abruptly from Clare's grasp, sprawled to her knees and began tearing the sheet away. "No!" she sobbed, "no!"

"Now, Mrs. Proctor," the doctor drew her to her feet and spoke gently but firmly, "he's gone. We'll take him to my office for the coroner's report." He got to his feet and signaled with his eyes for the waiting men to take Tobias away. He barred Alice from interfering. "He didn't have a chance, Ma'am. The lightning hit that big machine over there, and then slammed into Tobias. He got burned with electric shock, and it appears that he's broke all up inside from the hit. I can't get no pulse. Poor fella. I'm so sorry, Mrs. Proctor."

"Alice, dear, come with me, please." Clare choked, and tried to draw her away.

Alice made a small animal-like wail, tried to follow Tobias, and then collapsed in an unconscious heap at Clare's feet.

Clare dropped to her knees. She rubbed Alice's arms, her face. She gripped her hand and implored, "Wake up, Alice, please, dear! I want to take care of you, walk you to the hotel. Please, please wake up. This will be all right, somehow, it will be all right."

But Alice didn't respond. Clare closed her eyes and held her sister's upper body in her arms, her heart aching with pain for Alice. This was not fair, this was not right! The poor orphan boy from New York should not come to this dreadful end here in Kansas. It was criminal this should be happening to Alice, who'd been treated so badly by life already. She was much too fragile to withstand such tragedy as this.

"She's fainted," someone said.

"I know that," Clare answered in despair. "Now I just wish she didn't have to wake up to all this right away. She's going to take this very, very hard. Will someone help me carry her to the hotel?"

Gully Cahill stooped and eased Alice from Clare's arms into his own and stood up. He shook his head, looked down on Alice's still face, her closed eyes. "This poor woman. Only barely married. Who'd of thought lightning would strike Tobias, of all the folks it could hit?"

Dinger Toledo stood behind Clare, now on her feet, and she could smell his stench even above the sulphur smells of the lightning strike. He was saying, "I remember hearing tell about a boy struck by lightning. Out in western Kansas, it was. He was carrying a bucket in each hand when the lightning hit. He was all charred when they found him so that you hardly knew who he was. Folks tried to pry the bails of the buckets from his fingers and his fingers fell plumb off."

Another man began in a sonorous voice, "I heard tell of another fella who was so swole up and charred black you couldn't recognize him and—"

"Do you have to tell such stories right now?" Clare turned on them angrily.

Toledo looked at her from flat, olive eyes and he shrugged. The other man shriveled under her sharp glare. Others watching, who had a story to share, decided to save it for another time.

Doctor Williams touched Clare's arm as she prepared to follow the men carrying Alice. "I'll send a tonic over, something to help her sleep until she's ready to accept what's happened. And Mrs. Wade, you take care of yourself, hear?"

"Thank you, doctor." Clare wiped the tears and rain from her face with the end of her shawl. "I wish this day had never happened. This is so unfair to my poor dear, sister. And to Tobias. And his children—all of us have lost so much today."

He gave her shoulder a pat, "If you need a tonic for yourself, I'll send that along, too."

She shook her head. "I'm fine."

What she needed was for things to be as they were yesterday. And she needed Larkin. She must send someone to give him the sad news about Tobias, his partner and dear friend. Larkin. was another person who'd take this hard. She wished she could find him and tell him, herself. But Alice needed her, and then there were Tobias's children to be told.

Alice's eyes opened soon after she was put to bed upstairs at the hotel, but she was silent and unresponsive, as though all emotion and thought had fled her heart and soul. The medicine arrived from the doctor and Clare got a spoonful into Alice's mouth. She held Alice's hand, and begged, "Dearest sister, talk to me. Look at me."

There was no sign she heard. After a while, the medicine took effect and her eyes fluttered shut. She began to breathe deep in sleep. With a heavy sigh, Clare went to tell her staff that she must go out again.

"I'm going to see Alice and Tobias's children. I believe they are at home. They need to be told. I'll bring them here to the hotel to be with Alice."

"That should help her," Hattie said, and Flora and Rachel nodded agreement.

"I believe it will be better for the children, too, to be with Alice. If she wakes up, keep her here, please. She may want to pay respects to her poor husband and if so, Rachel, accompany her there, but let's pray she waits until later this evening. Other than that, give her anything she needs. I'll be right back."

Outside, the storm was over. The air was fresh and sweet, a gentle wind blew, but Clare hardly noticed. She was more concerned, on her way to the Proctor house on the edge of town, how she would tell Beth and Will about their father, about Alice.

As she approached, she saw young Will chucking stones at the woodpile at the side of the green-shuttered cottage. "Please come inside with me, Will, I need to talk to you and Beth." Inside, the house smelled of breakfast bacon Alice had cooked earlier that morning, and yeasty bread dough she'd left rising on the kitchen table. Beth played with paper dolls strewn on the floor. "I have some bad news." Looking at their sweet inquisitive faces, she realized that she couldn't tell them, yet, that their father was dead.

That could come later, and perhaps Alice would want to tell them herself. "There's been an accident due to the storm. I've come to take you back to the hotel with me, it's best that you two not be here alone."

"A man came for Mama Alice. He didn't tell her what happened, but just for her to come with him in a hurry," Beth said, her small face twisted in puzzlement.

"We were told to stay here out of the storm," Will said. "Did something happen to our father? Mama Alice seemed awful upset. Is she taking care of him? Are they all right?"

"You'll be told everything, I promise," she said around a thickness in her throat. "Alice is at the hotel—waiting for us. Come now."

Like little robots, Will and Beth obediently washed their faces and hands, and they started off for the hotel, one on each side of Clare, holding her hands. The bright sun was quickly drying the path to dust again.

When they reached main street, Clare immediately sensed a change in the mood of the townsfolk still milling about. There were smiles. Jubilant-seeming conversations. What on earth...? She hurried, pulling the children with her.

Gully Cahill was the first person she readied and she grabbed his arm and asked him, "What is going on? What is this that everyone is chattering about?"

"He ain't dead," Gully reared back, grinning widely. "Doc was getting ready to put Tobias in the cold box til he could fix him for burial. But Tobias twitched a little, tried to say somethin'."

"Really?" Clare gasped, "is this true?" Her hand pressed her heart.

"Tears the lightning bolt just knocked Tobias out. Maybe his pulse was just too weak for Doc to find it. Men carryin' Tobias to the doc's place thought they felt him move, but figgered it was their imagination. Doctor Williams says Tobias's heart is beatin' strong now, good as you please."

She covered her mouth with her hand. It was difficult to speak. "Are you absolutely positive? Tobias is alive?"

"Saw him myself," Gully chortled. "I didn't believe it at first, neither, but Tobias is breathing. He's in bad shape, Doc says, but with the right care, he'll likely live."

"I pray that's so! What truly grand news." Her heart was beginning to pound erratically with excitement. Thinking of the tiny little nubbin of a baby in her abdomen, she regained calm. She wanted so much to believe Gully, and the others around her exclaiming about the miracle. "Mr. Cahill, are you very sure?"

"Yup. He come back from the dead like, and as alive as you an' me."

"Thank you!" Clare said. "Oh, my goodness, thank you. Thank God! Come children. We must tell your Mama Alice what's happened."

"Can we see our daddy first?" Beth asked.

Clare hesitated, thinking it over. "Possibly. But understand, the doctor might not let us see him right away. We'll run and ask, but Alice needs to hear this good news too. The doctor gave her something to help her sleep, but by now she might be waking. We want her to know, right away that everything will be all right."

Mrs. Williams, cheery-faced and silvered haired, met them at the door to the doctor's combined office and home. "Doctor is with your father, now," she told the children. "Could you come back later? Doctor has asked me to tell visitors that Tobias will recover, but right now he needs the doctor's attention, and a lot of rest. All right?"

Will and Beth nodded in solemn unison.

"We have stick candy for visitors," the doctor's wife said, and handed them each a striped peppermint stick, bringing smiles to their faces.

"We'll return," Clare told Mrs. Williams, "if you'll send word to the hotel when the time is right for visiting. I'll bring the children with me, and Alice."

"You and your sister take care of yourselves," Mrs. Williams said, as she saw dare and the children out the door. "Mr. Proctor will be all right, with time and care."

A few minutes later, Clare hurried into the hotel and immediately asked Rachel, behind the registration desk, "How is Alice? Has she come around? I've brought the children."

Rachel looked bewildered. She brought both hands to her cheeks and shook her head, "None of us saw her leave, but Mrs. Proctor's not here anymore. We don't know where she is."

"Not here? But I have wonderful news for her. Tobias is alive, after all."

Rachel gulped, "Mr. Proctor's not dead?"

Flora and Cook came from the kitchen when they heard voices. Clare repeated her news, "The lightning must have weakened his pulse for a bit, or maybe Doc isn't experienced enough to have found it from the start. But Tobias is breathing, he's alive. His condition is still grave, but the doctor feels that he'll survive."

"Alice will be so happy to hear it!" Flora said. "We're sorry she slipped away from us, Mrs. Wade."

"She must be found right away. Did she seem all right? She was in such deep shock and confusion. I was glad for the medicine that helped her sleep."

"She come around," Cook told her, "but sad like a house had fallen on her. Odd though, she hardly shed a tear. Just looked empty and—crushed. Said she had to go home. I told her you went for the children and to wait here for you all. But she slipped out when we wasn't lookin'. I had a roast of beef startin' to burn in the oven, didn't want to set the place afire. When I went back to her room and found her gone, I reckoned she'd left to find you."

"I just came from her house, and then we went by the doctor's office. We didn't see her along the way." Clare warded off a wave of apprehension. "Maybe she meant she wanted to go home to my parents. That's it, surely. I'll look for her there. If I don't find her and she comes back here, please tell her about Tobias. She may have already heard, and is at the doctor's and we just missed one another at some point. I'll check for her at the doctor's first."

"You go on and don't worry a speck. We'll keep an eye out for Alice, won't we, children? I got some sandwich fixins' and a chocolate cake I baked and iced this mornin'. An' you can play checkers, if you want, in the parlor."

"Thank you, Hattie." Clare gave her shoulder a pat. "I'll be back as soon as I can."

Alice had not been to the doctor's office, nor had she been seen anywhere else around town. Clare got her team and buggy from the shed. Under a hot sun, she drove hard to the farm, praying over and over that she'd find Alice with Momma and Poppa. She had to be there!

"No," Poppa said, "we haven't seen her."

"She didn't come here to the farm today," Momma said. "Is something wrong, Clare? You're acting strange."

She told them about Tobias, that he'd been struck by lightning and that the doctor had pronounced him dead. "Doctor Williams told Alice that Tobias was dead. But the lightning had just knocked him out. Tobias isn't out of the woods yet, but he's alive and the doctor believes he will get well."

"Alice doesn't know he came—awake?" Momma frowned worriedly.

"No, she doesn't. Unless she's met up with someone, wherever she went, and they've told her. It seems odd that our paths haven't crossed either in town or on the road here. Very strange that you haven't seen her, that no one has."

"I vow, this is worrisome," Poppa said, dropping into a chair and reaching a shaking hand for his pipe on the side table.

"I am very worried. We have to find her. I'm going back to town and if she's not at the hotel, or the doctor's office—if no one's seen her, we'll ask for help to go looking for her. Make a wide search." She kissed her mother's cheek and held her hand for a moment. "Momma, I'd like for you and Hallie to stay here in case Alice comes to the farm. Poppa, will you bring Oakley so the two of you can help look for her?"

"I should come with you, Clare," Momma said. "I can help with tasks you want done."

"No, Momma, please stay here and wait for Alice. If she's on her way here, by some roundabout way, you'll want to be here for her."

"We'll come in our own wagon to search, maybe pick up other folks on the way," Poppa said. "You go on, daughter, but drive careful and don't worry too much. We'll be right behind you."

Clare nodded, feeling a nervous quiver in her stomach. Alice had to be all right, she just had to be.

Chapter Twenty-Two

CLARE HAD GONE A SHORT DISTANCE ON THE WAY BACK toward town, when she saw Larkin on his blood bay gelding loping to meet her. Relief to see him brought her close to tears. As they drew abreast, she halted the buggy. He drew his shuffling mount alongside, leaped to the ground and lifted her from the buggy into his arms.

"What a morning you've had, poor darling," he whispered against her ear. He kissed her and held her tightly for several seconds. When he drew away, his hand caressed her abdomen in concerned affection. "How's our little one?"

"The baby's all right. B-but, you know what happened to Tobias? You've seen him?"

"Yes." A shudder went through him. "Poor cuss, it was a close call. I don't know if I could've stood it, if he'd been killed. He's the best friend I ever had."

"Is he any better?" She wiped her eyes.

"He's conscious now and in awful pain. Doc is doing everything he can for him. I told him there's no limits. Whatever Tobias needs by way of medicine and such, he's to have it."

She lifted her gaze to her husband's beloved face. Holding her breath in hope, she asked, "Did you see Alice? Was she with Tobias?"

"No," he said solemnly. "I heard she's missing. No one in town has seen her. She wasn't at your Pa's place?"

Clare shook her head. "No, she wasn't. I'm so worried, Larkin. It's all very strange. She couldn't just vanish." Beginning to shake, she clutched at his shirtfront, "What are we going to do?"

"We'll find her, I promise you, Sweetheart. Just hold on and try not to get too upset. We can get the whole town out in a search for her."

His words soothed, and helped revive her determination. "Yes, we will find her! Poppa and Oakley are coming in their wagon right behind me. They may bring other folks with them to help in the search."

"Good. Keep hope, Clare."

"I will. I am." Her mind touched tentatively, then rebelled from, fears which no doubt would turn out to be groundless. Nevertheless. In the end, her deep concern won and she told Larkin, a tremor in her voice, "I'm afraid that Alice might have done something very, very foolish." He looked at her in growing alarm. Clare bit her lip and continued, "She loved Tobias with all her heart, and for all she knew, he was killed."

"You think she might—hurt herself?" He looked stunned, deeply worried.

She sighed, "I think it's possible. She suffered a great deal when she was separated from her first love. That episode changed her whole personality, her outlook on life. She was like a ghost, a hollow person, only going through the motions of being. Sometimes I think she wanted to die. Then she found Tobias and fell iii love with him, when it was the last thing anyone expected. I know she believed she'd never love again til she met Tobias." Tears filmed her eyes. "I hope it turns out there's a perfectly logical reason for her disappearance, that she's fine, and we'll all wonder why we worried so much."

A breeze tossed Clare's hair into her eyes and with tender fingers Larkin brushed it back behind her ear. His other hand rested on her waist.

"Like I said, don't give up that we'll find her alive and well. Maybe she's just very sad and confused and she wandered off to think—to get her bearings." He shook his head and said quietly, "But you could be right about—the other."

Clare explained that Momma and Hallie had stayed at the farm in case Alice showed up there.

Larkin nodded. "I sent word out to Ma about what happened and that she's to keep an eye out for Alice, too. Darlin' I want you to wait at the hotel. You need to take care of yourself, and think of our young one. Besides, Alice might come there."

"I want to help search for her," she was adamant.

"Clare, please," he grasped her shoulders. "The hotel would be the first place she'd look for you, and if she needs to talk, you'd be the one she'd want. I don't—"

Of course he was right that she should consider their unborn child and try not to get anymore upset than she was. She reached up to cover his hand with hers. "You're afraid I'll see something you don't want me to see, when Alice is found, that's it, too, isn't it?"

He didn't reply directly, but she saw the answer in his eyes. He pulled her to him. "It's best for you and our baby that you stay put at the hotel."

In the end he convinced her and she told him, "I'll help Hattie prepare sandwiches and lemonade for the search parties. They can come in shifts to the hotel."

"No telling how long the search will take. But we can hope we find her real soon."

———

IT WASN'T the search parties, but Hattie who found Alice's body that evening when she went to empty scraps into the scrap barrel in the alley behind the hotel.

Clare hurried from the lobby in the direction of the kitchen when she heard Hattie's stricken cry, "Clare! Mrs. Wade. Come. I found her."

Hattie explained, wild-eyed and distraught, "She's out there in the alley. Alice is dead, Mrs. Wade. I touched her. She's very cold, and not breathin'. I think she jumped from that room way upstairs, somehow." She grabbed Clare's hands, her voice was forlorn, "I wouldn't have seen her except that I spotted a bit of calico showing in that pile of stone leftover from rebuilding the front porch. The alley was likely searched, but she'd be hard to see."

The spark of hope Clare had held to tightly flickered out. She clutched the edge of the nearby kitchen work table and leaned against it. *Oh, Alice.* It was impossible to comprehend that this could happen, and yet, Clare realized, she had feared this very thing subconsciously for years. "I want Larkin found," she said through a tight throat, "and I suppose Sheriff Seavers will want to investigate. If you'll send for Doctor Williams, too, Hattie, I'll be grateful. As you know, he's Sweetbrier's undertaker, as well as healer. I'm going out to be with Alice. She shouldn't be alone."

Clare was sitting on a pile of stone beside Alice's body when Larkin arrived. Her throat ached with defeat, and she pounded Larkin's chest as he held her, "If only Alice had waited a bit longer! She would've found out that Tobias didn't die, that they still would have a life together."

He caressed her, his face taut with sadness. "I reckon the pain of loss—all that Alice supposed she lost—was just too great for her to carry. She couldn't go on."

Clare shook with sobs, tears streamed down her face. "What a waste, oh, Larkin, what a waste! She was a beautiful person, so good with children, so kind to everyone. Tobias and the children are going to be devastated. They'll miss her dreadfully, we all will. Dear God, why did she have to die?"

He told her with a catch in his voice, "Don't torture yourself, sweetheart. I'm afraid there isn't an easy answer, though in time we may come to understand this better, and the pain won't hurt so much."

"I won't ever forget her."

"No, you won't. Now, dearest, I want you to come inside. I'm going to find your family and bring them here to the hotel. They'll want to be with you. I'll take care of the rest."

Her anguish caused her to stumble as he led her toward the hotel's back door. She looked over her shoulder one last time, and whispered, "I love you, sister."

A while later, Sheriff Seaver arrived, his high-crowned hat in hand. He faced Clare where she sat on a sofa in the hotel parlor. She was numb, the cup of tea Hattie'd made for her was untouched on the nearby table. Her staff hovered, ready to do battle with anyone who might say, or do anything, to upset her further. She looked at the sheriff and asked in a faint, empty voice, "You have something to tell me, Sheriff?"

He nodded solemnly, "It's my conclusion and Doc's that Alice took her own life. From what we can guess, she went to the attic three stories up, climbed out of the window onto that narrow parapet, and closed the window behind her. God knows how she managed to crawl on up higher to the roof, but she did. That's where she jumped from. Doc said her neck was broken from landing in that pile of stone, that she died instantly and without pain."

Clare was too stricken to answer. Her hands went up to her face and she shook her head. Rachel knelt by her chair, "If there's anything I can do, just tell me."

"My family are on the way, and Larkin will be coming back. If you'd make a fresh pot of coffee, please." She squeezed Rachel's hand then let it go.

The sheriff waited, then said, "You take care of yourself, Mrs. Wade." He left a few moments later.

———

"I'LL WRITE home to Hobb's Mills of her passing," Clare told the family after they'd gathered in the hotel parlor to grieve privately. "All I'm going to tell Grandmother and the others is that Alice died in a fall, which is the truth. I will make it clear that she was very happy the last months of her life, that she had married a fine man with two children. Also true," she added in a faint whisper.

Momma, weeping quietly, nodded. "That's best. Thank you, Clare."

"Tobias is a good man," Poppa's spoke sadly. "He would've taken care of Alice. He'd of given her a fine life. If only she hadn't gotten it wrong that he was dead."

"That's true, Poppa," Clare said. She asked gently, "Hallie, would you like to say anything?"

Hallie, mute with grief, her eyes red from crying, shook her head.

"Oakley?"

"I just wish she hadn't done it." He mopped his face with the heel of his hand. "I wish there was a way to bring her back."

"I think that's how we all feel. It's going to be hard to go on without our Alice, but we must. Let's remember all the good things about her, I believe that's what she would have wanted."

"And love one another, she would have wanted that," Momma said.

Filially, Hallie spoke, "And keep Alice in our hearts, forever."

"Amen," came their united whisper.

———

LARKIN WANTED to wait until Tobias was stronger before telling him about Alice and Clare agreed that was best. Leaving out the harsher details, Clare and Larkin together told Beth and William that Alice had died in an unfortunate fall, but that she had loved them and they must always remember that.

Clare insisted on taking the children home to the ranch, until Tobias was well enough to care for them himself. Ma Wade welcomed the youngsters with the same warm heart she'd had for Larkin when he was handed to her—a baby in a basket.

The simple funeral was unutterably sad. Many from the community attended because they truly cared about Alice, about Tobias, and their families.

Others were anxious to be a real part of what they saw as an exciting and lurid episode of Sweetbrier history. Clare took note, but was too benumbed to mind.

A few stated self-righteously they couldn't possibly attend the burial ceremony because God did not welcome in heaven a person who chose to take her own life.

Clare maintained tiredly to herself that God would be more kindly than that. Who but He would have more intimate knowledge and understanding of how and why Alice did what she did?

The chief topic of conversation swirling about the community for days after the funeral was, "the woman who went mad and jumped off the roof of the hotel."

"Pay no mind to what they're saying," Larkin urged Clare, over and over. "They are fools and before you know it, something else will come up for them to gossip about."

"But it's all so ugly, that they keep talking about Alice this way. She wasn't 'mad', she was heartbroken and she couldn't handle the pain. I overhear the talk everywhere I go and it's sure to reach Momma and Poppa's ears. I hate them all for saying these things. They are wrong and it's hurtful!"

Work at both the ranch and at the hotel provided Clare mindless escape from grief that at times felt as though it would consume her. No matter that her good sense told her that life was for the living, that they must go on, her sorrow was akin to traveling a dark tunnel, the light at the end constantly moving from reach.

———

ONE DAY, the mayor came huffing into the hotel demanding to see Clare, his voice loud enough to carry to the kitchen where Clare was going over the food budget with Hattie. Larkin stood up from the kitchen table; he'd stopped by for a cup of coffee, as was his practice when in town. Together they went out to the lobby where Mayor Fuller ranted loudly, "Your father's finally done it, gone completely insane. You better come with me on over to the blacksmith shop, Clare Wade! See what Frank's done, now." Fuller saw Larkin then, and added, "Good tiling you're here, Wade, you can help hold Frank from doing more damage."

"Damage? What on earth are you talking about?" Clare asked, anxiety rising.

"Come on with me, and see for yourself! If Sam hadn't stopped him in time, Frank would have destroyed the blacksmith shop, put Sam Dorsey out of business. Somebody could have been hurt, killed."

"Nonsense, you can't know what you're talking about." A frown furrowed Clare's brow, her heart beat fast, as Larkin took her arm and they followed Fuller's hurrying figure along the plank walk to the blacksmith shop.

A few minutes later, Clare stared aghast at the mess. Buckets of nails had been dumped in wide swaths on the shop floor, bins and boxes of scrap iron were pitched helter-skelter, tools were thrown through a broken window.

Behind Clare, Larkin whistled softly.

"Poppa, did you have something to do with this?" she asked. "Sam, what happened?"

Before either could reply, Mayor Fuller declared, "Of course

Frank done it! The feeble-minded fool near ruined Sam's place. Would've if Sam hadn't stopped him in time. Something better be done about your father," he shook his finger at Clare, stepped over a pile of nails toward her, "before he ruins the town, or kills somebody in a rampage."

Larkin gave Fuller a hot look then asked grimly, "What happened here, Frank?"

Poppa, cowering near the forge where coals glowed red, looked mortified. A bruise was swelling on his jaw. "I—I—"

His brawny employer, Sam Dorsey, interrupted, saying angrily, "I asked Frank a simple question: did Alice's mind snap or was she always teched like some folks been sayin'. He didn't answer me, he waited a few minutes and then went crazy. Threw a hammer through the window. Started dumping out nails and scrap iron every-which-away. Dammit, I only asked him a simple question. He didn't have to do this! I had to grab him and sock him a good one to make him stop, or there'd be a helluva lot more damage."

"I'm not saying Poppa was in the right, but that was an unkind thing to ask him, about poor Alice! Do you wonder Poppa was upset?"

"Hell, I only wanted to know the facts! I went outta my way to give your Pa a payin' job." He waved his stout arms. "It ain't like he's not done a crazy thing or two since comin' to work here, gettin' my customers upset. I like to know what to expect. Since your sister jumped, some been sayin' yore whole family's teched. If that's so, I got to take measures to protect my business."

Clare chewed her lip, wondered if she could possibly help Sam understand. "Alice was frail, her heart ripped apart by news that Tobias was killed. For that very short period she didn't know what she was doing. Otherwise, she was as everyday normal as you, or me! We're not teched."

Larkin nodded. "I know Frank. I'd put money that his grief was his target, not you, or your business, Sam. Losing his daughter has been hard on him, but even so, he shouldn't have done this. We'll pay for the damage and extra for the trouble it's caused. We'll help Frank clean the place up." His lips tightened, "I have to say, though, I agree with my wife that your question was out of line."

The mayor, standing in the background, snorted, and muttered contemptuously, "You never know what to expect from a lunatic. They'll do anything. Commit murder even."

Larkin's eyes flashed anger at the mayor. "Watch your mouth!" He grabbed the surprised man's shirtfront and shook him hard, then shoved him aside as though disliking even to touch him.

"We're all very sorry," Clare touched Sam's arm. "This shouldn't have happened and it won't again. But I want Poppa to speak for himself, we can at least give him that." She turned, "Why, Poppa? Couldn't you see that you might have put Sam out of business, destroyed his livelihood?"

Poppa rubbed the sides of his head in consternation, thinking. He looked at Clare, at Sam Dorsey. His eyes avoided the mayor when he said, quietly, "I couldn't bear knowing what happened to Alice. She thought Tobias was gone, but he wasn't. It wasn't fair that she had that news he was killed when it wasn't so. A waste of such a nice daughter." He wiped his eyes on his sleeve and his lips quivered, "Ever since it happened I've been so mad I wanted to hit somebody—but I couldn't do that, I'd not hurt anybody. When Sam asked me if my girl, Alice, was crazy, I exploded. I should have just walked off to the creek, and cooled down. Now I wish I'd done 'zactly that. I'm real sorry, Sam. What I did was wrong, and foolish." He grabbed a shovel and began to scoop nails into a bucket.

"Damned tootin'!" Sam answered, ramming his fingers through his hair, his face crimson. "As good a smith as you are, I can't keep you on here anymore."

Poppa nodded, then said, "I want to pay for the window myself. I'll work here for no pay as long as it takes to make it up to you, Mr. Dorsey, then I'll go."

"Nossir, Frank. You can pay the damages in cash, right now, but I don't want you in my place at all. Mayor's been after me to let you go for a long time, anyways."

Alfred Fuller tasted the moment of Frank's firing like good whiskey. He nodded, said importantly, "Sam hired Frank out of the good of his heart. But I've seen the way Frank was from the start, he's crazy as a bedbug. Sam's right. I told him more than once he ought to let Frank go. Fire him, not put up with him like this was some Home For The Feebleminded."

"Would you stay out of this, please?" Clare turned on the mayor. "It's none of your business!"

"It is my business! It's my job to consider the folks of this town and see to their safety. Dear Lord, Frank might of taken after me, over the differences we've had time to time, and him being crazy. I've been lucky so far. If you're not going to see him locked in a home the way he should be, then you got my orders to keep him away from me, and out of Sweetbrier."

Clare was so angry she could have chewed a handful of nails and spit them at the mayor. He reminded her so much of her narrow-minded uncles back home in New Hampshire she wanted to scream. Manners were all that kept her from telling the mayor. *Maybe he should have taken after you! And when did you ever really think of anyone but yourself and your greed?*

Fuller wasn't ready to let it go. "Sam has been more than fair, but today proves it's a mistake to try and hire crazy people to do a job."

"Now, Alfred that's enough," Dorsey cautioned. "We done covered the matter."

"Poppa's not crazy!" Clare stated with fists clenched, barely keeping control. She implored the blacksmith, "Hasn't he done a good job for you, Mr. Dorsey, until this—this really upsetting time in his life?"

Sam said grudgingly, "Frank has done good work, I gotta say that. He's maybe the best blacksmith I ever run across. But there's been times that he got mixed up in his thinkin' and he got an order wrong or not done at all, upsettin' my customers."

"There's something else," Fuller hesitated and his eyes narrowed as he weighed his thoughts. "One night I came by the shop and saw a light flickering. I investigated, of course. It was Frank in the shop, behaving real strange and trying to steal your cashbox, Sam."

Sam Dorsey jerked to look at Frank, then Fuller. "What? When was that? How come I didn't hear about it before now?"

"It was last fall. I got there in time to save your cashbox for you, Sam. The idiot insisted he was just taking care of the money, but I had a hard time believing it. I still should have told you. That was a mistake on my part. Good thing you're getting rid of Frank now."

Clare was furious. She and Poppa could tell the truth of that night concerning the cash box but who would believe it, other than her family? She spoke quietly, "Mr. Dorsey, Poppa never tried to steal from you. The Mayor is lying but I don't expect you to believe that. All of you want to think the worst of Poppa and it's so unfair. He won't trouble you anymore. He'll be out at our ranch."

Mayor Fuller looked like a self-satisfied turtle.

"Go on back to the hotel, Sweetheart," Larkin said, "I'll take care of things here."

"All right." If she stayed here another minute she'd do something that would lead to her being called crazy. Clare sighed as she started for the door, "We're very sorry about this, Mr. Dorsey. You'll be paid in full."

Dorsey relented a little, saying after her, "I know your family's been through a lot lately, Mrs. Wade. But a man has to look out for himself and his business."

"I know. I do understand. I'm in business, myself."

Word of what Poppa had done spread quickly. James Myers gave the incident front page ink with an inch-high headline. Clare could not believe the firestorm of rumors that exploded, that she overheard at the hotel and on the street and on the road.

The community seemed of one mind, that they had seen from the beginning that Poppa was "touched." But they'd taken him in, accepted him, given him work they needed done, trusted him, and now look what he'd done before Sam stopped him. Of course, it wasn't surprising. Look what his daughter, Alice, did. Went crazy when she thought Tobias was dead and jumped off the roof of the hotel to kill herself. If that wasn't an insane tiling to do, what was? Whole family was nutty as a fruitcake, blind people could see that.

At the hotel, doing her work, Clare was stared at, as though she was expected to go off her rocker any second and do something wild and insane. On the street and in the stores she was given a wide berth, was seldom spoken to beyond a half-hearted "good day."

The night after she'd heard some women talking that her baby no doubt was tainted, would be born a half-wit, she cried in Larkin's arms. "Why are folks like this? I thought we left this sort of thing back at Hobb's Mills. But here it is, cropping up again. I know why Poppa did what he did, he was angry he hadn't been able to help Alice, he was in deep pain. Alice's mind snapped when she thought Tobias was dead, but she wasn't crazy in the accepted understanding of the condition. She was unhappy, emotionally empty, until she met Tobias. Then the worst happened and she thought she lost him—but that doesn't add up to crazy. Why don't they leave us alone and stop this stupid nonsense?"

"This foolish talk will die down in time, Clare." He held her face in his hand, wiped her tears with his thumb. "Human nature is pretty much the same everywhere. Folks latch onto a notion, like a dog with a critter in its mouth, and they shake it until nothing's left. It'll happen. They'll forget. Pay them no mind and go about your business. In time, they're the ones who'll feel like crazy fools for believing as they did. For the most part, these are good folks hereabouts. Give them a chance, they'll see you're one of the best things that ever came to Sweetbrier, you and your whole family."

"Thank you Larkin, I'm glad you see the situation how you do. God willing, you're right and all this will fade. I'll try to ignore the mean gossip and go on like always, but I can scarcely bear that they talk about our baby the way they do. I pray what they are saying doesn't go so far as to reflect on you, or Ma, or Nick. That would be so terribly unfair." She snuggled closer, her hand on his chest, feeling his heart beat. "You were all doing grand before we came."

"Don't worry," he turned and kissed her, "the whole world knows I'm crazy about one thing, and that's you." He stroked her hair back from her face. "If the talk doesn't die down quick, I'll have to pound some sense into a few fools. I'm here to take care of you, Clare."

"Just don't make any further problems for yourself. We have enough as it is."

He laughed softly and with his mouth on hers said, "I won't, sweet wife."

Chapter Twenty-Three

DURING THE NEXT SEVERAL MONTHS, CLARE TAUGHT HER staff the ropes for running the hotel so they could take over on the days she couldn't be there. After baby Andy's birth in January, she was able to spend entire days at home on the ranch with little Andy and Larkin. Now on this sunshiny day in May, she sat rocking on the veranda of her new house, her four-month-old baby nestled in her arms and nursing.

"Andrew Franklin Wade," she whispered, pulling aside the corner of her shawl to stroke his downy head, "you're the most delightfully perfect child in all of Rolling Prairie Township. Those folks who said you'd be otherwise are true fools!"

She was sotted with love for this child, as was Larkin. Baby Andy's arrival had brought a sweet return of joy, and peace to their lives. She sobered and her eyes filmed as she thought of Alice. How much she would've loved for her sister to see little Andy. Sadly, she didn't even get the chance to tell Alice she was expecting.

Engraved on her heart and mind was the deep sadness on Tobias's face, the desolation and heartbreak in his words when he was told about Alice's death.

"Two wives," he said hoarsely, "two of the finest women ever lived and I lost both of them. Nice women, good women. Couldn't have found me any finer women anywhere on God's earth." With tear-shiny eyes, regret in his voice, he added, "After I lost my

JoEllen I shoulda let it go at that. Not married Alice and brought her that bad luck. Alice would be alive."

They had assured him Alice's death was a terrible tragedy but not his fault. That their brief marriage was the happiest time of Alice's life. But his mind was set. "I sure as hell ain't goin' to see it happen again. No sir, enough is enough. Beth and Will are half-grown, they'll finish growing up without a mother. I'll be the best Papa I can be til they're on their own."

Larkin had insisted that with time he'd change his mind about remarrying, but Tobias was resolute. Clare believed he'd hold to his word. Although in this life, one couldn't tell for sure about anything.

Fortunately, Tobias's injuries from the lightning strike weren't as severe as first believed. Like his supposed death, his injuries were greatly exaggerated in the panic of the moment, although they were serious enough. The reddish brown color of his skin disappeared in a few days. He had suffered fractures in his right arm and leg, and contusions, but those healed in the year since.

Clare would always think of Tobias and his youngsters as Alice's family, and she dropped in to see them often.

Larkin had been right, when he said that situations involving other folks would come up to occupy gossipy minds. The major of which had been a supposed case of adultery last fall. The three-some involved left town together, leaving everyone to wonder who was guilty of what, or if there'd been any misadventure in the first place. Babies had been born, festivals had been held, crops planted and harvested, weather talked about— life went on.

Clare re-buttoned her bodice, and seeing that Baby Andy's wide blue eyes were on her face, she held him up to kiss him. She laughed when his tiny pink mouth quirked in a crooked smile. "Oh, you darling! You look just like your father and you'll be every bit the fine man he is, if I can just be a good mother to you."

How she wished Grandmother Hobb could see this boy! She would like to return to New Hampshire to visit her grandmother. Not the uncles and their families—she had no

desire to see them, ever again. If she and Larkin were to make the trip with their babe, it should be soon.

It was obvious Grandmother wasn't well and that she wrote her letters with effort. As often as not, her laborious scribble lamented what an enormous mistake it was that she had let Frank and his family leave. She blamed herself for not doing more to make them safe at Hobb's Mills, which was after all their home. Grandmother believed that Alice would be alive, if Frank and his family hadn't had to move to Kansas.

Clare wasn't so sure. Alice was an empty shell of a woman in New Hampshire. She'd then known true happiness with Tobias—until she thought he was dead. Clare wrote back in her letters all their many items of good news—Baby Andy's birth, their accomplishments on the farm, at the hotel, and on the ranch, but that never seemed enough for Grandmother. It was for Clare, who counted her good fortune in prayers every morning of her life. She had come to be almost as in love with Kansas as she was with Larkin. She'd never be sorry she came.

Humming softly, she went inside and put her now sleeping infant down in his cradle hi the bedroom. In the kitchen, she took a fresh-baked pan of bread from the oven and turned the loaves out on a dishtowel spread on her work table. She looked out the window to where Poppa sharpened scythes at the grinding wheel in the barnyard. Two of Larkin's shepherd dogs sprawled faithfully in the dust nearby. She smiled to herself. She was proud of Poppa, she'd had to uproot him from his home, his life, in New Hampshire, but he'd adjusted here in Kansas, even better than she'd hoped for. He still had mental slips, periods of confusion or forgetfulness, but he more than compensated by being such a hard worker and a loving husband and father. Spotting a cloud of dust moving along the lane to the ranch-house, she waited and watched until the buggy whipped to a dusty halt in the yard. She frowned, seeing the dust settle on her bed of blue iris she'd planted by the pump. The driver's pipe jutting from the shadows of his broad-brimmed hat told her that their guest was Marshal Seavers. If he was here to see Larkin, she'd need to call him in from the field by ringing the triangle hung by the back door.

Turning back for a moment to see that the baby slept, she hurried out to the yard. "Good afternoon. Marshal," she called cheerfully, shading her eyes against the sun. "What brings you to see us?" The wind whipped her skirts as she waited.

He touched his hat to her, "Your father, Mrs. Wade."

"What about Poppa?"

The marshal ignored her and strode to where Poppa bent over his work. Poppa's confusion, his distress, was immediate in response to whatever the marshal said to him, and he backed away from the law officer.

Clare was already setting the triangle to clanging. She gathered her skirts and hurried to where Marshal Seavers now gripped Poppa by the arm.

"What's going on? What are you doing with my father?"

"Sorry, Mrs. Wade, but I'm taking him in to the Sweetbrier jail."

"But you can't—why are you doing this—what on earth has happened?"

"Alfred Fuller's body was found this morning on the bank of Sweetbrier Creek, not far from here. He was bludgeoned to death. I'm here to arrest Frank for the murder of Fuller."

She felt the blood drain from her face, was stifled for air. "You've found the mayor—dead? But you can't possibly think my father had anything to do with it. This is nonsense." She looked to see if Larkin was coming, and spoke wildly, "Poppa has been here on our ranch nearly the clock around, every day for a long time now. Nights he's at home with Momma, in bed sleeping. He didn't do this, Marshal. If someone killed Alfred Fuller, it wasn't Poppa."

"We'll see about that. Your father had plenty of motive, and until we complete an investigation and learn exactly what happened, I'm keepin' him under lock and key. C'mon, Frank, get in the buggy."

He released Poppa just long enough for Clare to grab her father and shove him behind her. She spread her arms like a feisty hen ready to do battle.

"Don't even try to take my father off this property until you've talked to my husband! I rang for him to come, and you'll wait right where you are until he gets here. Larkin will tell you, himself, that Poppa didn't do this terrible deed, that it's not in Poppa to commit murder."

"Dinger Toledo says otherwise, that Frank has had it in for Fuller since gettin' fired from the blacksmith shop. Frank blamed the mayor for losin' his job, but your Pa got himself fired. He made mistakes right and left before that. He tried to steal the shop's

money box. When that didn't work out, he tore the place up out of
pure craziness."

"Lies, all lies. That's the story the mayor and Dinger would like
you to believe, but it simply isn't so. It was Mayor Fuller who was
stealing the money. I was there, and I saw it. The only reason we
didn't report his attempt at theft that night was because we knew
you wouldn't believe us. And fortunately we stopped the mayor
from taking the money so there was no crime to report. As far as
destruction of the shop, Poppa was broken up over my sister's
death and his inability to prevent it. All damages to the shop, by the
way, have been paid for in full and more."

Seavers didn't seem to hear her. He drew on his pipe and told
her gravely, "Another person might be plenty put out over losing
his job, then get over it. In a crazy man's mind, it'd grow like a
cancer, provoking them to do murder. Dinger says he's got no
doubt that's what happened."

Clare was about to protest that Dinger Toledo himself had
more reason to commit the crime, and there could be others with
motive, when a frantic glance showed Larkin riding hard across the
field, tails of dust in his wake. Seconds later he reined his bay to a
halt in the yard. Her relief was immense. She hurried to his side as
he slid from the saddle.

"What's going on?" Larkin demanded, shoving his hat back.
He pulled a bandanna from his back pocket and wiped his face.

Marshal Seavers repeated almost word for word what he'd
related to Clare.

Larkin whistled through his teeth. "Fuller is dead? It's murder?
Whoever did it, it wasn't Frank, I grant you that."

"I told the marshal that Poppa almost never leaves our place,
except to go home, and he couldn't have done this."

"Whoa!" the marshal held up his hand holding the pipe.
"There was the trouble just last month, between Frank and the
mayor. Your husband knows about it—tell her, Wade."

"There's been no trouble! What is he talking about, Larkin?"

"There was an altercation in town," Larkin admitted, flushed
under his tail and anger in his eyes for the marshal. "Frank had
gone to the stockyard looking for Fuller, to ask him if a package
Eugenie had ordered had come in on the train. Cuttings of bushes,
flowers and such, that she asked her family to send from New

Hampshire. In the conversation that followed, Fuller made threats against all of us. Frank ordered him to leave us alone."

"That's all? And why threats now? The troubles were well over." She stomped her foot as her anger flared hotter. "Something's been going on without my knowing? Why didn't you tell me, Larkin?" She clenched her apron in her fists. Poppa hovered behind Larkin, gazing at the ground.

Larkin sighed, "You'd been hurt badly by Alice's death and by so much more. I didn't want to add to it if I didn't have to. Besides, I'm the real sticker, or was, in Fuller's craw. Not you, and not your pa."

"What do you mean?" She paced, exasperated, looked at him again, and waited, hands on her hips.

"I'm trying to tell you, Sweetheart. For quite a while, the mayor imagined that I was trying to rob him of his place in importance to the community. He hated losing face. I already had the ranch he wanted. Finally, he held it against me for bringing inspectors to Sweetbrier to investigate his cheating at the railroad's shipping scales. He was slick, and he dodged being fired, but he was put on probation by the MKT officials. They've come to check on him every few months this past year. It didn't sit well with him that he could no longer steal from the farmers and ranchers hereabouts, the way he'd always done, to build his nest egg."

Clare was thoughtful, a deep frown set into her brow. She'd known about the dishonesty at the shipping scales, and that Fuller had wanted this ranch before Larkin came. "I suppose I just didn't realize Fuller was trying to get to you, through Poppa. What about this recent problem at the stockyard between Fuller and Poppa? So my father told Fuller to leave us alone. Where's the harm, why shouldn't he stand up for us? That hardly leads to suspicion of murder, for heaven's sake!"

The marshal spoke up, telling her but keeping his eyes on Frank, "When your father tried to tell the mayor off, Fuller started pushing Frank around and calling him a lamebrain, an idiot. According to witnesses, Fuller shouted at your pa that Larkin— all of you—were going to get your comeuppance. He was going to see to it."

"What did Poppa do, other than tell Fuller to leave us alone?"

"Nothin'. He didn't put up no fight at all. Fuller knocked him around, shoved him into the muck of the stockyard."

Tears sprang to Clare's eyes but before she could speak, the marshal held up his hand, "I admit the mayor had his faults, he was a moocher and a cheat, and probably a sniveling coward to boot—picking on your father when it was Wade, here, he hated. But that's no call to kill the man."

"Poppa didn't do it. He couldn't have, I tell you!"

"Take it easy, Clare."

Larkin reached to take her arm but she shook him off and turned on him, blood pounding at her temples. "Anything involving my family, large or small, I should always be told." She turned back to the marshal, "You have no right to take my father, when he didn't do anything wrong."

The marshal clapped his hat back on. "You weren't there, Mrs. Wade, and you can't say what did or didn't happen as fact. Like I told you a few minutes ago, it wouldn't be the first time somebody not all there made a mountain out of molehill and got to stewin' over the matter. Add to that your pa also figured he was savin' you all from whatever harm Fuller had in mind to bring on you."

Larkin swore under his breath. "This misunderstanding is my fault. I should have settled with Alfred Fuller a long time ago. Frank came and told me about the incident at the stockyard, the threats Fuller made. But the mayor always talked big and I didn't expect anything to come from the slimy coward. I did let Fuller know that if he ever did anything like that again, to Frank, he'd live to regret it. Clare—" his gaze implored her to understand, "Frank wasn't hurt, and he didn't want to upset you with the story any more than I did, and frankly, we saw no need to tell. Marshal, if you have to take somebody in for this, take me."

Seavers looked surprised and actually laughed. "You? Hell, Wade, you could handle the mayor with both your hands tied behind your back and chained to a post. He was no match for you. You didn't kill him."

"Neither did Frank! My father-in-law wouldn't kill a flea. You said yourself that Frank didn't fight back when Fuller jumped him at the stockyard."

"That was before Frank got to thinkin' and stewin' about everything in his mixed-up mind. I have to take him in, until we have an investigation and prove the facts one way or another." His jaw jutted, "If he's guilty, he'll hang or be sentenced to the state penitentiary. Unless he gets off on an insanity plea in which case he'll be sent to the Topeka insane asylum. Now step back, folks, and let me do my job, please."

"No," Clare cried, "you can't take him to jail! Poppa's innocent. You can't punish him for something he hasn't done. Larkin, please, make him release Poppa, please."

"Let him go marshal. We guarantee to keep him right with us until you've completed your investigation. We'll keep an eye on him. He won't be going anywhere. Your investigation will prove that Frank is innocent, I guarantee."

Marshal Seavers seemed to waver but only for a second. He took a puff on his pipe and shook his head. "No, I got to take him in. Other folks besides the hired man at the train station corroborated that there was bad blood between Frank and Alfred Fuller, even before the latest set-to. Plus the fact your father-in-law ain't right in the head. I got to do my job. C'mon, now, Frank, don't give me no trouble."

"I didn't do this, Clarie, I didn't," Poppa implored, but he allowed the sheriff to lead him toward the buggy.

She trailed alongside him, "I know you didn't. Poppa. We'll get you out of this as soon as possible. They have no right to hold you." She whipped around Poppa and grabbed the marshal's arm to try again, "Please don't take him. Leave him here with us. I promise he won't be out of our sight as long as you need to carry out your investigation. Don't take him."

The marshal shook her off, "Now Mrs. Wade, I've already explained to you that I have to take him in. You're only making this harder for us all."

Larkin hurried to her side, caught her waist and held her tightly. "Seavers is the law, Sweetheart. We have to do what he says. We'll get your Pa back, though, as soon as we can."

"Don't be afraid, Poppa," she called as Seavers pushed him up into the buggy. "We'll come get you right away. Don't worry, and don't be scared."

Larkin pulled her back against him, whispered in her hair, "I'm so sorry, Clare. I wouldn't have had this happen to you, not for anything. I'll make it up."

She wiped her eyes and turned to face him. "I shouldn't have yelled at you for this. I know what happened isn't your fault. I'm just so angry that Poppa would be accused because of folks' ignorance." She sobbed, fists pounding his chest, "Oh my God, Larkin, they're going to lock him up! Lock him behind bars like an animal in a cage. He'll not know how to handle it, what to think, or do."

"Shh, darling, shh. It's going to be all right."

But she couldn't be stilled. "Such treatment will only make him sicker. My poor fa titer. He doesn't deserve this, he didn't do anything."

As the marshal's rig disappeared into the distance, the world spun away. Larkin caught her as she collapsed, gathered her up into his arms and carried her to the house. He muttered several dark words against the law officer and a world in general that kept hurting his wife.

Clare's eyes fluttered open and met Larkin's concerned gaze as he sat on the edge of their bed looking down at her. Seeing that she was coming around, he lifted her hand and kissed it. "Nice to see that you're awake, Mrs. Wade," he said softly, his expression affectionate yet grave.

"What happened?" She felt as though she'd been dropped into a deep dark hole and was slowly climbing out into a vague and fuzzy cloud.

"You fainted, darling."

"I don't faint. I never have before."

"Maybe that's because you've always managed to keep your family safe. This time the thing you've always fought against, happened, and you couldn't stop it."

Her mind began slowly to clear and then in a crushing wave she remembered, "Poppa! Marshal Seavers took Poppa away. He accused him of murder!" She sat up and grabbed at Larkin. "We have to go get him out of there, Larkin, he can't be in jail. He's innocent. He didn't do anything wrong."

"I know," he caught her hands. "But let's stay calm. I've sent one of my hands to fetch Ma here to stay with Baby Andy while we ride into town. We'll pay whatever bail the marshal asks for, but your father is coming home with us."

He helped her off the bed, held her close for a moment before she struggled free. She tore off her apron, and made the most rudimentary fixes to her hair. "We have to hurry. I don't want Momma to know any of this until it's over and he's home again."

"I thought we'd stop on the way to town and tell her what happened. Better she hear it from us than some gabby neighbor."

Clare considered. "No. If she knows the marshal has taken him, she'll worry herself sick. We'll go get him out and then tell her what happened."

He shrugged. "If you think that's best."

"I do." She checked on the baby at the same time she heard Ma Wade coming through the back door. Baby Andy was sleeping soundly. She leaned down to kiss his velvety, sweet-smelling cheek. When she looked up, Mabel stood at the bedroom door, a deep frown creasing her usually placid face. Clare put a finger to her lips and tiptoed toward her.

In the hall, she allowed Mabel to draw her into her arms for a few seconds. "Oh, Clare, honey, Larkin told me what's happened. I'm so sorry. But you two go on and get him out of that place. Buncha' nonsense, accusing your daddy of murder, I vow! Don't you worry about a thing here. I'll take care of Little Andy. He knows me already, he knows his Grandma and he'll be happy with me til you get back. Now go on, and try not to worry more'n you have to."

"I'll be back by the time Andy wakes and is hungry. If not—"

"I know what to do. Milk's in the cooling box in the well, nipple and bottle in the cupboard. Go on, now."

"He'll need changing when he wakes up. I did the laundry today, there's plenty of clean didies."

"There you go then, everything will be fine."

In town at the small, rustic, stale-smelling jailhouse, Seavers, in his cubbyhole office, turned them down flat at their offer to pay bail so Frank could go home to his wife.

"Too chancy. If Frank is guilty as I suspect he is, I'd be real stupid to let him loose until such time as we can send for a county judge to preside over a trial. Frank could kill somebody else. He stays here under lock and key while I do my investigatin'."

"It shouldn't take long to prove my father innocent," Clare said frostily, hiding her deep concern for her father. "Not long at all. There are many folks in the community who will vouch for his character. There are ranch hands at our place who'll tell you truthfully that he's hardly ever out of their sight, except to go home to supper and his bed. My father hasn't a mean bone in his body toward another human being. He never has had and he hasn't now."

"That's your say so, ma'am. You got to admit you're prejudiced where your pa is concerned. This may take more time than you like, but that's how 'tis. I have to talk to folks, line up witnesses one way or another. Secure evidence. A county judge will have to be notified to come here to Sweetbrier and hold a trial when he can get to it. You folks are just goin' to have to sit patient an' let me do my job."

"I want to talk to him."

"I'll let you visit him for a few minutes, but take my advice and don't give Frank no hope that he'll be gettin' out any time soon. That ain't goin' to happen til the time is right and it likely won't happen at all—dependin' on what I find."

"Just let my wife and me see him," Larkin ground out angrily.

Chapter Twenty-Four

THEY FOLLOWED AS THE MARSHAL UNLOCKED A ROUGH wooden door and led them into a dim, bad-smelling back room that contained three small barred cells. Clare closed her eyes for a moment and wished that what she saw was a bad dream. Poppa sat on a crude, dirty bench, head bowed, his hands hanging between his knees. He seemed to stare at nothing. She bit her lip and fought against tears.

"Poppa, we're here."

He looked quickly around and then got to his feet, half-crouched. In the dim light, Clare and Larkin were but shadows to him. "Clarie? Clarie?" He stumbled to the front of the cell and his face brightened. "I didn't do what the marshal says." He curled his fingers around the bars. Tears wet his cheeks. "I'd never kill no one."

"I know you wouldn't, Poppa, and so does Larkin. Marshal Seavers will find that out when he talks to other folks. He'll learn the truth."

"Then I'll come home." His look was so hopeful it nearly broke her heart.

"Y-yes. But they may keep you awhile. Momma will want to come see you."

"No!" he gripped the bars, and his mouth puckered above his

beard. "She's not to see me in here. It would be too hard for Eugenie. Give her my love. You tell her not to worry."

"She'll want to see you, Poppa, and I'm not sure I can keep her from coming here."

By lamplight in the Hobb kitchen later that night, after reassuring Poppa the best they could that everything would be all right in a few days at most, and telling him goodnight, Clare had the difficult task of telling Momma, Hallie, and Oakley what had happened.

At first. Momma wouldn't believe it. Wringing her hands, frowning deeply, her eyes filled with concern, she looked at Larkin and Clare. "I wondered why he was so late coming home. I thought maybe it was extra work that kept him, and he'd be home anytime. I kept his supper warm." She clutched at Clare's arm, "He's not coming at all, tonight? They've locked him up? Don't tell me such things, Clarie! Don't!"

Tears clotted in Clare's throat. "I'm sorry, Momma. The marshal says he must keep Poppa until an investigation can be completed. And possibly until a trial can be held."

"This is not good for your father. Not good at all. We can't leave him there alone!" She hurried to where her shawl hung by the kitchen door. "Take me to see him."

"We can't do that tonight, Mrs. Hobb," Larkin said gently, taking the shawl and passing it to Clare to return to its hook. "Frank is handling this pretty well so far. He'll be all right tonight and Clare needs to get home to our little one. I promise we will take you into town first thing in the morning."

"Poppa doesn't want you to see him in jail, Momma." Clare hung the shawl and turned back to take her mother's shoulders gently in her hands.

"Anywhere Frank is, I will see him," Momma said firmly, her eyes flashing with uncommon fire. "No one can stop me."

Clare's mouth dropped and for a moment she could only stare quizzically. This was new, seeing her delicate mother behaving with such strength of will.

"All right, Momma," she shrugged, "Whatever you say."

When Clare and Larkin arrived at her parent's farm just after dawn next morning, Momma was dressed in her best navy blue frock and matching hat and was waiting calmly for them in a chair facing the door. Outside, Larkin tried to help his mother-in-law into the back of the buggy but she'd hurried ahead and climbed in without assistance.

On the way into town, holding Andy close, Clare stole several glimpses over her shoulder at Momma, who sat ramrod straight, shadows under her eyes from lack of sleep, but chin jutting. Had Momma all along had more backbone under her ladylike demeanor than they suspected? Or had Kansas hardships made her stronger? In any event, this surprising quality in Momma was fascinating to observe.

"I can give you ten minutes," Marshal Seavers told them, as he led them to Poppa's cell.

"That won't be enough," Momma said with a gracious tilt of her head. She touched the marshal's arm with her gloved hand, "I'm sure you'll allow us more."

When Poppa saw Momma, his eyes teared and he hung his head. His gnarled fingers nervously combed his beard on his chest. "You shouldn't have come here, Eugenie. I don't want you to see me here."

"Nonsense." Momma hid her dismay at sight of him behind bars in the dim, smelly cell. "You're here by mistake, but until it's corrected, I'm here to be with you. I love you, Frank, and I came to tell you to be strong. You're not to worry about a thing. Clare and Larkin will get you out of here, very soon." She reached through the bars and caught his hand, "There now, there now, every tiling's going to be all right."

Much too soon, the marshal came to inform them time for the visit was up and they had to go.

"I beg your pardon, but I'm not finished talking with my husband." Momma fluffed her skirts. "Bring me a chair, please."

"What?" His pipe came close to dropping from his mouth.

"I said to bring me a chair, please, Mr. Marshal. I'm staying here with my husband until I'm good and ready to do otherwise."

"I can't get you a chair and let you set here. This is a jailhouse, it ain't no parlor and we don't serve tea."

Clare was about to object to his being nasty to her mother, when Momma's back stiffened and she spoke for herself.

"Then let my husband out here with me, or let me in there behind those bars with him. I stay with my husband."

Clare swayed to and fro to keep her gurgling baby content in her arms, and protested, "Momma, you can't—"

"Yes, I can. You go on back home, Clare, or to the hotel to tend your work there if that's what you need to be doing. Larkin, you can go back to your ranch work. Poppa and I don't want to keep you from your chores."

"Eugenie, you can't stay here, angel," Poppa implored, gripping the bars.

"You're not in a position to stop me, Frank. I've spent my whole life at your side from the time I was a girl. I won't be leaving it because the fool marshal here hasn't the good sense to know you're a kindly soul who is innocent of what he accuses. Clare, tell Oakley to make sure he sees to his chores on time. Tell Hallie that when she's finished redding the house, I'd like for her to fix a nice stew and to put some in one of our small empty lard pails. Tell her to make sure the lid's on tight. She can wrap some plates and utensils in a dish towel. Oakley can bring the food basket here so I can have supper with Poppa. Go on, now, all of you, and do as I say."

Clare watched in amazement as the marshal got a chair and Momma thanked him graciously. Momma then kissed the baby nestled on Clare's shoulder, and waved them off.

Outside on the plank walk, headed for their rig tied at the hitchrail, Clare adjusted small Andy to a more comfortable position in her arms and said, "I've never seen Momma act like that before. I'm shocked at her, Larkin, but more proud than I can say. I was sure she'd crumple, and cry, and have to take to her bed over what's happening to Poppa. I was the one who fainted, not Momma."

Larkin chuckled as he helped her into the buggy. "Maybe Kansas is changing her, toughening her up a bit although I'll wager she'll always be a real lady. At any rate, I feel sorry for the marshal if he tries to make her leave. Did she actually ask you to send her knitting along with the supper Hallie is to fix?"

"She did. I think she's settled in for as long as they intend to keep Poppa. I just hope we can get her to come home to her bed, nights!"

"Frank will convince her to do that, I'm sure. In the meantime, it will do him good to have her close and your mother knows that. She'll be happier where she can keep Frank's spirits up. And Clare, darling, I think with your mother underfoot all day long, the marshal just may move faster to get this over with."

They both laughed, and for the first time in the last twenty-four hours, Clare felt better. She recognized, at the same time, that getting Poppa freed could involve an ordeal bigger than any of them ever had to face before.

––––––––

"It's ALL RIGHT, Rachel, my wife has given her okay for us to have a look in Alfred Fuller's room. And the marshal, here," Larkin quirked an eyebrow and jabbed a thumb in Seaver's direction, "has the right even without Clare's permission as owner of this place."

Rachel wrung her hands and shook her head, "That's not the problem, Mr. Wade. We don't have a key to get the door open. Mr. Fuller had his own key, and he only allowed us in the room when he wanted to, and when he was standing by, watching us."

Marshal Seavers pulled a ring of keys from his pocket and jangled them. "These came from the corpse's pocket."

Rachel's eyes went wide, she shivered and rushed off back down the hall.

Seavers tried several keys and then the door opened. "What the hell?" he muttered. "Wade, you better stay out here."

"I'm coming in. This hotel is still my wife's property."

"Where'd all this come from?" Seavers asked himself, staling at the room packed wall to wall with furniture and goods of every sort. Paths to the bed, bureau and armoire were narrow. Reaching the room's one window would be impossible.

Larkin sucked in his breath as he looked around. There were gilt-framed mirrors and paintings, a gold-plated birdcage, pewter plates, fancy bookends holding leather-bound books, statuary and bronzes of every sort, all stacked on top of the finest furniture Larkin had ever seen.

"He said the furniture, most of the stuff, was inherited," he told Seavers, "but others figure it could be stolen. It came to him mighty mysteriously, each time he made a trip out of town."

The marshal opened a mirrored armoire that stood next to a grandfather clock. Suits were on hangers, hats on a shelf above, shoes below. He went over to a bureau, tried several keys before he could unlock the drawers. He whistled under his breath, ran his hands through a drawer filled with jewelry, necklaces, brooches, pendants, watches, rings. From another, deeper drawer, he pulled out record book after record book.

"Interesting," Larkin said, looking over his shoulder. "I'll wager that a good study of those records will reveal exactly how Fuller cheated the farmers and ranchers in this county, all those folks who shipped their crops and livestock through Fuller's station."

Seavers pursed his lips. "Might be," he admitted.

They pulled from under the bed a metal box, five inches deep and two feet square. When Seavers unlocked it, so many greenbacks and coins filled it that the paper money spilled over.

Larkin chuckled drily, "And there you have the money our good mayor and station agent has cheated out of folks, for a long time—and, if you get my meaning, Marshal—got away with."

The marshal stood up. "I won't argue with you on this, Wade. You're probably right that most everything in this room coulda been stolen. But that don't answer who killed the mayor, and whoever did is goin' to pay for the crime. I intend to see to that."

"As it should be, Marshal, but let's make sure it's the right man, or woman, that pays."

The marshal had gone and Larkin stood in the lobby talking to Rachel and Flora, advising them to not let anyone near Fuller's room until the marshal had taken inventory of its contents. "He locked the room, and has the key, but somebody determined to get in could do it with a crowbar."

The words were no more than out of his mouth when Dinger Toledo came through the hotel door, saw Larkin, and started to duck back out.

"C'mon in, Dinger," Larkin motioned. "Something on your mind?"

"I thought I might got some things up in Fuller's room. Thought I'd have a look and see is all," Dinger answered, sheepish and belligerent at the same time.

Larkin told him, "Marshal's already been here, looked it over, locked it up. Sorry we can't help you, with whatever up in that room you think is yours."

Dinger's face closed. He shrugged. "Mebbe there ain't nothin'. Just thought I'd have a look."

"There were several ledgers up in the mayor's room. Records he kept of weights and measures over at the stockyards, you know what I mean, Dinger?"

"You won't find nothin' about me in those books!" Dinger blustered. "Nowhere in 'em!"

"If you're lucky, we won't. But just in case, I'd walk on eggshells for a while, and I wouldn't try to leave town if I were you."

Dinger thought that over and then his olive eyes gleamed with malice, "Hell, I ain't leavin' Sweetbrier. No, sir. I'm stickin' around to see your pappy-in-law hang for Alfred's murder."

THAT NIGHT, Larkin told Clare what they'd found but left out what Dinger had said about Frank hanging. "The marshal says that if the records show how Fuller skimmed shipping tallies, and prove who was cheated by how much, they'll get their money back. Anybody who can properly identify an item stolen from them by Fuller, can claim it."

"And the furniture and art that came in from elsewhere?"

"Marshal says he'll do what he can to trace it. If the rightful owners can't be found, the goods will be sold at auction and the money will go toward building the new courthouse Fuller promised the town."

LARKIN THOUGHT Clare should take more days off from work, due to recent turmoil, but she told him, "I'll be fine. And it's easy enough to keep Baby Andy with me at the hotel so I can feed him and care for him. I can't expect Hattie, Flora, and Rachel to keep doing my work, they have enough to do. I want to be in town, where I can visit Poppa at the jail. Momma's insisting on spending time there and I can't let that go on—it isn't fair to either of them. I want to talk to folks, maybe hear something that will tell us who is really responsible for Alfred Fuller's death."

"Marshal Seavers says he's doing all he can to find out what took place."

"We both know that isn't half enough! He's convinced Poppa did it."

He shrugged and frowned, "You're right. He's not much of a law officer, to my mind, or he'd be hot on the trail of a whole bunch of suspects. Maybe he means well, but he's far too satisfied that your father killed Fuller, and his job is all but done." He sighed, "Wish there was a good lawyer here in Sweetbrier, but there's none at all. I'll get somebody from one of the larger towns in the county, but there's not a lot of glory for an attorney in a small town like Sweetbrier. It might not be easy to get one to come."

"He's going to need the best lawyer we can find."

"He'll have the best, I'll turn every stone until we find the right man, and soon."

In the next several days, Clare talked to people who were sympathetic to her cause, but seemed privately to think Poppa might be guilty. The mayor had had his difficulties with others, namely the Cahills and their friends, who had held it against him for never coming through with the courthouse he promised. Many folks disliked him for his cheating and stealing and mooching, or pawing their wives. Dinger Toledo loved playing the big man at the railroad station in Fuller's place. But nothing seemed a solid enough motive for killing the mayor.

A week passed. Despite it being one of the busiest seasons on the ranch, Larkin got away as often as he could in his search for a lawyer to represent Poppa. Although Seavers claimed he was doing plenty to look into every aspect of Fuller's murder, he seemed content to hold Frank in jail as the most likely suspect, into infinity.

EUGENIE LOOKED up from her knitting and found Frank watching her through the iron bars, wearing a whimsical smile. "What is it, Frank?" She returned his smile, her chin lifted in curiosity. She lay her knitting aside, her heart glad to see that he was having one of his better moments: thoughtful, almost his old self.

"I was thinking. About the day we met, Genie. It was a boating party. Ayuh, on Lake Winnipesaukee! You were the most beautiful girl on the boat. I could hardly stand up, looking at you made my knees so weak."

She laughed softly, "Oh, Frank, dear, that was the movement of the boat made it hard for you to stand. The lake was rough that day, remember? A chilly wind blew. I was foolish not to bring a warmer wrap. You lent me your coat."

"Ayuh, I did." He nodded, satisfied.

Her eyes shone. She sighed, "Such a long time ago and yet it seems like yesterday. I fell in love with you, Frank, that very moment you gave me your coat. You were so handsome, with your blue eyes, your broad shoulders in a hickory shirt, and the wind in your hair. Not to mention how considerate you were, and funny. Your brother, Simon, was trying to catch my eye that day, he was quite the flirt. You fibbed and told him I was your girl, that you and I were acquaintances of long standing. I think he was afraid of you, you were so fierce about it."

They laughed together, then Eugenie went on, her eyes filled with affection. "Later you told me privately that it wasn't a lie at all. We had met, in your dreams. I was the girl you had pictured to be your wife, spend the rest of your life with. And that counted, as fact, in your book."

He chuckled, and stroked his beard. "I was a smart aleck, wasn't I?"

"A bit, but I didn't mind. I was afraid I might never see you again. But the very next day you came to my house to ask if you could court me. Two months later you asked my father for my hand. He had no qualms about you at all, he told me how lucky I was to 'land such a fine fellow.'"

Frank shrugged, leaned against the bars, and held his hand through for her to take. She stood, and nestled her hand in his. "When you took me home to Homestead House to live," she shook her head, "I wasn't sure I'd fit in with such a large and prosperous family. I was a simple doctor's daughter, after all. But gradually, it all worked out, and then our babies came, such wonderful children. You kept things running magnificently at the mills, and on the farm. Your mother was so proud of your skills. According to her, Hobb's Mills wouldn't have been half so successful iii anyone else's hands. It was a very good life, Frank."

His hand tightened. "Until I got hurt in the head." His eyes filmed. "I'm sorry, Genie. I wish that hadn't happened. You deserved better than what you've got out of me."

"Don't be foolish, Frank! I wouldn't have had you hurt, for anything. But it did happen and it wasn't your fault. You're still the young man I married, you're the love of my life." She leaned forward and kissed him through the bars, their tears mingling.

He said so quietly she could barely hear him, "Genie, if anything happens, if they put me away, remember me the way I was. Back when I was normal. Remember me that way, please, not the way I am now, and I won't care what happens."

"Oh, Frank my love, don't talk that way. You're my life, Frank, you're my life."

ONE AFTERNOON, Clare made a swift decision, wrapped little Andy in a blanket, and walked four streets over from the hotel to speak with Liddy Goodlander, the minister's wife. Alfred Fuller had taken meals at the Goodlander table for a long time. Maybe Liddy could tell her something helpful toward Poppa's case.

The Goodlander dwelling —the yard surrounded by the beginnings of a low stone fence—was small and bare of paint. Heat and silence hung heavy over the place. A pot of yellow and orange nasturtiums was a bright spot by the door.

Liddy opened the door a mere crack to Clare's knock. The pale, pretty woman bit her lip in surprise when she saw who it was. "Hello, Mrs. Wade." She looked like she might close the door without further conversation.

"May I come in, please? I'd really like to talk to you."

"What about?" Liddy was nervous, and continued to hold the door almost closed.

Clare adjusted little Andy in her arms. "I hoped you could tell me something about Alfred Fuller. You know, who might be angry with him, hold something against him, want him out of the way? I'm sure you know that Marshal Seavers is holding my father in jail, has accused him of murdering Alfred. But Poppa is innocent. If you can tell me—anything that might help, I'd be so grateful."

"I don't know what happened," she answered softly, her eyes averted and her face flushed. "There's nothing I can tell you, and I'm very busy today, Mrs. Wade."

Clare persisted, "When did you last see the mayor?"

"I—can't say for certain. My husband had asked Alfred to take his meals somewhere else—" She hesitated, like she might say more, but changed her mind.

"If we could just have a nice long talk, it's possible we'd come up with something. Please, may I come in and sit down, for just a while, please?"

"I don't mean to be rude, Clare. I will pray for the truth of your father's innocence to come out. I'm certain that it will." She said in aside, with a faint smile, "You have a pretty baby. I must tell you good day, now." She closed the door.

Clare's shoulders slumped. For a long while, she stared at the door, resisted the urge to lift her fist and pound on it again, insist that Liddy talk to her. Finally, in defeat, she headed back toward the hotel and her work awaiting her there. On the way, she bounced little Andy in her arms, telling him, "Liddy is right about one thing, you're my handsome little fella." She was rewarded with a grin, his first tooth resembling a tiny pearl in a sea of drool.

———

SHE TOLD Larkin that night at supper in their kitchen, "Liddy is hiding something, I know she is. I can sense it."

"She's a shy, quiet person. It would be hard for someone like her to discuss her private life, which included the mayor. She was plenty embarrassed that Fuller lusted after her. If you remember, the reverend had to call him off for it."

Clare took a sip of water and nodded, "I can understand why that would bother her, it would bother me, too. But there's more, I'm positive. I'll give her a chance to come to me, and if she doesn't, I'll be visiting her again." She sighed, and pushed her plate back. "Do you know if Seavers has found a judge to hold court here in Sweetbrier? Has a date been set for a trial? Seavers won't tell me anything. He doesn't like it that I don't make Momma stay at home."

"I gather that the marshal is having as hard a time finding a judge, as I am a qualified lawyer."

"I hope both happens soon. Poppa's not getting any younger sitting in that jail! It's hard on him, even with Momma there to keep him company. I want both of them home where they belong!"

Clare's exasperation at the slow wheels of justice didn't abate when another week passed and Poppa was still being held.

She was sweeping the hotel porch with a fury one afternoon when the train from the east chugged into the station across Front Street. She brushed her hair back from her eyes and rested, watched passengers as they stepped from the train. Some were greeted by friends or family, others headed alone back toward the baggage car to retrieve their things. Among the latter group was a pair of nattily dressed men who looked familiar. Her throat dried and she tried to convince herself that she was imagining things. She stared hard, and nearly dropped her broom.

Sweet heaven, it was them. Uncle Edward? Uncle Simon? Here? She stumbled to lean against the porch rail and watch them, wide-eyed, stricken with disbelief.

They retrieved their bags, seemed to be looking across at her hotel sign. She melted into the shadows of the porch to stand near Andy in his cradle, waiting, as they started to cross the dusty street toward her.

Chapter Twenty-Five

"WH-WHAT ARE YOU DOING HERE?" CLARE DEMANDED FROM A closed throat. She felt sick to her stomach. She fought for composure and glared at her uncles standing below the steps of her hotel porch. The two of them smiled amiably—if somewhat uncertainly —up at her. She repeated in a demanding voice, "Why are you here?"

"We're here in Kansas to see our brother, Frank," Edward told her cordially. "We've missed him and Eugenie, and you, Clare, and your siblings." He added solemnly, "We were very sorry to hear about dear Alice. We came as soon as we could."

Edward had grown more stout in build, his hair had thinned over the past few years, but he was the same kindly-faced, affable Uncle Edward. As he'd always appeared on the outside, giving him an advantage. She wondered what selfish interest motivated him this time, to bring him and Simon all the way to Sweetbrier from Hobb's Mills? Did they know Poppa had been jailed?

Simon seemed to read her mind. He said, "When we got the wire that Frank was in serious trouble, we lost no time in making arrangements to come here and offer moral support and—other aid." Simon was so finely turned out, every gray hair in place and mustache so neatly trimmed, it was hard to believe he'd traveled a thousand miles to be there. It was as though Kansas dust didn't dare land on dapper Uncle Simon.

"We don't need you, and I'm not aware of anyone wiring to ask you to come. I know I did not. My husband and I are taking care of the situation. Poppa is innocent of the crime and we'll prove it. Whoever contacted you has wasted your time."

"Young Hallie sent us the telegram."

"Hallie?" Clare clutched her broom tighter for support. Of course. She fought back anger at her younger sister. "She shouldn't have bothered you with our troubles."

"Now, Clare, of course she should," Edward said expansively. "In many letters Hallie has told us how bad life is, here in Kansas. Numerous times she's begged that we come for her, and bring you all home again to Hobb's Mills. We couldn't, until now. When she sent the wire saying that Frank has been jailed for murder, and may hang for the offense, we knew we had to come and make sense of this mess, find some way to get your father out of it."

"How generous of you! You came to save Poppa? You came because Hallie just asked? Sorry, I don't believe you. Oh, I don't doubt that Hallie has slipped letters off to you without our knowing what she wrote, or that she wired you that Poppa is in serious trouble. But you have other reasons for being here than to help Poppa and his family." They could have done that ages ago and they hadn't.

"We've always loved Frank," Simon claimed with a tidy frown, his gray fedora held to his chest. "Whatever we've done, it was in his best interests. Every decision we made was meant to protect him from himself and care for his family in the kindest way possible."

"Hogwash!" It was all she could do not to swat Simon's fine head with her broom. "How do you like that word, hogwash? I learned it since coming here to Kansas. Fits what you're saying, both of you, fits what you've claimed against Poppa for years. We don't need you, so the best tiling you can do is rum around and catch the next train headed east. Hallie was a fool to ask you to come. And once again, I don't believe that her request to come get us, to come help Poppa, brought you all this way. Not that I expect you to tell the truth."

Edward turned red. He sighed and rested a foot on the bottom step. "Give us a chance, Clare. Stop fighting us. It's not becoming to a young woman and it isn't necessary."

She looked at him, aghast, and exploded, "You still believe you can order me how to think, how to behave?" She flew a couple steps down to face him, "Well, think again, Uncle Edward. I'm my own person now and your rigid rules no longer apply."

He flustered for a moment, before he managed a very earnest expression, "We've come with the best of intentions toward you all. Why can't you believe us? We're here to support your father. He'll want to see us. Ask him."

"It will frighten him into the next century to know you're here! Have you both forgotten how you mistreated him, blamed him for Samuel's death when everyone knows that it was an accident? Have you so conveniently put it from mind that if we hadn't left our home, pulled up our roots at Hobb's Mills, you would have placed him in an institution? I have nothing but pure dislike for you both! You drove us away, with my aunts urging you on, so that the greedy lot of you could have Hobb's Mills to yourselves."

"Well, now—" Edward began, his expression suddenly closed. Simon brushed imaginary lint from his trousers-leg.

Clare was about to light into them further when realization hit. She drew in a sharp breath. Somehow, their being in Sweetbrier had to do with the dispensation of the Hobb's Mills properties on grandmother's death. Grandmother had issued an ultimatum of some sort. That her other sons got less, or nothing, if Frank wasn't restored to his birthright? Her broom clattered to the step. She grabbed it up, returned to the porch, and dropped into a chair to catch her breath. "It's Grandmother who's sent you, isn't it? She's never been happy that we were forced out."

Edward came tentatively onto the porch and sat down. Simon cautiously followed. "Yes, you're partly correct, but please believe that we came because we wanted to, to help your father. Your grandmother isn't well and hasn't long to live. She's asked us to bring Frank back to her before she dies. Of course, we have to get him out of this trouble, first, in order to fulfill her wish."

How could she believe him, considering the past? If her uncles had wanted to help their brother and his family, if they had any true concern at all, they'd have done something for them long before now. At the same time, she was so tired of making the family decisions. She wished Larkin were here to help her decide what to do. She thought of Momma, lately showing a strength of determination not often evident in the past, though she'd always been wise.

"I don't believe half what you're telling me," she stood up and faced her uncles square on, "but I'll find out if my parents want to see you. In their place, I would not. In fact, I wouldn't have cared if I never laid eyes on either of you again. My hotel has a dining room. You may go inside and wait. You'll be served coffee or tea and something to eat if you're hungry."

"Your hotel?" Simon studied her in surprise.

"You thought I was just the maid? Well, once I was. Now I own this hotel with Momma and Poppa. They also have a small farm that provides decently for them. My husband and I have a good-sized ranch." *As I said, none of us need you.*

Andy, needing her attention, started to whimper and squirm in his cradle at the end of the porch. "I'm taking my son inside and after I've taken care of him, I'll go to the jail to speak with Momma."

"Eugenie is in jail, too?" Edward exclaimed, eyes wide, "Well now, Clare, this situation your father has gotten into is much worse than we thought."

She would have sworn he found appeal in the idea, despite his show of shock and disbelief. It would be convenient for her grasping uncles to have Momma out of the way, too. That would leave Clare and her siblings, who could somehow be disposed of, disinherited.

"They are both jailed?" Simon sat forward in his chair. "Eugenie was his accomplice?"

Clare said, gritting her teeth, "Like I told you, Poppa is innocent. He committed no crime. Momma is not in jail, she's at the jail. She spends her days there with Poppa, to keep him company, and his spirits up."

That announcement seemed to strike them dumb, and frankly, Clare decided, no wonder.

"The poor woman, in a place like that, because of Frank. A bloody shame." Edward shook his head.

"I wouldn't waste time worrying about her," Clare said crisply. "In the time she's spent there, she's wrought miracles. She orders the cuspidor emptied regularly, the floors swept clean and mopped, and insists on better food for Poppa. She has the marshal and his deputy hopping. Now, please excuse me. Do make yourselves at home in the dining room and I'll ask Cook to bring you refreshment."

Poppa was napping on the bench in his cell when Clare arrived; Momma was engrossed in her needlework spread in her lap. Next to Momma's chair was a table and oil lamp she had insisted the marshal provide. Taking much care in the telling, speaking quietly so as not to wake Poppa, Clare revealed that her father's brothers were in town.

Momma looked as though she'd been struck. She paled and with hands shaking she put her needlework down. She stared at Clare, too stunned to speak. Then she drew a deep breath and whispered, "Well, I wouldn't have expected that. Why are they here did you say?"

"They claim they've come to help Poppa. And they want to take us all home to New Hampshire on Grandmother's orders."

"How odd. They've never lifted a finger to help us since we came to Kansas, they could hardly wait to see us leave Hobb's Mills." Momma's brow knitted in thought, "Grandmother Hobb has been ill, her letters have been fewer and she seemed to have difficulty writing them. She could have had Polly or Julia write for her, but I gathered she wanted to write them herself. She sent Edward and Simon?"

"The question is, Momma," Clare broke in quietly, "do you think Poppa will want to see them? Would it bother him, make him worse? Or help him, do you think?"

Momma sighed, "He'll want to see them. They are his brothers, after all. Do you think they are actually here to help him, Clare?"

"Truthfully? I think they are here for more than that. I think Grandmother has finally put her foot down against Simon and Edward, has told them they will treat Poppa fairly, or else. If she believes her time is close, she may be threatening to leave them out of her will if they don't bring Poppa home to Hobb's Mills for his fair share. Now that would bring them here to Kansas. They can't risk losing Hobb's Mills. They depend on the mills for their livelihood, to take care of their families."

It pleased her no end to add, "While we, the unlucky branch

on the Hobb family tree, have found good lives here in Kansas, despite this latest nonsense against Poppa."

Momma smiled, she spoke softly, "I never dreamed I'd be content, in Kansas. I can't say these past days have been pleasant, they are truthfully trying to one's very soul. But I was getting used to this country, the people here. Mabel is my dear close friend, she's become like family, a sister to me. You have your Larkin and baby Andy, my first grandchild."

"Are you saying you might be willing to stay here in Kansas, and not return to Hobb's Mills?"

"I'm saying I like it here more than I ever thought could be possible. But to jump to conclusions about anything else right now would be rather foolish, don't you think, dove?"

"Yes, Momma, it would." At a small sound, Clare looked and saw that Poppa was stirring.

His eyes fluttered open. Seeing Momma, he smiled. "You should go home, Eugenie. Be with our children. Be where you're comfortable with your own things. Please."

"I'm most comfortable here with you, Frank. When you're free, we'll go home together."

A hopeful look came to his eyes and he sat up. "Has something happened?" he asked with childish eagerness. "Marshal Seavers is going to let me go?" He got off the bench, and with a closer look at his wife's face, concluded, "No, it's something else you have on your mind. You're worried, Eugenie. What is it?"

"Frank, your brothers are here in Kansas. They say they've come to help us out of this trouble."

"Here? In Sweetbrier?" above his beard his lips trembled. His face lit up. He clutched at the bars. "Edward and Simon? They've come to help me?"

Momma sighed, "Yes, that's what they say they've come for. Would you like to see them, Frank?"

"You're thinking that I might not want to—because they weren't very kind to me back home?"

"Yes." "

"They're my brothers, my kin. I want to see them, Eugenie. But I wish I was out at our farm, when we visit. I wish I wasn't here in jail." He started to cry and then wiped furiously at his tears.

Clare stepped forward, touched his hand gripping the bars. "We're doing everything we can, Poppa, to get you out of here. I wish you could be home right now, too, but the marshal says you must stay here until a trial can be held."

"Bring my brothers to the jail," he said sadly, wiping his nose. "I'll see them here."

Momma whispered to Clare as she was leaving the jail, "I'm scared."

Clare nodded. She was frightened, too, to her core. Things were bad enough for Poppa. His brothers could make matters worse, despite their declaration that they wanted to help. Maybe she should have ordered Edward and Simon back onto the afternoon train; and never told Poppa and Momma they'd come.

But that seemed wrong, too, and Poppa wanted to see his brothers. God willing, they would help him, not add to the problems.

Back at the hotel, she gave Edward and Simon the news that Poppa welcomed their visit. She registered them for rooms before they walked with her to the jail. She introduced them to Marshal Seavers and his whiskery, elf-like deputy.

"You're Frank's brothers?" the marshal was surprised, "come all the way from New Hampshire?" He shook their hands. "Wish I had better news for you gentlemen, but I haven't found a single lead that anyone else could have committed the crime. I'm sorry."

"That doesn't mean you've ceased your investigation, though?" Clare asked pointedly.

"Oh, no, not at all. I'm digging all the time, hoping to uncover new facts. I'm just not having any luck at it."

Edward shook his head solemnly. "Too bad, too bad. I can't believe what's happened here."

Simon sighed heavily, "We'll get to the bottom, though. That's why we're here, to help."

Clare gritted her teeth, "My uncles would like to see Poppa."

"Of course, of course."

Poppa's faded eyes lit up at sight of them, but he pulled nervously at his beard in embarrassment. Eugenie insisted on chairs being brought for Simon and Edward. They turned down the marshal's offer of a cup of coffee. Simon pulled out a handkerchief, and made to wipe his eyes but held the cloth close to his nose to shut out the smells of the jail.

"We're going to take care of you," Edward told Poppa, exuding compassion. "You're not to worry about another thing. We'll get you out, somehow. And Eugenie, you really shouldn't be here, this is no place for a woman of your refinement." In this regard, he was genuinely shocked.

"My place," she smiled, "is with Frank."

"Well then," Edward's eyes shifted, "we must work to get Frank free all the sooner."

"How is mother?" Poppa asked. "What's happening at the mills, and on the farm? I missed home, when we first came to Kansas. I still miss Sandwich, sometimes."

Simon didn't like hearing that Poppa missed Hobb's Mills. His tidy mustache twitched with a smile that didn't reach his eyes. "Mother isn't well, and in fact she asked that we visit you. Mother would like to see you. In the meantime, she sends you her love. We've brought small gifts for all of you. The mills and the farm—well, work proceeds as usual. Profits aren't what they once were but that could change. Edward and I, and our employees, put in very long days. It requires that, you know. Long hours of intelligent application to the jobs."

Clare was so angry at that smite at Poppa she could have struck Simon.

———

SHE SHARED her concern with Larkin that evening at home. "Poppa was glad to see Edward and Simon, although he was embarrassed to be in jail."

"Poor fella."

"They gave every indication they were glad to see him, though it seemed false to me. I don't trust them, Larkin. They wanted badly to be rid of us back at Hobb's Mills. For all their show of concern for Poppa, and the rest of us, I'm truly fearful they have ulterior motives they aren't revealing."

"Did they say or do anything to indicate what they're actually after?"

"They admitted to me that on top of a wire Hallie sent to tell them Poppa was in trouble, that Grandmother wants to see Poppa. They are to bring him to her. They don't say that it has anything to do with her will on her passing, but I suspect it does. I think she's insisted on them doing right by Poppa, or be left out of her will. Something like that."

He whistled softly. "If you're right, and if they are as callous as in the past, they might see it to their advantage that your father is found guilty of murder. He'd be committed, or—" he didn't finish.

"They could go back to grandmother and say they did what they could for Poppa, but the courts took the matter from their hands. Dear Lord, Larkin, I believe they could be that coldblooded, if they thought it would mean they'd not have to share Hobb's Mills."

"We have to find out who really killed Alfred before your uncles destroy your father, intentionally, or otherwise."

She shivered as she said, "I don't think Marshal Seavers is trying hard enough to find out if anyone else did the deed. He's so sure Poppa murdered Alfred, he gives his attention to proving that. I overheard him telling that squirrel of a deputy to keep searching for the murder weapon. To not leave a stone unturned."

"I wasn't going to mention it, but Ma tells me the deputy has snooped around the ranch when we weren't there. Oakley told Nick that the deputy was at your parents' farm, too, asking questions, looking around. Oakley ordered him off with a fist in his face and told him not to come back until he had an official search warrant."

"I hope Oakley didn't make things worse, if they can be any worse. Larkin," her eyes filled with tears, "what's all this coming to? Is there a chance they can find Poppa guilty, despite his innocence?"

"No, darling, no. A good, honest, lawyer will bring sense to this mess and get your father freed. The next attorney I talk to could be the one." He gathered her close with a soft murmured endearment. "You're cold."

They held one another tightly, until her trembling eased. "I don't know what I'd do without you, Larkin," she whispered tearfully. "The last years have been so difficult, your love is the blessing that keeps me sane. Your love, and our little Andy."

He smothered her face with kisses. In bed a few moments later, they made love fiercely, conquering for the time-being the demons that would dare to darken their happiness.

Two days later, Clare knew positively how dangerous it was for Poppa that his brothers were in town. With an overblown show of concern for him, they were methodically relating to anyone who cared to listen—Mr. Jackson at the general store, Cahill the hardware man, Dorsey the blacksmith, James Myers at the paper, and numerous others, that they believed their brother was likely innocent. But if the tragedy had indeed occurred at Frank's hands, they needed to remember that he was not responsible due to his lack of mental capability. They asked Sweetbrier folk to pray for Frank, to have compassion for him.

No one in Sweetbrier had heard before that an older brother, Samuel, had died in a tragic accident due to laxity on the part of their mentally troubled brother, Frank. Now, everyone in town and for miles around knew, thanks to Edward and Simon. The town was abuzz with gossip that gained momentum with each passing hour.

Clare saw with growing alarm what was happening, but didn't know how to stop it. Edward and Simon were everywhere doing their dirty work, spreading their version of what happened in New Hampshire to make her father look as bad as possible.

The details changed so much with each telling and retelling that the latest versions held no resemblance at all to the truth. But Edward and Simon achieved their goal.

Many in the community had already thought that Frank Hobb might be guilty of killing Alfred Fuller. Now they had Frank's own brothers'—compassionate gentlemen to the core—confirmation that he was responsible for their brother's death in New Hampshire. The family had fled to make a new life in Kansas where no one would be aware of that ugly truth. By coming to their town, Frank Hobb escaped punishment for the awful deed, or being institutionalized as he should have been. The people of Sweetbrier had been duped, had been made to believe that Frank was only mildly retarded and could do no harm to anyone.

Weeks before, James Myers wrote in his newspaper that the killer was likely a mysterious outsider, now his articles pointed a finger almost directly at Poppa. The stories quoted her uncles at length.

Folks who had been sympathetic before did a total about face. They angrily believed, with this new evidence of his past, that Frank for sure was the one who murdered their mayor.

Clare had never been so angry, or so frightened.

Chapter Twenty-Six

LARKIN SHOOK HANDS WITH THE ELDERLY, BUSHY-HAIRED, Junction City lawyer. "Thank you, Mr. Mahony. My wife will be happy you're coming to Sweetbrier to defend her father." It took all of his gumption to say it, because this man's background fell far short of what he'd hoped to find in the lawyer he hired.

Mahony was honest in telling him that his legal training was minimal, that he'd started out many years ago as a school teacher who in the off months studied for the bar in the office of an established lawyer. Which was sufficient to getting the job done, Mahony felt, his chief qualification being common horse-sense, anyhow, gained in years of practice.

From the moment Frank was jailed, Larkin had sought a younger man, one who had studied at a really good law school. A fighter with experience in criminal law. But a lawyer of that standing had no interest in trying a small-town case that would do little for his reputation.

John Mahony looked up at him from clear, intelligent blue eyes, his silver caterpillar eyebrows squinched in a frown. "I'm gettin' old to travel so far from home to work on a trial, but your father-in-law's story intrigues me. I feel for any feller my age, regardless. And from what you tell me, he's bein' railroaded right into a hangman's noose, or the Topeka asylum. Like I told you, I don't get offered many criminal cases. I argue private law. Personal injury suits, business affairs, land swaps, petty thievery, and the like. But I like a challenge now and then, and your father-in-law's predicament sure as hell fits that bill."

"Um-yes." With a deep sigh, Larkin hedged toward the door. "I'll send word as soon as we know a date for the trial."

"I'll try to get down to Sweetbrier before that, do some snoopin' around of my own. Only thing stop pin' me might be a case of lumbago, which lays me low for a day or two now and then. Or a law case that runs longer than it ought, that could keep me leavin' soon as I'd like. But I'll be there, an' I'll do my best for your wife's pa, you can count on it."

Larkin stepped out onto Junction City's main street from Mahony's small cramped law office and took a deep breath. He wished he could take Clare better news. That he'd finally found the best lawyer in Kansas to help her father. Truth was, he'd contacted several, in Topeka, Council Grove, Junction City, and Manhattan, Kansas. Mahony was the only one to say yes. The only one. God help them.

——————

WHILE SHE WAITED for Larkin to return from Junction City, praying that he'd found a lawyer on this recent trip, Clare continued to ponder who else might have had motive to kill the mayor. Her mind kept going back to Liddy Overlander, the minister's wife. Not that she thought shy, sweet-natured Liddy killed him, or even had reason to, but when she'd talked to Liddy before, the woman had seemed to hold something back. Some knowledge of Mayor Fuller that she wasn't sharing.

The fact that Liddy had the mayor into her home several times a week put her into a position of knowing more about him personally than others might. Whether he had enemies unknown to the community. Someone from his past or somebody he met on one of his mysterious trips away from Sweetbrier. Perhaps a stranger came to town unseen, had killed Fuller, and left again without anyone witnessing what happened.

Of course, it was possible the reason for Liddy's reticence was that she simply didn't want to say any tiling unkindly about the mayor, if she didn't have any helpful facts to offer. Clare had to know, one way or the other. Leaving her napping baby with Rachel, at the hotel, she hurried to the Goodlander house. Although Clare knocked several times, there was no response. A pall of silence hung over the cottage. Disappointed, Clare turned back the way she had come. Liddy could be away from home at any number of places, or she could be hiding in her house to avoid being questioned.

As she walked away, Clare considered who else she might talk to about the crime. Larkin had grilled Dinger Toledo on the subject of the murder, and so had the marshal, but Clare wanted to hear for herself what he had to say. She found Dinger at the depot scales, weighing a farmer's squealing pigs for shipping out. When she declared her mission, he looked up from the task for only a second, his expression belligerent.

"I've said all I've got to say about Alfred's murder, to Marshal Seavers. I'll be honest, I believe your Pa done it. Now do you still want to talk to me?"

"My father is innocent." *Maybe you're not? And that's why you refuse to talk to me?* "We'll prove his innocence, too. You were a friend of Alfred's, so I believed you might want to help find the true murderer." She waved an insect away from her face.

He turned red behind his rough whiskers. "I'm busy here, Mrs. Wade," he puffed, "and I got no time to talk about somethin' useless to discuss."

———

THE EVENING FOLLOWING Larkin's return from Junction City, Tobias came to visit them at the ranch. Tobias had been named acting mayor until an election could be held. Clare was pleased to see him in the new role. He was good at the task, he'd been a resident of Sweetbrier for years and knew the community's problems inside and out. He was still grieving his loss of Alice. Filling his mind with town concerns would help in the healing, Clare believed.

"We've finally found a judge who'll preside over Frank's trial," he told them. "Judge Wilson Royce has agreed to come down from the county seat. We feel lucky to get him.

He can be blunt and quick in his decisions in runnin' a trial, but he's a fair man. Unnecessary argument without facts gets his back up. We should have the trial over within a few hours. I feel pretty sure that the jury will vote in Frank's favor. They got to, because there's a lot of us know that he's innocent."

"We have a trial date then, and the judge is coming for sure?" Clare asked, glad the ordeal would soon be over, and scared at the same time.

"Yep to both questions. Judge Royce wants the trial six days from now, an' he figures from nine to eleven in the mornin' will be sufficient. Since we don't have a courthouse, we've suggested the trial be held in your hotel."

When Clare hesitated to speak, Larkin said, "Your hotel is the only building in town with enough room. It'll do fine."

"Marshal Seavers was in favor of having the trial at the saloon or at the schoolhouse, but both are too small," Tobias told them. "He didn't believe the judge would agree to holdin' the trial in the accused family's place of business, but Judge Royce said that wouldn't affect any decision of his, or the jury's, he's sure. He was testy on the subject in his wire. He wants the trial over with."

"I'm glad the trial will be soon, and I'll be as happy as anyone when it's over and Poppa is free. But is two hours enough to hear all the evidence?"

"The marshal thinks so. Of course what he has is lined up against your father. If you need any more character witnesses for Frank, I'd be glad to talk to some folks for you."

"Thanks, Tobias, we appreciate that." Larkin readied over and clapped his shoulder.

"How's Frank takin' all this? I've been to visit him a few times at the jail. Your mother is always there, insists the deputy or marshal bring me coffee." He smiled. "She usually has some cookies from home. If I didn't know it was a jail, and your Pa behind bars, sometimes I'd think it was a tea party."

She returned a wry smile and said with chagrin, "Poppa isn't happy where he is, in fact he's miserable. But he's not really worried about what will happen to him. He knows that he didn't kill Alfred Fuller, and believes as soon as everyone else figures that out, he'll be able to go home. Momma's worried, but down deep she believes that justice will prevail. It's hard for her to believe anyone could think Poppa could commit the murder, in the first place."

"Your uncles are still in town? They stayin' for the trial?"

Larkin grunted in disgust and looked at the ceiling. Clare answered. "Unfortunately, they'll be there. Despite the damage they've done to Poppa's reputation since they came, they insist that they'll be character witnesses for Poppa. I tried very hard to get them to return to New Hampshire, gave them my opinion of their so-called 'help' but they refuse to go. I don't trust either one of them farther than I could throw an elephant."

The men chuckled in agreement coupled with concern. Tobias said, "Your uncles are plumb two-faced, to my thinkin', claimin' they have your father's interests at heart, then they turn around and spread gossip that he caused the death of their older brother back in New Hampshire! I don't know why they're plantin' the possibility in folks' minds that Frank could have had something to do with Fuller's murder, but sure as shootin' that's what they're doin'."

"It's complicated," Clare sighed, "but I'm convinced they'd like nothing better than to have Poppa out of the way of their inheriting our family's mills and homestead back in New Hampshire. I hope the jury will see them for the cold-hearted, selfish buffoons they are and pay them no mind. My Uncle Samuel's death was a tragic accident! I want to testify. I'll explain clearly what took place."

Larkin smiled and squeezed her hand.

———

LARKIN STEPPED BACK into the shadows of the barn. Normally, he'd go on about his business and not eavesdrop, but when he heard Nick and Oakley speaking in low tones in the area of the horse-stalls, something about Alfred Fuller, he listened.

"Gordy Goodlander was pretty mad. Said he'd like to take a gun to the mayor, shoot his brains out, for tryin' to paw Gordy's Ma," Nick was saying.

"When Mrs. Goodlander tried to collect what the mayor was past due payin', ol Fuller said he had plenty to give her, more pretties than she could dream of—all she had to do was leave the reverend and come with him," Oakley scoffed.

Nick said in agreement, "Gordy's ma is a nice lady, she'd have no truck with the mayor that way. She ordered him off their place, said she'd never leave Gordy's Pa, not for the mayor or anybody else. Told that slimy reprobate not to come back when her husband, the reverend, wasn't to home. Gordy said if Fuller did come back and try anything with his ma, he'd take his shotgun and blast the son of a bitch to kingdom come."

The boys dissolved into a fit of laughter. "Kingdom come, pretty good place for a preacher's son to send somebody," Oakley guffawed.

"Gordy was mad, sure as hell," Nick said.

"What are you boys talking about?" Larkin strode to where they lay in a pile of hay, covered with chaff, chewing on straw, red-faced with laughter.

"Nothin', Larkin." Nick stood up fast.

"We was just talkin'," Oakley said solemn-faced as he got to his feet more slowly.

"I heard what you were saying, and using some bad language to boot that you both ought to be skinned for. What about Gordy and the mayor? Do you boys think Gordy had something to do with the killing?"

"Nope, not Gordy, he'd never do nothin' like that, he just talks," Nick said seriously. "Anyhow, Mrs. Goodlander run the mayor off. She took care of it."

"Have you told anyone else about this?" Larkin asked.

"No," Oakley shook his head. "We swore a blood oath to Gordy we'd not tell anybody else. It'd embarrass his ma, if folks knew." His face was crimson. "I wouldn't want talk like that going around about my Ma."

Larkin sighed. "All right. Go on back to work. And mind your language, both of you."

He told Clare about the incident later that night.

"The boys may be right that it was just tough talk coming from Gordy. That he was speaking out of anger toward the mayor, but would never take action on his words." Clare paced their kitchen, while Larkin sipped coffee at the table. "Even so, I'm going to visit Liddy one more time and see if she'll talk. If what the boys say is true, it's not her fault the mayor had wrong ideas about her." She was remembering Doctor Plummer's assault on her. "And it shouldn't shame her."

———

CLARE FELT GROWING alarm when for the second time, Liddy Goodlander was not at home. She had called out Liddy's name over and over, knocked several times, only to be met by total silence. She walked around the house, shading her eyes to peek in the windows. She observed tidy, sparsely furnished rooms, but no sign of life. Something wasn't right about this, not right at all. She noticed now that the small flower bed in front of the house was slowly dying. She was standing there, trying to think, when a hearty woman's voice spoke behind her.

"You looking for the Goodlanders?"

Clare whirled, "Oh, Mrs. Lang, it's you." She took several deep breaths, hand on her heart to calm her breathing. The Goodlanders' next door neighbor, Minerva Lang, a friendly woman with unkempt hair and a soiled apron spread across her broad figure, stood there smiling.

"Yes, I'm looking for Liddy, do you know where she is, Mrs. Lang?'

"She ain't to home."

"I gathered that. But do you know where I can find her?"

"Finding Libby right now would be hard as searching for a pea in a hayfield, is my guess. Liddy, and her boy, Gordy, took off a few days ago. Hired a rig from the livery in town. Said they were going to join up with the Reverend—wherever he's preaching this week. They was going to have to track him down."

"Do you know why they left to join Reverend Goodlander?"

"Didn't say. Wasn't really none of my business. I just naturally figured they was headed to be with him for some social doin', a weddin' or buryin' or some other special service."

"I suppose. But you say they've been gone for two or three days?"

"Yes'm, but I expect to see them fore' long. The reverend is due back in Sweetbrier for his monthly preachin' in another week."

"Yes, that would be true. Thank you Minerva."

"No thanks needed." Minerva suddenly fluttered her apron in both hands. "My, would you look at Liddy's nasturtiums! If it ain't too late, I'll be bringing my dishwater over to water 'em."

"Good idea." Minerva could be right that Liddy and Gordy

had gone to join the reverend for social reasons. Or—they could be fleeing trouble. Running from a crime? Clare found that hard to believe. But how to be sure, with them absent?

If Fuller had been bullying the family in his efforts to win Liddy from her husband, she supposed anything was possible. If Fuller had tried to force himself on Liddy, that could be considered assault. It wouldn't be against the law for her to defend herself, or for Gordy to come to her defense.

With all that, it was next to impossible to envision any of the Goodlanders taking a life. Maybe Minerva Lang was right in her belief that it was a social matter behind Liddy and Gordy's leave-taking. And maybe, she, Clare, was mistaken to believe that Liddy had information that would help Poppa.

John Mahony arrived on the train from Junction City two days before the trial. Clare liked the stoop-shouldered old lawyer from the moment he introduced himself. After he'd registered for a room at her hotel, he went to the jail to question Poppa. He had a long relaxed visit with him, and Momma, over coffee and cookies.

Following his stop at the jail, Mahony strolled the town, chitchatting with folks on the street, in the stores, at the livery, and blacksmith shop. That night, he had supper with Larkin and Clare.

"Your husband, here, has told me your father's story. I've spoken with Frank and your mother, and with folks around town. I believe he's innocent and I'll do my utmost to prove it. I'd like to hear what you have to say, Mrs. Wade. Have there been any recent developments, or is there anything in particular on your mind that you'd like to tell me?"

"First of all my father is innocent." She told him about Fuller's helper, Dinger Toledo, who had inherited the head position as station agent on Fuller's death. "I don't know that he had anything to do with the mayor's death, but I don't like how confident he is that Poppa is guilty."

Mahony nodded. "Mr. Toledo will probably be called as a witness by the prosecuting lawyer. I'll ask to cross-examine. Maybe I can get Toledo to tell us things he'd rather we not know. Never can tell. Sometimes the prosecution's witnesses turn out to be a big help to defense."

She told him about Liddy Goodlander, that the preacher's wife, trying to make ends meet, had prepared meals for the mayor.

That there was indication the mayor wanted the reverend's wife for himself and that had led to troubles for the Goodlanders. Mahony looked thoughtful, his thick brows bunched. "Sounds like we have good cause to subpoena her, though it's late for that."

"If she can be found." Clare revealed that Liddy and her son had left town.

Larkin explained, "Her husband, Milton Goodlander, is a circuit minister who travels and preaches over quite a bit of country. If Liddy knows something but doesn't want to talk, she might've decided that she and her son would be better off close to the protection of her husband. Wherever he is. It's possible they know something about the murder and will just disappear. We may never see them again."

Clare looked at him in deep concern. "I hope you're wrong about that."

Chapter Twenty-Seven

THE DAY BEFORE THE TRIAL, MAHONY HAD BREAKFAST IN THE hotel dining room but remained in his room the rest of the day, making notes, studying them, deep in thought as he stared out the window at the blue Kansas sky. Clare personally took his lunch to him, and in mid-afternoon, his coffee.

"I appreciate very much that you're here to help Poppa," she told him.

He smiled at her, and nodded.

She stood with the empty tray in her hand. "You might like to know that Judge Royce and the prosecuting attorney, a Mr. Julian Snyder, an acquaintance of the marshal, arrived about an hour ago and have registered here at the hotel."

"Thank you. I'll be wanting to talk to the judge about that subpoena for Liddy Goodlander, if she can be located. He may not give it, even if she shows up, since it's only hours now before the trial begins. I hope he will, I'd like to see Mrs. Goodlander on the stand, ask her a few questions."

"I, too, hope she'll be there."

"Mrs. Wade," he said, just as she reached the door.

She turned.

"I don't think your husband has much confidence in me. I don't think he believes I can get your father off."

Her eyes twinkled. "And I believe you're going to prove my husband wrong."

He chortled, deep in his throat, "My God, for a beautiful woman like you, I'm prepared to die trying!"

Out in the hall, Clare sobered. When you really looked at it, John Mahony was about the only hope they had.

Clare had never felt such terror as next morning in her hotel dining room, now transformed into a packed courtroom where her father's fate would be decided. Death, lock-up for probably the rest of his life, or—God willing—freedom.

Taking a seat next to Larkin, she surveyed her friends seated near and was mildly comforted that Eva Cahill, Mabel Wade, and Carrie Spencer had earlier shared their belief that Poppa would be found innocent. Muriel Fayne on the other hand had been a staunch supporter of the mayor, believing implicitly in his moves for town improvement. Clare caught Mrs. Fayne's eye for a brief second. Mrs. Fayne began to sniffle behind her handkerchief, her eyes turned now on Poppa. If looks could kill, he would have died that moment. Clare decided in relief that for now it was a blessing women couldn't serve as jurors, Muriel would have voted Poppa be hung!

It was impossible to read the minds of the twelve male jurors, rustic farmers, ranchers, townsmen, eyeing Poppa sitting at a table with Mahony, then Marshal Seavers as he prepared to testify for the prosecution from his chair next to the Judge's table.

Snyder, the prosecuting lawyer asked, "Marshal Seavers, would you tell us how you first learned of Alfred Fuller's death, where the body was found, and the condition of the body when you went there?"

"Some boys playing down by the creek were the ones to find the body. They run and told Stanley Adams, whose land borders the creek right there. Stan come and got me."

"And condition of the body? On examination, how would you say Alfred Fuller met his death?"

"He was hit, hard as hell, in the head with a blunt instrument. Once on the side of his head and once in back." He demonstrated with motions. "Couldn't say exactly when Alfred was killed. His body was kind of swole up when we found it. Nobody'd seen him around or knew where he was, til those boys found the body. Probably killed that same day, or the day before which was a Sunday. He was dressed in his best suit, a little orange flower in his button-hole. A dried up dead flower, of course."

"The instrument of death, what would you say that was?"

"I got no doubt about that. He was killed by a blacksmith's hammer."

There was a unified gasp in the room, eyes again on Poppa, a blacksmith. None looked Sam Dorsey's way. Although a black-smith, he was not the one on trial.

Listening, John Mahony shook his grizzled head, but before he could make a protest the prosecuting lawyer pressed on, "What makes you so sure that it was a blacksmith's hammer?"

"Well, in the first place, the mark on the side of his head was kinda square—when you got the flies and caked blood cleaned off. A blacksmith's hammer has about an inch and a quarter square head."

"Did you find the weapon?"

"No sir. Me and my deputy searched everywhere. Down at the creek where the body was found. Other places, too. But that don't mean much. The hammer could have been washed clean and put back in its place."

"Its place?"

"The blacksmith's shop here in town, or in the shop out at Larkin Wade's ranch where the prisoner did some work. Or it could have been cleaned up and hid away in the accused, Frank Hobb's, barn."

Poppa frowned in puzzlement at that.

Mahony jumped to his feet, late. "I object. The marshal's testi-mony is hearsay—both as to supposed weapon and where it might be."

Judge Royce waved him silent, "Sustained." He asked Snyder, "Are you finished with this witness?"

Snyder nodded and smiled at the judge. "I am. Marshal, you're excused for now. I'd like to call Sam Dorsey to the stand."

Sam looked uncomfortable as his short brawny form settled in the witness chair. He nervously smoothed his bald head with huge hands after he removed his hat. He looked at Poppa with at least a shred of sympathy, Clare thought. Poppa returned a quiet, trusting smile.

In answer to the prosecutor's questioning, Sam related that Frank Hobb attempted to tear up his shop in a crazed rage. That he made other mistakes on occasion. Mixed up orders, forgot what he was doing and didn't finish a job on time. "I had to fire him before he took me out of business."

Snyder looked down his long nose at Sam. "Would you say that the accused, Frank Hobb, is—not right in the head?"

Poppa looked embarrassed, but he nodded his head at the question not intended for him.

"Well, that ain't for me to say," Sam answered, looking at the floor. "I'm not a doctor. Frank could get awful mixed up sometimes, yes. But he's a good worker, a good family man, and I just don't think he killed Fuller. You see—"

"That's all, Mr. Dorsey, thank you," Snyder quickly dismissed him. "You may return to your seat."

"Your honor, I'd like to question this witness." Mahony drawled, and got to his feet.

"Proceed," the judge said, barely looking up as he scribbled a note.

"Mr. Dorsey—Sam, you indicated you don't believe the accused killed the victim. Why is that?"

"Frank Hobb might be mixed up in the head, and it's true he made a mess of my shop. But I got to know him pretty good while he worked for me. I just don't figure he's got it in him to kill nobody. I can't see that. He didn't give me no argument when I had to fire him. He was real sorry for the damage and it was paid for, prompt."

"Thank you, Mr. Dorsey, you're excused." Mahony returned to his seat. He looked thoughtful as he pulled at the loose skin below his chin.

Clare gripped Larkin's hand tightly when Snyder called Dinger Toledo to the stand.

"First, Mr. Toledo would you give the court your opinion of the victim, Alfred Fuller, tell the jury what you—his close associate— knew of him."

"Alfred Fuller loved this town. He was like family to everybody. He got invited to sit down to supper by different folks, oh— three, four, five times a week. He did nobody no harm, but he did a lot of good for Sweetbrier, as mayor. You look at the clean streets, that's because of his order. He had work goin' at the town square, where we would've had us a new courthouse built, if—" he glared at Poppa who sat with his head down next to Mahony, "if Alfred hadn't been beat to death by a crazy man. Ask Frank Hobb's own brothers about that, they know he should have been put away, years ago."

"Mr. Toledo," Mahony took his turn to cross-examine, "first of all, let me congratulate you in your new position. Going from mere stock handler to station agent is an impressive promotion."

"If you're tryin' to say I had somethin' to do with killin' Alfred so I could take his place, you're lookin' down the wrong road. I had nothin' to do with it!"

"Sorry, I didn't mean to indicate that you did." Mahony looked with innocence at the jury and smiled. He studied his fingernails. "But we really need to get to the bottom of who killed your associate, the deceased, Alfred Fuller. Please describe your duties at the depot and stockyards, Mr. Toledo."

"My job don't have nothin' to do with what happened to Fuller! Do I have to have to answer, Judge? Hell, I see that stock is penned, fed, watered. I see that they're weighed and got onto the freight cars. Awright, yes, Fuller cheated on the weights of stock and grain, too, sometimes, an' pocketed the difference, but I had nothin' to do with that and nobody can prove otherwise. You want the killer, he's sittin' right there, Frank Hobb!"

"Didn't mean to get you riled, Mr. Toledo," Mahony said calmly, "and I apologize. I thought perhaps you might have ideas about other folks—connected in some way to the work you and Mr. Fuller performed—who might have had motive to commit the murder." He smiled, rocked back on his heels with his hands in his pockets. "It's interesting to learn from you that Fuller cheated farmers and ranchers at the shipping scales. Seems to me that others might have motive to do Fuller in." Mahony glanced at the judge. "I'm not convinced that Marshal Seavers tried as hard as he might to learn if someone other than the accused committed the crime." He gave the man in the witness chair the briefest wave. "That's all, Mr. Toledo."

Mahony then called Tobias Proctor to the stand for the defense. Tobias was sworn in and sat forward to answer Mahony's request to tell what he knew of Frank Hobb's character.

"Frank is the kind of fella who'd turn loose a ladybug to be rid of it before he'd squash it. He wouldn't kill nothin' or nobody. Somebody else took Alfred's life, it wasn't Frank."

In cross-examination, Snyder asked Tobias, "But didn't Mr. Hobb nearly destroy a man's business, as we just heard? Sam Dorsey is a big man, and strong and was able to stop him. But if it had been someone else with Frank that day his insanity cut loose, wouldn't he likely have killed that person?"

"No sir, that's not right, not right at all. He was bothered to the end of his tether over the death of my wife, but he wouldn't have hurt a soul over it."

"It's understandable, Mr. Proctor, that you still grieve the loss of your beloved wife and you sympathize with her father and that would cloud your thinking. But in actuality, didn't your wife also exhibit symptoms of insanity? Didn't she jump to—"

"You won't talk about Alice that way!" Tobias leaped to his feet, beet-red with fury. "She loved me and she thought I was dead. She was as fragile as a garden lily, but she wasn't crazy!"

Judge Royce banged his gavel repeatedly to quiet the uproar in the room.

Half of the spectators were on their feet, Clare among them. Larkin pulled her back into her chair. "You don't want the judge to make you leave," he whispered.

She sat back, trembling from head to toe. "I'm afraid for Poppa. Mahony is no match for that wily Snyder who keeps twisting things folks are trying to say."

Mahony called two more witnesses for Frank, simple farmers who'd had work done by Poppa at the blacksmith shop. They tried to help, giving a good opinion of Poppa. Then Snyder, in cross-examination, ripped their comments to shreds until they admitted it was possible that Frank killed Alfred.

Clare cringed, her face hot, as first Edward and then Simon were called to the stand for the defense. With less than believable conviction, they hemmed and hawed their belief that Frank was innocent of this crime, but yes, he did have a hand in their older brother's death. That they had put up with his mental failings from the time he was kicked in the head and left simple. Trying always to be fair, of course, as they wanted to be now.

Mahony looked out into the room at Clare and she nodded. *Please put me on the stand, please.*

Pale, but earnest and determined, she described the runaway that killed Uncle Samuel. "I've always blamed myself for what happened that day. I was meeting my lover in secret, my husband, now, when I could have gone with my father to make his delivery." In the audience, Momma's hand went to her mouth, Hallie gaped, and Oakley grinned. Poppa turned slowly to look at her.

She continued, "It's taken me a long time to realize that what happened to my uncle was no more my fault than it was Poppa's. It was a terrible accident that happened because of my uncle's temper and his mishandling of a skittish horse." She finished quietly, "Uncle Samuel's death was a tragedy that haunts our family and always will but it truly was no one's fault, it was an accident."

"Your witness." Mahony sat down.

Snyder shook his head, and peered over his glasses at Clare with mirthful disdain. "Now, Mrs. Wade, be truthful. Haven't you always covered up for your father? Still the dutiful daughter, trying to protect him now, as you covered up for him when his brother Samuel was killed?"

"Absolutely not. Poppa didn't commit this crime, and he didn't cause my uncle's death, either."

"But wait a minute, now. Didn't you and your family leave New Hampshire to escape your father's guilt in the accident? Haven't you tried to hide the fact of his insanity in a new life here in Kansas?"

"Escape? Hide?" She could hardly breathe she was so incensed. "We didn't come here to Kansas to run away from what happened, or hide from guilt on my father's part. We were forced out of our home." She explained Edward and Simon's part in that, and concluded, "We're happy in our new life in Kansas, and none of us, not even Poppa, whose mind can slip on occasion, would jeopardize that happiness by hurting another human being."

Snyder said that he was finished with the witness and nodded Clare back to her place among the spectators. He looked smug as he said, facing the jury, "Mrs. Wade is clearly a biased witness, whose testimony must be discounted. She loves her father, to that we agree and we admire her for it. But her prejudice clouds her vision of the truth."

"I think," Mahony scratched his grizzled jaw, "it's time we heard from the accused. I would like to call Mr. Frank Hobb, to the stand."

Poppa stood up, looking uncertain, and scared. He caught Momma's eye and she smiled at him, nodded at him with an expression that encouraged him to be strong. He made his slow sure way to the witness chair, looked again at Eugenie, and sat down.

At the judge's admonition, he raised his hand and swore to tell the truth and nothing but the truth.

Mahoney addressed him with a gentle smile, "Mr. Hobb, Sir, would you give us your opinion of Mayor Fuller?"

Poppa was a while answering. "He was a good mayor, I heard folks say that about him. He did fine things. He cared about Sweetbrier, making it a good place." He looked at the judge, at Snyder, at Mahony, and finally at his family to check if his answer was the right one.

"Did you and the mayor have differences, arguments?"

Poppa touched his ear, then put his hand down in his lap. "He didn't like my work sometimes. He was a hard man to please. He made me hurry when taking my time would have done a better job."

"How did that make you feel, what did you do?"

"I tried harder to please him. Ayuh, I wanted to please the mayor."

"You don't feel you had reason, then, to take his life?"

"No, no! I would never kill another soul, not ever."

"I thought not." Mahoney smiled and indicated he was finished questioning Frank Hobb.

Snyder took over, not pleased with the direction the trial was taking, "Mr. Hobb, didn't Alfred Fuller, the mayor, catch you trying to steal from your boss, Mr. Dorsey, one night at the blacksmith shop?"

"No."

"No what? He didn't catch you?"

"No, it wasn't me trying to take the money. It was him, Mr. Fuller. My daughter, Clarie, was with me. She saw him. She can tell you what really happened. The mayor said he was taking the money box because I was careless with it and he wanted to put the money where it'd be safe. He lied."

"Excuse me, Mr. Hobb, Sir, but the deceased is not the one on trial. You are. You trashed the blacksmith shop. The mayor thought you should be fired over that and other incidents and he was right. Sam Dorsey let you go, and you held that against Mayor Fuller." Snyder's voice rose to a near shout, "You wanted to blame him, not your own shortcomings, for your being fired. In a second rage, when the mayor said something against your family, you took it on yourself to kill your enemy, Alfred Fuller. Isn't that right?"

Mahony was on his feet, objecting, as spectators noisily discussed the matter among themselves. A calm resonant voice from the back of the room spoke so all could hear, "Frank Hobb did not kill Alfred Fuller."

There was a giant rustling noise as everyone in the room turned to see the three Goodlanders who had just entered the room. Clare said a silent prayer of thanks, and gave Liddy a nod. Whatever information she brought, it would indicate someone other than Poppa had done the deed, Clare was sure.

Mahony requested that Liddy Goodlander take the witness stand. She remained frozen in place as her husband advanced into the room. "I'm the witness the court needs to hear from," he said quietly. "I'll take the stand, your Honor, if you please."

The judge, as surprised and fascinated as everyone else in the room, leaned forward, "You have facts pertinent to this case?"

"I do."

"Your name?"

"Reverend Goodlander, Milton Goodlander. I'm a circuit preacher but my home is here in Sweetbrier. That's my wife, Liddy, and son, Gordy, who came in with me."

"You swear to tell the whole truth?"

"I do."

"My witness," Mahony said quickly before Snyder could get a word in.

Judge Royce nodded, "Proceed."

"Reverend Goodlander, please tell us what happened, as you see it."

"To start with, all of you know that I'm on the road a good lot, preaching to my flocks around three counties. It's not an easy life, nor does it pay well, but I'm doing the work I was called for, the work of the Lord. As soon as my wife heard that Alfred Fuller had been found murdered, and got to thinking about it, she and my son made ready to come searching for me. There had been an altercation between me and the mayor the last time I was home. It's possible our tussle resulted in his death."

A shocked babble arose throughout the courtroom. The judge banged his gavel for order.

"Continue, Reverend. Why were you and the mayor fighting?"

"Because he—he had designs on my wife. In his own fashion, I suppose he was in love with Liddy. He was insistent that she deserved better than a life with a poor minister who was often absent. He was convinced he could win her away from our marriage with promises of fancy gifts, nice things that I'd never live long enough to give her. Beautiful objects that he'd been 'collecting' with her in mind. His dream was to be a rich landowner, master of his own mansion. He saw my Liddy as the woman to complete that dream, as his wife."

"The altercation," the judge reminded.

"Yes, well, he watched and waited until the next time I was back in Sweetbrier from my preaching rounds and he appeared at our house for a showdown. Dressed up right smart, he was, like he'd come courting and I guess in his mind that's how he saw it. He insisted that I give my Liddy up for the finer life he could provide. He honestly and foolishly believed that she would choose him, although both my wife and I had—for a very long time—done everything possible to convince him that would never happen."

The room was dead quiet. Every spectator was at the edge of their seat as they listened, a mouse squeak would have sounded like thunder.

"He meant to have Liddy, just take her. When she refused to go with him, he started to manhandle her, to force her to his bidding. I went to her aid and managed to free her and move her aside. That's when Alfred pulled out a knife and came at me. I had to stop him. I yanked out my revolver from under my coat."

"Your revolver?" The question hung in the air, a preacher carried a revolver?

"I carry a gun, but it's never loaded because I could never

intentionally kill anyone. I've been beaten up a few times while making my circuit, by drunken rowdies, by others simply hostile to religion. A show of the gun is usually enough to stop my attackers."

"But showing your gun didn't stop Fuller?"

"No, it didn't. I turned it around in my hand as quickly as I could and just as he jumped at me I struck him on the head with the butt of the gun. It slowed him, but he kept coming, hacking at me with his knife. I knocked the knife from his hand and I shoved him off of me. He fell backward and struck his head on some limestone we have in our yard for building fence. He laid there, not moving."

"He was dead?"

"No, not at all. In fact, after a minute or two he got to his feet. I helped him back on his horse and ordered him to leave, get to town and see the doctor, and to stay away from my family. He rode off, bent over the saddle, his head bleeding, but cursing me roundly over his shoulder and threatening to get even with me yet. I don't know what happened after that. He might have gotten mixed up, got lost, ended up down by Sweetbrier Creek where he fell off the horse, lay down and died. The wound I gave him might have helped bring on his death, but he was alive when I last saw him."

The silence in the room was long and heavy. Liddy wept without sound, a handkerchief to her mouth. Gordy eyed his father with pride and slipped his arm around his mother's shoulder.

Mahony cleared his throat, his expression wise as an owl. "Thank you for coming here, today, Reverend Goodlander. An innocent man was about to be hung for something he didn't do."

"I know. I wasn't aware that Fuller had died until my family came for me. My wife told me he was dead and that Frank Hobb had been accused of killing him. I came here to clear Frank, because I sincerely believe he didn't do this. It was what I did to Alfred, trying to protect my wife, that brought about the mayor's death."

A babel of surprise and pleased exclamation arose in the room and the judge banged his gavel. "Order in the court! We'll have order!" When the room was silent again, he continued. "I rule the case against Frank Hobb be dismissed. In my opinion, the death of Alfred Fuller most likely happened in the way the reverend just described. He was defending his wife with damn good cause, and the deceased died of head wounds received in that altercation. I have no need to hear more. Marshal Seavers," he addressed him, "if you have any more bodies turn up suspiciously in your jurisdiction, you damn well better try a little harder to find the true facts. Court dismissed."

Clare whirled on the bench to wrap her arms around Larkin. "He's free, Poppa's free!" She rushed to hug Poppa next, but he was surrounded by folks clapping him on the back, and shaking his hand. Momma was circled by women hugging her in turn, saying how happy they were for her, how sure they'd been of Poppa's innocence all along.

Then Clare looked up to see Uncle Edward and Uncle Simon approaching. They attempted to smile, but in fact both looked sick. She laughed softly, waiting to hear what they would say this time.

Chapter Twenty-Eight

CLARE AND LARKIN SAT IN THE SHADE OF THE HOTEL PORCH looking out on the town that lay drowsy and peaceful in summer sunshine. Her slippered foot rocked baby Andy's cradle while he napped. Feelings of perfect bliss filled Clare. Larkin winked at her as they listened to the retreating sound of the east-bound train with her uncles aboard.

"You should've heard them, Larkin. Uncle Simon and Uncle Edward stuttered and stammered how happy they were for Poppa, but their words were as empty as a broken rain barrel. I don't think they liked Kansas much, what happened here in Sweetbrier these past few days."

He laughed. "Can't blame 'em, darlin'. The trial was their last hope and they lost. If your father had been found guilty, he would've been hung or put away to rot, and the promise to your grandmother would've been taken out of their hands."

She nodded. "Yes, with Poppa out of the way, the pot of gold—the family mills and homestead—would be theirs."

"Well, anyhow, they got in a real good visit with your Pa while he was in jail. He seemed to like seeing them."

"Truthfully, he did. And I think they observed for themselves how much better he's doing here in Kansas, even behind bars. He's able to think more clearly when he's not being shoved around and badgered for his mental failings. He's fine when he's simply accepted for how he is."

"Your mother had a lot to do with how he saw things, while he was in jail."

"Bless her heart, she wouldn't leave him there alone, and it did help him. On top of that, Poppa was smart enough to know he was innocent. He had faith he'd be freed." She was thoughtful a moment. "I don't fool myself. I realize that Poppa will have mental lapses from time to time, for the rest of his life. But the fact remains, he's the happiest he's been in years and Kansas did that for him."

"He looks forward to going home to visit his mother, though, doesn't he?"

"He's thrilled, as the rest of us are, to be leaving next week for the trip to New Hampshire to visit Grandmother." She smiled and caught Larkin's hand across their chairs, "I can't wait for her to see us as a married couple, and to meet our little Andy."

"Will there be trouble with Hallie wanting to stay back east?"

"I don't think so. I believe she's finally conceded that Kansas is the place for what she calls the 'unlucky branch of the Hobb family.'" She giggled. "I'm going to enjoy my aunts' and uncles' discomfort at having all of us under the same roof again. They would be so happy if we'd just disappear off the face of the earth. Actually," she mused, "It's no never mind with me whether or not Poppa accepts his share of Hobb's Mills when the time comes, but if he does, it serves his brothers right."

Larkin sat up straighter and reached over to take her hand. "What with the trial and all, I don't think I've mentioned that Ma got word recently that she owns another piece of property back there, in another county near Sandwich."

"What?"

"Ayuh, she does. Not a real big piece, but it's in a beautiful setting, lake edging the property, mountains behind. Ma wants me to look into the situation while we're there. Could be there's another buyer looking for a good spot to put up one of those resort hotels, she says. The money would come in handy. She's as eager as me to keep expanding out here on the prairie. She says, 'what if we had ten thousand acres, son'."

Clare burst out laughing. "Good heavens, Larkin, who would've dreamed our lives would come to this?"

"I would've," he answered softly. "I always knew."

"No, you didn't. How could you? The troubles we've been through—I can't even bear to think of them." Her hands went up to her cheeks and she shook her head. "I'm just so thankful they are past."

He was looking at her closely, his eyes gleaming with love. "I found it the other day."

"Found what?"

"This." He reached into his pocket and drew out a crumpled piece of paper, yellowed with age. "I've believed what it says from the day I found it skittering along the street, and then later met you." He handed it to her. "It's for you."

Clare opened the paper and her heart overflowed as she read the barely visible scrawled message, *Love endures all things.* She smiled at her husband, and whispered as she nestled into his arms, "For us, no words could ever be more true. I love you, Larkin, I always have, I always will."

A Look At: The Women of Paragon Springs

The Complete Series

THE DUST, THE WIND, THE PAIN

Award winning author Irene Bennet Brown introduces the four women of the thriving western Kansas town, Paragon Springs.

Cassiday Curran, Meg Brennon, Aurelia Symington and Lucy Walsh all found themselves in Paragon Springs in different ways, but they all have one thing in common: homesteading in a small western town while battling their own problems and the issues of life in the late 1800's.

Running from abusive husbands, falling in love, grief and ridicule are only some of the everyday struggles these women face. How they find their way through the struggles are what pull you into these heartwarming stories.

Women of Paragon Springs includes: Long Road Turning, Blue Horizons, No Other Place and Reap The South Wind.

"If you enjoy western novels, such as Little House on the Prairie and Lonesome Dove, you will enjoy this series by Irene Bennett Brown."

AVAILABLE NOW

About the Author

Irene Bennett Brown was born in Topeka, Kansas but has lived in Oregon's beautiful Willamette Valley from the age of nine. As a young girl, she play-acted days away in grand adventures on the banks of Muddy Creek and in the nearby Cascade Foothills, galvanized by favorite books like On to Oregon. With help from Gene Autry and Roy Rogers movies. Interest in the West, particularly the Kansas heartland, grew with the years and is the setting for most of her books.

Considering her nine YA novels a warmup to writing adult fiction, Irene Bennett Brown is thrilled that they include four Young Adult Literary Guild selections, an International Reading Association Young Adult's Choice nomination, a Western Writers of America Spur Award, and a nomination for the Mark Twain Award.

The significant role women and children played in developing the West against incredible hardship, intrigues Brown. Her historical novel, The Plainswoman, carries that theme and was a finalist for a Western Writers of America Spur Award for Best Original Paperback. In the author's critically acclaimed Women of Paragon Springs series, a group of women decide the way to survive, and make better lives on the raw Kansas frontier, is to build their own town. Following actual history, Long Road Turning, Blue Horizons, No Other Place, and Reap the South Wind takes the story from 1870's sodhouse days to their part in the birth of aviation in Kansas forty years later.

In Miss Royal's Mules, the adult sequel to Before the Lark, Book One in the author's new Nickel Hill series, a young woman takes work with a mule drive to earn back her farm lost to the bank in 1900 Kansas. "A time and place rigorously evoked down to every minor character and filmic detail". Miss Royal's Mules is a Will Rogers Medallion Award Winner.

Irene Bennett Brown is a longtime member of Western Writers of America and is a founding member of Women Writing the West. When not writing, reading, or exploring historic places, she likes attending sports events and concerts with her growing family.

She enjoys small-town life in Oregon with her husband, Bob, a retired research chemist, and their rescue cat, Quigley—The King of Everything.